# The World Walker

## by

## Ian W. Sainsbury

**The World Walker**

Copyright © Ian W. Sainsbury 2016

The right of Ian W. Sainsbury to be identified as the author of
this work has been asserted by him in accordance with the
Copyright, Designs and Patents act 1988.

This book is a work of fiction. Names, characters, places and
incidents are the product of the author's imagination or are used
fictitiously. Any resemblance to actual events, locations, or
persons, living or dead, is purely coincidental.

For Ruth

# Chapter 1

## Los Angeles
## Present day

It's never a good day to die, whatever they tell you in the movies. Then again, scriptwriters are paid to deliver snappy, memorable dialogue, not universal truths.

Legs dangling over the edge of the building, Seb Varden could still just about hear the last chorus of Forgotten Blues, as the band cranked up the volume six stories below.' Clockwatchers - not too many years ago considered the biggest band in LA - still finished every gig with the same song, and Seb smiled picking out the snish of Dan's high-hat and thrack of the snare as he slowed the band into the final few seconds. Worked into a frenzy, the crowd screamed for more, despite knowing they'd never get it. Refusal to play an encore was a Clockwatchers trademark. Lead singer Meera had always had an instinct for stagecraft, and her notion of playing under a huge clock that counted down the band's time on stage had proved a winner from their first gig. The hands of the clock moved backward toward midnight, ignoring real-world time. The song they started before the hands met at the top of the dial was always their last. Seb leaned forward, listening more intently for the end of the ritual.

"Watch the clock," came the familiar words, drifting up through dark, heavy, summer smog, "because the clock is watching you." Seb frowned. The words were right, but the voice saying them was unexpected.

The metal fire-escape ladder rattled and the heady smell of marijuana smoke drifted across the rooftop.

.

"Hey, Meera," said Seb, "not like you to miss the sign-off."

Meera picked her way carefully across the rooftop, graceful as a dancer, despite permanently negotiating the world through the haze of a habitual dope smoker. She sat next to Seb and offered him the spliff. He shook his head, smiling.

"Still on a health kick, huh?" she said, drawing deeply, the red glow brightening and revealing her dark eyes, just visible under heavy bangs and enough mascara to make a goth feel naked. They sat in silence for a few minutes, then Meera looked behind her across the Burbank rooftops out to the lights of LA; a glittering bauble dropped in the valley, blotting out the night sky with a million tiny stabs of light. She turned back to the dark mountains before them.

"You're looking the wrong way, you know," she said.

Seb carried on gazing toward the Verdugo Mountains. The bar was right on the edge of the city. The neon sign below announced "Badlands" to passing traffic, and the owner was only half-joking.

"You sure?" he said. He couldn't hear anything other than the sounds of the dispersing crowd and the hum of a thousand cars, but he knew a couple hours' walk would bring him to a place where the clearest sound would be the suss of the wind through the leaves and the creak of shifting wood as the trees stretched and groaned.

Meera lit a new spliff from the end of the last one and inhaled deeply. She sighed melodramatically.

"Go ahead," said Seb. "Ask me." Meera absently brushed hair away from her eyes and looked at him.

"What's really going on, Seb?" she asked. "If Scrappy or Dan suddenly said they'd decided to give up music and move to Europe I'd believe them, but you? Well, maybe not

Scrappy. He still thinks Europe is an imaginary land from *Lord Of The Rings*. But Seb Varden, white soul boy, best songwriter on the west coast?"

Seb snorted but Meera just raised an eyebrow. "Hey, what the hell do the critics know? And come on. Five minutes without access to a piano and you'll be climbing the walls."

Seb sighed and flicked some of Meera's ash off his jeans.

"It's just time for a change, Mee, is all," he said. "Nothing more to it than that."

Meera took a long pull on the joint and said nothing for a while.

Abruptly standing up, she ruffled Seb's hair fondly and started back across the rooftop.

"You're full of shit, Sebby," she called. Seb grimaced. "And stop pulling faces," she continued without looking back at him. "Whatever it is you're really up too, it sure as hell ain't giving up music and moving to Italy or where the fuck ever."

"You always did have a wonderful vocabulary, Mee," he said.

"Yeah, and you always played your cards a bit too close to your chest, but hey, you've got my number, you could always use that phone-shaped object you carry around to actually call me," she said, the rungs of the fire-escape rattling as she made her way back down.

Seb waited another 30 minutes or so, until he heard the band's van roaring off down the street. He stood up and turned back to the permanent glow of the city. There was so much he was going to miss. Meera was right, of course. He wasn't going to Italy. Or where the fuck ever.

Two hours later and Seb was close to his favorite place in LA. Officially, the Verdugo Mountains weren't in LA at all, but Seb always thought of them that way. The steep, scrub-lined dirt paths, the tough vegetation that looked like it had taken hold before humanity had made its way out of the slime; the mountains were a reminder that the city was a cheap ornament Nature could brush away at any time. The mountains had a permanence and a silence that drew Seb in. Popular with hikers during the day, he had found the solitude he craved by walking the paths at night. The threat of mountain lions or coyotes discouraged most people from heading out after dark, but Seb found the local wildlife treated him with the same respect he gave them, keeping their distance.

He shrugged the backpack off his shoulders and realized he had managed the entire hike without once thinking about what he was about to do and why. Now, finally reaching the spot he'd picked out weeks before, looking back at the city, he reviewed the last six months quickly and calmly.

The initial headaches had been nothing unusual at first. His occasional willingness to experiment with drugs had led to some spectacular hangovers over the years. And he was 32 now, not 19. Hangovers wiped out entire days and no amount of water, fresh fruit and Tylenol seemed able to ease the process. It was when the headaches started manifesting on the days when he'd been nowhere near any substances that he thought something might be wrong. A suspiciously fast referral to a specialist by his doctor heightened his suspicions, and by the time the diagnosis came in, he was already preparing for bad news. As it turned out, the news couldn't have been worse.

Certain impressions, however trivial under normal circumstances, stand out when someone tells you something that alters the course of your life. The specialist was attractive, Latin, intelligent and beautiful. Seb's urge to flirt had deserted him totally, but he found himself obsessively focusing on her nipple, clearly outlined beneath the medical white of her jacket. There was nothing sexual in his gaze, but he found himself unable to look away as he registered her words. Brain tumor. Inoperable. Less than a year. She had said a lot more that afternoon, covering his options. There would be loss of memory at first, some balance problems, weakness in the limbs. He might experience fits as the tumor grew and pressed on different parts of his brain.

Seb sat down, his back against a tree, and opened the backpack. He pulled out a heavy glass tumbler and a bottle of Johnny Walker Premier. A few weeks back, he'd decided that if he was going to die, he was going to do it on his own terms, and after enjoying a few glasses of $200 whiskey. He poured an extremely generous measure and inhaled, taking in the caramel, honeyed woodiness, the almost savory richness. There was a certain irony to the words that came into his mind just then: treat every moment as if it might be your last. He smiled to himself, raised his glass and toasted the night, drinking deeply and with unfeigned enjoyment.

The specialist had been worth whatever money the insurance company had paid her. Within a few weeks, Seb had noticed some balance problems. He felt as tired when he woke up as if he had barely slept. Life became increasingly unreal - colors muted and washed out, food bland. Even his libido had packed its bags and left without a backward glance. Only the strongest tastes, such as a lovingly crafted Scotch, still gave him enjoyment. He'd only had one seizure, but it had been enough. Exactly seven days ago, sat in front of the love of his life - a nine-foot

Bosendorfer grand piano - he suddenly lost all awareness of where he was and what was happening. He had been playing a chord sequence that had been plaguing his subconscious for weeks, threatening to turn into the chorus of new song. Suddenly, his entire existence seemed to tilt and shift, his vision narrowing rapidly to a pinprick. He woke minutes later, under the piano, his shoulder throbbing where it had hit the floor. Carefully picking himself up, Seb's first thought was to play, but the chord sequence had gone. Worse, he found he could no longer coordinate his hands on the keyboard. He caved, giving in to self-pity for the first and only time, lying face down on his bed and weeping. When he finally got up, he accepted the inevitable. The remainder of the week had been spent arranging the end of his life so that he wouldn't leave a mess for others to clear up.

Seb took out his phone and cued up the last piece of music he ever expected to hear. When he'd started learning piano, it was the first thing he had ever managed to play all the way through - he remembered performing it in the children's home where he'd grown up. He selected the loop function and reached for his headphones. Not a fan of earbuds, Seb wanted total immersion when he listened, so his headphones had taken up much of the space in the backpack. Along with the Scotch. And the craft knife.

He pulled out a piece of paper and unfolded it, putting it on the floor next to him, held in place with a stone. He knew Bob would be the one to discover his body. No one else walked their dogs at 5am every day, and the two of them had progressed over the years from wary looks to a nod of recognition, then finally some brief conversations and even a shared nip of the hard stuff from the flask Bob carried.

Seb smoothed out the note and took another sip of Scotch. Taking out a Sharpie, he wrote,

"Sorry it had to be you, Bob, but I knew you'd be able to cope ok. All the best, Seb."

He recapped the pen before changing his mind and adding,

"PS. Help yourself to the Scotch. It's good stuff."

Finally sitting back, finishing his glass and taking the protective covering off of the razor-sharp blade, he pressed play. Bach's Prelude in C Major. Just a series of arpeggios, never repeating, so simple yet impossibly evocative of something half-remembered, half-seen. He'd never got bored of it, never stopped marveling at its ability to move him. And moved was exactly the right word, since he never finished listening to it in the same place as he'd started. It was the Glenn Gould version. The guy might grunt a bit while he played, but, man, no one played Bach like Glenn Gould did.

Seb took the knife in his left hand and unhesitatingly drew a deep gash across his right wrist before changing hands and doing the same to his left. He wondered if he should feel grief, bitterness, anger, maybe even anticipation or happiness. But he felt none of these. He just felt resigned to the anonymous inevitability of fate as he sat back and let his blood seep into the dry dusty earth of the mountains.

At 3:13am, he opened his eyes sleepily. A mountain lion stood about ten paces away, watching him. Seb raised his head, thinking for a moment that he was hallucinating. Realizing he wasn't, he called out to it, his voice sounding far away and disconnected.

"Shoo!"

The mountain lion cocked her head to one side, considering whether this was a fight she wanted to take on, before abruptly padding away into the darkness.

At 3:49am, Seb opened his eyes again, much more slowly this time. His brain felt like it was trying to communicate with his body from the bottom of a dark, wet well. He struggled to focus, but when he managed it, he *knew* he was hallucinating. A huge thin figure stood in front of him. A huge thin glowing figure who looked exactly like the guy who stepped out of the spaceship at the end of *Close Encounters of the Third Kind*.

"Welcome to Earth," said Seb. "I would get up, but," He lapsed into a bout of weak coughing, his breathing shallow and rasping. Man, it was getting hard to breathe. Seb decided it was time to stop making the effort. His hallucination would just have to get along without him. The hallucination, however, had other ideas.

# Chapter 2

The facility had originally been built during the Second World War, as part of a national strategy to provide the United States Government with a series of well-equipped underground bolt holes from which they could continue to govern in the event of a nuclear strike. It was an expensive strategy, involving the construction of thirty-seven such buildings across the country, and the irony wasn't lost on President Truman that if they hadn't invented the damn bomb in the first place, they could have saved millions of dollars. Still, throughout the Cold War, many workers in the higher echelons of public office took comfort in the fact they were rarely more than an hour away from a safe haven.

Like most ultra-secret facilities, the Los Angeles DF1 Suites (named after DefCon 1, the state of emergency which would automatically trigger their use) were hidden in plain sight. In the State Department's experience, huge fences, barriers, heavily armed guards and warning signs kept out all but the most curious; but it was the most curious who were crucial to keep out. So the government had started placing its most important facilities near to more prominent, traditionally guarded ones. Then they'd come up with cover stories to deflect the curious. LA's DF1 Suites had a better cover story than many. Sitting on top of a vast warren of underground rooms was a long, low building displaying a simple sign: FMR. There was a fence, of course, and a guard - usually a retired cop catching up on the sports pages or taking a nap - but no one ever came near the place because of the smell. The guard was well paid due to the stench, which was pumped out to the surrounding countryside day and night. FMR stood for Fecal Matter Research. The locals all knew it as the Shit Station.

For over fifty years, the secret rooms beneath the Shit Station had housed a single occupant. This occupant was watched - initially - by a 12-person team of scientists plus nearly fifty highly trained guards, all unaware they were embarking upon the most tedious job they'd ever draw a pay check from. The guards lost interest within weeks and, over a period of decades, their numbers fell as budgets were cut. The professional fascination of the scientists took years to begin to diminish, but eventually, even they reluctantly accepted the inevitable. By the time Seb took his final stroll just over a mile away, the Shit Station only got one scientific visit a month and that was purely a box-ticking exercise.

The occupant had arrived on US soil at Roswell, New Mexico on July 7th, 1947. He (although it had no discernible gender, 1950s American attitudes pretty much dictated the masculine epithet) had unceremoniously created a 500 ft wide crater in a thinly populated area, scared a few farmers and provided the raw material for decades of conspiracy theories. He had even been named: Billy Joe. This was in honor of the half-drunk old guy who'd come "for a look-see" about an hour after impact. The military response had been swift, a cordon was in place, but no one could prevent him seeing the figure standing in the wreckage. The old man had taken one look at the giant gray creature, spat on the dirt and stumped away, calling back over his shoulder, "Only came up to see Billy Joe, and that sure as hell ain't him." One of the soldiers raised his weapon as the drunk walked away, but an officer put his hand on the barrel and pushed it toward the ground.

"Let him tell his story, son," he said. "Couldn't wish for a better witness."

A thousand accounts of what had occurred that night sprang up in the years following the incident. The story got some attention at first based on the evidence of a number of reliable witnesses who had seen lights in the sky or heard the shriek of tearing metal as something big tore into the New Mexico desert. But the lack of any material evidence ensured the story was never given much scrutiny. If something had crashed, where was the wreckage? Even if the US government had somehow pulled off the fastest, most thorough cleanup operation in modern history, some fragment would have remained, some tiny piece overlooked. But nothing ever came to light, and years of alien-hunters with magnifying glasses, metal detectors, and increasingly complex technological equipment had failed to turn up any evidence.

The platoon of soldiers first on the scene were the only witnesses to the truth, and their exceptionally generous pension packets, coupled with some not-so-thinly-veiled threats, ensured they would never break their silence. But not a man among them would ever forget what they had seen. Colonel Harkett's statement from that night was still on file at the Shit Station and every scientist who had subsequently spent any time with Billy Joe had read and reread it so many times, they could have quoted it verbatim in their sleep.

"The alien stood in the middle of the wreckage, looking around itself. And glowing. It didn't seem to see us, or, if it did, it sure as hell didn't care. The wreckage spread out a fair distance, around 500 feet in diameter. You could feel the heat, but there was no fire. You ever seen a plane crash? Looked like that in some ways, the way the wreckage was dispersed, the gouge in the ground made by the impact. But I couldn't stop thinking, where are the seats? This guy's come from another planet, right? You telling me it stood up for the whole trip? Couldn't see any controls, neither. Every bit of wreckage looked the same, like it was the hull or something. Just plain metal. After a while, the alien closed its eyes and knelt down, putting its hands flat on the ground. That's when it happened, and Christ, I don't mind telling you I'm just glad you got other witnesses, 'cause I wouldn't believe it otherwise, in your shoes. Its whole body was glowing - did I mention that? It seemed to get brighter and for a second I just looked at it. Not an everyday sight, right? Then one of my men shouted and I looked back at the nearest piece of wreckage to me. It was getting smaller. I could see it happening. Now I've heard a couple of the guys say it sank into the ground but that isn't right. I know exactly what it reminded me of. You ever poured hot water on an ice cube? That's exactly how this looked. Like someone was picking it apart in tiny pieces. Then it was gone. All of it. And your gray fella was stretched out on the ground. Not glowing any more. We all figured it was dead."

To all but the educated observer, the alien *was* dead. No discernible breathing, no pulse. But even the relatively unsophisticated diagnostic equipment available to medical professionals in the 1940s detected enough signs of life to make it worth transferring Billy Joe to the Shit Station, the best hidden secret facility on US soil.

Billy Joe's arrival at the Station was followed by months of study by the cream of the American scientific community. Their initial euphoria was matched by the excitement and fearfulness throughout the select few in government who shared in the knowledge of what had really happened at Roswell. However, the reports emerging from the secret facility; daily at first, then weekly, monthly and finally six-monthly, contained many words, some of them extremely long, but just one message: we've got nothing. No news, no reports, no details of the alien's physical makeup, no change in his condition. Zilch.

The best scientific minds literally grew old and died trying to solve the enigma of the creature. The problem was they couldn't get a single sample to work on. Asked by an irate White House advisor to sum up his report in language they could actually understand, one esteemed professor simply scrawled across his original words,

"Doesn't eat. Doesn't shit. Skin like a tank. Questions?"

The strange thing was, if you touched the alien's skin, it felt warm, pliable, soft. But if you tried pushing a needle into it, the area where the needle touched the flesh suddenly became totally unyielding. Scientists noted it was almost as if the skin immediately pushed back at them, became rock hard. And throughout it all, the alien lay as if dead, stretched out on the slab, monitored by cameras and recording equipment.

There had been one near-disaster in 1982, where no less than a Nobel-winning professor of physics succumbed to a moment of madness resulting from years of fruitless, frustrating observation. Snatching a gun from the holster of a guard, he fired three rounds into the alien's body before a second guard shot and killed him. As the professor's body was dragged away, the medical team rushed into the room in a blur of professionalism. Within seconds they had stopped short, staring. There were no wounds on the alien's body. No bullet holes. No blood. No change in his condition. If it hadn't been for the fact they'd witnessed the professor's murderous attack, and later had seen the three empty chambers in the guard's gun, they would have doubted the evidence of their own senses. The bullets themselves had undoubtedly entered Billy Joe's body as there was no sign of them elsewhere.

The occupant of the Shit Station became the eighth wonder of the world. It was just a shame this was the only one no one could talk about. As successive governments came and went and presidents retired, died, or got caught screwing the American people metaphorically, or - in at least one memorable case - literally, Billy Joe lay on a slab in a secret facility just outside Los Angeles. Once every six or seven years, a vigilant Chief Of Staff with a desire to actually know where many of the larger drains on the national budget ended up would trace a chunk of change to the Station and demand some answers. He or she would subsequently be given the tour, allowed to poke the star attraction, given a strong drink and asked how exactly they might better spend the tax dollars. Given that the alien's body itself was no nearer to giving any answers and the craft that had apparently whisked him from God-knows-where to New Mexico had vanished without trace a few hours after crashing, successive Chiefs Of Staff reluctantly came to the same conclusion. They had to wait until human technology caught up with the alien. Or until the alien did something: spoke, moved, yawned, broke wind. Anything would do. Until then, they just had to sit on their hands and throw money at it. And stop anyone finding out. On that they all agreed.

So when, at 5am one Sunday, Billy Joe swung his legs off the slab, stood up and walked through a solid wall 150 feet underground, no one was quite prepared for it.

There were two guards on duty, both three years into a 10-year assignment at the Shit Station. Each displayed the kind of vigilance that might be expected from well-trained soldiers asked to babysit someone who hadn't moved a inch in over half a century. They were playing poker. Chad may have missed the alien's initial movements, but he was chasing an unlikely flush that would bring him a ten-buck pot if the final diamond hit. As it happened, the river card was the Queen of Diamonds, but Chad never saw it, his eyes having finally flicked to the monitor. Carl was staring at the cards disgustedly, having suspected the flush all along, but when he glanced up and saw the expression on his partner's face, he swung around and checked the monitor before assuming an identical expression, mouth hanging open, eyes bulging.

"What the f-," managed Carl before Chad stood, knocking the cards flying. He unholstered his gun, punched a combination into the airlock and was in the room just in time to see Billy Joe's heel disappearing into a solid steel wall, a faint glow lingering in the spot for half a second before fading.

"What the hell do we do now?" said Chad, his gun pointing at the empty slab. Carl managed to gain a little equilibrium, swallowing hard.

"We get topside," he said. "You make the call."

As the elevator doors opened at ground level, Chad hit send on his cell phone, calling the number he had been trained to call should the alien's condition ever change, however minor that change might be. Chad guessed this probably qualified. It was picked up immediately.

"Tell me exactly what's happened, soldier," came the calm voice at the other end of the line. Chad swallowed. He'd never met the owner of the voice, but had been briefed by phone when he was first assigned to the Station. It was the voice of someone who demanded unquestioning obedience, someone who could bypass the usual channels, someone who got the job done, whatever the job might be.

You either did what you were told or you got yourself suddenly disappeared. Permanently.

"It's Billy Joe, sir," said Chad. "He's gone." There was a fraction of a second's pause before the voice continued as calmly as it had before.

"Describe precisely what you saw." Chad did as he was told, including the impossible exit through a solid wall. Carl listened to his partner's account while checking his ammunition. He handed Chad some night-vision goggles.

"Which direction was he heading in when he exited the facility?" said the voice. Chad hesitated, licking his lips nervously.

"Wake up, soldier and answer my question; and I need you to be precise. Which wall did he walk through?" Chad thought for a second, sweating more.

"At the foot of his bed, sir." Another brief pause.

"Then he's heading west. Get out there. Do a five-mile sweep. If any civilian has made contact, bring them in. Report every ten minutes. I'll be there within the hour."

\*\*\*

In a wood-paneled home office in a gated Los Angeles suburb, a man in a dressing gown looked at his cell phone and frowned, thinking, before making another call. He spoke as soon as it was answered.

"It's Westlake," he said. "I want a five-man team and a chopper immediately."

He nodded at the answer and went to the closet to get dressed. He picked out a snub-nosed Glock to tuck into the holster under his armpit. As he laced his shoes, he could already hear the rhythmic throb of the approaching helicopter. He smiled grimly and went out to the helipad at the back of his lodge.

# Chapter 3

As the tall glowing alien stretched out a hand with impossibly long fingers, Seb felt no fear at all. Part of him coolly noted that this was probably not a normal reaction. He put it down to the fact there was more of his own blood currently enriching the dry soil of the trail than still weakly pumping through his veins. He wondered why an extraterrestrial should want to make contact with a dying man. Well, it made as much sense as plucking Mid-West farm boys from their solitary late night hooch-consuming sessions, giving them a quick tour of the old spaceship before sticking high-tech probes up their anuses. What was it with aliens and anuses anyway?

Seb blinked and looked into the huge dark eyes of the creature. He was about to die, and didn't want his last thoughts to involve anuses. He tried to reach up to grasp the alien's hand. *What am I going to do? Introduce myself and offer him a shot of the Scotch?* He half-laughed, half-coughed and a mixture of dark, thick blood and spit flopped onto his chin and ran onto his shirt. His hand twitched slightly in response to his brain's command to move, then lay still. Too much blood loss. He felt his vision suddenly beginning to narrow and heard his pulse slow to a funereal pace. Ah, the famous tunnel. The glowing figure in front of him seemed to dim as did everything he could see and hear around him. It was as if reality had no more significance than a TV playing quietly in another room. Seb knew it was there, but it held no interest for him. The tunnel was real. *Will I get to see a light? Meet Mom and Dad? Do orphans get to meet the parents they've never met? Could be awkward. Still, might get to meet Jesus if the TV evangelists are on the money. Not much chance of that. Oblivion it is, then.* He sighed, feeling the last shred of life slipping away, and closed his eyes.

The alien grasped both his hands. The huge black eyes closed. The touch was icy. Dimly, Seb wondered how he could feel anything at all in fingers no longer connected to his bloodstream. Then, suddenly, the sensation changed to one of warmth, then heat, then a rush of pain as if red-hot lava was sliding up his arms. Not just on the surface - inside, as if the spilled blood was being replaced with boiling, spitting oil. He took in a huge, ragged breath, oxygen hitting his dulled senses in a rush of color, humming, blurring, his whole body vibrating with a massive surge of adrenaline.

The alien suddenly pulled Seb to his feet, the light emitting from his glowing gray body seeming to pulse in time with the beating of Seb's heart, which was accelerating every second, back from the brink of stopping altogether. Seb's breathing got faster and drops of sweat appeared on his forehead. He felt no fear, caught entirely in the moment, a man who had chosen to die feeling more alive than he ever had before.

All sense of time passing slowed, then stopped.

Seb had been to summer camp when he was twelve and had learned to dive from a board. The swallow dive was his favorite. There was always a moment in the dive where he'd reached the top of the arc, the moment between rising and falling, the best feeling, weightless, when anything seemed possible. It felt like that moment now - poised in time, just before the fall began. But Seb knew there was a choice here. He didn't have to fall. He could fly.

He just had to say yes.

But yes to what, exactly? Life...and something more. Something other. Something that would change him forever. Seb realized that were he to accept this invitation, he would be opening a door through which no human being had ever stepped. He would be alive, alone...and yet...he wouldn't be alone, quite. Somehow, he could feel others, tendrils of awareness brushing his consciousness.

He hesitated, his mind settling like a pond after the last ripple from a thrown pebble has washed gently against the reeds.

He felt the tug of time, of expectation, but also the lure of death, which he had faced and accepted. In the last months he had learned to truly let go; of possessions, of friends, of the future and the past. And death was just the last step of letting go. He had made his decision with no expectation of an alternative. And yet...

Time unfroze. The Bach prelude started again and Seb heard it as if for the first time, as if each note was unfolding in every moment.

Bach. How could he leave life when it had Bach? And The Beatles. And Frank Zappa. And Randy Newman. And Thrash Metal.

Seb smiled. He said yes.

***

The two soldiers were nearing the limit of their five-mile search when Chad saw a glow from the trees ahead. He spoke softly into the mic on his lapel. "600 feet northwest of my position. That glow. It's got to be him."

The voice in his ear sounded calm but he had known Carl long enough to hear the tension.

"Stay where you are."

As Carl came alongside him, Chad pointed ahead to where the trees thinned revealing a clearing near a path favored by joggers and dog-walkers. The two men parted without speaking, heading toward the target in a pincer movement, weapons drawn and ready. Chad reached the edge of the clearing, looking to his right, his night-vision goggles revealing Carl moving silently into position and nodding. He nodded back and turned toward the glow.

Billy Joe stood in the clearing, his back to Chad. The soldier narrowed his eyes, trying to see what was happening. He wondered how he was supposed to persuade the alien to play nice and come back to his comfortable cell.

"Can you see what he's doing?" he whispered.

"There's someone with him," said Carl. "He's - Jesus!" Chad gasped and both men ripped the goggles from their faces as the glow suddenly brightened.

"What the-," Chad pressed the call button on his phone. It was answered immediately.

"Report."

"Sir, we've found him. He's not alone. It's a civilian. They're...um...they're holding hands." The pause on the other end of the line was no more than half a second but Chad had visions of his career being flushed down the toilet.

"I have your position. We're ten minutes out." Another pause. The line went dead. Chad stopped holding his breath.

Seb felt a pain unlike any he could ever have imagined. It lasted no more than a fraction of a second, but it was as if his entire body had exploded, every atom separated from its neighbor then sucked back into place. There was a roaring in his ears, his eyes burned and his skin felt as if it was changing from millisecond to millisecond: now soft, now liquid, now a vapor, now impervious, diamond-like, now fluid again, rising and falling like a tide on the screaming muscles beneath.

The two watching soldiers yelped with pain and covered their eyes as the two figures suddenly flickered, then shone like the midday sun. The glare only lasted an instant, but when they looked back they could see nothing. It took nearly half a minute before their eyes adjusted and when they could see clearly, they doubted their own sight. Billy Joe was only glowing faintly now, but his whole body seemed less substantial. It wavered and rippled, as if being seen through water. He was no longer touching the civilian. His hand came up and made a slow cutting gesture in the air. Then he turned sideways and slid out of existence.

"Chad?" came Carl's voice in his ear.

"Yeah," said Chad, "I saw it too. What the hell do we do now?"

"We grab that guy. That's what we do." Both soldiers moved cautiously out of the cover of the trees, their weapons raised.

Seb watched the alien disappear. It was as if he had just walked right off the planet. Seb took a couple of deep breaths, tasting the air, the unique mixture of mountain oxygen and LA pollution. He took a small step forward and stumbled slightly. He remembered his wrists, his dead fingers. Looking down, he slowly raised his arms, searching for evidence of the deep cuts he had made only hours before. His skin looked unmarked. He raised his wrists closer to his face, dimly aware of someone shouting.

Chad saw the guy lift his arms. "Weapon!" he shouted. Carl dropped to one knee, bracing the assault rifle against his shoulder, narrowing his eyes, still trying to see clearly through the residual glare. Chad kept his rifle pointing at the man and called out to him.

"Drop your weapon!"

Seb looked at the unmarked skin on his wrists and smiled. The Bach prelude continued evolving in his brain. He heard shouts again but could only truly see and hear what was in front of him. He grabbed his right wrist with his left hand, his thumb exploring the area which should be an open wound.

"DROP YOUR WEAPON NOW!"

Seb was alive and feeling better than he had in years. He threw back his head and laughed.

The soldiers fired at the same moment and eight rounds were emptied into Seb's body, one reducing his heart to a mass of shredded tissue.

"Well, there's an irony," Seb had time to think before pitching face forward into the dirt.

# Chapter 4

**14 months previously**
**Berlin, Germany**

Despite holding the comparatively junior post of Minister for the Environment, Nature Conservation and Nuclear Safety, Dietricha Strennbourg occupied an office in the Bundeskanzleramt second in size only to the Chancellor's. The German press had christened Dietricha 'Bou-Dietricha', a particularly ineffective pun that had, somehow, stuck. It was supposed to be a reworking of 'Boudicca', Britain's first-century Celtic warrior queen. Dietricha had spent three years studying at Oxford University, and, early on in her political career, a story had surfaced linking her with undergraduate Pagan organizations. The press found a photo of her in a druid-like cloak, holding a carved wooden staff. She had laughed off the speculation, said it was a fancy dress party, and, as no naked photos of her participating in nature rituals at Stonehenge had appeared, the story went away. The name stayed, however. And, secretly, Dietricha liked it. She even had a name plate on her desk, carved with rune-like letters, spelling Bou-Dietricha.

Her rapid rise from intelligent but unproven small-town lobbyist, to a central government position within a few short years had taken many political commentators by surprise. It was no surprise to those who knew her well. She was driven, ambitious, single-minded and ruthless. The environmental lobby had championed Dietricha's career early on. She was an outspoken advocate of green policies, refusing to give an inch on her principles, even when under pressure from big business. She spoke well, she looked good, and, best of all, she intimidated the opposition. It didn't hurt that she was six feet tall, but it was really the force of her will that took people aback when they met her. She didn't so much negotiate as demand, and her utter self-belief convinced many an opponent to concede more than they had planned. She was formidable, and the media loved her. All who worked with her professed great respect and admiration for Dietricha Strennbourg. No one had a bad word to say about her, on or off the record. Journalists marveled at this rare universal approbation for a politician. Not one of them guessed the real reason for it: fear.

In Dietricha's opinion, fear was an underused, undervalued concept in public office. In her opinion, politics was all about power and power was all about fear. Respect, love, they might get you a few rungs up the ladder, but keeping opponents terrified was a far more effective tool for advancement. Dietricha knew she would be Chancellor some day. Every other politician she'd had dealings with knew the same. The Chancellor herself certainly knew it, and had quickly agreed to move Dietricha's office from its traditional home in Bonn, to Berlin, the political heart of Germany. The only reason Dietricha was still content to remain - in the view of the public, at least - an underling, was the fact that her network was still growing. As she moved through the ranks, she met more and more influential people from all parts of Germany. She also met senior figures from other European countries and superpowers like America, Russia and China. She contrived reasons for private meetings with as many of these people as possible. Once she had spent some time alone with them, they were hers. All in all, the plan she had first begun to conceive during those pagan rites in the

Oxfordshire countryside had fallen into place with barely a single hitch. Because the newspapers had been right about the paganism after all. Although she had thought of herself as more of a Druid at the time. Now that she was more self-aware and less self-deluding, she was perfectly happy to call herself by the most fitting epitaph, with no sense of shame at all. Quite the opposite. Bou-Dietricha was proud to be a witch.

She woke at 5:29am, turning off the alarm before it sounded. The young man beside her, Johann? Jonathan? stirred briefly before resuming snoring. No one seemed to be able to match her sexual stamina or appetite, so she had taken to satisfying herself with two visitors a night. She wasn't a fan of group sex - too many options, but she was never satisfied with one or two orgasms and had yet to find a single man who could give her what she needed. She approached her sexual needs with the same kind of thorough determination and detailed planning as she had embarked upon her political career. In practise, this meant two lovers a night during the week, three on Saturdays. She took alternate Wednesdays off so she could watch Friends box sets. For some reason, it was the only show that could make her laugh, despite the fact that she felt no empathy at all for any of the characters.

Dietricha got straight into her running gear. It was Saturday morning, cool and clear on the deck outside her weekend chalet at the foot of the Harz mountains. She stretched and sipped water, looking up at the majestic giants, densely wooded, ancient geological marvels that must have looked much the same for thousands of years.

Tying her hair back as she set off, she quickly settled into an easy loping rhythm that looked lazy to a casual observer, but was actually faster than it seemed, her long strides taking her quickly out of sight.

The light was improving every minute as Dietricha ran. She followed a rough track that would take her a few hundred feet higher before looping back along the side of the lake. The trees at this level were primarily wood-rush or common beech. Further on, when she came to the lake, there were a few sycamores, then the real reason Dietricha had chosen to build her chalet here: English oaks. A ring of them, ancient, silent and watchful. A place of power. The place she visited weekly to be filled with the ancient energy that enabled her to pursue her ambitions. She had also found a place in Grunewald, closer to work, that could provide the same power, but the oaks lent gravitas to the ritual. She quickened her pace, longing to be there.

She felt more at home, more herself, running in these woods, than at any other time. An animal amongst other animals in the forest. Her mind cleared. Firstly, details of work she had scheduled for the following week lost their urgency and drifted away. Any thoughts of the people in her life were next to go. Finally, with a pure sense of excitement thrilling through her like a potent drug, language itself vanished along with the last vestige of logical thought. Dietricha was simply running, a graceful, dangerous beast in its natural habitat. Anyone who'd ever seen her immediately after one of her morning runs instantly understood why she had chosen to champion the wild, making the environment ministry her political vehicle: she seemed barely human, unable to speak until she'd had a long shower and a large coffee. She felt no particular kinship with her fellow humans at the best of times. But in the mountains, humanity started to look less like family, more like a parasitic growth.

When she rounded the corner before the lake and the reassuring bulk of the seven oaks was finally in sight, she allowed herself to break into a sprint, her powerful legs pounding the soft earth, her lungs full of sweet mountain air. She felt joyous, alive. She emitted a noise that was part-shout, part-roar of satisfaction.

Then, suddenly, she slowed, her brow furrowed. She had seen movement ahead, between the trees. She slowed again, to walking pace, took a gulp of water from her canteen and squinted, shading her eyes. She hadn't been mistaken. There were two or three figures moving in the natural hollow surrounded by the ring of oaks. She experienced a rush of rage. It seemed like desecration that others should dare enter the sacred space. She felt cold logic and reason returning as she neared the grove. They were probably hikers. They'd be moving on soon enough. She'd stay out of sight and wait. She certainly didn't want to have to speak to anyone.

A strange, unfamiliar sound came from up ahead, along with a flare of light. Dietricha frowned at the combination. It seemed familiar, she'd heard such a sound before. But where? When? The sound came again, a kind of harsh rush of air, some crackling, accompanied again by a flash of illumination. She stopped and thought. Her memory was usually exceptional, but this was something unusual, something out of the ordinary. Then she remembered. It had been a demonstration of confiscated or banned weapons four years previously. She knew that sound. She started sprinting.

Dietricha burst into the clearing to have her fears immediately confirmed. Three young men were walking slowly around the ring of oaks. They might have been taken as hikers at first glance, but Dietricha knew better. On their backs, instead of backpacks, were tanks of high pressure propane and natural gas designed to be released in white hot jets of fire from the nozzles carried by the men. The use of matches and cigarette lighters was banned in the area: flamethrowers would guarantee a significant prison sentence for these idiots.

She cursed her habit of leaving her cell phone in the chalet. Then she shrugged and smiled grimly. If she couldn't take care of three men armed with flamethrowers on her own, she might as well retire now and take up watercolor painting.

"Take the weapons off and put them on the ground," she shouted. "You will answer to the police for this."

The three men seemed unsurprised by her sudden appearance. No, it was more than that. They were expecting her. What was going on? She had little time to speculate as all three men swung toward her with practiced movements, squeezing their triggers as they moved, sending three superheated jets of flame straight at her. She had less than half a second to react, but Dietricha's instincts were honed to a very rare degree indeed. She jumped fifteen feet into the air, flipping backward as she did so. She landed in the oak tree behind her and immediately sprang forward, over the heads of the men, who had yet to react to her first move. As she flew through the space over them, the flames reached the tree behind her and the 300-year-old wood began to crackle and burn immediately. Dietricha screamed with frustration and drew on her power. She chose a template she had constructed with years of practice, meaning she could transform quickly.

Her shoulders thickened and widened as her neck, chest, arms and legs grew great slabs of muscle covered in thick hair. Her head became slightly bigger, the mouth becoming snout-like, filling almost instantly with hundreds of sharp, serrated teeth. Her ears were now those of a wolf, her eyes the predatory amber of a panther. Even as her paw-like feet touched the earth, she sprang, her fangs laying open the neck and shoulder of the nearest man, his life blood pouring out fast enough to render him unconscious before he started to fall. He would be dead within a minute. The second man was beginning to turn, so Dietricha simply slashed a taloned paw across his face, ripping out one eye and temporarily blinding the other as it was filled with blood from the gash in his forehead. She spun toward the third man. She knew he'd had time to react and could feel the heat already as the flame came closer. She gambled he would go for maximum damage and aim at her upper body and face. She dropped to a crouch and sprang low. He was as predictable as she had hoped. The flames passed over her, singeing a few hairs, nothing more. As her outstretched fingers reached his feet, she brutally ripped out the tendons from the back of both legs simultaneously. He made a choking, agonized sound and dropped, bleeding to death.

The second man was still flailing around, his flame the only one still ignited. He was turning in a circle, trying to hit Dietricha. She stayed behind him, then brought her hand up to the tank on his back and twisted the nozzle anti-clockwise. The flame died and the man swung around to face her. She bit his face off. He fell without a sound.

Breathing heavily, she surveyed the scene quickly. The only oak to have suffered had lost a few branches, but some rain the previous night had ensured the fire didn't spread. Dietricha felt the rage start to subside a little. She glanced at the bloody mess around her. She was going to have some cleaning up to do.

Then she heard it. Someone was clapping. She turned in disbelief. A red-haired woman almost as tall as herself, wearing a long black cloak, dropped down from a thick branch on the other side of the clearing and walked toward her, applauding and smiling.

"What a display, Fraulein Strennbourg," the female said as she got closer. "I'd heard rumors, of course, but seeing your work at first hand...well, it's an inspiration. Bravo."

Every hair on Dietricha's body rose and she snarled involuntarily. Her animal instincts were telling her plainly that danger was approaching, that it was fight or flight time. She had never been one for flight. But her brain fought her instincts. What possible threat could this woman represent, despite her confidence and seeming lack of fear?

"Oh, you're right to be scared," said the woman. "I am here to kill you, after all."

Dietricha decided that was probably enough talking. She had to get this over with and destroy the evidence, before a vacationing walker stumbled across the bloody scene and raised the alarm. She crouched slightly, then sprang at the woman, swiping a taloned claw at her unprotected head. She missed. It had never happened before. Although it had rarely come as far as this, as one look at her in wolf form was enough for most people to decide they would rather be her friend than her enemy.

Dietricha hit the ground, rolled and came straight up again, lips drawn back from her vicious incisors. The red-haired woman hadn't dodged, she had simply melted into the air. Now she was in front of her again. Dietricha didn't hesitate, just sprang a second time. The woman reached out, caught her by the throat, slammed her to the ground, then straddled her. Dietricha's yellow eyes widened in disbelief. How could this woman have strength like this? She tried to move, but the woman's knees pinioned her. She thrashed, but it was like being held down by iron manacles.

"Did you think all this power was just for you?" said the woman, shaking her head. She held out the hand that wasn't gripping Dietricha's throat and one of the flame-throwers slid across the soil into her grip. She pointed it directly at Dietricha's face. "Shame," she said.

Dietricha made one last attempt to free herself, putting all her strength and power into the effort. She could feel the ancient magic of the oak circle entering her body, increasing her power. The woman above her faltered for a moment, and Dietricha felt the balance of power shift suddenly in her favor as her strength seemed to double, then double again. But even as she began to push the woman off her, the flame ignited, white-hot burning gas was released full into her face, devouring hair, skin, muscle, tissue, bone and finally brain, and suddenly it was all too late.

# Chapter 5

**Los Angeles**
**Present day**

The sun rose at 5:43am that summer morning. Unusually, Bob Geller didn't have his labrador with him as he climbed the path. That may have saved his life. Marcie had been kept overnight at the animal clinic after a minor operation, but Bob was a man of rigid habits and nothing would keep him from rising at 5, showering, downing the first of many coffees then heading up into the Verdugo mountains.

Bob had spent the best part of his life in the military, only leaving when an Iraqi land mine left him with one leg shorter than the other and a lifetime of nightmares. His career had cost him his marriage. His grown-up daughter had stopped even the pretense of staying in touch nearly a decade ago. Now in his late fifties, he kept his life simple. Healthy eating, exercise, a few nips of the hard stuff every day to distract him from the dull pain in his leg. He had never been a romantic - the first time he'd bought flowers for his ex-wife was when she died. He knew he lavished more time and affection on his dog than he ever had on another person, but Marcie just loved him whatever mood he was in, never asked him if he wanted to talk about it and never gave him *that look*. Even when he came home late twice a month after his regular visit to a semi-retired call girl.

"Don't even know if I can call her that," he said to Marcie one morning. "Can I call her a call senior?" Marcie had wisely kept her own counsel.

The only regular human contact he had other than the prostitute was Seb - the young guy he met regularly on his morning hike. Seb liked his own company, too - wary, reserved. Bob knew a fellow loner when he met one. It had taken months for them to get beyond the nod and grunt greeting and on to a conversation of sorts. But there was something about Seb - a kind of dreaming, thoughtful quality combined with a grounded down-to-earth nature that Bob couldn't help but warm to. He often met Seb on the weekends, after the younger man had been playing with his band. It gave Bob another reason to get outdoors on the occasional days when the whisper in his head asked why he bothered getting up at all.

Seb had been spending weekend nights walking the mountain trails more often lately, but he'd been quieter, paler. There was obviously something on his mind, but Bob knew better than to ask. Seemed like it was what you were supposed to do these days, talk it through, talk it out, communicate, even - God help you - reach out to someone. But Bob knew the value of a friend who let you talk when you wanted to talk and didn't ask questions. Seb was just happy to walk, throw sticks for Marcie and share a few warming sips from the flask.

Bob was a little surprised when Seb wasn't around that morning. And he was even more surprised at the figure he found walking ahead of him on the trail. She was short, slim, Asian, her hair a slow-motion explosion of black, purple and bleached white. She was wearing a denim jacket with the words 'Crushed Asians' on the back. A flicker of memory stirred in Bob and he stopped short, watching the woman as she pulled a cell phone out of her pocket and peered at the screen.

Just as he decided to call out to her, a flash of light briefly flickered over the whole scene, as if sheet lightning had suddenly decided to break all the rules of physics and start manifesting at ground level.

"What the f-!" yelled Meera and dropped her phone. As she bent down to find it, Bob took a step toward her.

"Meera?" he said. The woman straightened, brushed her hair away from heavily made-up eyes and glared back at Bob.

"Who the hell are you?" she said. Bob gave her a measured stare and took his time replying. Underneath the horror-show makeup, fright wig and up-yours attitude was just another scared kid hoping a show of bravado would keep the bad shit away.

"Name's Bob," he said. Meera made it obvious she was unimpressed by this information by raising an eyebrow and chewing ostentatiously.

"I'm a friend of Seb's," he said. Meera grinned - it transformed her face and suddenly Bob understood what Seb had seen in her. She looked like a cat who had not only got the cream, but had discovered a permanent source of free cream and was about to get started on it.

"Well, ok then," she said. "How'd you know who I am?"

"Seb mentioned you," said Bob. Meera raised an eyebrow and Bob colored slightly.

"Nothing, um, personal," he said. "But he told me about the band - and about the original name." He waved his hand at her jacket. She snorted.

"Yeah, Clockwatchers turned out to be a bigger crowd puller than Crushed Asians. Who'd a thunk it, eh? Thought a name like that would have 'em lining up around the block." Her eyes narrowed as she looked at Bob, her head on one side. *Looks a lot like Marcie when she does that.* He resisted a sudden urge to throw a stick and see if she'd fetch it.

"Not like Seb to talk about the band," she said. "Not like Seb to talk about me either." She sighed. "Not much like him to talk at all, really. He must like you. Guess I'll give you the benefit for now. So. Any clue at all what the pyrotechnics were all about just then? I'm no weather expert, but that was pretty weird, right?"

Bob shook his head. He was trying to tune in to her English accent. She walked toward him, pulling a spliff from behind her back and taking a huge toke. She waved it in Bob's direction.

"Sorry - thought you were a cop to start with. You've got that look about you. No offense. Want some?"

"No thank you," said Bob. "Tried it once and it made me fall asleep in the middle of a wedding."

"Yeah, it can relax you," said Meera, "but where's the harm in that?"

"It was my wedding," said Bob.

"Oh God!" said Meera, laughing. "OK, that's not so good."

"You looking for Seb?" he said. "I normally see him here about this time."

"He's here," she said. She held up her cell, which showed a map with a flashing green dot. They walked up the trail. The light changed as the sun began to slice through the clouds, smog and trees. Everything around them was a sombre monochrome and it was eerily quiet. Bob heard a distant throb that made his guts churn. Too quiet. He grabbed Meera and half threw her under the canopy of a nearby tree, clamping a hand over her mouth when she tried to protest. The joint had fallen from her fingers and he ground it under his boot, making sure it was out.

Gunshots suddenly broke the silence. A burst from an automatic weapon - no, two bursts.

"What the hell is going on?" said Meera.

"Quiet!" Bob hissed. "You're going to have to trust me." Her eyes widened as the low throb Bob had heard became the unmistakable sound of an approaching helicopter, although much quieter than any he knew. Almost immediately a camouflaged helicopter blocked the light through the trees as it hovered less than a hundred yards away. A dozen heavily armed figures jumped out and formed a defensive circle within seconds with an ease born of years of practice. Seconds later, a tall man joined them, his eyes immediately scanning the area as if to pick out any details his highly trained team might have missed. He spoke quietly into a head mic and the team cautiously moved forward, weapons at the ready. The tall man paused briefly, then followed.

Bob leaned forward until his mouth was brushing against Meera's ear.

"Listen," he whispered. "I don't know who those guys are, but they're not wearing any kind of official uniform and the bird they arrived in had no markings. We could be in several hundred kinds of trouble here. I think our friends here may be the 'shoot first, don't bother asking any questions' types, so we need to get out while we can. We don't really know if Seb is here at all, so let's go."

Meera shook her head furiously. "He's here," she said. "I know exactly where he is."

"What?" said Bob. "Where?"

She pointed to a clearing half hidden by bushes. "There," she said. Bob already knew which direction she was going to point in. It was precisely where the guys with half a million dollars' worth of advanced weaponry had just gone. Where, minutes before, some poor fool may have got himself shot. Bob considered his options. Meera saw him hesitate and snorted.

"You do what you like," she whispered, "I'm going to help Seb." She stood up and started to walk.

Bob grabbed her arm and pulled her back.

"I want to help him too," he said, "but we won't be much help dead." She looked afraid but determined. *Crazy, stubborn kid.* Bob shook his head. He couldn't help liking her.

He looked around quickly before glancing upwards, coming to a decision. He pointed at the tree.

"Can you climb that?" he said.

Thirty seconds later, they were both halfway up the tree, hidden by the summer foliage. Their vantage point gave them an excellent view. Six of the soldiers had taken up positions around the clearing. The rest of them had formed a ring around something lying on the floor. The tall man was talking to two uniformed soldiers. One of the men pointed at whatever was on the floor and the tall man seemed to be asking questions. Bob knew enough about body language to see that the two men being questioned were terrified of the taller man. *Who the hell is this guy?*

Just then, two things happened simultaneously that made Bob feel like his heart might stop beating. First, one of the soldiers moved and he could see it was a body on the ground between them. Second, one of the two scared soldiers handed a backpack to the tall man. Bob recognized it immediately. He turned to look at Meera and the tears running silently down her face told him she recognized it too.

The tall man turned toward the body and the other soldiers made room as he approached. With every minute, the light improved and Bob could now see clearly. More clearly than he wanted to. Seb's shaggy brown hair hung across his face and his body was surrounded by blood-stained earth. Bob had seen enough fatalities to know when someone was gone. He felt a deep quiet anger burning away his fear. *What the hell was going on here?* Seb was one of the gentlest people he had ever known. None of this made any sense.

The tall man knelt beside Seb's body, putting a couple of fingers on his neck. He said something into his head mic and within seconds the sound of the rotors was back. Bob guessed it must have gained altitude to be out of hearing until needed. Two soldiers went to Seb's head, two to his feet. As they flipped the body over, Seb's face came fully into view and Meera choked back a sob. Bob glanced at her and as he did so, her eyes suddenly widened in disbelief. There was a shout from the clearing. Bob snapped his head back.

Seb opened his eyes. The soldiers around him involuntarily took a step backward in shock. He sat up and looked around him, spitting out a mouthful of dirt. He remembered falling. He remembered shots. He stood and the soldiers backed up a few more steps, their guns pointing at him.

"Don't shoot!" came a voice. Seb turned as a tall man walked toward him, exuding authority. He eyed Seb steadily and motioned at the men. They all lowered their weapons.

"Son, I represent the US Government. You and I need to have a little talk." He nodded toward the helicopter.

"Shall we?"

Seb barely knew what he was thinking. In fact, the thought that he didn't know what he was thinking was the only thought his brain seemed capable of handling. He looked at the tall man. Behind him, Seb saw two vaguely familiar faces. The men who had shot him. He had no idea what was going on, what had happened to him, whether he was really dead or alive. The whole scene might just be a lucid dream as he lay dying, his blood pouring from slit wrists as he sat under a tree in the Verdugo Mountains. But he felt alive and he knew these guys were far from friendly. He made his decision. He ran.

The soldiers began to raise their weapons but it all seemed to happen in slow motion for Seb. He was out of the clearing and crashing through the bushes before the first gun barrel had been raised more than an inch. By the time the tall man had screamed "Follow him!" Seb was out of sight. As the soldiers began their pursuit and the tall man jumped back into the helicopter, Seb was running faster than he had known possible. He felt stronger than he had in years and would have laughed out loud if he hadn't needed all his breath to draw enough oxygen to keep his legs pumping. It seemed - but couldn't possibly be - only a few minutes before he rounded the corner of his block. He wasn't aware of the moment he stopped running, he just found himself walking through the door and heading up to his apartment, vaguely aware he'd just run faster than he'd thought possible. And he wasn't out of breath.

Back at the clearing, all the soldiers gone, Bob and Meera climbed down in silence and stood facing each other. Neither knew what to say. In the end they both spoke together.

"We have to -"

"Seb needs _"

They stopped talking. Bob nodded.

"Whatever just happened, Seb's in trouble. And now he's on the run. We have to find him." He moved into the clearing and started looking at the bushes, peering at bent branches and patches of flattened grass.

"What are you doing?" said Meera.

"I know one or two things about tracking," said Bob. Give me some time and I think we can find him."

"He's in his apartment," came Meera's voice behind him.

"Possibly," said Bob, "but we don't know that for sure. We need to -"

"No," said Meera, "he's in his apartment."

Bob turned and looked at her. She had her phone. She turned the screen to face him and he saw the map with a pulsing green dot.

"I gave Seb my old phone," she said. "He never was much of a geek. Never even changed the password. So I just used 'find my iPhone'. He's in his apartment. Even though that's impossible."

"I'm not much of a one for technology either," said Bob. "You telling me you can find him with that thing?"

"As long as he has his phone with him," said Meera. Bob put down the twig he had been studying.

"You're the boss," he said, then stopped. "What do you mean, it's impossible?"

"Seb's apartment is about three miles away," she said. "What did he do? Fly?"

# Chapter 6

Seb stepped into his apartment and leaned heavily against the door. He closed his eyes and slid to the floor. *What the hell is going on?* A jumble of images raced through his head: the half empty whisky bottle slipping out of blood-drained fingers, the mountain cat eying him hungrily, the tall, graceful alien creature that had somehow saved his life, the look on the soldiers' faces as they emptied their weapons into his body. The soldiers had looked scared.

*But they still shot me.*

He opened his eyes and walked over to the kitchen. Pouring a large glass of water, he took it through to the open-plan living space and sat on the piano stool, his back to the instrument. He had never gone for more than a day without playing it until his illness had forced him to stop. He drank deeply, tasting the fresh, cold liquid in a vivid way he'd never experienced before. Setting the glass on the floor, he suddenly shocked himself by bursting into laughter. He'd packed most of his belongings into boxes over the last week, so his laughter bounced off bare floors and walls. He laughed and laughed at the sheer joy of being unexpectedly alive. He laughed until his chest ached. He put his hand up to his shirt pocket and felt the bullet holes. His laughter slowly subsiding, he walked over to the mirror. He unbuttoned his shirt, unsure what to expect. Moving closer, Seb ran his fingers over his chest. He remembered the bullets ripping into him from left to right. He remembered the sensation of his heart bursting and all the blood in his body succumbing to gravity, no longer driven by his pulse. He remembered all of this, yet his chest was totally unmarked. Not a single blemish. In fact, his body looked like it did in his early twenties, when he was working out five days a week.

"What the-," Seb took a step backward in shock, his fingers moving to his belly, looking for the scar that had run from his hip to his navel. The scar that Jack Carnavon had given him in New York at the age of 15 at St Benet's Children's Home, pulling a knife from his pocket to settle an argument the only way he knew how. Seb touched that scar dozens of times every day. It reminded him where he came from. But now his skin was unmarked, anonymous, clean. He gasped.

"No," he whispered. He stared at his reflection, numb with shock. His mind started to dart around like a frightened animal, refusing to settle anywhere. His old scar. Jack Carnavon's face. Melissa turning away from him. Meera taking a huge toke from a fat joint. Father O'Hanoran's office. The girl who had unexpectedly kissed him at that club in Manhattan. The Burning Man festival where he'd snorted something that made him talk like Stephen Hawking for two days. The scarred face he sometimes dreamed about, wondering if it was his father. His first show with Clockwatchers. The famous video call he'd made to the rest of the band after writing *Sunburst Sunday* - forgetting he was naked.

Seb groaned and walked closer to the largest window, pulling up a hard wooden chair. He sat facing the morning light and closed his eyes, feeling warmth as he looked at the deep red behind his eyelids. He took three long breaths, inhaling through his nose, exhaling through his mouth.

Father O'Hanoran had taught him the technique of contemplation when everyone else seemed to be writing him off as a disturbed teen. Although the weekly meetings had begun as a tedious chore for Seb, he'd soon realized that some of the things Father O talked about made sense. Sense was the last thing 15-year-old Seb had expected from a Catholic monk, but as he gradually overcame his initial misgivings, he began to try the technique he was being taught. He had let it slip lately, but now his body and mind moved quickly into the first stage. Within minutes, he had taken a step back from his chaotic thoughts and was calmly watching them enter and leave his consciousness.

Thirty minutes passed as Seb watched his thoughts and his breath. At the deepest point of awareness, he found something new. A presence - passive but awake, vast, powerful - waited for him in the place of silence. He felt no threat, no fear. He was there and he/she/it/they were there. He opened his eyes. A feeling of someone being close to him lingered for a few seconds, then dissipated. He stood, stretched. His hand went to his scar and his eyes widened when he discovered he could feel it again. Turning to the mirror he confirmed its reappearance, the thin white line curving slightly where, 18 years earlier, Seb had grabbed Jack Carnovan's wrist and stopped him carving him up like a joint of meat.

He walked into the kitchen and drank three glasses of water. He was hungry - hungrier than he should have been considering the amount of sushi he'd consumed the night before thinking it was his last meal. Opening the ice box, he found a bag of spinach that had probably been there since he moved in. Tearing open the plastic, he began tearing off dark green chunks and stuffing them into his mouth, crunching them like cookies. His cell phone rang.

"Hi, Mee," he said, his mouth full of frozen spinach. "Guess what? I don't have sensitive teeth any more."

"No shit," came Mee's East London tones. He could hear her smiling. "And that's the most important thing going on at the moment?"

"Well," he said. "It's pretty weird, don't you think?" He poured another glass of water and washed down the last handful of spinach.

"I think I've had to redefine weird this morning," said Mee. Seb looked at his watch.

"Mee!" he said, "it's before noon. What are you doing out of bed?"

"It's a long story," she said, "but you and I need to talk. The main thing is, are you ok?"

"That's another long story," said Seb, "but the short answer is yes. Come on over."

"Be there in ten," said Meera.

Seb sat at the piano and gently placed his hands on the keys. He smiled and began to play, the music flowing again, his fingers moving seemingly ahead of his brain's signals as he improvised. Almost immediately he felt himself approach a similar state of consciousness to when he sat in contemplation.

A phone rang. He put his hand on his pocket. Not his. He ignored it and went back to the piano, but it continued to ring loudly. He sighed and stood up. The noise was coming from the door of his apartment. He checked the spy hole but there was no one in the hall. He opened the door cautiously and looked down. On the floor outside his apartment was a cell phone, still ringing. He picked it up and held it up to his ear.

"Mr. Varden, my name is Westlake. I represent the United States Government. I know you're scared, but I am not here to hurt you in any way. Please come to the window of your apartment and look outside." Seb walked to the window but hung back, remembering the soldiers. He flattened himself against the wall, then took a quick glance before jerking his head back. No uniforms, just one guy in front of a long black car. The tall guy from the clearing. *Well, if he has a long, black car, he must work for the government.*

"The soldiers with you shot...at me," said Seb. "Why? What the hell's going on?"

"Mr. Varden, believe me, what they did was contrary to their orders and they will be dealt with. I have sent my squad away. It's just me and a driver. I have answers to some of your questions, but you're going to have to trust me and come down here."

"Give me a couple minutes," said Seb and hung up. He considered his options. He could run again, but this guy had found him pretty quickly. He certainly didn't trust him, but maybe he could get answers to a few questions. Start with the simple ones like, "Did you see that alien?" and, "Any idea how I can recover from massive blood loss and survive being shot in the heart?" before moving on to the tougher stuff like, "Think my brain tumor's disappeared too?". And Mee would be turning up soon. He didn't want this Westlake guy knowing about Mee. He could send him away, agree to meet later. He opened his closet and pulled out a black suit and shirt. A girlfriend had once called him vain because he wore black so much, not realizing that he only did it because he hated shopping and buying everything in one color made life easier.

Five minutes later he walked out of his apartment building. Westlake stuck out a hand. Seb stayed out of reach. Westlake shrugged.

"I can't blame you for being cautious, Mr. Varden," he said.

"You said you have answers," said Seb. "Well?"

Westlake shook his head slightly.

"Not outside. What I have to say concerns information vital to American national security. Step into the car, please."

"Oh, come on," said Seb, "there's no way I'm getting into a car with you. Despite the national security bullshit." He thought of Meera again. "There's a coffee place around the corner. Let's go there."

"Very well," said Westlake. He took a step toward Seb. He spoke quietly. "But there's one thing I need to tell you right away."

Seb leaned in. Westlake's right hand was in his pocket and as Seb came closer, it came out fast. Westlake was holding something and Seb flinched as it headed toward his face. Even as he recognized it as some kind of small aerosol can a fine spray hit him as he was breathing in. He staggered, his legs suddenly unable to support him. The taller man caught him by the shoulders as he stumbled, maneuvering him in the direction of the waiting car. An old couple with bags of shopping hesitated as they watched Westlake push Seb onto the back seat. Westlake turned toward them.

"Likes his drink a bit too much," he said. The old woman grimaced and pulled her husband away. Westlake got in and pushed Seb into the far corner of the car. He shut the door and caught the eye of the driver in the rear view mirror.

"Go," he said.

Ten minutes later, Bob and Meera walked into an empty apartment. Meera had kept a key for a couple of years, partly because she occasionally stayed over, partly because Seb would occasionally leave his somewhere on one of his lost weekends.

"No sign of a struggle," said Bob, picking up the water glass and sniffing it. He turned to Meera, who was looking at her phone.

"He's ten blocks away," she said. "Think he's gone for another run?"

Seb felt like he was at the bottom of a deep well, lying with his head lolling uncomfortably on his shoulder. Drool slid down one cheek. The well was pitch black and he had the sense that he was moving. He could hear a man's voice, muffled at first then quickly getting clearer.

"Asgert acwurwf," came the voice. A picture came into Seb's mind of a tall, dangerous man. "Yus, na prublush. Yus, sir. I've given him enough to knock out a horse. He'll sleep like a baby for about 12 hours. Agreed. Yes, sir. I'd suggest the Shit Station. Everything is in place there, our security hasn't been breached. No witnesses and any shots can be dismissed as a training exercise."

Seb was now fully conscious. He kept his eyes shut and breathed deeply, listening intently.

"That's right, sir, they both confirmed he had been shot. No doubt at all, sir. Well...not as such, sir, no...but he was lying in a pool of his own blood...No, I have no idea, we're running background checks now. Seb Varden, 32, an orphan - no really close friends. Musician. Yes, sir, thank you, sir, I'll brief the team at the Station."

The car slowed. Seb carefully opened his left eye. They were approaching a traffic light. His fingers brushed against the door handle and he pulled gently, ready to run. Nothing. The door was not only locked, there was no conventional lock at all in sight. Seb guessed anyone who got a ride in the back of this particular model often did so against their will.

"No sign at all, sir. The soldiers' statements agree on every detail but it doesn't help us. The creature has gone. We never found a way of tracking it anyway. Yes, sir, this is our best chance. Whatever the connection is, we'll find it. We'll trace any known associates."

Seb tensed slightly. He was aware of Westlake suddenly turning toward him.

"Wait a second, sir," he said. Seb introduced a slight snore to his breathing, hoping he wasn't overdoing it.

"It's nothing. Yes, sir, will do." Westlake leaned forward and spoke to the driver. "Take the freeway. Break some traffic laws."

Seb felt the car accelerate. He began to panic and forced himself to keep his breathing steady. He drew on his contemplation experience and drew his attention back to his breath. As he stilled his mind, his awareness seemed to broaden slightly, a tilting in his consciousness, as if he had simultaneously withdrawn from the moment and reached out toward it. His fingers against the door seemed to melt into it - there was no gap in sensation - the metal and flesh both reacted to his impulses.

Opening his left eye again, he saw the freeway as they pulled into light traffic. He guessed their speed to be around 80mph as the car accelerated again. The outside lane of the freeway was closed for repairs, but there was no evidence of any work being done - just a long stretch of cones. Seb felt something in the door begin to move - metal begin to melt away from the lock and the hinges. The freeway began a long curve to the right and, as the car turned, Seb saw his chance. He tensed. Westlake reacted next to him, his hand coming up to grab him. Seb put all his weight against the door and pushed with his shoulder. There was a moment when he seemed to hang in space, Westlake's face a mix of shock and anger as he reached across the empty back seat.

Then the door - with Seb now crouched on top of it, hit the surface of the freeway with a scream of metal and a shower of sparks.

By the time the driver had started to stop, Seb, kneeling on the car door, had slowed to about 50mph as he shot through the cones, sending two of them flying into the air. He was aware of the sound of screeching tires and honking as the door slowed further and he could see he was heading directly toward a parked tow-truck. He had two, maybe three seconds before he hit it. With no time to think, Seb launched himself off the car door, sending it spinning and flipping into the truck. He crossed into the opposite lane in mid air, managed to right himself and landed on his feet, skidding to a stop. He had just enough time to congratulate himself on the style of his landing before he looked up to see a van, its driver's face a mask of shock as he stamped fruitlessly on the brakes.

The van hit him. It must have hit him. He had no time to avoid it. But there was no pain, no noise, no sensation of impact. He just heard a hurricane rush in his ears, felt his stomach feel like the world was turning upside down and his head spin in a split second to a tiny point of consciousness which winked out like a blown match.

Then nothing. Again.

# Chapter 7

**17 Years Previously**

St. Benet's Children's Home, New York

In the TV room, Jack Carnavon was holding court, as usual. At 17, he was two or three years older than most of the other boys, which gave him a physical and mental advantage. Not that he needed it. If he had been ten years old and a foot shorter than everyone else, he would still have emerged as a leader. Some people seem to carry off an effortless charisma just in the way they hold themselves. Jack Carnavon wasn't particularly tall, at 5'10, he was almost exactly Seb Varden's height, despite Seb being two years his junior. But where Seb was still skinny and awkward, Jack was compact, wiry and surprisingly well-muscled. He moved gracefully, with an easy charm. He teased the Sisters in a way that equally horrified and thrilled his peers, though he was careful not to overstep the mark.

Since arriving at St. Benet's a few months previously, Jack had quickly put his power structure in place. It had been a subtle process, showing favor to certain boys who bore grudges against other, bigger, rivals, then delighting his new lieutenants by dealing out minor humiliations to those who had wronged them. His background was unclear and he obviously enjoyed the mystery, occasionally hinting at a violent - but romantic - past.

Like a new alpha in a pack of chimps, Jack knew he would have to see off a challenge at some point. The way he dealt with it, when it came, showed him to be a ruthless enforcer, not just a tough, good-looking kid with a winning smile. To no one's great surprise, it was Stevie who took him on.

Stevie was a bully, no one would deny that. He took what he wanted, he used violence liberally, although it was never serious, just a case of pinning someone on the floor until they gave up their soda, their comic book, the couple of dollars they'd saved. But Stevie's bullying was a product of his environment. It wasn't nature, it was nurture. He wasn't that bright, he was overly sensitive, he stuttered. But he was heavy, strong and could take punishment. His personality made him a natural victim, his build gave him the opportunity to avoid that eventuality. So he became a bully. And, contrary to the prevailing wisdom about bullies, he wasn't a coward. You could punch him and he would just swat you away as if he hadn't felt it. So when he saw Jack Carnavon establishing himself as de facto boss, he knew he would have to be pre-emptive, put him in his place. Hard. He was no planning genius, but knew enough to understand his move would have to be public - he had to humiliate Carnavon, make his fair-weather friends desert him. Isolated, he would be easy pickings.

The TV was on, but the sound was muted as Jack was reading the funnies. The four boys in the room were keen to earn his favor, and it was only ten minutes, after all. Stevie walked in, glanced around the room, then strolled over to the TV and put the volume up. Loud. Jack looked up from the paper.

"Stevie," he said. "Be a pal. I'm reading here. Just kill the sound for another few minutes, ok?"

"Watcha reading?" said Stevie, ignoring his request and walking over to where Jack was sitting. Stevie wasn't tall, but he was broad and squat. A wrestler's build.

"Stevie, please," said Jack, not even lifting his eyes from the paper. He waved his hand casually toward the TV. "The volume."

Stevie responded by leaning forward and snatching the paper from Jack's other hand. "Thanks, Carnavon," he said, "I haven't read that yet."

He walked slowly to the door, then turned back toward his audience. "You make sure that volume stays up," he said.

Jack sighed theatrically and smiled at the boys, shrugging slightly as if to say, "Hey, I tried to be polite, I gave him a chance." He picked up the remote and muted the sound again.

"Put it back on," said Stevie, scowling.

Jack responded by getting up and stretching ostentatiously before walking toward Stevie. The room fell silent. Everybody stood up. A couple of older boys started to follow Jack, but he motioned for them to stay where they were. He stopped just out of reach of Stevie. "There's no excuse for being rude," he said. "And no one likes a bully, Stevie."

Stevie was so tensed up, the veins on his neck were throbbing. He opened his mouth to respond, but didn't get the chance because Jack's fist hit him so hard, two of his teeth flew out. There was a collective gasp in the room. Stevie took a step backward, which put him just into the doorway. He knew he had to respond, and he knew it would have to be good. He launched himself forward, his hand extended to get hold of Jack's collar. Jack was expecting this and stepped nimbly aside, grabbing the open door. He slammed it as hard as he could, his whole body spinning anti-clockwise, lending extra momentum to the move. The door hit Stevie just below the elbow, instantly breaking his arm. The impact was so hard, the bone broke the skin, exposing glistening muscle and fat as the white splinter poked through. One of the boys threw up as Jack moved forward and clamped a hand over the mouth of the white-faced Stevie, now sweating and shaking with pain. Suddenly there was a knife in Jack's hand. Jack's body blocked everyone else's view, but he showed the knife to Stevie, waiting until he could see Stevie had seen it. He leaned forward and whispered.

"You tripped, ok? When they ask. You tripped. Anything else, any more trouble, I'll visit you when you're asleep and I'll slice off your balls."

The atmosphere after Stevie had been taken to the hospital was false, forced, strange. Jack had crossed a line. The boys of St. Benet's were keen to appear self-reliant, tough even, but pretty much all of it was bluster and bravado. Everyone knew a fight would never get serious. Threats were just threats, extremely unlikely to escalate into any real trouble. So Jack did more than break Stevie's arm, he broke the unwritten laws of St. Benet's. At that time, there were 19 boys living there, but those in the TV room after Stevie had been taken away were the top of the tree. They were the oldest boys in a place where age generally implied seniority. The Sisters might run the place, but if you wanted to fit in at St. Benet's, you followed the rules set by the older boys. There was a tense quiet in the room. Everyone knew Jack had gone too far, no one wanted to say it. If they were going to walk away from him, it had to be now.

Jack sensed the mood and dealt with it quickly. He sat on the sofa and buried his head in his hands, saying nothing. After about thirty seconds, his shoulders started heaving and, when he lifted his head, fat tears were running down his face.

"I never meant to hurt him so badly. Oh God, I swear, I never meant to hurt him."

One of the boys sat next to him and put a hand on his shoulder.

"I thought he was going to kill me," said Jack, sobbing. "Did you see the look on his face? He'd gone crazy. Psycho. I thought I was going to die." Two more boys moved back toward Jack and made conciliatory comments.

"It was self-defense."

"No one blames you, Jack."

"Don't be hard on yourself, you had no choice."

The only boy who hadn't moved was Seb Varden. He had seen the look on Stevie's face very clearly. It was the look of a scared boy who'd suddenly realized there were people out there for whom violence was not just a way of life, but a passion. He had seen the pleasure Jack was gaining from hurting him and it terrified him. Seb knew the other boys had seen it too. They'd just chosen to rewrite reality in a way that allowed them to carry on being friends with Jack. Seb saw through Jack's performance after the incident, too. The tears were real enough, but Seb had once read an interview with an actor who could cry whenever he needed to. On demand. Jack obviously had the same ability, since through his tears Seb had watched him looking around, seeing what effect his performance was having, playing the crowd like a pro.

Seb felt disgust. Mostly with himself. He had chosen to hang around with Jack Carnavon, had told himself he was a fascinating guy, with some experience of real life. But really, he had known from the start that Jack was something else entirely. He'd felt coldness and emptiness radiating from him. For someone so talkative, who had so many stories, so much to say, he never revealed anything personal.

Not really. Seb felt sure no one would ever get to know the real Jack Carnavon. And now, seeing a glimpse of the heart of the boy, he was convinced it was time to walk away.

He stood up and went to leave. The boys surrounding Jack were starting to joke around a bit again, diffusing the tension. Jack was joining in, but still feigning weakness and regret, puffing up the other boys' egos so they felt needed by him. But those cold, quick eyes followed Seb as he left the room and he knew his desertion wouldn't be forgotten or forgiven.

The trouble - when it came - was worse than Seb had anticipated. He had managed to avoid Jack as far as possible for a few days. Not too obviously, but enough that the clique of boys at the top accepted that he had voluntarily left their number. Seb was popular with the others, quiet but loyal and with a self-deprecating sense of humor. And he was always willing to listen, which was a truly rare quality. So when he deliberately isolated himself, spending more time at the piano and listening to music, his decision was respected by everyone. Everyone but Jack.

The boys slept in two dormitories, 8-12 boys to a room. A locker beside their bed held clothes, toiletries and a few personal belongings. One late afternoon in Fall, Seb was lying on his bed, supposedly reading but actually thinking about the girl who'd been doing some voluntary work with the Sisters around the Home the past few weeks. St. Catherine's, a local Catholic girls' school, regularly sent small teams of volunteers to help with odd jobs, gardening, or decorating. New faces around the place were nothing new, and Seb was used to exchanging a nod or a polite "hey" with unfamiliar people during the day. But, nearly three weeks ago, that had all changed.

Melissa Rae was the most beautiful sight Seb had ever seen. He liked to think of himself as a bit of a man of the world at the age of 15. He had talked with girls on four or five occasions without tripping over his words, blushing uncontrollably or completely losing the power of speech. It had taken work to get past those stages, which had previously crippled his efforts at getting close to females at the various social events organized by the children's home.

The Sisters running St. Benet's were considered progressive by many of their peers, allowing reasonably free mixing of the sexes when possible. They justified their position to their more conservative critics by pointing out that any claim to be "good" or "morally upstanding" was suspect if never tested. Easy to be pure if no one had ever offered you a chance to be dirty. That wasn't quite the phrasing they used at the Motherhouse Symposium they attended annually, but that's what they meant. "Would our Lord *be* our Lord if he hadn't been tempted?" was the provocative - and often unpopular - question they posed to their colleagues.

Seb and the other half-dozen hormone-driven boys and young men currently residing at the Home, naturally cared nothing for any scriptural or theological justification, as long as the outcome was the same: girls were made available. They could be spoken to, smiled at, even flirted with. Seb knew of the Sisters' thoughts about temptation, but secretly wondered if Jesus would have been quite so quick to avoid it if he had met Melissa Rae when he was 15. He felt terrible for wondering, but he wondered just the same.

Lying on his bed that afternoon, eyes closing, Seb decided he was finally ready to ask Melissa out. Their conversations had drifted to the subject of romance recently, and Seb knew that Melissa didn't have a boyfriend.

A sci-fi feature was playing at Cap House (no one could remember the real name of the shabby movie theater two blocks away) and he was going to ask her to go with him. His stomach was in knots, but he was ready. He would ask her tomorrow morning.

He smiled and opened his eyes. Jack Carnavon stood over him, a nasty self-satisfied smirk on his face. Seb sat up against his headboard and closed his book. Jack sat down on the end of the bed. He reached over and picked up the book.

"Poetry?" he said, and laughed humorlessly. "You're just such a sensitive soul, Seb. I bet your suffer from inner torments. Don't tell me, no one understands you, right?" Despite knowing the cliche would apply to any 15-year old, Seb still felt the sting of an accurate taunt. Jack examined the cover of the book.

"Philip Larkin?" he said. "Looks like a fag." He read a little of the blurb on the back. "A British fag, too. Thought poets were meant to be sexy. This guy looks like a librarian." Seb considered telling Jack that Larkin was, in fact, a librarian, but decided any attempt to educate him would be wasted. He just patiently held out his hand for the book and waited until Jack returned it.

"What do you want, Jack?" said Seb, putting the book in his locker.

"Hey, why do I have to *want* something," said Jack. "Can't I just hang out with my buddy? Haven't seen so much of you lately. Me and the guys miss you, is all."

"Yeah, well, sometimes I just don't feel too sociable," said Seb. He didn't want to spend any more time in Jack's company than was necessary, but there was no point in antagonizing him. In less than a year, Jack would turn 18 and have to leave St. Benet's. Seb could wait him out. After all, how much damage could he do in such a short time?

Jack stood and looked at Seb, that false smile still on his face. "Ok, pal, that's your choice," he said. "Guess we've got to respect that. But you're missing a bunch of fun." He walked to the doorway, then turned back.

"Speaking of fun," he said, "you checked out that redhead from St. Catherine's? She's some piece, ain't she?"

Seb felt the color rise to his cheeks and his heart rate rise. Melissa was the only girl with red hair - a gorgeous, deep auburn. "Don't think I know who you mean," he said, feigning a yawn.

"Oh?" said Jack. "Someone said they saw you talking to her. Must have been mistaken, I guess." He opened the door to leave.

"Um, what about her?" said Seb, hating himself for being drawn so easily, but incapable of not asking the question.

"Oh, nothing much," said Jack. "Just got talking to her myself today. Melissa - that's her name. Tidy little body, great eyes. Surprised you don't know her. Anyway, I asked her out tonight."

Seb had always assumed the expression 'his blood ran cold' was a gothic exaggeration that had nothing to do with real life. Not any more.

"The Sisters think I'm taking her to a ball game," said Jack, the smirk on his face never touching the cold eyes that were locked on Seb's. He laughed. "They're so easy to play. Thought I might take her to a bar or two, find out how many drinks it takes before I can get into those tight jeans of hers. What an ass on that girl! Gotta go now, enjoy your fag poetry."

Seb clenched his fists and dug his nails into his palms to stop him shouting in rage as the door closed softly behind Jack. To his shame, his first thought hadn't been concern for Melissa's safety, but *why the hell did she say yes?*

# Chapter 8

**Present day**

The sun hung low and pale in a winter sky. Frost-held grass crunched under his feet as he walked toward the water. On either side, ancient trees, dark, silhouetted and austere, their branches a bold typeface on the blank fog. Geese broke from the surface of the pond ahead in a flurry of purposeful activity, lifting into a V heading North-East.

"Shouldn't they be heading south?" thought Seb. His hands were cold. He reached into his coat pockets and pulled out some heavy black gloves. A tube ticket fell to the ground and he picked it up. All Zones. He remembered being here. Turning slowly, he saw a herd of deer grazing obliviously about a hundred yards behind him. Behind them, acres of grass, trees and pathways dominated the foreground. Further on rose the skyscrapers of the city: the Shard, the Gherkin, Canary Wharf. He was in Richmond Park. He was in London.

Eight years ago, Meera had brought him to this very spot after promising "a day in the country". After a short train journey, he had followed her out of a dirty dark station into a busy street and had questioned the sincerity of her promise. Five minutes later, he'd laughed as she led him through the gates of Richmond Park. 2,500 acres nestled alongside the Thames in South London, the Park had seemed magical to him, particularly when the first stag bellowed from the trees, disturbing a bird which - as it flew over him - turned out to be an escaped parrot.

Now, as he turned slowly to take in the remembered winter landscape, he realized what was different this time.

*There's no one here.*

The fog was patchy, drifting, dreamlike, obscuring his view for a second or so. *No one.* Like the opening of a post-apocalyptic movie, he shared the park with the birds and animals, but not a single person was in view, and - even taking into consideration the way fog could dampen sound - the only noise was the calls of birds and the creaking of frost-hung branches. He had always been attracted to the scenarios in those movies, something inside him yearning for the silence, the emptiness, the absolute loneliness. But now he had a taste of it, he felt panic rise up suddenly, an animal fear, an immediate craving for human company.

He licked dry lips and shivered. He knew vaguely that he shouldn't be here, he remembered the trip in the car with Westlake, the impromptu body surf across the freeway and the wide eyes of the van driver just before impact. But he couldn't remember an impact and it just didn't seem important. He knew - logically - that he couldn't be in Richmond Park, South London in winter, since he was in Los Angeles in August, but he was equally convinced that he was - somehow - here. He carried on slowly turning, each detail of the landscape before him convincing him this was no dream. Finally he turned back to what he realized now must be Pen Ponds, where Mee had unpacked her idea of a picnic: two packets of salt and vinegar crisps, a slab of fruit cake, a packet of chocolate-covered rich tea biscuits and a bottle of gin. He smiled at the memory then froze as he looked again at the pond. Someone was there.

On the bench, sitting with his back to Seb, a man was throwing bread for the ducks, who were fighting visciously over every piece, despite being perhaps the fattest ducks in Britain. The man was wearing a dark coat, his collar turned up. As if aware of Seb's gaze, he half turned and looked over his shoulder. Seeing Seb, he gestured for him to come closer. He looked familiar. As Seb walked toward him, he turned back to the ducks, throwing the last few pieces of bread into the water. Seb reached the bench and the man patted the seat next to him. Seb sat down and looked at his companion. The face was one he had seen countless times before, but it was so unexpected, and so subtly different that it took a few moments for Seb to register who it was. The eyes - while young - seemed ancient, wise, sad. The features were strong and the way the coat hung hinted at a muscular torso beneath. The man was taller - Seb had to look up slightly. Which was odd, as the face was Seb's own.

"This seemed like the best place to chat," said Seb2.

"So it is a dream," said Seb. "It just seems so real."

"Not exactly a dream," said Seb2, "more a useful construct. Since reality is only what we decide it is after we apply various filters, it's a simple task to make the brain accept something as real."

"You know what?" said Seb. "I love asking philosophical questions as much as anyone, but there's a time and place. Dream or not, who are you and what the hell is going on? Are you me?"

"Yes," said Seb2. "Well, part of your consciousness. You're another part. I'm deeper, you operate closer to the surface but we're both me. Or you."

Seb stared at Seb2. Abruptly, both men burst into laughter. They stopped just as quickly, but still perfectly in sync, which led to another outbreak, both men laughing until they were gasping and wiping tears from their eyes. As they began to calm down again, Seb2 put his hand gently on Seb's shoulder.

"I know it's ridiculous," he said, "but that's how it is. Now, I brought you because I need you to know a bit more about what's going on."

"Just a bit more?" said Seb. "Tell me everything."

"I can't," said Seb2. "Different parts of our self do different jobs. Your job - first point of contact with reality - would be compromised if you tried to take in all the information I've been given. Most of which I can't begin to understand. You have to trust me on this. Mostly because I'm you."

"Doesn't stop you being a pain in the ass," said Seb.

"That's a given," said Seb2.

"Ok, stop for a second," said Seb. "What happened in the mountains? Was that an alien? Where's the brain tumor? And while we're on the subject of miraculous recoveries, what about the bullet holes? Oh, and wasn't I just hit by a van?"

"Slow down," said Seb2. "Ok, lots of questions, but I only have ideas about the answers."

"Well, you're a big help then. Start with the van."

"I can half-answer that one. It didn't hit me. Er, you."

"Oh, come on, there's no way it could have avoided me. It was about six feet away."

"Yeah, but you moved."

"No, I didn't," said Seb. I closed my eyes just before the fender hit my skull at 50 miles per hour."

"Yeah, you did," said Seb2. "You, I, we 'moved'. We left the freeway. In a few minutes, you're going to open your eyes in the bathroom of an Amtrak train just pulling out of Union Station. Well, it'll be minutes for you, but a whole day will have passed out there."

"Out there?" said Seb. "Just back up a little. Where exactly am I now?"

"We're...between places. In the cracks. Buying some time."

"Buying time by keeping me here - in the cracks? Can you try using words and ideas that I might actually understand?"

"I'd love to, but I don't understand them myself."

"Oh, give me strength," said Seb, rubbing his forehead.

"Ok, this much I know," said Seb2. "Yes, that was an alien. It came to me - you - us - specifically. When it took your hands, it transferred something to you. Something that merged with you, body and mind. You're not just you any more. You're something new..."

"Me - specifically?" said Seb. "Why?"

"Now that I can't answer," said Seb2. "Because we weren't ready. Your suicide attempt forced its hand. If you'd been ready, you'd know how to use this - gift, you'd know what to do. But Billy Joe had to act because you would have died if he hadn't?"

"Billy Joe?" said Seb.

"The alien," said Seb2. "It was a nickname. He found it funny."

"Billy Joe," said Seb. "Of course. Back up - you talked to him? When did that happen?"

"No, I didn't talk to him. When Billy Joe transferred the power, a message came with it. Not in words as such, but some of it was loud and clear. Other parts - well, it's like trying to watch TV with the sound down and not being able to lip-read. I get bits of it - not enough. He's been waiting a long time. He tried to find you - or someone like you - before. He's...ancient...and he's an outsider. There are so few like him. And I'm - we're - one of them."

Seb stood and walked to the water's edge. The ducks had long since lost interest and drifted away toward the middle of the pond. The pale reflection of the winter sun rippled on the surface.

"Anything useful in this message? Like how to avoid people trying to kill me or experiment on me? And how about what I'm supposed to do with this power? And what if I don't want it?"

"Don't try to kid me," said Seb2. "I am you, after all."

"What do you mean?" said Seb.

"You want it all right," said Seb2, leaving the bench and joining Seb by the water. "All those comic-books, all that science fiction and fantasy - you've always wanted this. What about the vampire phase - you were half-convinced they were real and used to hang around graveyards hoping to be bitten."

"Oh, please," said Seb. "I grew up."

"Yeah, yeah," said Seb2, "but you always had a bit of a 'chosen one' complex, even after you 'grew up.'"

"Doesn't everyone?" said Seb.

"How would I know?" said Seb2. "Anyway, you lucked out. You've been chosen. Now we have to decide what to do about it. As for people trying to kill you, you can relax. Can't be done."

Seb took a deep breath, his head aching.

"I can't die?" he said.

"So far as I can see, no, you can't," said Seb2. "But, like I said, I'm operating with limited information here. Your body can repair any damage, that much I'm sure of. So the brain tumor, the damage done by the bullets, we hardly broke a sweat. Problem is, you have no real control at the moment."

"Tell me something I don't know."

"Billy Joe would have come to you much, much later if it hadn't been for the tumor and suicide attempt. I think you would have been an old man when he came to you. I think he saw something in you that hadn't yet developed, a seed only he could detect. He hopes you will grow into this power."

"He hopes?"

"My impression is you're needed in some way, he took a huge risk passing this to you now, but his hand was forced in some way. And the risk was made worse because he can't help you, he had to leave and he won't be back any time soon."

"So what the hell am I supposed to do?"

"I think you can find him...when you're ready....but everything is partial, foggy. There's so much of his message I can't understand. It was meant for me - you - when we were ready."

Seb2 stretched a hand out toward the water. Close to the edge, it began to bubble, then suddenly grow calm. Seb2 took a step forwards and stood on the surface of the pond. He smiled.

"Always wanted to be able to do this," he said. He took a few more steps, then turned to face Seb.

"You're not helping the messiah complex any," said Seb. He looked on as Seb2 stood on a column of water, rising to a height of about 12 feet.

"You need to learn to do some of this stuff," called Seb2.

"Great," said Seb. "I'll get right on it. Just as soon as I've mastered flying and shooting lasers out of my fingertips." Seb2 dropped gracefully to the surface of the pond and stepped back onto dry land.

"No need for sarcasm," he said. "Ok, I can't hold this any longer. You have a train to catch. Listen for a minute. That Westlake character wasn't playing games. He'll have the airports, bus stations and train stations watched. You can't rent a car without a credit card and I'm guessing he'll get a heads-up if you use it. Stay away from ATMs. Oh, and don't bother trying to use your phone."

"Why not?" said Seb.

"They might be able to track us using it," said Seb2. "Maybe that's how they found the apartment so fast. It travelled with us, but when you wake up, I'll dump it. They'll probably find it, but we'll be on our way by then."

"Wait a second," said Seb, "if you can beam me up to Union Station, why not make it somewhere further away, somewhere they won't find me."

"Would if I could," said Seb2. "Problem is, I can only reach out a few miles in any direction. I don't make the rules. I don't even know the rules. I'll get back in touch once I can figure out a way to do it without you getting run over. Get off the train at Albuquerque."

"Where am I going?" said Seb.

"Where do you think?" said Seb2. "Alien central. Roswell, New Mexico."

# Chapter 9

## Los Angeles

"His cell's still off. And when I say 'off', I mean completely off the grid. I should be able to find it with this app, but it's not finding anything." Meera put the phone down and searched her bag for rolling papers and hash. Bob moved around Seb's apartment, lifting the lids of cardboard boxes. He picked a book out of one - Zen And The Art Of Motorcycle Maintenance.

"Tried three times to read this after a buddy said it was amazing," he said. "Never got past page thirty." He looked over at Mee. "You do too much of that stuff."

Mee lit up and inhaled, blowing a sweet cloud through her nostrils.

"So they tell me," she said. She peered at Bob. "If you want to make yourself useful, the coffee's in the tin on your right and the grinder's under the sink.

"Yes, Ma'am," said Bob and started rummaging around the worktops for cups.

"If you really want to know," said Mee, "Reality is sometimes just a bit too real to deal with." She inhaled again. "This helps."

"Yeah, well I prefer to face reality with all my faculties functioning perfectly," said Bob, emptying the beans into the grinder.

"OK," said Mee, "and how's that working out for you? Happy?" Bob thought for a second before answering. He poured water into the coffee maker and turned it on.

"Yeah," he said. Mee said nothing for a long time and when he finally turned, she was looking directly at him, the challenge clear in her dark eyes.

"Well, mostly. Mostly happy." She still didn't speak.

"No," he said. "Not happy at all." He poured two cups and brought them to the table.

"I never expected to be happy," he said. "I just wanted to know that things worked the way they should. Good guys win, bad guys get punished and kids grow up feeling safe."

"That why you joined the army?" said Mee.

"The marines," said Bob. "Yep. Pretty much."

Mee sipped her coffee and sighed appreciatively. She tried Seb's cell phone again - not available.

"I still say we should call the cops," said Bob.

"No way," said Mee. " First, you were the one who said those military guys could be working for anyone. How do we know they weren't cops?"

"Too well trained, for one," said Bob.

"Second, Seb hates cops. Doesn't really trust anyone in authority - and I'm with him there. He had a pretty bad experience when he was growing up."

"What happened?" said Bob.

"He won't talk about it," said Mee. "All I know is a kid died and he blames himself for it."

"Did he kill this kid?" said Bob.

"Like I said, he won't talk about it," said Mee. "But he doesn't seem the killing kind to me. Anyway, this isn't helping us find him any faster."

They'd spent most of the day searching as much of a ten block radius as they could. They'd asked questions but no one had seen Seb leave the apartment. It was as if he had vanished. There had been a pileup on the freeway about ten minutes after they'd spoken on the phone, but calls to local hospitals drew a blank. Finally, tired and dispirited, they had made their way back to Seb's apartment, hoping he might be waiting there.

Meera's phone suddenly vibrated and uttered the word, "plectrum".

"Private joke," said Mee to Bob's silent question, then snatched up the phone excitedly. "It's a message from Seb." Bob got up and came around to her side of the table to read the words on the screen:

**Sorry to panic you. Change of plan. Going to lie low for a few weeks. I need to figure some of this out on my own. Give me some time. Sorry. Seb x KWPTOW**

"KWPT what?" said Bob.

"Keep Walking Past The Open Windows," said Mee. "It's from a book we both love."

"So it's from Seb?" said Bob. "I mean, no one else would know that, right?"

"It's definitely Seb," she said.

"So what now," said Bob. "Shit, I was ready for a fight. Where the hell's all this adrenaline gonna go?"

"Well, cowboy," said Mee, standing up and grabbing her jacket, "how about taking it to Union Station for starters?"

"That where he is?"

"According to my iPhone," said Mee.

"But he wants to figure this out for himself," said Bob. "So we should back off. I mean, it's his decision, right?"

"Right," said Mee, opening the door, "but that doesn't stop me being pissed with him. At the very least, I want to find him so I can tell him that. You coming?"

Bob gulped down the rest of his coffee and followed her out.

*\*\*\**

Union station was busy - it was evening now and the last of the commuters were heading home, joined by tourists and a fair amount of people who, judging by their bags, were heading further afield. The brick walls rang out with the echoed reflections of a thousand footsteps on the tiled floor. As Mee hurried forward to look at the departures board, Bob caught up with her and grabbed her arm.

"I don't like it," he said.

"Don't like what?" said Mee. Bob scanned the area then leaned in close and spoke in an undertone.

"The guy with the news paper at 10 o'clock, plus the guy on the phone at two o'clock," he said. "They're not here to catch a train."

"Oh, for God's sake," said Mee, "this isn't a spy movie. Just tell me where they are."

Bob nodded toward the men he had spotted. Sure enough, the thickset guy holding the LA Times looked like he found reading a challenge, as he kept returning to the same paragraph over and over, spending more of his time scanning the faces of passengers. His colleague on the other side of the hall was holding a cell phone up to his ear but seemed to have forgotten he was supposed to speak occasionally as he watched the stream of faces go by. Mee jumped when he looked straight at her, but quickly reminded herself that - if these guys were the ones from that morning - they'd be looking for Seb, not her. She took out her cell phone and consulted the screen.

"He's on a platform in that direction," she said, "so if those bruisers are looking out for him, they're not doing a great job. Come on." Mee walked away. Bob took another quick look around before hurrying after her.

On the first platform she tried, the Amtrak train was pulling out of the station, due to arrive in Chicago 45 hours later. Meera checked her phone again as the last car followed the curve of the rails and pulled out of sight, the evening sun winking from the windows.

"Bugger," said Mee. "Bugger! His cell's disappeared again."

Bob looked at the platform screen.

"Chicago?" he said.

"Or any of the stops on the way," said Mee. "If he's on it at all. Dammit."

"Come on," said Bob. "It's been a long day. I'll buy you a coffee."

"Sounds like a good idea. I think I'll join you." The voice came from behind them. Bob and Mee turned to see the tall man they'd seen standing over Seb's body that morning. He was flanked by the two heavies they'd already spotted.

Five minutes later, Mee and Bob were sitting opposite the man Seb was running from. He was stirring a third sugar into a large black coffee. One of the heavies sat next to him, the other blocked Bob and Mee's exit.

"My only vice," he said, spooning in even more sugar.

"Who are you?" said Mee, her arms folded across her chest.

"My name is Westlake," he said, holding out his hand. Mee just glared at him, but Bob shook it, figuring they'd better not show too much animosity toward the man. He had no idea they'd seen the events unfold that morning, so acting like they hated the guy might come across as a little over-hostile. He nudged Mee but she just snorted.

"Bob Geller," said Bob, wincing a little at Westlake's iron grip.

Westlake raised an eyebrow at Mee but she just stared him out, despite Bob kicking her under the table.

"Well, that's the pleasantries out of the way," said Westlake. "Here's my ID".

He slid an open wallet across the table. Underneath his photograph it stated 'Field Director. United States Of America Secret Service.' Mee snorted again. Bob coughed discreetly.

"Ok, you claim to be working for the President. Impressive. But my friend and I would like a little more proof than a plastic card from someone who is threatening us," said Bob, nodding toward the heavies.

Westlake tapped the number on his ID. "I'm on the White House roster. They're used to people checking up. Go ahead, call."

Mee took out her phone and brought up the browser.

"Think I'd rather find the number myself," she said. Westlake said nothing. She clicked on the number and waited.

"Hi," she said. "I've got someone with me who claims to work for the Secret Service, who do I need to speak to? Thank you." She looked directly at Westlake as her call was transferred. "Yes, hi, He says he works for the Secret Service. He's ugly, arrogant and rude so I'm inclined to believe him but it's always best to check. His number? Yes, I have it here." Mee read the number aloud while Westlake sat impassively. "No, thank you, ma'am."

"Satisfied?" said Westlake.

"Rarely," said Mee.

Westlake took his wallet back. "I need to ask some questions," he said. "At this point you are under no obligation to answer them. However, with a little inconvenience for me and a great deal for you, I can have you taken somewhere where you will be so obliged. Do you understand?"

"Are you - " began Mee.

"Yes," said Bob, giving Mee a look which she tried to snort at but changed her mind halfway through, ending up trying to cover it by blowing her nose. "We understand. But we don't know what you could possibly want with us."

"You're here looking for Sebastian Varden," said Westlake. "Why?"

"What are you talking about?" said Mee. "We were just planning a trip together."

Westlake said nothing, just held out his hand. The heavy on his left gave him a tablet. He tapped the screen and scanned it quickly, his eyes flicking from left to right.

"Bob Geller, 58, retired Marine, most likely contact with Sebastian Varden his early morning hikes in the Verdugo Mountains." Westlake's eyes flicked up, but Bob showed no reaction.

"Meera Patel," said Westlake, "singer, regular marijuana user. Dual nationality - British father and American mother. Stage name Mee Jane."

Bob raised an eyebrow and turned slightly toward Mee.

"As in 'you Tarzan, me Jane'," she said.

"Ah," said Bob. "Funny."

Westlake continued reading information on the screen.

"On-off relationship with Mr. Varden. Played together in the band 'Clockwatchers' for three years."

Westlake passed the screen back to the impassive heavy.

"Now," he said, "let me just clarify your position. You have had close contact with someone suspected of having links to certain terrorist organizations."

"That's utter bollocks and you know it," shouted Mee, standing up and pointing a finger at Westlake's chest. Several heads turned at neighboring tables.

"Sit down, Ms. Patel," said Westlake.

"Or what?" she said. Westlake leaned forward and looked at Mee's pointing finger. It was shaking slightly.

"The last person to touch me without my consent spent six months in the hospital," he said.

"Are you threatening me?" said Mee, her voice rising slightly.

"Absolutely," said Westlake. "The report said you were intelligent - it's good to see our information is accurate." His voice dropped slightly but he made sure every word was clear.

"Over the last five years, I have personally killed 14 enemies of the state. Five of them were women. I have no misguided sense of chivalry, Ms. Patel. My job is to pursue those who threaten the security of our nation. Now sit down."

Mee sat, her hand automatically going to the pocket where her next ready-rolled joint was waiting. Suddenly, she just wanted to go home.

"Although your mother is American," said Westlake, " you spent all of your formative years in Europe. I wonder where your loyalties lie, especially when you are associated with a known terrorist."

"Known terrorist?" said Bob. "Two minutes ago he was only accused of having links with terrorist organizations."

"Mr. Geller," said Westlake. "You're a soldier. You understand the chain of command. I am not here to share information with you. I am here to get information from you. Where is Sebastian Varden?"

"I don't know," said Bob. Westlake turned to Mee. She shrugged.

"Give me your phone," he said.

"What?" said Mee. "No." Westlake nodded to the heavy at her side. With a turn of speed surprising for someone with the frame of a heavyweight boxer, he grabbed her wrist, simultaneously reaching into her jacket pocket and pulling out her cell phone.

"Ow!" said Mee, rubbing her wrist. The heavy handed the phone to Westlake, who checked the list of outgoing calls.

"Hmm," he said, "maybe you are telling the truth. A lot of unanswered calls here." He flicked back to the home screen and clicked on Messages.

"Ah," he said. "A message from Mr. Varden. Apparently, he's lying low for a few weeks. Any idea where that might be, Ms. Patel?"

She shook her head sullenly.

"I thought not," he said. "Mr. Geller?"

"Nope," said Bob.

"So why come here?" asked Westlake, staring straight at her. Meera stared back and hoped the twitch that had just developed in her eye wasn't noticeable.

"We had to start looking for him somewhere," she said. There was a long silence.

Finally Westlake nodded and put the phone onto the table. Mee grabbed it, stuffing it into her jacket pocket.

"Here's how this is going to play out," he said. "You two are free to go, but know this. You are now under observation. Every call you make, every email you send, anyone you talk to, I'm going to know about it. Until Mr. Varden has been found, you won't be able to take a crap without a report about it landing on my desk. If he gets in touch, we'll know. If he asks to meet, say yes. We'll be there. If you try to warn him, I'll make sure you spend at least ten years in a federal institution. This is not a game. Do we understand each other?"

Bob sighed and leaned back. He looked at Mee. She was doing a pretty good job of looking defiant, but he could see she was terrified.

"Yes, sir," he said. "We understand."

Dismissed by Westlake, a subdued Mee and a quietly angry Bob made their way out of the station. As they left, Mee saw one of Westlake's men jump down to the train tracks, grab something and pass it up to a colleague. It was an iPhone.

"Oh, Seb, how am I going to find you now?" she muttered. She turned and hurried out of the station, Bob jogging to keep up. A few seconds later, an anonymous sedan started up and cruised slowly behind them. Unseen by Bob, Meera, or Westlake's men, a small figured emerged from the shadows, pulled a hood over her head and followed.

# Chapter 10

**Nine months previously**
**Sydney, Australia**

Byron stood in the middle of the darkened stage, walking slowly backward while making small mystical gestures with his hands. He had worked on those gestures for hours; first in front of a mirror, then filming himself on his phone in his front room while his show music - mostly mid-80s synth pop - played through his stereo. At first his movements had been self-consciously theatrical, but he'd quickly admitted how ridiculous they made him look. He was, after all, in his fifties, not his twenties, and his body was hardly athletic or graceful. 'Portly' was the term journalists seemed to have settled on. He knew they meant fat but he didn't care.

His favorite gesture, a dismissive flick of the wrist, was delivered by his left hand over his right shoulder while facing the audience. He was doing it now. He loved this bit because what was about to happen was utterly impossible, and, at some primal level, the audience knew it. Yes, they'd paid good money to see 'Byron: Twenty-first Century Wizard' (the national tour sold out within an hour), so they expected him to be *good*. In fact, they expected him to be *great*. But no one was ever really prepared for what he delivered night after night, up and down the country.

The audience gasped. Every last one of them in perfect unison. From his vantage point downstage, Byron looked carefully at the individual faces, his eyes darting around the room. Every single mouth hanging open, eyes popping in disbelief. He allowed himself a small smile. He remembered the first time he had consciously attempted this trick. It wasn't on stage, it was in his bathroom. It wasn't a huge cloth made of parachute silk, it was a hand towel. And the animal that had appeared under the towel had been a hedgehog, rather than an elephant. Then again, he was just plain Brian then. Byron thought bigger.

The sounds of admiration turned to sudden screams of panic as the huge beast on stage which had just risen up from the floor draped in silk, apparently became enraged and broke away from its handlers. Byron stepped nimbly aside as the huge shape charged. As it reached the edge of the stage, it leapt the footlights and sailed toward the audience, trumpeting at ear-splitting volume. The screams reached new levels of panic, as people started to climb over each other in their hopeless attempt to avoid the acrobatic pachyderm.

Byron blinked at the flying elephant. It turned into a million pieces of glitter which fluttered slowly down on the front five rows of the audience. There was a shocked silence. Then a long pause. Byron counted silently, still with that small smile on his face.

"One elephant, two elephant, three elephant, four elephant, five elephant, six ele-,"

The place went berserk. Every man, woman and child flew out of their seat, clapping, cheering, whistling, shouting, screaming, whooping, fist-pumping. The roar of 2,500 people screaming themselves hoarse began to find a rhythm, becoming a pulse, a chant; incoherent at first, then clearer and clearer.

"Byron, Byron, Byron, Byron BYRON, BYRON, BYRON, BYRON, BYRON!"

Byron blew a little kiss and walked into the wings. The calls for an encore would go on for 10-15 minutes.

They always did. But not giving encores was one of Byron's little rules. Along with not appearing on TV. Or giving any interviews. Col, his manager, thought he was crazy. Had almost decided not to represent him after all. Then Byron gave him a demonstration and he changed his mind. "Just do that for every newspaper editor," he said, " and they'll give you all the publicity you'll ever want. And then some."

Col was waiting in his dressing room. "Fantastic, Byron, as always. Now look, I've had another call from America. They've doubled the offer."

Byron dabbed at his face with a towel, the brown makeup staining the white cotton.

"You know my answer, Col," he said. No shows outside Australia was another little rule.

That last rule was the one Byron knew he would never dare break. He could make a pretty good living touring his native Australia, without venturing abroad. He had always wanted to travel, so it was ironic that the very secret that had made him such a massive success also tied him to his home country. And not just his country. He couldn't even go more than a day's travel away from his little house near Sydney. Not without losing all his magic, he couldn't.

The tiny two-bed house on the edge of a new development had been all Byron could afford after his divorce. Marjorie had left him for a juggler. All that time moaning about him being a magician and she'd left him for a freaking juggler. It had hit him hard at first and his life had settled into a pattern of late-night solitary drinking and ignoring the bills piling up on his mat. For a while, it looked like he would end up losing even the pokey little house he'd spent his last bit of money buying.

Then, after one particularly heavy night with a bottle of vodka, he'd crawled out of bed around noon, grabbed a beer, put on his sunglasses and decided to take a seat in the yard. He had lived in the house for nearly three months, but this was the first time since viewing it with the realtor that he'd actually stepped into the yard. He dragged a chair from the kitchen, planted it in the middle of the paved space, facing back at the house. He sat there, sipping the beer, looking at the only thing he could call his own after 27 years of marriage. He decided he wouldn't be performing at the children's party booked for that afternoon. He just had a very strong feeling that, assuming the damn kids didn't pass out purely from the toxicity of his breath, he might finally give in to the urge to strangle the little bastards with his balloon animals. Better to stay home. Better yet, stay home and drink some more beers.

He got up to take a leak, but hesitated. Something seemed to be gently pulling at his consciousness, like an invisible thread pulling a playing card out of a deck. He turned and squinted into the corner of his yard. For some reason, he very much wanted to go and stand there. He squinted a little more, making his headache pulse more insistently. He really needed another beer. But this pull was hard to resist, despite it leading him to nothing more than a square foot of dirt with a few tufts of coarse grass trying to push through. He belched and walked over to the corner of the yard. With every step, things changed. He felt better. He felt happier. He felt...right.

Finally, standing where the mysterious pull seemed to insist he stand, he smiled without knowing the reason why. He felt excited, like a kid spotting the biggest present under the Christmas tree and knowing it was for him. For a moment, he wasn't sure what to do. He just stood there with this strange quizzical smile on his face. Then, obeying some strange impulse, he knelt down and put his palms flat onto the ground. Instantly, energy seemed to flow from the earth into his fingers, his hands, his arms, his body, his head. The hangover burned away like mist as the sun comes up. His teeth buzzed with the energy that poured into him.

As quickly as it had begun, it stopped. He stood up. Not so much stood, as *bounced*. Something had changed. He felt 20 years younger. And, suddenly, he wanted to go to that kids' party.

Later, as he drove home with an extra $100 tip in his pocket, he tried to rationalize what was going on, but reason seemed to have little place in the afternoon's events. He knew something had happened in the yard. And he knew those kids had just seen the best magician they were ever going to see. He knew that, because what they had seen was real magic. He had gone through his usual repertoire - good enough, funny in places, made them giggle, got them shouting, did his job. Then he got to his finale, where he pulled Rodney the mind-reading rabbit out of his hat. The younger kids loved that bit, especially when he pretended to hypnotize Rodney. He'd revealed the card the kid was thinking of, was about to say goodbye, then changed his mind. Reaching into his top hat one more time, he pulled out a puppy. Then another. Then a third. Thirty seconds later, the room was full of puppies, the children screaming with delight. The adults were in the kitchen, probably hitting the vodka themselves. Byron knew they'd be back to see what the noise was about. How was he going to explain this? With a performer's instincts, he snapped his fingers. The puppies immediately became cuddly toys, just as the mother of the birthday boy put her head around the door.

"What a lovely touch!" she said, as the children scooped up a toy puppy each. One very happy customer.

Byron drove straight home, giggling. His only concern was that what had happened might be temporary.

This fear seemed to be justified later when, after magically producing various small mammals in the bathroom and the front room, he found he couldn't do it any more. He had gone cold. He didn't think he even wanted to go on living without this new power. Magic was real, just like he'd imagined when he got his first magic set, aged seven. It couldn't be taken away from him! He had stumbled out to the yard in the moonlight and knelt in the same spot, hardly daring to breath in case what had happened was a one-time deal. He felt the energy buzzing almost immediately and wept with relief.

Now, just eight months later, he was the best-known, busiest, and wealthiest magician in Australia. No more kids' parties for Byron. He walked out of the stage door, past the fans who'd lined up four deep behind the ropes to get a close look at the miracle worker. They never screamed, shouted, called out or asked for autographs. They were too much in awe of him. It was enough just to see him. Deep down, they all knew what they had just witnessed was no trick.

Byron climbed into the two-seater Mercedes. The cream leather squeaked as his bulk settled into it. The engine made that slightly angry roar he loved as he turned the key. He headed home, Col's last words still echoing in his head.

"America, Byron. Europe. Royalty, film directors, musicians, actors. They all want you. Think about it."

He wished he could go. But he knew all his power would be gone within a day or two unless he could get back to his yard. He sighed and tapped the steering wheel, lowering the automatic roof to enjoy the balmy evening. He had booked himself a little "entertainment" for the rest of his evening. He might not be able to leave his native country, but being fabulously wealthy brought some compensations.

After he had been home an hour, he'd checked his watch in frustration, then called the agency.

"Where the hell is she?" he said, when they picked up. He listened as he walked through to the kitchen and opened the fridge to get a beer. Alcohol didn't seem to affect him the same way these days, but you couldn't beat a cold one.

"Yeah, well, I don't care how reliable she is normally, she isn't here now and-," Byron stopped talking and looked out into the yard. In the moonlight stood a naked woman. An incredible looking naked woman with the most amazing body he had ever seen. She was beckoning him. He licked his lips.

"Never mind," he said into the phone. "She's here."

Out in the yard, he shivered slightly. He looked hungrily at the naked woman. Other than the perky nipples, there was no evidence that she felt cold. She smiled at him coquettishly.

"Going to show me some magic, Brian?" she whispered.

"It's Byron," he said, angrily, his excitement waning rapidly. The agency was supposed to make sure the girls were submissive. He had had enough lip from Marjorie to last a lifetime, thank you very much. He moved closer to the naked woman. She was still smiling at him. Perhaps the back of his hand would make her a little more respectful. He drew himself up to his full height. The heeled shoes he'd taken to wearing made him nearly five foot nine, but this woman was still an inch or two taller.

"I can see I'm going to have to teach you some manners," he said. She looked at him and laughed. *Laughed.*

"Oh, dear," she said, her perfect breasts bobbing disconcertingly as she chuckled. "What a waste. All that potential, all that power, and such a silly little man."

Enough was enough. The agency charged a fair bit more if he bruised the merchandise. Byron decided tonight was going to be expensive. He slapped the woman across the face. Hard. She laughed again, shook her head, then held up a wagging finger, tutting at him.

"My turn," she said. She swung her hand toward his neck. He had time to see the hand darken and change shape, the nails elongating and sharpening to become micro-thin and razor-like, before the blow neatly decapitated him. His head retained consciousness long enough to see his body fall backward into the yard. As the scene dimmed and disappeared, he realized she had been right about him being a silly little man: his last thought was, "ta-da!".

# Chapter 11

## Between Los Angeles and Albuquerque
## Present Day

As Seb opened his eyes, the floor beneath him moved and he lurched to one side, his arms coming up to stop him falling. He grabbed a handrail and steadied himself. He was in the bathroom of a train. There was a shower attachment on the wall and a round mirror over the tiny basin. He ran some cold water and splashed it on his face. Looking at himself, something seemed wrong. He frowned, trying to work out what it was before he realized.

*I haven't shaved in three days.*

He rubbed a hand over his baby-smooth, stubble-free chin, frowning. His hands looked manicured, the nails short and clean. Backing up as much as he could in the cramped room, he saw that he was wearing a dark suit with a white shirt, unbuttoned at the neck.

*Nice outfit,* he said to his reflection. *Where'd ya get it?*

He pulled on the lapels, straightening the jacket over his shoulders. He frowned again. There was something in his pocket. Reaching into the jacket, he pulled out a cardboard folder and his wallet. He opened the folder first. Tickets from LA to Albuquerque. Superliner bedroom. Seb opened the bathroom door. Sure enough, he had his own sleeper, small but private, with a seat by the window and a couch/bed. *Well, Seb, whatever the hell else is going on, the good news is, you're doing it in style.*

His stomach growled and he checked his watch. Dinner time.

The dining car was busy and noisy. At first, Seb thought there were no spare seats, but when he moved to one side to let a waiter through he realized he had squeezed into an empty bench. He had to look twice, as he was sure he'd seen a figure dozing there, leaning against the window. No - the seat was definitely empty. On the other side of the table, a man nursing a large red wine waved the glass in Seb's direction.

"It's free," he said, "join me."

Seb slid gratefully onto the seat. The man opposite pushed a menu across toward him.

"Steak's overpriced, but passable," he said. "If you're hungry." Seb was hungry. Really hungry. He couldn't remember the last time he'd eaten properly. He glanced at the menu. The steak was more than $25. He would normally pay with plastic, but if Seb2 was right, he was going to have to rely on cash, which he generally didn't carry much of. He took out his wallet and glanced at the bills, flicking through them.

What the hell? There were 20 $50 bills neatly folded in his wallet. Seb guessed the magic money came from the same place as the magic suit and the magic tickets.

"One piece of advice," said the man opposite. He looked to be in his early fifties, well groomed, gray hair, an expensive dark blue suit. His tanned features were set off by warm, intelligent brown eyes. He had the look - and Seb could find no other way of putting it - of someone who knew something you didn't. A whole bunch of things.

"What's that?" said Seb.

"Don't bother with the house wine if you have the steak. Help yourself to a glass of this." He tapped the bottle next to him. Seb read the label.

"Screaming Eagle?" he said. "Sounds...interesting. I'm sorry, I know nothing about wine."

The man smiled and put out his hand. "I'm Walter Ford. Walt." Seb shook his hand.

"Seb Lewis," he said, momentarily smug as he'd remembered to give himself a false surname. Varden was unusual - might easily be remembered. He stopped feeling smug when Walt raised an eyebrow in polite disbelief.

"Nice to meet you, Seb," said Walt, smiling. Seb swallowed, shaking his head slightly. No point being paranoid. There was no way this guy could know he was using a false name.

"Screaming Eagle is one of the better Napa Valley Cabernet Sauvignons," said Walt, pouring some for Seb. "Try it." He raised his glass and drank as Seb did the same.

"Yeah, it's good," said Seb. "Smooth," he added, feeling slightly ignorant. Walt nodded.

"I think it's undervalued," he said. "Save some for your steak." His eyes flicked up to the waiter who'd just appeared. Seb ordered a rare steak with an extra portion of fries.

"So where are you headed?" said Walt.

"Albuquerque," said Seb.

"Business?" asked Walt.

"No, just wanted to do some traveling," said Seb.

"Can't say I blame you," said Walt. "There's so much of this country that most of us never see. Some of the most unlikely places can take your breath away but you'll never find them sitting on your ass."

"Guess that's true," said Seb.

"Of course, it's also possible to see more of life than 99% of the population by doing nothing other than sitting on your ass." Walt began carefully folding his napkin.

"What do you mean?"

" 'Without going out of my door I can know all things on earth,' " said Walt.

" 'Without looking out of my window'," continued Seb, " 'I can know the ways of heaven'."

"Lao Tzu," said Walt, almost simultaneously with Seb's "George Harrison."

"Who?" they both said at once. Both men laughed. Seb took another sip of wine. Walt pushed his napkin between his hands, making a loose ball.

"5th Century BC Chinese philosopher, reputedly the founder of Taoism," said Walt.

"Are you seriously telling me you've never heard of George Harrison?" said Seb. "Paul McCartney? John Lennon? Ringo Starr? The Beatles?"

"They were a band popular in the sixties, right?" said Walt.

"Popular in the sixties? Popular? Yeah, I guess you could say they were popular. You're kidding me, right?"

Walt carefully placed the napkin on the table in front of him.

"I was busy in the sixties," he said. He put his hands in front of him, palm down, about ten inches above the napkin. "Wanna see some magic?"

"Busy?" said Seb. "Busy enough to miss The Beatles? Man, you've got some catching up to..."

Seb's voice trailed away. Walt's napkin had begun to move, swelling and receding in an eerie sinuous motion that reminded Seb of a TV show he seen once when a pregnant woman had shown the baby moving under the stretched skin of her stomach. Walt slowly closed one hand into a fist and the napkin mirrored the movement, closing in on itself until it was a tight ball. Then Walt opened his hand again, and as the napkin unfolded itself, he began moving both hands as if he was a puppeteer. The napkin responded to every move of the older man's hands, dancing gracefully side to side, then slowly pirouetting. Seb was entranced, although he knew the secret must be some kind of ultra-fine thread. Even knowing how it was done, it was hard not to be impressed by the convincingly lifelike movement exhibited by the napkin, which was now rising upwards. Seb caught Walt's eye and smiled.

"Hmm," said Walt. "Not really impressed, I see."

"The opposite, actually," said Seb. "I mean - wow - it's amazing. I love close-up magic. Really."

"It's ok," said Walt, "you're not supposed to be impressed yet." Slowly, deliberately, he folded his arms and sat back in his chair. The napkin very slowly folded in on itself and curled back onto the table.

"Seriously," said Seb, "you've got some chops. Fantastic."

Walt held up a finger. It seemed a casual gesture, but Seb detected the crowd-controlling skill of a long-time performer. He looked at Walt. The man's face had taken on an aspect of absolute concentration. He was staring at the napkin. Seb had once read that a magician was actually an actor playing the part of a magician. If that was true, this guy was De Niro. He looked utterly composed, focused and serious - the look on his face was that of an athlete about to attempt a world record. Seb felt a palpable sense of power and he could swear the space around Walt's face was shimmering like a heat haze. He looked at the napkin just as it began to unfold itself again. It seemed to coil itself into a crouching position, one white cotton corner pointing toward Seb. Then it began to move. Not a dance this time, more the purposeful, quiet movements of a predator. It crawled slowly across the table, each step hinting at some kind of ancient, instinctive, deadly intent. Seb tried to swallow, but found his throat suddenly dry. Absurdly, he couldn't tear his eyes away from the thing long enough to reach for his wineglass. He was aware of Walt's presence opposite: he wasn't moving a muscle - there was no way this was being controlled by threads.

*Some sort of animatronic exoskeleton? Wires sewn into the napkin itself?* Even as he forced himself to be logical, a deeper part of him registered what was actually happening. This was real. Walt was somehow imbuing the napkin with its own physicality. Not only was it real, it was dangerous and it was headied straight for him. He tried to move, but his fascination seemed to have locked his arms and legs in place. The thing rocked back, muscles rippling under the surface of the napkin.

*Oh, God, it's going to spring. It's going to attack me.* He braced himself for the inevitable pain even as a tiny part of him tried to dismiss the whole scenario as ridiculous. Just before the creature could move, a hand appeared on top of it. His view momentarily obscured, Seb managed to look up.

"Your steak, sir," said the waiter, plucking the napkin from the table, shaking it out with one hand, then draping it efficiently across Seb's lap. Seb flinched as it landed, then he grabbed it and kneaded it with his fingers. No wires, no threads.

"Are you all right, sir?" said the waiter, placing a steaming plate in front of him, followed by an extra bowl of fries. Seb reached for his wine and took a long swallow.

"Fine, thanks. Yes. Fine."

The waiter nodded and left, dodging his way through a family coming the other way with an ease borne of years working the railroad. Seb looked at Walt, feeling suddenly embarrassed as the fear he had just experienced dissipated.

"Didn't think you could bring your own wine on board," he said. Walt smiled and raised his glass.

"We have an understanding," he said. "Don't let your steak go cold."

"That...trick," said Seb. "I've never seen anything like it."

Walt sipped at the wine, twirling the stem of the glass slowly through long fingers.

"I've loved magic all my life," he said. "I'll tell you about it while you eat. Bon appetit."

Seb noticed that Walt didn't ask him whether he actually wanted to hear his story, just assumed he did. He was right, of course. Seb had always slightly envied those who seemed so sure of themselves, of their place in the world. That sense of entitlement. Some people just seemed to have it, while others had to nurse a sense of self-worth so fragile, it sometimes seemed barely present. Seb picked up the steak knife and cut a huge slice, washing it down with the Cabernet Sauvignon, which was beginning to taste better with every mouthful.

"I grew up poor in Chicago," said Walt. "I'm not looking for sympathy, I didn't know anything different. Where I grew up, rich meant you got meat more than once a week. There was no education worth the name - I was expected to earn my keep as soon as I was able. For me, that meant running errands for the local mobster. Well, not for him directly. I was so far down the food chain, I didn't even qualify as bait. I got all the jobs no one else wanted - taking messages, picking up parcels, but mostly cleaning up, fixing drinks. Sometimes, I got to hear things I shouldn't hear, see things I shouldn't see. Passing information like that to the right pair of ears could get you some real money. I was smart enough not to take sides and careful enough not to get myself killed. I had no loyalty to these thugs.

They were dangerous and - worse - they had no style, no finesse. They were short-sighted, greedy. Not one of them had the sense to know when to stop, to know when they were attracting too much attention. So their life expectancy was pretty short. Luckily, I developed an instinct for that kind of danger and was always long gone before the inevitable hit the fan.

"In my teens, they let me join the protection run once a week. We were assigned a street and had to collect protection money from the owners of the businesses. 'Business' is too grand a word for what these people did - struggling to make ends meet in one of the hardest periods this country has ever faced."

Seb wondered what period Walt meant. There was no way he was any older than sixty. More likely mid-fifties, which would make him a teenager in the sixties. A teenager in the sixties who hadn't heard of The Beatles.

"The cut we took from these shopkeepers kept them just above the breadline," continued Walt. "I didn't much like it, but I needed to feed myself. And - by that time - it was all I knew. Until one day I realized we were avoiding one of the businesses. Nothing special about it, just a small florist. Bernbaum Flowers. Not only did we never get any protection money, we just pretended it wasn't there. No one ever mentioned it. One day I plucked up the courage and asked why. Manny - who headed up the protection boys - told me Sid Bernbaum was an old friend of the boss. I started to ask another question, but the look he gave me stopped me dead in my tracks. 'We don't talk about it, ok?'. I kept my mouth shut but I already knew I was going to find out more."

Walt paused while he filled up both glasses. Seb looked at the bottle. It was still half full, although he was sure they must have drunk it all by now. Another mystery.

"By this time, I'd learned a few useful skills. Late one night, I picked Bernbaum's lock so I could search the shop. Didn't know what I was looking for, couldn't even have put into words what drove me to do it, but I knew I didn't want to spend the rest of my life as a middle-ranking mobster and I'd half-convinced myself this guy might know something that would help with my career progression.

"The shop was dark, warm - the thing that really got me was the smell. You ever noticed how some plants don't release their fragrance until night? Well, this place was so heady, I could hardly breathe. I went further in, decided I'd poke around a little. Then I remember just stopping dead in the middle of the store. I'd barely questioned the compulsion that had led me there, but I suddenly started to wonder what the hell I hoped to achieve. I got cold feet, decided to leave, but it was too late."

Walt sipped his wine, seemingly lost in his own story. The train was slowing. Seb glanced at his watch. 9:08pm. He realized he didn't even know what day it was. He looked out of the window.

"Victorville," said Walt. "Not much to see. But the Chicago train never stops here. I wonder what's going on?"

As the train rounded the bend, a concrete apron in front of a rudimentary station building came into view. A few people were huddled together at one end, looking toward the oncoming train. As the rest of the platform came into view, Seb saw about a dozen armed men, FBI logos on their arms and caps, waiting for the Southwest Chief to stop. Seb froze for a moment, then jerked his head back as he recognized a tall figure looking in his direction. Westlake. How the hell had he got here?

Seb got out of his seat. A couple of nearby passengers glanced at him as he lurched to his feet, panicking.

Walt twirled the stem of the glass between manicured fingers.

"Friends of yours?" he said. Seb didn't reply. His mind raced through the possibilities. He could go back to his cabin - but were they coming on board? He could see if any passengers were leaving and try to slip off unnoticed. He scanned the dining car: no one else was getting ready to disembark. He could get out on the other side of the tracks and make a run for it. But he could hardly do that without other passengers giving him away, and he didn't think he would be able to stay hidden long in an unfamiliar place with trained officers searching for him. What the hell could he do?

"Sit down," said Walt, nodding at the seat opposite.

Seb shook his head.

"No," he said. "I can't. Those people. I've done nothing wrong...but...I have to leave."

The train had almost come to a stop. The armed figures were heading for the train doors. Seb moved toward the aisle but Walt's hand shot out and caught him by the wrist. Seb turned.

"I can help you," said Walt, "but you're going to have to trust me. There's no way you can outrun those guys. Now sit down."

Seb hesitated - he knew Walt was right about not being able to outrun the uniforms, but he hated the idea of just sitting and waiting to be dragged off the train by the same guys who'd already killed him once today.

"Sit down," said Walt again, "and I'll show you some real magic."

# Chapter 12

**17 Years Previously**
**St. Benet's Children's Home, New York**

Melissa didn't show up at St. Benet's the next Monday. Or Tuesday. On Wednesday, Seb plucked up the courage to ask Sister Theresa if she had seen her.

"That beautiful red-haired girl?" said the nun. "You like her, right?"

Seb blushed to the roots of his hair. Romance was not a subject he'd ever feel comfortable discussing with someone who'd devoted herself to a life of celibacy.

"Um, I guess so, a little," he said. Sister Theresa smiled and winked at him. She was a portly women in her fifties.

"Ah, don't mind me teasing," she said. "I might have sworn my life to God now, but I did have a life before coming here and taking the vows, you know." To his embarrassment, Seb realized he'd assumed the Sisters had always been nuns.

"Aha!" said Sister Theresa. "Gotcha! You thought I was born in a habit, right?" she laughed good-naturedly. If it had been possible for Seb to blush any more, he would have done so. As it was, he just shook his head in dumb denial.

"Don't you worry," she said, "I'm not going to embarrass you with sordid stories of my life out in the world. I'm just saying anyone with eyes in their heads could see you'd taken a fancy to that girl. She has a lovely nature, that one. I'm sure she'll like a nice, well-mannered, sensitive boy like you, Sebastian."

Seb looked everywhere in an attempt to avoid the kind, interested gaze of Sister Theresa. "Um, I haven't seen her these last couple of days, Sister. Do you know where she is?"

Sister Theresa pulled a notebook out of her pocket and consulted it briefly. "Well, looks like her shifts have been covered by another girl. And they're finishing up this Friday, so my guess would be she won't be back. Maybe she got sick. I'm sorry." She patted Seb on the arm. He managed to thank her and walked off, his hands stuffed in his pockets, thinking furiously.

All weekend he had managed to avoid Jack Carnavon. The older boy would have gloated and supplied details of his 'date' with Melissa, whatever had actually happened. Jack had been given an evening pass that Saturday and Seb had heard him come back at midnight. Jack had stopped at the end of Seb's bed and chuckled quietly, but Seb had feigned sleep, his mind and stomach churning. For once, Sunday Mass, instead of annoying him and provoking his innate distrust of religion, had actually calmed him and let him think through the situation with a clearer head. He decided to talk to Melissa when she came in on Monday. Tell her he had intended to ask her out, but assure her he would not be upset if she liked Jack. Although, of course, he would be. Upset and scared for her. But he hoped with every atom of his body that she would reject Jack in favor of him.

By the time he'd managed to talk to Sister Theresa on Wednesday, Jack had contrived a couple occasions to find Seb and casually mention his 'hot date' and how 'quiet girls always turn out to be the horniest'. He could feel the rage building up, but wasn't going to give in to this animal impulse. He might want to smash Jack's lying face against a brick wall, but not acting on that desire was what was going to help him grow into the sort of man he wanted to be. Which was someone completely unlike Jack Carnavon.

Wednesday afternoon, Seb signed out of St. Benet's, saying he was headed to Ted's Music Store. The Sisters were used to him hanging around there, talking to local musicians and were happy to let him meet others who shared his passion, so long as he wasn't back late and kept up with his schoolwork and chores.

Exiting the gates, he turned right and walked toward the intersection. When he got there, he darted a quick, guilty look back at St. Benet's, then turned right again instead of left. He walked quickly toward St Catherine's High School, feeling bad about deceiving the nuns, but his need to see Melissa was greater than his fear of committing a sin.

He timed his walk to reach the school at about the time the girls would be leaving. He watched them leave in twos and threes, wrapped up against the cold. Some were met by parents and climbed into cars, others boarded the yellow bus for their trip home. Melissa had told Seb she only lived a ten minute walk from school, so he hoped he would get a chance to see her without any adult intervention.

The rush for the gates slowed first to a trickle then stopped entirely. Seb wondered if Melissa was really sick. In his gut, he thought her absence was more likely something to do with her date with Jack, but he was scared to think through the consequences of this. He decided to wait another five minutes.

Just as he was about to give up, his patience was finally rewarded. A side door of the main building opened and Melissa came out, her hair blowing across her face as she wrapped a long scarf around her neck. She was talking to a teacher who looked concerned, reaching out and squeezing Melissa's arm while she asked her something. Melissa just shook her head a few times in response to the questions, then smiled and turned to leave, walking toward the gates, where Seb stood leaning against an old gnarled tree. That was when he saw the black eye.

At first, Melissa wouldn't even speak to him. Her eyes widened when she saw him step out from beside the tree, then she pulled her coat tighter around her and walked quickly away. He stood there for a moment, his mouth hanging open and his hands spread in a conciliatory gesture. Then he jogged after her.

"Melissa," he said. "Melissa, please stop." She said nothing, head down, her short breaths making small clouds in the cold air. Seb stopped again, wondering what to do, then ran to catch up, coming alongside her at the corner. He walked alongside her for a long couple of minutes in silence.

"Look, whatever this is about, it can't be about me because I haven't done or said anything to hurt you," he said, finally. "I wouldn't...couldn't do that to you." Seb found his shyness evaporating as fast as his desperation became more solid. "I really enjoyed talking to you, Melissa. I don't talk to many people, not properly, not the way I did with you. I lie awake nights thinking about you, wondering if you're doing the same. I was going to ask you out, it took me all week to build up the courage. Then...then he got there first and I felt sick. I've been worrying about you all week. Please talk to me."

Melissa's march slowed a little and she glanced at him. She took a deep breath and stopped. She looked straight at him. The black eye was puffy, ugly, raw. Seb winced but didn't look away. Slowly, she unbuttoned her coat and lifted her sweater and school shirt. Seb felt his mouth dry up as he saw the smooth skin of her stomach and side, tiny fine barely-visible hairs in a thin line under her navel. Then she pulled the clothes further and he saw the underside of her ribs. The left side was one big mass of bruising; yellows, blues, purples and blacks mapped out their territory across her skin. Seb felt his eyes fill with tears. He blinked them away against the cold wind. Melissa was dry eyed, impassive. It was as if she was showing him a school book. She seemed completely unemotional. When she saw the horror and concern in Seb's eyes, she dropped the sweater back and re-buttoned her coat. She looked at the floor.

"He said you had told him to ask me out," she said. "He said you thought I was his type, that you liked me as a friend but you were...you preferred boys."

Seb snorted. "He's some piece of work," he said. "Couldn't you tell how much I liked you?"

"Yes. No. Well, I hoped you liked me, but you never said anything, so...well, I didn't want to believe him, but he was so convincing. He said you were his best friend, that you'd do anything for each other." She looked up at Seb. "He lied, right?"

"He lied," said Seb. "I don't like him, I hardly know him. He's not someone I want to know. Melissa, did he do this to you?" he reached out a hand to her, but she stepped backward. He stopped and stood still again. After a while she continued speaking.

"I told my folks I was meeting a girlfriend. They're not quite ready for me to start dating. He said he was going to take me to a book signing. He said he'd got tickets and that it was a famous author. He wouldn't tell me who, he said it was a surprise." Melissa's voice was toneless and flat. Seb noticed she hadn't said Jack's name once. "We stopped at a bar on the way. I said I wouldn't go in, but he said they did the best hot chocolate in New York and I had to try it. I let him persuade me. It tasted funny. I think he put something in it. I felt a bit light headed when we came out."

She stopped talking and walked off again. Seb walked alongside her, keeping his distance.

"Melissa," he said. "Did he do this to you?"

She stopped again. He stopped alongside her. When she spoke, she looked straight ahead.

"He pushed me into an alleyway. He tried to kiss me. I said no, tried to make a joke of it. But he thought I was laughing at him. His eyes went horrible. Cold. He turned away and left me alone. I said I was going home. Then he turned back and hit me in the ribs. It hurt so much, Seb."

Seb thought about moving closer again, but she sensed it, glanced at him, shook her head. She faced forward again.

"I couldn't breath. I hunched over. I thought I was going to throw up. Then some guy came out the back of one of the restaurants carrying some trash. He wanted to know if everything was ok. Ja- he told the guy I had had too much to drink. He made some joke about it and the other guy laughed and walked away. I tried to go but he pushed me back against the wall. That's when he showed me the knife. He told me what he wanted to do to me. Then he told me I was frigid and ugly. That he could have any girl he wanted. I was so scared, I didn't say a word. I just looked at that knife and listened to his voice. He said if he saw me at St. Benet's ever again, he would kill you, Seb. He said if I saw you or spoke to you again, he would kill you. Then he would come for me and do all those things he wanted to do. Then he would kill me too."

Seb felt two warring emotions fight for control. Overwhelmingly, he wanted to put his arms around this girl and hold her and promise to protect her. But he also wanted to kill Jack Carnavon.

"He meant every word, Seb,"she whispered. "He's crazy. But he wanted to make sure I would believe him, so he hit me again. I didn't see it coming. I fell over. He crouched over me, said I'd slipped on leaves and fallen down some steps. Made me repeat it. Told me again what would happen. Showed me the knife again. Said if I went to the cops, he would get away with it. I'd lied to my parents about where I was going. He'd told the Sisters he was going to see his uncle. He smiled at me. Then he just walked away."

Seb could barely form a coherent thought. He could feel his heart racing. He had seen the look in Jack's eyes when he attacked Stevie. He knew he was capable of worse. Far worse. What the hell was he going to do?

"I can't see you again," said Melissa.

"No, please," said Seb. "We can't let him - ,"

"We have to," said Melissa, finally facing him. Her beautiful, solemn face looked up at him, the bruising doing nothing to detract from the impact she had on him. He wanted to hold her, to stroke her cheek, to kiss her lips. "I'm transferring," she said.

"What?" said Seb.

"I'm leaving St. Catherine's. Told my parents I'd been unhappy for a while, but had been hiding it from them. I'm moving in two weeks."

"Where to?" said Seb.

"Oh Seb, you know I can't tell you," said Melissa, her voice shaking. "This isn't the movies. He could really do what he said he would do. And we couldn't stop him. This is the only way to be sure." Seb just stood there, trying to think of something to say, his mind racing. "Goodbye, Seb," she said.

She walked away and this time Seb let her go, watching her as his brain seemed to slow and become numb. It was as if he had been drained of any life force, like he was watching himself from outside his own body. She stopped once, at the corner.

"I really like you, too, Seb," she said. Then she rounded the corner and disappeared. It was the last time he ever saw her.

# Chapter 13

**Victorville**
**Present day**

Westlake stepped forward as the train slowed to walking pace. He turned to face his team. The FBI uniform was one of a number of options open to him when he needed to move openly. It was more than just fancy dress. If a concerned member of the public called the FBI to check, it would immediately be confirmed that a team was working in the area. Westlake reached into his pocket and pulled out a photograph of Seb, holding it up.

"Sebastian Varden, age 32," he said. "It's possible he's not on this train, but unlikely. Make a thorough sweep. When you find him, let me know. Do not, I repeat, do not attempt to bring him in yourself. He may be dangerous. Go."

The figures moved to the train doors and, on a nod from Westlake, got on board. Westlake stepped away from the train and watched, his eyes scanning the cars.

On board, passengers reacted just as they should when confronted by a uniformed man with a gun. They were helpful. One Chicago businessman seemed to be sweating a lot more than would be considered normal in an air-conditioned railway car, and appeared more relieved than most when the FBI guys checked him and moved on. He had recently begun embezzling his employers in order to pay for a mistress in Los Angeles and - although he knew it was very unlikely the US Government would waste money arresting him using what looked to be a SWAT team - he wondered how he would be able to explain away the handcuffs, clamps, gags and whips in his luggage.

The dining car was one of the last places the team checked. Every cabin had been opened, every bathroom gone over. Two burly men stepped into the restaurant car and stopped at each table, checking faces carefully. They muttered the same insincere pleasantries.

"Sorry to disturb you, won't take a moment, I'm afraid we can't tell you that. Thank you for your time, have a good trip." They moved purposefully and always had one hand close to a holster.

"Sorry to disturb you, sir."

Walt looked up at the black-clad linebacker towering over the table.

"No problem at all, officer," he said, smiling thinly. "Should I call you officer?" He looked at the insignia on the man's arm. "You are... with the FBI, aren't you?"

The man didn't answer, but stared at Walt who met his gaze, unblinking. "Well, we must help you fellows preserve our national security, mustn't we?"

The FBI officer turned to look at the man opposite Walt. He seemed to be asleep. He leaned in for a closer look.

"My father," said Walt. "It's been a long day and he needs his rest. Please don't disturb him."

The officer ignored Walt and shook the shoulder of the man. One eye opened, pale blue, watery and bloodshot. The face was heavily wrinkled and pale, the skin so thin he could make out red and blue veins just under the surface.

"Sorry to disturb you," he said. "You folks have a good trip."

"Thank you," said Walt, "I'm sure we will."

Their search complete, Westlake's men left the train. After a short debrief, Westlake made a call. The train engine roared into life and the Southwest Chief peeled away from the platform, resuming its journey east. Westlake watched it disappear before turning back to his team.

"The chopper will take you back to LA, after which you will resume your normal duties," he said. He turned back to the rail track as his men jogged away from the station to the waiting helicopter, before turning and following them.

\*\*\*

Seb kept his eyes shut until he was sure the train was a few miles clear of Victorville. He had never been so scared in his life, which was ironic considering the day he'd just had. There was something about the slow, inevitable closing in of a net that brought him out in a sweat. Seb distracted himself by attempting to re-establish contact with Seb2. He tried calling a silent "hello", but quickly recognized no conscious effort was going to work. Judging from the conversation that morning, it seemed extreme physical danger or impending death might be the only way to get in touch with his subconscious.

"They're long gone," said Walt.

Seb cautiously opened his eyes. The restaurant car was clear of uniforms and everybody had resumed their conversations. The heightened pitch of most voices testified that they were discussing the unexpected interruption. No doubt, there would be some speculation about who the FBI were looking for. Seb saw three or four people checking their phones, looking for news of escaped convicts or terrorists on the loose. *Try googling 'suicidal musician cured by alien still at large'.* He smiled.

"Care to share?" said Walt.

"Oh, I was just thinking about the day I've had," said Seb, "you wouldn't believe me if I told you."

"Try me," said Walt.

"No, you first," said Seb. "You just met me. You know nothing about me. Why did you help me back there? I could be an escaped lunatic for all you know. And that FBI guy looked right at me and didn't recognize me. What the hell was that? Jedi mind trick?"

"Now that was a movie I thoroughly enjoyed," said Walt. "The Force - wonder where he got that idea from? But - sadly - I can't influence anyone's mind directly. The stunt I just pulled was far more basic."

"How did you do it?" said Seb. "Why did you do it?"

Walt topped up both glasses and sat back.

"The easiest way I can explain is by finishing my story."

Seb sat up impatiently, disliking the feeling of having no control. He'd had no time to absorb what was happening to him - hell, he didn't even know exactly what *was* happening to him. And meeting the enigmatic Walt just as he desperately needed help couldn't be a coincidence. He looked across at the older man. His face was relaxed, intelligent, alert. Who was he? Seb had so many questions, he didn't know where to start. He sat back again and deliberately slowed his breathing, calming his mind.

"Go ahead," he said. "I'll save my questions for a little while."

"Thank you," said Walt. "I will answer them, I promise." He closed his eyes for a second, gathering his thoughts.

"I remember that first encounter with Sid Bernbaum. I'd decided anyone who was allowed to avoid paying protection money to the mob was probably someone I shouldn't mess with. The problem was, I didn't come to this conclusion until I had picked his lock and was standing in the middle of his store." Walt chuckled softly. "I was far too curious when I was a kid. Usually, I had enough sense not to put myself in danger unnecessarily, but for some reason I disregarded all the warning signs that night. When my gut finally got round to telling me I needed to be somewhere else - fast - I turned and went back to the door. But it had gone."

"Gone?" said Seb, startled. "What do you mean?"

"I thought I was losing my mind, to start with," said Walt. "Instead of the florist's front door and shop window, there was just a mass of green. It was like I'd walked into a jungle. Where the door should have been was just leaves, branches, tendrils, flowers. I froze for a second, then I saw the door handle. It was just visible although some kind of creeper had coiled itself around it. Then I realized the plants were moving. Two paces closer, and suddenly they all seemed to rear up at once. I stopped short, then backed up again. It was as if I was facing some kind of massive snake about to strike."

Seb's mouth twitched as he remembered the sensation he'd felt earlier as the napkin had come toward him.

"I could see the individual plants making up some kind of body," continued Walt, his eyes closed as he remembered. "I saw geraniums, roses, carnations, rubber plants, orchids. It would have been funny if it hadn't been the scariest thing I'd ever seen. I just stood there, gaping, sweating, practically hyper-ventilating. And - for the first time in my life - I didn't know what to do. I'd always lived on my wits and now they deserted me. I felt a sensation I'd never felt before: panic. I could taste acid in my throat. I thought I was going to collapse. And that's when Sid finally spoke. He was hidden in the shadows behind the counter.

" 'I'm afraid we're closed, young man,' he said. 'If you're after a bouquet for a lady friend or a button hole to smarten yourself up, you should come back during business hours. The sign on the door makes it perfectly clear. Or is there something else I can help you with?'

"I could hardly form a rational thought, let alone speak in coherent sentences, but I blurted something out about taking a wrong turn, didn't mean to be there, how it was all an innocent mistake. Sid said nothing, just let me tell my lies and make myself look more and more ridiculous. I didn't dare look away from the plants. They were still swaying slightly and I was convinced they were watching me. At the edge of my vision I saw a wizened old man shuffle past. He was bent over a silver-topped cane. Only a few wisps of white hair clung to his wrinkled skull. He went right up to the plants and stroked what looked to me to be the head of a snake, muttering either to the greenery or himself, I wasn't sure which. Then he turned to face me and the plants slowly withdrew, the only sound a faint rustling as the door and window slowly came into view again. I blinked quickly, sure I couldn't be seeing what I was seeing. Funny. When something happens so far outside our world-view, we'll often accept any explanation, however unlikely, as long as it doesn't challenge our preconceptions. I leapt to the conclusion I must have been drugged somehow, or gassed. I looked at this frail old man standing in front of the door and thought I must have imagined the whole thing. I decided I had to clear my head, I had to go home.

" 'I'll leave,' I said. 'I'm sorry for any trouble.'

Sid shook his head. 'No,' he said, 'stay a while. We need to talk.' I swallowed hard.

" 'I have to be somewhere,' I said. Excuse me.' I lurched toward the door, but just as I began to move, creepers shot across the floor and wrapped themselves around my ankles. I screamed and fell, tearing at them, but even as I pulled some away, more took their place until they had pinned my hands to my ankles. I lay there in a fetal position and sobbed in frustration, just a scared kid.

" 'I'll make some tea,' said Sid as he shuffled back past me. 'Tea helps one think clearly, don't you agree?'

Walt had closed his eyes again and was smiling while he spoke. Seb was transfixed. This guy really knew how to tell a story, and - despite his initial impatience - Seb was a sucker for a good story. Especially one that might shed some light on the strangest day of his life.

"Sid went off to make his tea and I struggled to get free for a minute or so before giving up. I managed to get a grip, control myself a little, accept the fact that, for the first time I could remember, I had been out-maneuvered and wasn't in control. I was a smart, streetwise kid, remember. I thought I knew it all. But this tiny, ancient Jewish guy had me powerless in seconds. My world view was going through some fairly serious revisions while I lay there. The main one being an acceptance of the reality of what I had just seen. I've always been a realist, and when I'd first seen those plants move, I tried to convince myself it was only happening in my mind. But I knew different. It was clear this guy was a genuine, bona fide magician, wizard, sorcerer. Whatever. I didn't know any words to describe him that didn't come straight out of a first grade picture book, but he couldn't have been more wizardy if he had worn a pointy hat and waved a wand. But - ever the pragmatist - I soon moved on from this conclusion to wondering what he would do to me. No one knew I was there. I was breaking and entering and he had caught me red-handed. I couldn't help wondering if wizards went in for human sacrifices.

"When he came back into the room, I felt myself being raised from the floor. The greenery twisted itself into a structure like a chair, lifting me into it. A green table formed in front of me and as Sid put the tray down, my hands were released, although my legs were still firmly tied to the 'chair'. As he sat, vines and fronds rose up from the floor and supported him.

" ' I rarely have visitors,' he said, pouring the tea into a china cup, 'so I don't buy milk. I'm afraid you'll have to take it black.' I didn't trust myself to say a thing, just nodded, picked up the cup and took a sip.

" 'Now, tell me why you are here.' I thought for a second, opened my mouth, but he held up his hand to stop me. 'Think carefully before you speak,' he said, 'then tell me the truth.'

"I did as I was told. I wasn't going to mess with this guy. As I thought about my boss, the weekly protection money racket, and the fact no one ever bothered Bernbaum's Florist, I realized the real reason I was there. I remembered the pull from the shop every time I'd passed it, the compulsion to go in which had built ever since I'd first set eyes on the faded awning outside his shop.

" 'You called me,' I blurted out. 'You wanted me here.'

"Sid's eyes widened a little, then he nodded. 'Good,' he said. 'Very good. You are intelligent as well as gifted. This will make things much easier. How old are you?'

" 'Seventeen,' I said. He just looked at me, sipping at his tea. 'Fifteen,' I said.

" 'That's better,' he said. 'A little old, but talented. Hmm.' He stood up and gestured toward me. The 'chair' raised me into a standing position and the plants binding me loosened and fell away. I felt the blood returning to my legs. The old man was just staring at me. I didn't say a word. After a while, he seemed to come to a decision.

" 'I have been watching you for a while, Walter,' he said. 'You're a bright boy and you've managed to avoid getting yourself killed so far, but it's only a matter of time.' He walked back to the counter and put his hand palm up on the surface. A pot plant next to him slid out fresh new buds, leaves and vines. They covered his hand. He looked at me and I heard a voice coming from the plant nearest to him. If I hadn't been scared half out of my wits, I would've laughed, it was such a shock. I was so taken aback, it took me a while to realize it was Buddy Hanlon's voice. Buddy was a few rungs up from me in the Mob. A dangerous character. It was disorienting hearing his rough Irish voice coming out of a geranium. But after a couple of sentences, I focused on what he was saying.

" 'Yeah, that Ford kid - Walt,' said the plant/Buddy. 'Manny saw him talking to Benny K last week.' I felt my insides turn to water. Benny K ran the East side for another family. Being seen with him would mean I was finished. And finished with these guys didn't mean a party and a gold watch. Buddy was wrong - I wasn't stupid enough to talk to Benny K - but Manny was a liar and he'd never liked me. Then another voice came from the plant. The voice of Al Strollo. Al 'the strangler' Strollo.

" 'I'll take care of him,' he said. I was a dead man.

"Sid smiled at me and the plant slid away from his palm.

" 'What I can do, only a few can learn,' he said. 'I have been here for over thirty years and the urge to pass on my knowledge before I die has been strong. But you are the first. The first in thirty years. There are others with this power, but...ah, you will learn more about them. If you accept.'

" 'Accept what?" I said.

" 'What I am offering you,' said Sid. 'An apprenticeship.'

"I thought about Strollo the Strangler's hands around my throat.

" 'Yes,' I said immediately. "I accept.'"

Walt picked up the wine bottle and refilled the empty glasses. The bottle was still half full. Seb raised his eyebrows and tapped the bottle.

"The wine?" he said.

"Yes," said Walt. "We could sit here drinking all night, offer everyone on this train a few glasses and it would still be half full. And each glass just as good as the last."

"Well, I'm glad this ability of yours turned out to have some practical use," said Seb. "Can you make plants talk, too?"

"Yes, I can do that," he said, "although I never got to be as adept as Sid was. He had a real way with nature, he seemed to work with the plants, rather than just impose his will on them. My talent turned out to be more powerful, but I could never match his finesse."

Seb leaned across he table. "Back there, when they were looking for me," he said, "what did you do?"

"Parlor trick," said Walt. He closed his eyes. Seb was suddenly aware that Walt's face had brightened. No, that wasn't it. It was more like the dining car lights had dimmed. He looked around quickly, but when he turned back to Walt, his features were still normally lit. Walt's face began to change.

It only took one or two seconds. Walt's tanned features lengthened slightly, his hairline moving forward, the hair itself darkening, thickening and growing three or four inches. Brown eyes became light blue, eyebrows thinning and lifting slightly. Walt's mouth became more generous and a couple days worth of stubble appeared on a distinctly squarer chin.

Seb whistled in admiration as he stared straight at the most famous young actor in America - as well-known for the sheer volume of equally famous actresses he had dated as he was for the eye-watering pay checks he picked up for his blockbuster movies.

"Man," said Seb, "that's incredible." A young woman walked past, glanced at them, then looked back at Walt, her eyebrows nearly leaving her face as she realized who she was looking at. She screamed in delight, than fell over her own feet and took a dive into the middle of the dining car, her vodka tonic ending up in the lap of a very unhappy businessman.

"What the hell are you doing?" the business man said, half-standing and dabbing at his pants with a napkin.

"I'm sorry," she squeaked, "I'm sorry, it's just, it's just that, well -" She backed up a step and looked over at Walt. Walt - his face now his own again, smiled innocently up at her.

"Can I help you, Miss?" he said. Her face colored and she coughed, her eyes darting all around her in a desperate attempt to locate the missing celebrity. When she accepted she couldn't possibly have seen what she thought she'd seen, she practically ran for the door, knocking the irate businessman back into his seat as she passed.

Walt chuckled. "I gave you something a little less ostentatious," he said. "It has to be someone I can picture easily. You should be honored. I gave you Sid's face."

Seb realized that - despite the quantity of wine he'd drunk - he felt completely sober.

"Look, Walt," he said. "Thank you for what you did. Don't think that I'm ungrateful. But I feel like I'm losing my mind here. I've been attacked, now I'm being hunted."

He leaned forward and grabbed Walt's wrist, his voice cracking. "Nothing - nothing is what I thought it was. Something has happened to me - I've changed. I don't know. Everything is different. I feel like I should have lost my mind, but I'm just about holding it all together. And now you. You seem to know what's going on, you just happen to be on this train, just happen to be sitting at the only table with a free seat, just happen to be able to change my face - my face! - when the bad guys come calling. Don't take this the wrong way, but why the hell should I trust you?"

Walt opened his mouth, but Seb leaned further forward, his face only inches from the other man. Was that a sudden flash of fear in Walt's eyes?

"I'm not stupid," said Seb. "Who are you - and how did you know I was here?"

Nearly half a minute passed in silence as the two men stared each other out.

"Ok," said Walt. "Ok. It's true, it's no coincidence." Seb released Walt's wrist and sat back.

"But I didn't find you," said Walt.

"What do you mean?" said Seb.

"You found me."

Walt stood up. "Look, Seb," he said. "I don't expect you to trust me right off the bat. But you're here for the same reason I walked into Sid's store that night. I didn't come looking for you. I was on this train before you were, right?

Seb frowned. He had no idea how long he had been on the train, or where he'd been before he boarded. Was 'boarded' even the right word?

"You found me," repeated Walt "You need me. But I knew you were coming. Look, it's late, we're both tired. Sleep on it."

Seb laughed. "I don't feel like I'll ever sleep again."

"Take my word for it," said Walt, "you'll sleep like a dead man tonight. Sorry," he said, as Seb winced, "bad choice of words. I'm getting off at Albuquerque. You?"

Seb remembered the tickets. "Me too," he said.

"Let me give you a ride tomorrow. There's something I want to show you. And I have a proposition."

Seb hesitated. Walt put out his hand. His face was serious and sincere. Seb sighed, reached out and shook the older man's hand.

"You're going to find it next to impossible to find anyone who understands anything about what you're going through. And friends can be few and far between when you've discovered Manna, believe me. Go to bed. We'll talk in Albuquerque." He turned and walked out of the dining car.

Seb looked after him for a long moment. *Manna?*

Getting on the superliner bed fully clothed, he stretched out and sighed. He had never been a good sleeper. And after the craziest day of his life, he was convinced he wouldn't be able to sleep at all.

Three seconds after his head touched the pillow, Seb slipped into the deepest sleep he had ever experienced. And - for the first time in as long as he could remember - there were no dreams.

# Chapter 14

The day was well established by the time Seb opened his eyes, sunlight flickering through the flimsy curtains. Never a morning person, he marveled at the energy he felt as he sprang out of bed and went into the bathroom. He didn't need a shower to make him feel invigorated, but took one anyway. He rubbed his chin. Still no stubble. Shame, he had always thought he looked better with a couple days' growth. He grabbed a brush and looked up at the mirror again, immediately dropping the brush, stepping backward, slipping and nearly ending up back in the shower.

Five seconds earlier he had been clean shaven. Now he had stubble.

*This is going to take some getting used to.*

The dining car was half full, the breakfast crowd having thinned out. Seb ordered a coffee and watched the landscape roll by the window. Halfway through his second cup, Walt slid into the seat opposite.

"Sleep ok?" said Walt.

"Unbelievably well," said Seb.

"Told ya," said Walt. "So what do you say? Going to give me a chance?"

Seb shrugged. "I don't know who you are," he said. "And I'm not stupid. But you were right about friends. I can't even get in touch with the ones I have. I know they'll be watched. Whoever is after me seems to have the FBI at his disposal. I can't risk contacting M-, er, anyone. My options are limited and I do want to find out what's happening to me. I guess I could come with you today."

"Love that enthusiasm," said Walt.

"No offense," said Seb, "but I don't trust you. Yet."

"You'd be crazy if you did," said Walt, smiling.

It was just before midday when the Southwest Chief slowed to a stop in Albuquerque. Seb stepped off the train, a slim case in his hand. The case contained a wash bag and his clothes. He had felt terrible cramming such a beautiful suit in there, but when he took it out to refold it, he realized it looked freshly pressed. As did the shirt. All the clothes appeared to be recently laundered, too. Seb had a fun couple minutes screwing the suit and shirt up as much as he could - even stamping on them for a while, then shaking them to find they looked brand new again.

When he climbed down from the train, Walt was on the platform, handing his suitcase to a short, dark-haired man. As Seb approached, Walt turned.

"This is Steve, my assistant, accountant, chauffeur, concierge. Steve, this is Seb."

"Good to meet you,"said Seb, shaking his hand. Steve eyed him impassively.

"Steve doesn't speak," said Walt, "but he listens real good."

They followed Steve to Walt's car, a black Chrysler 300. Steve held open the door and they both got out of the heat into the cool, air-conditioned leather interior.

"This thing makes me feel like a gangster," said Walt. As the car pulled away, he pushed a button and thick security glass slid up between them and Steve. Seb was a little surprised at Walt's choice of vehicle, but said nothing.

"There's little Steve doesn't know about me," said Walt. "He knows I'm a successful magician performing mostly for Hollywood royalty and CEOs, and an even more successful gambler who cheats to maintain his luxurious lifestyle." Walt laughed. "And the rest of it he pretends he doesn't see. Now, settle back and enjoy the ride."

"Where are we going?" said Seb.

"Mind if I keep that a secret a little longer?" said Walt. "I think you're gonna like it. It's going to take a few hours to get there and I promised to finish my story." He reached forward and pulled a couple of bottles of water from a small fridge in the center of the car. Seb accepted one gratefully.

"I'm not going anywhere," said Seb.

Walt sank back into the soft leather, his memories coming alive for him as he continued his story.

"Sid Bernbaum was the most powerful man in Chicago. It only took me a couple weeks to realize that. He understood that information is power, and whoever held the most information ultimately held the most power. He knew the Chicago underworld better than anyone. He also knew everything that was going on in the police department, the mayor's office: every level of local government."

"How?" said Seb.

"He spent the first week showing me what he'd set up. The florist store was the perfect cover for his real business. And no one ever suspected a thing. How could they? It was beyond their comprehension. Sid pretty much implemented a covert bugging operation before electronic bugs were invented. He started by sending flowers to the wives or girlfriends of the Bosses. Once a bouquet was in the house, the Manna would infiltrate any other plants in the vicinity. Then, unless the plants died or were thrown out, he could listen in on any conversation in town."

"Manna?" said Seb. "Magic?"

Walt nodded. "It's been called many things over the hundreds - possibly thousands - of years since it was first used. Magic is one. Still gets called that occasionally, although it's usually Magick with a capital M and a k at the end. The Power Of The Gods, or The Great Power was popular in the 18<sup>th</sup> and 19<sup>th</sup> centuries, but faded out of use. The Craft still remains fairly popular. I - and many others - use the word 'Manna'. We don't know what it is, but using a word associated with an ancient mystery reminds us of our ignorance and our quest to know more."

"We? How many of you are there?"

"A handful. Possibly no more than a few hundred on this continent. Thousands worldwide. With varying degrees of talent, both shut-eyes and open-eyes."

"Woah," said Seb, "you're going to have to explain some of this."

"Open-eyes use Manna knowingly, shut-eyes have abilities but don't know it. Sometimes they survive car wrecks or become aware of events that have happened thousands of miles away. Most call them miracles and leave it at that. Some explore their talent. Then one of the groups or the Order pick them up."

Seb frowned and Walt laughed.

"I'm sorry," said Walt, "I know it's a lot to take in and I'm not going to be able to explain every last detail now. Just let me fill you in a little more about my background, then we'll see where we are."

Seb nodded and motioned Walt to continue.

"Sid showed me how his network of living plants and flowers gave him power over everyone of significance in Chicago. After secretly listening to them for months, he would contact them individually, hinting he had information about their enemies. Politicians, newspaper moguls, mobsters, they would treat him to lunch in the swankiest restaurants, be liberal with the champagne, try bribing Sid with money and women. He'd reveal enough to convince them he could bring down their rivals. Then, while their greedy minds plotted the downfall of their enemies, he would quietly tell them something he knew concerning them personally. He had enough dirt on each of them to ruin them forever. Then the conversation would take a different turn, the tone would get ugly. Threats would be made. But Sid was way ahead of them. He told them he had documents in lawyers' safes all over the country, ready to be sent to the press on his death. After they'd finished ranting, most asked what would happen if he died of natural causes. I used to enjoy that bit. He told them the press got the documents no matter how he died, so it was in their interests to keep him healthy."

Walt chuckled at the memory. "Sid used to laugh about this all the time. Because if he ever got even a cold, he'd be checked into a private clinic and treated like a king. Funny thing was, he was just messing with them. I don't think he ever really got sick - not while he was using Manna."

Walt looked up at Seb, who raised an eyebrow.

"Yeah, it keeps you healthy, too, as long as you keep it topped up. Manna users need to replenish their supply regularly. For some, this means every day, for others every few weeks or even a couple months. Sid could go six months at a stretch, he was famous for it. Don't ask - it'll be easier to show you.

"Sid didn't ask for much in return for keeping his knowledge to himself. He lived above his shop rent-free, someone else picked up his tab at local restaurants and stores, his bank account was always healthy although I never saw him deposit more than a few dollars. He didn't do it for the money, he did it because he could influence those with influence. He was a realist like me, he knew he couldn't clean up the city, but he also tried to keep innocents out of harm's way. He made sure no Boss ever got too powerful. In his own quiet way, he ran Chicago. "

"How did he teach you?" said Seb. "I mean, what did you do, day to day?"

"You have to be trained by an adept to learn to control Manna," said Walt. "Women are supposed to make the best adepts, but a higher proportion of women join the Order, and their teaching is very formal. They have a system, and no one outside the Order can use it as it involves a collective...ah, it's complicated. It's enough to know that training outside the Order is more hit-and-miss, but the most powerful users have been developed our way. Sid said I'd need patience and discipline, neither of which were my favorite word.

" 'Just sit with me, boy,' he said. 'Sit, don't ask questions and be aware of your mind. It will fight you. It will do everything it can to stop you simply being here, simply sitting, simply letting pure awareness be present.' "

Seb realized with a start that Walt was describing Contemplation perfectly. Contemplation, belying its name, was anything but relaxing. It involved constant vigilance, awake-ness, being entirely centered in the moment.

"Sid was an incredibly patient man," continued Walt. "Which was lucky, because I would have driven anyone else crazy. I threw myself into the training for the first few weeks. Every day, I'd spend hours sitting with Sid while he used Manna. But he might as well have been asleep for all the sense I could make of it. I couldn't sit still for five minutes. My mind would race. I'd start thinking about my life before I met Sid. It had been dangerous, sure, but at least I was out there doing something, not sitting silently next to the oldest Jew in Chicago. I'd get frustrated about life drifting away, all my opportunities going down the plughole. Fortunately, I was as stubborn as they come.

Every time I thought about leaving, I'd remember the alternative - a brief encounter with a professional strangler - and I'd sit my ass back down. And slowly, real slowly, I started to feel something. It's different for everyone. For me, it's like a buzz - a vibration - I feel it in my face, behind my eyes, in my cheekbones. And one day, while we were sitting there, I stretched out with this buzzing sensation."

Walt stopped talking. Seb turned toward him and noticed immediately that the area near Walt had darkened again. A silence had suddenly captured the space around them. It felt like a physical presence, reality becoming a movie still. A newspaper tucked behind the seat in front of Walt slid slowly out from the pouch, falling between them. It opened and the pages moved although there was no breeze, just the subtle waft of the AC. As the newspaper reached the center pages, four sheets peeled away and floated upwards, folding as they did so. Seb watched corners furl and edges tuck under, the movements crisp and precise. Within a few seconds, the first two sheets had become perfect simulacra of tropical fish, swimmingly lazily around the car. The effect was so startling that Seb took a breath to convince himself they weren't underwater.

The other two sheets came together and rapidly took on the outline of a hungry predator stalking its prey. A perfect scale model of a great white shark began circling the oblivious fish. It was so realistic that Seb flinched when it flicked its powerful tail and passed close to his face. It was as if someone had shrunk a real shark and wrapped it in the LA Times before releasing it into the wild. One of the fish was near the door handle on Walt's side of the Chrysler. The shark lunged with incredible speed, its mouth opening, then shaking violently from side to side as it ripped the fish apart. Confetti drifted around the car.

Seb realized he was seeing more than just the darkening effect he had noticed the previous night. He could make out smoky dark tendrils coming from Walt's head and body connecting with the paper shark and the surviving fish. Walt looked over at him.

"You feel it, don't you?"

Seb nodded.

"Reach out," said Walt, "try to take over the shark."

"How?" said Seb.

"I have no idea," said Walt, "only you know how."

"Well, thanks," muttered Seb, but he turned back to the shark just the same, which was now hovering close to the thick glass screen between them and Steve. He let go of his thoughts and just watched the shark, carefully letting mental distractions slide away from his awareness. Nothing happened. Disappointed, he slumped back in his seat. He closed his eyes and tried to remember the sensation when he escaped from Westlake, the way he'd seemed to become one with the door, the car. He opened his eyes again, feeling an echo of the fear he'd felt on that highway the day before. He felt a surge of...something...head away from him toward the shark.

With a noise like an explosion, the glass screen shattered, tiny lumps of safety glass falling to the floor of the car. Steve swerved violently and the Chrysler left the road. The rear of the car twitched violently before jackknifing. Seb lurched against Walt as the car side-swiped a utility pole before coming to rest in a cloud of dust about 20 feet from the highway, its rear suspension causing it to sag drunkenly in the dirt.

Steve was out of the car first and opened the door next to Seb to let them out. They walked around the vehicle and assessed the damage, Walt holding a silk handkerchief to his face as the dust began to settle.

"You ok?" said Seb. "I'm sorry, I don't know what happened." Then his mouth dropped open. The car he was looking at wasn't a Chrysler 300. It was a Lincoln Continental, but bigger, sleeker, and more luxurious than any he had ever seen. And it was white, not black.

"What the-?"

Walt smiled. "I'll explain in a moment," he said, his fingers tracing a huge dent in the side of the car where the impact had buckled the metal. He shut his eyes and laid a hand flat on the side of the car. For a moment the air seemed to darken and Seb thought the metal began rippling under Walt's hand. Then the older man frowned, shrugged and stood up again.

"Best thing you can do is get straight back on the horse," he said. "Look, son, I'll be honest with you, what you just did in the car would have been beyond my capabilities after a year with Sid. You need to learn some control before you hurt yourself. Or someone else."

Seb looked at the crumpled metal and the shattered glass still covering the back seat. He remembered tapping into a sense of fear the moment before the glass had exploded.

"Don't worry," he said, "it'll be a while before I try anything like that again."

Walt turned toward him and shook his head.

"You don't get away that easy," he said. "We need this car back on the road and I haven't paid a mechanic's bill in a long, long time."

"What?" said Seb, "you want me to...?" He gestured at the car and Walt nodded.

"No," said Seb. "I'm more likely to make things worse."

Walt shrugged.

"It's a write-off," he said. "How much worse can you make it?"

Seb grimaced. "You really want to find out?" he said.

Walt said nothing, just moved away from the damaged car. Seb took his place by the crushed wing and put his hand on to the damaged metal.

"Ok, then," he said, "it's your dime."

He closed his eyes, thinking back to the sensation he had felt when his body seemed to merge with the car door in LA. Nothing happened. He tried to remember his exact mental state...that was easy enough: he'd been terrified. So maybe fear was the key. His mind flashed back to the fear he'd felt when the two soldiers had raised their weapons the day before. There was a bang. He opened his eyes. The Lincoln was 15 feet away, tracks in the dust where the tires had scraped across the rough surface. Seb looked round. Walt and Steve took a step back. He walked up to the car and knelt next to the dented metal again. He closed his eyes.

*Maybe fear isn't the only emotion that can trigger this...Manna.* He briefly wondered what might happen if he allowed himself to get angry. What might rage produce? For the first time, the fear that had gripped him intermittently since Westlake had started pursuing him took on a new aspect: fear of what he himself might do. His lack of control might be seriously dangerous to anyone nearby.

Taking a deep breath, Seb turned his attention to the movement of air through his nostrils into his body and back out again. The thoughts whirring around his mind, the unanswered questions, the fears and hopes for what the future might hold - they all began fading into background chatter as his attention on his breath deepened. He offered up a silent prayer of thanks to Father O'Hanoran for teaching him Contemplation when he was a teen who might have ended up pursuing a very different path. More quickly than usual, he reached that place of emptiness. He tried to reach out toward the car with his mind, but it was like grabbing a handful of mist. He could feel a presence again, a hum of possibility under the surface, like the charged atmosphere before a huge storm. He was about to try reaching out again, when he had an idea. He gently allowed Bach's prelude to begin sounding in his mind. Bach had always elicited strong emotions in Seb. Emotions he couldn't name. They just rose up inside him in response to that particular arrangement of the twelve notes in the Western scale. As he listened internally to the music, the composition seemed to provide a structure through which he could reach out again with the Manna. This time - as his mind stretched out - it was as if the metal gave way like butter. There was a moment when his awareness seemed to expand; his sense of self shrinking. He was unworried, calm, doing what needed to be done right now, this moment.

"Well," said Walt from behind him, "that's a pretty nice job."

Seb opened his eyes and stood up, stepping backward from the car. There was no evidence of any damage. In fact, the Lincoln looked like it had just rolled off the production line. It gleamed in the sun, the alloy wheels painfully bright.

"I even prefer the color," said Walt. Seb looked again. The car was a deep midnight blue. Three minutes earlier it had been white.

Walt narrowed his eyes and cocked his head to one side as if listening.

"I wonder..." he murmured. Picking up a rock, he hefted it in one hand for a second, then snapped his arm back and threw it at the Lincoln. It sailed through the air before landing squarely in the middle of the hood, bouncing off and leaving an egg-sized depression with some surrounding scratches where the bare metal showed through.

"What are you doing?" said Seb, but Walt just held up a hand, his eyes never leaving the car.

Seb looked too. The dent began to move, the area around it looking briefly like water rippling on the sunlight. Within a second the hood was perfect again, no evidence of the damage visible.

"Thought so," said Walt. "Wonder how long it'll last?" He walked over to the car and held the door open for Seb. Steve's impassive features showed no surprise at what he'd just witnessed.

"Imagine if you could patent that," said Walt. "You'd make a fortune."

Steve started the engine. Walt tapped the newly replaced security glass. It slid smoothly down.

"Someone on that train might remember seeing you leave," said Walt. "And this Lincoln is not the kind of car you forget. It's still supposed to be just a concept car. I had to pull a few strings to get it. So I gave it a little disguise. Then I had Steve drive us a few miles south. Anyone looking for you will guess you're headed for Mexico in a black Chrysler. I'm a magician, Seb. I just made you disappear."

*Roswell. New Mexico. That is where I need to go. But maybe not straight off, if Westlake thinks that's where I'm going.*

"So where are we heading?" said Seb, as the big Lincoln swung around to face the other way.

"My place," said Walt. "Las Vegas"

# Chapter 15

## Los Angeles

Bob knocked back a shot of bourbon, the liquid burning his throat as it chased the seven bottles of beer he had already sent down there. He held up his finger for a refill.

"Are you sure you need another?" said Rachel, owner of the Heroes And Villains Bar and Grill. Her clientele had tended toward the Villains end of the market as the neighborhood got rougher and the only grill in the place these days was the one she pulled down at the end of the night to stop the window getting a brick through it. Bob was a regular - one of her favorites. He had even shared her bed occasionally. Tonight, though, he was worrying her. He'd never been a serious drinker. One or two beers then home, Marcie barking goodnight as he headed down the street. Now he was drinking with a kind of grim determination she didn't much like.

"Give me a break, Rachel," said Bob, only slurring his words very slightly. "I know my limits. One more and I'm going home, anyway."

Rachel suddenly realized what was missing. The first thing Bob usually asked for was a bowl of water to take outside for his dog.

"Where's Marcie?" she asked. Bob looked up and held her gaze before sighing and staring at the empty shot glass.

"She's dead," he said and slid the glass toward her. She put her hand on his and placed the bourbon bottle in front of him.

"It's on the house," she said. He looked up again and nodded at her, not trusting himself to speak. Rachel moved away down the bar and found some glasses to polish. She hadn't run a bar for thirty-five years without learning how to tell when someone needed some space. She watched Bob refill his glass and drain it.

It had happened the previous night. Bob had decided a little research into Westlake and his mysterious soldiers might help him understand what Seb had got himself into. And he didn't believe he was being watched, despite Westlake's threat at the station. It had to be a bluff - the sheer expense of 24 hour surveillance on someone pretty much guaranteed it. About 20 minutes internet research had uncovered nothing of interest. In fact, he'd found nothing at all. No Westlake listed anywhere, despite trying various government departments. He had half-expected it. The sort of work Bob suspected Westlake to be involved in required a degree of invisibility.

Bob had stopped to brew fresh coffee then changed tack. He trawled through some conspiracy sites, looking for sightings of military personnel with no traceable link to the US Government. Things started to get more interesting. Sifting through various reports after dismissing the obvious paranoid fantasists, there were three or four instances in the last year where unidentifiable military types had been seen in action. All of the reports were categorically denied by the military and no evidence could be presented to prove otherwise.

One report in particular caught Bob's attention. Three years ago, an Idaho farmer claimed to have shot dead an intruder who was part of a group of armed men he'd seen advancing on his house. He had called it in to the local sheriff and, when he'd arrived, had led him to the edge of his field where they found the corpse of one of his horses. Ballistic evidence had matched the bullet to the farmer's rifle, but he had sworn blind the gun wasn't his - he claimed they must have been switched. What made the story interesting was the sheriff's statement. First, he'd pointed out that it was a full moon - hardly a night where someone might mistake a horse for a man. Second, the farmer was an ex-Navy Seal. His testimony was detailed, thorough and convincing. Third - and most compelling for Bob - the Sheriff had heard a helicopter as he left for the farm. The official report had been unable to reach a definite conclusion. Bob wondered why the Sheriff or farmer hadn't pursued it further, but a quick search of their names revealed they had both died with three months of the incident: the previously healthy sheriff from a heart attack and the farmer in a car wreck.

The phone rang. Bob picked it up absently, his attention still on the screen. The voice at the other end was chillingly matter of fact. "Stop it. Or you're next."

"Who is this?" said Bob to a dead line. *You're next? Who...Oh my God. Meera.* He realized he had no way of contacting her. She knew where he lived but they hadn't even swapped numbers after the discussion with Westlake. He suddenly needed some air to clear his head.

"Come on, Marcie," he said, grabbing his jacket along with her leash. He stood by the door for a few seconds.

"Come on girl," he said. "Let's walk it out." The silence told him what he couldn't bear to admit to himself. He had just said the word 'walk' and Marcie, far from leaping up and running for the door, hadn't made a sound. He went back to the living room and looked at her bed on the floor. She was perfectly still. She might have been asleep if it hadn't been for the ever-widening pool of blood spreading out under her sweet, trusting head. Bob looked at the window, always left open this time of year. A light clicked on and off in an apartment in the building opposite. Bob stood absolutely still for over a minute, fighting his instinct to grab his gun, run across the street and put a bullet in the sniper who'd killed his best friend. But he knew he'd be long gone. Instead, he turned off the lights, knelt by Marcie's cooling body, stroked her soft fur as she slowly stiffened and cried as he had never cried before.

\*\*\*

"What does a girl have to do to get a guy to buy her a drink?"

Bob turned, knocking an empty beer bottle with his elbow and sending it flying off the bar. Before it reached the floor, Meera snatched it out of mid-air.

"Reflexes of a cat," she said. She turned to Rachel, who had stopped polishing glasses and was eyeing the young Asian girl with more than a little suspicion, Mee could hardly blame her. Glen Campbell was playing on the jukebox, a couple of old boys were halfway through a game of pool and the TV was on a channel that was apparently dedicated to re-runs of Cheers. Meera was wearing bondage trousers, a Sex Pistols tee shirt and her hair seemed to be making a bid to leave her head in order to find a more conservative area in which to settle down. It might not draw much attention in the bars she usually frequented, but Mee realized everyone in the place was staring at her, a couple with their mouths hanging open.

"What?" she said, "I normally go butt-naked painted green with a peacock feather up my ass, but Bob told me it was dress-down Friday."

There was a moment of stunned silence before the dozen or so customers returned to their drinks and tried to pretend they weren't talking about her.

"Could I get another glass, please?" she said, and Rachel set her up after looking her up and down slightly disdainfully and raising an eyebrow at Bob.

"Meera," he said.

"What a gift for recall," she said, "although only my mother calls me Meera. Call me Mee."

"Mee Mee?" said Bob.

"Just Mee is fine," she said before narrowing her eyes and sipping at the bourbon. "God, this stuff is rougher than a bear's backside. No wonder you're drunk."

"Not drunk," said Bob, shaking his head. He slid off the stool and took a quick corrective step to stop himself falling over.

"Well, maybe a little drunk," he admitted.

Meera grabbed his arm.

"Let's get you home," she said. "I need to talk to you. You can pack some stuff. We're going after Seb"

Bob suddenly looked around the bar, searching for unfamiliar faces.

"Are you crazy?" he said. "Westlake wasn't playing games. Were you followed?"

"No," she said.

"Are you sure?" said Bob. "These guys aren't amateurs and they're dangerous."

"Well," said Mee, "they scared the shit out of me at the station so I didn't take any chances. Climbed out of the bathroom window at the club during the break. Then I borrowed a car from Mrs. Reynolds. She's 92 and thinks I'm dating her son. He died twelve years ago."

Bob looked at her.

It's complicated, ok?" said Mee. "All you need to know is, she won't report the car as stolen. She probably won't remember she had a car."

Bob didn't move.

"Come on," said Mee. "I've been sitting around like a pussy for two days, but I'm not letting those fuckers tell me what to do. Now let's swing by your place, pick up some clothes and your dog and get going."

Bob said nothing but something in his expression got through.

"Oh God, what happened?" she said.

Bob told her. As he spoke, he could see her getting angrier and angrier. He started to feel ashamed that his own reaction had been to crawl into a bottle.

"So who do you think these wankers are?" she said, white-lipped and almost shaking with rage.

"I don't know," admitted Bob, "but they're well-funded and run on military lines. No one just flies around the country without anyone knowing about it, even if their chopper has some kind of stealth technology. For once, I think the conspiracy theorists are probably right. Whatever they're doing, the government must know about it."

"So what do they want with Seb?" she said. "And what the hell happened the other morning? I thought he was dead."

Bob thought back to that first glimpse of Seb's body on the forest floor. He hadn't been breathing.

"I was sure he was dead," he said. "Ok. You're right. Let's go find him then we can ask him ourselves. You been in touch with him?"

Mee frowned. "Nope," she said, "He dumped the phone at the station. My gut tells me he was on that train to Chicago."

Bob grabbed his jacket, feeling more sober by the second.

"Well, they're probably still watching my place," he said. "Hold on. How did you find me?"

"No answer from your apartment when I buzzed," she said. "This is the third bar I've tried."

"Shit!" he said. "They will have followed you here from my place. They'll kill us both. I mean, it's not like you blend in."

"Easy, tiger," said Meera, shaking out a bundle she had under one arm. It was a shapeless poncho-style raincoat with a hood. She put it on, stooped slightly and began walking away from him. Bob burst out laughing. Nothing of the feisty lead singer of Clockwatchers remained. She was an old bag-lady, shuffling, muttering and occasionally stopping to inspect something on the floor.

"That's incredible," he said. "I wouldn't have believed it if I hadn't seen it."

"I left my phone at home, so they can't find us that way," she said, straightening up and flinging back the hood. "But I've brought my old cell. It's pre-paid, first one I had when I came to the States. No way they'd know about it. Car's parked a couple blocks away. This place got a back door? I assume they'll have someone watching the front."

"Maybe the back, too," said Bob, impressed at Meera's street smarts. "These guys are serious."

Bob felt more sober still as they ducked out of the Heroes and Villains fire door and walked toward the car. As they passed a dumpster he suddenly stopped, grabbed Meera's arm and pulled her behind him.

"What are you - " she said, then stopped when she saw the two men step out of the shadows.

"It's ok," said Bob with relief, knowing immediately from the way the men moved that they were local muggers, not trained professionals.

"It's not ok," said the bigger of the two men, pulling a hunting knife out and passing it from hand to hand. "Put your hands where I can see them." He had heard the relief in Bob's voice. He was used to hearing fear. Fear was good, he enjoyed the fear he provoked in his victims almost as much as the money he took from them. But this guy wasn't afraid and that was making him angry. He clicked his fingers and his companion stepped alongside him, a heavy metal bar in his hands. He was going to have to take this guy's money and hurt him a little to teach him a lesson.

Bob looked squarely at the bigger man and smiled.

"You ever play Rock, Paper, Scissors?" he said.

The smile was too much for the bigger guy. He stepped quickly forward. Meera held her breath, then let it out as the big guy stopped, suddenly looking much less sure of himself. She looked at Bob. From nowhere, a gun had appeared in his hand. She had barely seen him move.

"Gun beats knife," said Bob. "You lose. Toss your weapons in the dumpster." The men did as they were told.

"Now empty your pockets," said Bob. Their hesitation at obeying him only lasted a second, during which Bob cocked the pistol. Then they couldn't comply quickly enough.

"Go," said Bob. The muggers looked at each other briefly before running. Bob stepped forward and looked at the haul. A few wallets, some money clips. He took the cash and threw everything else in the dumpster.

"About a grand," he said. "We're probably going to need it."

"Well, aren't you just full of surprises," said Meera, taking his arm. "Oh shit."

It seemed that the muggers had only made it as far as the corner before running into the rest of their gang. The two Bob had humiliated were now heading back toward them, followed by four others. Two of them had guns. The rest carried baseball bats, metal bars or chains. Bob did some quick calculations. He figured he could draw his gun, take one of the armed guys out, roll and tag the other one before the others knew what was happening. But if the second guy got a shot off, it would stand a pretty good chance of hitting Meera. And - goddammit - he was 58, not 25. 58 and drunk. Shit.

"Toss the gun over," said the first mugger, swinging a baseball bat casually by his side. "Nice and slow, Pops."

"You're a tough guy now?" said Bob, taking his gun and putting it on the floor in front of him. "Amazing how quickly you grew a pair once you found your buddies."

"Shut up and kick the gun toward us," said the mugger.

Bob looked at Meera. "Sorry," he whispered. She shrugged but he could see she was shaking. He kicked the gun away.

Another one of the gang spoke up.

"Was that a friend of yours watching the back door?" he said. Bob glanced at Meera. It must have been one of Westlake's men. They were watching his apartment and could spare two men to cover both exits of the bar? *This operation must be costing a fortune.*

"I re-arranged his face a bit," said the gang member, swinging a hammer and grinning. The leader punched him lightly on the arm and sneered at Bob.

"After you've watched us have our fun with your girlfriend, I'm gonna break every bone in your body." The gang started to walk toward them, an unpleasant smile on the mugger's face as he smacked the baseball bat repeatedly onto his palm.

"Get behind me," said Bob, "and if you see a chance, run like hell." Meera moved behind him and Bob took up a fighting stance. *Reckon I can take a couple of them.*

"Excuse me?" The voice came from the shadows behind the dumpster. The gang stopped moving as a small woman walked out between them and their intended victims. She wore sweatpants and a hooded top, her face in shadow.

"Go home, kid," said one of the gang. "Before you get hurt."

"I'm no child," said the woman. Her voice was quiet and calm.

The lead mugger looked back at his fellow gang members, shrugged and swung the bat straight into the stranger's body. Only - somehow - when the bat should have connected with flesh, there was just air. He felt a sharp pain in his wrist and yelped. He looked for the woman but she was gone. He turned round. She was standing between him and the gang, his baseball bat in her hand. She stooped and placed the bat on the ground, turning her back on him and facing the others.

"Put your weapons on the ground and leave in peace," she said.

In answer, a heavily tattooed bearded muscle-guy took two quick steps toward her, his massive fists clenched. He threw out a flurry of punches with the assurance of a trained boxer. None of them landed and - much to his surprise - he suddenly found himself lying on his back as the tiny woman approached the rest of his gang.

"Shoot her!" he screamed in frustration. The gang members he had gathered around him over the last few years may not have been the brightest, but they had learned to obey orders, which was how they had survived as long as they had. Two shots rang out. The woman dropped to the floor. He got to his feet and walked over to her. She raised her hands and placed them on her chest, where the bullets had torn into her.

"Finish her," commanded the bearded man. The two armed gang members stood over her body and raised their weapons. In a blur of speed, her hands shot out and grabbed the guns before throwing them to one side as she leapt to her feet. The gang froze in sheer disbelief, no one daring to move. She backed slowly away from them.

Bob and Meera watched her. She stopped a couple feet in front of them and pulled her hood away from her face. Her head was closely shaven. She stood no more than five feet tall.

"Leave," she said simply. Her voice betrayed no anger or fear. "Now."

A couple of gang members stepped forward, led by the bearded boxer. Then, as if someone had thrown a switch, they all stopped dead in their tracks, staring at the woman's face, their expressions flicking rapidly from disbelief to absolute terror. They looked as if they had suddenly seen their worst nightmares come to life in front of them. They dropped their weapons and ran as if chased by the hounds of hell.

When they had gone, the woman turned to face Bob and Meera. They both flinched, expecting to see something horrific. Instead the face smiling at them was that of a young woman with slightly Asiatic features.

"You are Bob?" she said.

"I guess I am," said Bob.

"And Meera?" Meera just nodded, swallowing. Unexpectedly the woman laughed, a joyful carefree sound completely at odds with what had just happened.

"My name is Lo," she said, holding out her hand. In a daze, Bob and Meera shook hands with her, Bob looking down at the top she was wearing. Two bullet holes.

"You want to find Seb?" she said.

"Yes," said Bob, not knowing what else to say.

"I too want to find Seb," she said. "He is in danger. I can help him."

"Who are you?" said Bob. "How did you find us?"

"What's happened to Seb?" added Meera. "And that...thing...you just did. How did you, I mean what did you, er - ". Her voice trailed away. Lo's smile was genuine, open.

"May I answer your questions on the way?" she said. "Do you have a car?" Meera coughed, shook herself and tried to regain a little equilibrium.

"Follow me," she said. She led them to the car - a 1972 Ford Galaxie 500 with dents on just about every panel.

"One careful lady owner," said Mee, smiling a little shakily. They got in - Lo climbing into the driver's seat and starting it up.

"Where to?" said Bob, remembering the train at Union Station. "Chicago?"

Lo's face broke into another smile.

"Not Chicago," she said. "Las Vegas."

# Chapter 16

## Six months previously
## Japan

Shibata lived in a rudimentary hut on the steep side of a hill commanding a stunning view of Kaimondake, a dormant volcano that had last erupted in 885AD. The hut was small, built in the traditional Japanese way by erecting wooden columns on a flat, packed earth foundation. There was one main room and a bathroom. A natural spring supplied water. There was no electricity.

He got up when it was light and he slept when it was dark. This meant Shibata slept far longer in winter than summer, but over many decades his body had grown used to the rhythms of the seasons. He never felt tired, each morning found him fully alert, his mind as clear as the water he drank with his breakfast.

He was an old man, his face so lined that his lucid dark eyes were almost lost in the folds of skin surrounding them. He used a cane when he walked. He was often seen hiking slowly around the mountain, a small cloth bag on his back. The bag contained paper and pen. He enjoyed sketching what he saw: the mountains, trees, streams, plants, birds and animals. Occasionally even humans, although they were usually portrayed as insignificant figures in the corner of the drawing. He didn't display his sketches, they went in a box in the corner of the hut. Sometimes over the years, hikers who had strayed from the path would find Shibata. He would make them tea and, before they left, give them one of his sketches.

Visitors were few, however, and the box contained many hundreds of his simple drawings. He had lived there so long that the generation in the nearest village who might have known of him had long since died or moved away, replaced by those who did not even suspect his existence.

Shibata was neither happy or unhappy. He had vague memories of these concepts. A long time ago, he had surely been a child, had played with his friends, gone to school, met a girl, fallen in love. These events must have occurred, but the passage of so many years living alone, observing the patterns of nature, had caused those early years to be washed almost completely away, a smudge on the edge of a picture.

Now there was only eating, sleeping and being. No happiness, no unhappiness, just *mu*. Shibata would never have attached a word to his state of mind, but '*mu*' - a Japanese word meaning 'neither *this* nor *that*' - was surely the closest language could come to describing it.

As a young man, he had met a stranger who had told him about the Tao, the ancient way of life. He had, of course, already heard of Taoism - along with Shinto and Buddhism it represented a good deal of Japan's wisdom tradition. But it had just been background noise, he had never spent any time studying it. After meeting this man, who said little but radiated such a deep, non-judgmental calmness, Shibata found his parents' copy of the Tao Te Ching and began to read. He wasn't sure what to expect from a religious book, but the first sentence jolted him so thoroughly, he never again experienced a single day without thinking about it.

"The Way which can be spoken of is not the true Way."

It was as if the very ground beneath his feet had been removed. His psyche experienced a deep shock, and for many days he did not leave his room. He remembered his parents' concern, he remembered saying goodbye, but he could no longer remember their faces, or even the name of the town he had walked away from so long ago.

Many years of traveling had followed, a hundred menial jobs, a thousand journeys on crowded buses or trains. A gradual quieting inside. Then, one day, he found the hut, and bought it with the little money he had saved.

Since then, the rising and setting of the sun, the ever-changing unchanging mountains, a bird in the sky, a rat in the vegetable garden, the sound of rain on a wooden roof.

The hut never needed repairing. He used to wonder about that, just as he used to wonder how plump vegetables grew all year around in his garden, despite the fact he never planted a single seed. Gradually, questions such as "how?" or "why?" faded away. Eventually, language itself disappeared, and his very few visitors were greeted with nods and smiles rather than words. His sense of time beyond the seasonal evaporated like shallow puddles in summer. He had no way of knowing he was over 160 years old, and the numbers would have meant little to him had he still been able to comprehend their meaning.

He lived the Tao, the Way, but he never spoke of it.

One summer evening as he knelt on the earth in front of his hut, watching mist fold itself gently around distant Mt Kaimon, seven figures approached. He watched them come closer. They stopped walking on the edge of the path leading to his door. Shibata returned his attention to the mountain.

A few minutes passed, during which time, the figures separated, six of them lining up, facing him. They were not hikers, they wore the wrong clothes: dark robes. Their faces were set, tense, serious. Their minds were confused, busy, hurting and wanting to hurt. The seventh figure was different. Her mind was free of much of the confusion of those around her, but she had an aura like that of stagnant water in the forest. Somewhere that may once have been lush and fruitful, now overgrown, dark and poisonous. Shibata saw this and remained kneeling. When the woman walked toward him, he stood.

She spoke as she approached him. Had he retained any clear memories of human behavior, he would have identified deference, even respect in her mannerisms and the tone of her voice. Her head was slightly lowered. She seemed regretful. Shibata put his head on one side, just as the bear cubs who lived in a nearby cave did when they saw him. He stood quietly, hands by his sides, and considered his visitor. He needed no language then to understand why she had come. She was here to kill him. He looked at the other figures. They had not been sure he would die easily. He made an odd, guttural noise in the back of his throat which, decades ago, might have been the beginning of laughter.

The woman seemed to have made up her mind to act. Shibata held up a hand and she stepped back, puzzled. She was afraid. He bowed low to her. There was nothing to fear. His death was the inevitable conclusion to his life. Now was as good a time as any other. There would be no need for violence, he would die as naturally as each season dies before the next begins. Turning his back on her and her companions, he walked slowly toward his vegetable garden. With every step he took, the ground became softer, more giving. First solid, then spongy, then quicksand, finally like water. Within six steps, only his upper body was visible above ground level. Another five steps, and the earth closed over his head and all was quiet.

The woman glanced at her companions, then walked in the same direction Shibata had walked. The ground was solid. She stood on the exact spot he had finally disappeared. She knelt, put the palms of her hands flat on the earth, then stood again, brushing soil from her hands. She remained still for a few minutes, her eyes shut in concentration. Then she nodded at the others.

Rejoining her companions, they turned and retraced their steps down the path that would lead, eventually, to the village where they had left their rental cars. No one spoke during the four-hour hike.

The mist had finally cloaked the distant mountain. Rain began to fall. The hut sagged, the wooden structure visibly rotting. It lurched to one side, the roof tiles sliding off, becoming dust as they hit the ground. After five minutes had passed, the ruin that remained looked like it had been that way for many years. The rain got harder and the rats that had made their home under the hut squealed as they ran for cover in the forest, looking for a new home.

# Chapter 17

**Red Rock, Nevada**
**Present day**

"Red Rock Canyon. This place was probably first inhabited by Paleo Indians 10,000 years before the birth of Christ," said Walt, sipping from his bottled water as Seb got out of the car. "You can see it from the Strip, so around a million tourists take a look when they've grown tired of losing their take-home."

Seb stretched and yawned. It had been a long drive.

"As fascinating as that sounds, right now I'd kill for a shower and a cold beer," he said.

"And you shall have both," said Walt. "Soon. First, I need a top up. You too, I'd imagine. Follow me."

They'd parked the car off the loop of road which guided visitors through the conservation area. The calico hills rose sharply to one side. Seb was surprised by the clear delineation between colors on the rocks. It was as if a child had colored them in - first sandy then a deep red. Hardy-looking shrubs defied the desert temperatures to thrive in the shadows of these rocks. He squinted back through the haze and saw Las Vegas shimmering in the distance, looking like a cheap toy left on a beach.

When he turned back to follow Walt, he had gone. He looked at the rock outcrop on his right. It varied in height between nine and 15 feet. No handholds - no way the older man could have climbed over them in the few seconds he had been looking away, even if he was in good condition. And ahead and to the left, open desert with no hiding places.

"Walt?" he called. He turned back to the car, where Steve was standing impassively, shaking his head.

Seb walked a few paces on, looking more closely at the rock. After a few yards, he stopped short. There was a passageway between two rocks, but the colors were so perfectly blended that it was totally invisible until you were a few feet away from it.

"Wow," said Seb and stepped through.

A natural basin sloped down from where he stood, a circle of about 30 feet diameter, surrounded by rock. If you didn't know exactly where to look, you'd never guess it was there. Walt stood with his back to Seb, slipping off his jacket. He turned and nodded before carefully placing his jacket on the ground, then kneeling beside it on the hot sand.

Seb opened his mouth to speak, then thought better of it. The atmosphere had changed somehow. It wasn't the weather conditions; the sun still blazed onto the tableau before him, the shadows cast by the rocks not quite reaching the kneeling man. With a jolt, Seb suddenly remembered what the scene reminded him of. It was like being in church. Father O had persuaded Seb to attend Mass at least once a month. He had felt uncomfortable with the rituals but loved the atmosphere. A palpable silence the words of the worshipers stood no chance of disturbing. It was exactly the same now, out in the open under the baking Nevada sun. It wasn't the fact that Walt was kneeling, it was the stillness and silence around him.

Walt bent forward, laying his head on the dust, his hands palm down on either side. Now the religious parallels became transparent, the posture looking exactly like a Muslim at prayer.

Seb heard - felt - a thrumming start to sound in the basin and in his body. It was as if a billion tiny insects had started buzzing at once. The area immediately around Walt darkened, especially near his outstretched hands. The thrumming became more intense and Seb gasped as he saw tiny threads of light appear under the surface of the desert floor. It was as if the ground was alive and the glowing threads were the veins sustaining...what? Even as he wondered, Seb's question was answered for him. The veins of light flowed up to Walt's fingertips and Seb could see the light tracing a path through his companion's body, starting at his hands, then following the network of veins and arteries in his body. After about a minute, the light was dancing through Walt's skull, the web of his neural network lit up like a science display.

Half expecting an impressive end to all of this, Seb was slightly disappointed when the light vanished as if someone had flicked a switch, the thrumming ceasing at the same moment. He waited a couple seconds, then took a step forward. He stopped abruptly when Walt unexpectedly launched himself into the air like a man half his age, threw his head back and started howling. For a second, Seb thought there was something wrong with him, then the howl became a laugh.

"Whooo!!" howled Walt, beating himself on the chest with his fist. "That feels good! God, I'll never get bored of it! Ha!" He jogged around the perimeter of the basin, laughing before stopping in front of Seb and grabbing his shoulders.

"Seb, come on! You have to try some of this. And to think that folk pay money for crack cocaine when this is just lying around the place. Ha ha!" His eyes were gleaming, his grip on Seb's shoulders almost painful.

"Come and get it," he said, jogging back to the center of the basin.

Seb followed him warily. Walt was pointing at the dust beneath their feet.

"Just put your hands flat on the ground," he said. "Reach out, like you did back there with the car. But don't try and make anything happen this time. Just open up. And wait." Walt backed up a little, giving Seb some space. He was still twitching slightly and bouncing on the balls of his feet, like a man who'd just had a massive hit of something very powerful.

Seb knelt. He took a deep breath then placed both of his hands palm down onto the sand. He deepened his breathing, watching his breath and letting his awareness sink under the level of conscious thought. The thoughts were still there, but they became blurred, indistinct, nebulous. He paid them no attention. The beginning of the C Major Prelude began to sound in his head, but he turned his attention back to his breath and let it fade away into nothingness. The thrumming was back.

It was different now that he was so close to the ground. He could see the glowing threads appearing, but there was a far greater impression of depth. He could see them forming four or five feet beneath the desert floor, individual tendrils of light, fragile and translucent. They surged toward his fingertips and he waited without fear, wondering vaguely how it would feel when they merged with his body. Ten thin tendrils reached for his fingertips. 20 centimeters, 15, 10, 5, 2, then...nothing. The veins had stopped precisely at the moment they touched his fingertips. There was a pause of about a second, then the lights suddenly winked out and were gone.

Seb stood up, brushing the dirt from his knees. He looked at Walt, The older man was frowning.

"Weird," he said. "Never..." his voice trailed away. He seemed about to say something else, then changed his mind. "Well," he said finally, motioning back to the gap in the rocks they had entered by, "guess you just don't need any yet."

"What do you mean?" said Seb. "This place is like a gas station, right? People like you - and me - fill up here?"

Walt disappeared through the gap and headed back to the car, talking over his shoulder.

"That's the theory. But I don't know it all. Only the parts Sid knew and some more I've figured out over the years. But almost all of it is guesswork. We tend to be loners, we don't share much information. And - if you ask me - no one really knows much about Manna. How to use it, sure. But where it comes from? Why so few people even know it exists? I think we're all guessing."

Seb caught up with Walt just as they reached the car.

"So what's going on? Why couldn't I...connect back there? Is something wrong with me? And you said you'd tell me how you found me. Or I found you. So talk to me."

Walt looked at Seb.

"I know you've had a strange couple days, but things will get easier. I don't think there's anything wrong with you. But I do think there's something different going on. Something new."

"New how?" said Seb.

When someone uses Manna for the first time, we all feel it," said Walt.

"Who?" said Seb.

"Everyone who uses Manna. It's like..." He hesitated, searching for the right words. "Imagine you're in the middle of a dark forest in the middle of the night." Seb flinched slightly, thinking of where he had been two nights previously.

"Well," said Walt, "it's like someone turning on a flashlight a few miles away. You see it out of your peripheral vision first, then swing around to take a look. After a few seconds it's gone. But you know where to look."

"So you saw me like that?" said Seb, "and set out to find me?"

"Actually, it was a bit easier in your case," said Walt. "You weren't exactly a flashlight."

"What, then?"

"You were a flamethrower,"said Walt and got into the car.

The ten-minute ride to Walt's apartment passed in silence until Seb cleared his throat and looked at Walt quizzically. Walt turned slightly to face him and raised an eyebrow.

"Shoot," he said.

"Well," began Seb, hesitantly, "it was back when you were telling me about Sid. The way you described Chicago. The whole gangster scene, the poverty."

"It was a pretty brutal time," conceded Walt, flicking a sun visor down and checking his reflection in the mirror.

"That's what confuses me," said Seb. "The timeline. The people you described, the conditions. It sounds too long ago. I mean you're - what - 52, 53?"

Walt laughed and said nothing.

"Ok," said Seb, "I guess you could be in your early sixties."

Walt pointed upwards.

"Wow, ok," said Seb. "Past 65? Possible, I guess, with a personal trainer and a decent plastic surgeon."

Walt chuckled again but didn't comment.

"Even so," said Seb, "that would mean you would have met Sid in the mid-sixties. And there was no financial crisis I ever heard about. People were too busy taking acid, dropping out and enjoying all that free love. And they were all listening to The Beatles."

Seb stopped and leaned a little closer to Walt. There was a healthy look to his skin that surgery couldn't fake. If anything, he looked younger than he had the day before.

"Except for you, of course," said Seb. "Apparently, you're the only human being I ever met who knows nothing about the Beatles."

Walt smiled. "I know who they are," he said, "but that kind of popular music was never my thing. Guess you never really get away from the music you love while you're growing up. First girl who ever let me kiss her - we were dancing to Mark Isham and his Orchestra singing *I'll See You In My Dreams*. Sure don't write 'em like that anymore."

"When was that?" said Seb.

"That would have been in the early months of the Depression," said Walt.

"The Great Depression?" said Seb, eyes widening. But it can't - I mean you can't be - er, wouldn't that make you..."

"I'm four months shy of my hundredth birthday," said Walt, smiling.

"Wow," said Seb, conscious that his mouth was hanging open. "I want some of whatever you've got."

"Son," said Walt, "you might have more than I ever dreamed of."

# Chapter 18

**17 Years Previously**
**St. Benet's Children's Home, New York**

Hindsight is, of course, a frustrating rather than a wonderful thing. To know the course of action you should have taken in a given situation, or, more usefully, to identify what you should have avoided is a fairly useless exercise. This is because the decisions that look foolish in hindsight, tend to be those made when under stress. Hindsight is a calm and considered process, applied when the brain is capable of reason, rather than acting purely on instinct. So, much later, when Seb was in a fit state to look at the events of that afternoon without being overwhelmed by anger, grief, sadness, regret and residual rage, he knew he should have gone to the Sisters and Father O'Hanoran first. They would have called the police, Jack would have been arrested, Melissa would have told them the truth. Jack would hopefully have ended up in prison and they would never have seen him again. But that's hindsight for you. Frustrating.

Seb ran the half mile back to St. Benet's and raced through the building when he got there. One or two Sisters called after him as he flew by, not so much angry as surprised to see their quiet musical prodigy flying through the halls, sweating and panting, his face grim.

It was Wednesday evening - movie time in Fall when the light failed too early for outdoor activities to continue. Almost every kid in the place would be in the dining room; the tables pushed back against the walls, chairs lined up in rows and - more often than not - the smells and percussive sounds of corn popping in the kitchen, ready to be brought out in steaming bowlfuls. Seb had forgotten what day it was and ran straight to the dormitory, barely seeing where he was going, the image of Melissa's battered ribs and bruised face burned into his mind.

Stevie looked up when the dormitory door was suddenly and violently flung open. Seb tore in, breathing heavily. Stevie, his arm still in plaster, had barely spoken to anyone since coming back from the hospital, avoiding company whenever possible. He quickly looked down again, ashamed that Seb would have seen the terror in his eyes before he recognized him.

"Where is he," said Seb, still gasping. Stevie didn't ask who he meant, just pointed into the hallway.

"Trunk room," he said and returned his attention to the comic book he was reading, his hand shaking as he did so.

The trunk room was really the attic. It had never been called anything other than the trunk room by the occupants of the dormitories below it, because that was where your cases went when you arrived at St. Benet's. When you left, your case left with you, although that had not always been true, judging by the dozen or so old wooden trunks still there. Some were banded with iron hoops, fastened with huge padlocks, others tied with rope. All were covered in a thick layer of dust. A great deal of St. Benet's folklore originated from the romance of the trunk room. Where had those boys gone? Did they die and never leave - is that why their luggage remained? Was the scratching sometimes heard at night really mice and squirrels, or were the bones of young Hodgkins trying to free themselves from his padlocked trunk in the cobwebbed room above? Ghost stories and adolescence have always gone together and the dim attic provided plenty of material for generations of St. Benet's boys.

The trunk room ran the length of the hall and the two dormitories beyond. The only access in or out was a trapdoor reached by a stout old wooden ladder, usually hanging on hooks fastened to the wall. Today the ladder was in place, the trapdoor open and a faint smell of cigarette smoke detectable from below.

"Jack," said Seb, and began to climb.

Many of the boys smoked at St. Benet's. A rite of passage for the younger boys, it was also a symbol of maturity and - just as it was in prison - a common currency. The older boys had recently started aping the way Jack Carnavon held a cigarette: the filter pinched between thumb and first finger, the lit end heading back into the cupped palm. Seb guessed Jack thought it evoked the war heroes and spies often portrayed on TV, smoking like that to avoid detection as the burning end was hidden by the hand. Seb had often wondered why the spies or soldiers didn't just give up smoking and avoid any possibility of detection, but smart-ass opinions were usually best kept to yourself in an institution full of boys and young men.

As he climbed the ladder, Seb could hear the rhythmic *snick, snick, snick* of Jack's Zippo as he flipped the cover of the lighter back and forth with the pad of his thumb. Jack was smoking in his trademark style; Marlboros, of course, like the eyes-narrowed, lean, king-of-the-world cowboy on the billboards. Jack had made himself a seat by pushing a few soft cases up against the back of a metal trunk, which he'd leaned against the rafters. He looked up at Seb as the younger boy climbed through the trap door, then dropped his gaze back to the porn magazine he held and sneered, blowing a slow thin trail of smoke through his pursed lips.

"Sebastian," he said. "Hoped I might be seeing you sooner or later. Thought your curiosity would get the better of you. Well, don't you worry, I don't mind sharing some of the details of my date with the hot redhead. I should warn you, though, you missed out there, she was practically a nymphomaniac. Just couldn't get enough. Here, pull up a pew, take a load off." He kicked out a leg, lazily sending a suitcase skidding a few feet across the dusty boards. He glanced up as he did so and realized - too late - his mistake. If he had been watching Seb while he spoke, he would have noticed his initial absolute stillness, born of a pure single-mindedness of purpose. He would have seen Seb's hands slowly begin to clench into white-knuckled fists as he was talking, and - most telling of all - he would have read in Seb's eyes the intention to act recognized instinctively by every living being on the planet. It was fight or flight time and Jack Carnavon was so complacent in his alpha male role that he was utterly unprepared for the onslaught that followed.

Seb ran the few feet separating them and launched himself at Jack. He had never been in a serious fight, just a few scuffles now and then. He had no plan, no thought of defense against whatever resistance Jack might put up. He had only a pure, mind-cleansing rage which admitted no possibility of failure. Jack Carnavon was going down. Seb jumped as Jack began to stand up, intending at first to strangle him, but changing his mind as his momentum grew, instead tucking his hands back and raising an elbow. It would have caught Jack in the throat had he not been moving, but instead hit his sternum, driving him backward into a roof strut. His head missed it by a fraction of an inch but as he fell, his shoulder took the impact and spun him sideways. Both boys fell, Seb onto his knees, Jack face down in a pile of cases. The older boy howled with pain, then suddenly went quiet and still.

Seb got up and looked at Jack. He wasn't moving. The trunk room was silent other than Seb's deep breaths. The sudden silence after the noise of the scuffle was eerie: Seb felt his skin tingling, his teeth clenched together, the pulse throbbing in his neck. He took a step toward Jack's body. That's when he noticed Carnavon's left arm. It was broken. It had twisted behind his body when he fell and was now draped across his shoulder blades. Jack was making small whimpering noises. Despite his initial intention to do as much harm as possible, Seb felt the rage drain away at the sight of his enemy helpless and in pain.

"Jack?" said Seb. "Can you move? Don't try, you might make it worse. I'll go and get the nurse." He turned to go but Jack called his name and he turned to see the older boy trying to get up. As he got into a kneeling position, the arm behind his back swung to his side and he screamed in pain.

"It's dislocated," hissed Jack, his face pale and beaded with sweat. "Just help me up, will you? I think I've hurt my leg, too. Please."

Seb hesitated, but he could see the pain in Jack's face and blood on his leg. The trunk room had nails, screws and other assorted ironmongery dating back at least a century. Jack must have caught his calf on something when he fell, and the blood had run down his leg and was beginning to pool in his socks and white sneakers. As Seb watched Jack try to stand, his anger continued to ebb away, replaced by guilt at the damage he had inflicted. As his head cleared and he began to regain some capacity for rational thought, he decided it wasn't too late to do the right thing and get the authorities involved. He would take whatever punishment was meted out for his treatment of Jack Carnavon. He felt a sense of relief as he made the decision and knew it to be the right one. He walked to Jack's side and held out his hand.

"Come on, then" he said. Jack took it and, with Seb's help, pulled himself to his feet. He stood for a moment taking short breaths and screwing his eyes up with the pain.

"Are you ok?" said Seb. "Can you walk?"

"Yeah, I think so," said Jack. He put his right hand at the top of his injured leg and shuffled forward half a step. Then he winced, paused and tried to take a second step. This time, he shouted with pain and looked as if he was about to fall. Seb made a grab for him, avoiding the damaged arm and trying to support him around his waist. As he did so, he felt a sudden searing pain in his stomach. Jack hadn't been supporting his injured leg, he had been going for his pocket. Seb looked down and saw Jack Carnavon's knife. The hilt was in Jack's hand and about an inch of blade was visible. That meant the other two inches of steel were in Seb's stomach. Seb gasped in agony and looked up at Jack, whose eyes were narrowed in fury.

"You dislocated my shoulder, you prick," he said and, using all the strength in his right arm, drew the knife in a half cutting, half sawing motion across Seb's stomach, down toward his hip. The cut was deep, ragged and ugly, and blood was already welling up from the wound, livid and purple, drenching Seb's shirt and soaking Jack's hand. Jack wrenched the knife out, twisting it as he did so. If it had been a serrated hunting knife, that action might have done enough damage to kill Seb. As it was, it opened up the cut and increased the bleeding. Seb staggered backward, fell and sat clumsily, both hands holding his stomach. His fall was one of the contributory factors toward his survival, as Jack missed him with the follow up thrust aimed at his heart.

"Spoke to your little girlfriend, did ya?" said Jack. "I warned her what would happen. Gonna finish with you, then I'm going to pay her a visit. After that, I'll be gone. It's a big world out there, Sebby, you know as well as I do they won't catch me. Christ, it'll be good to be out of this dump, anyway."

Seb didn't answer. The edges of his vision had darkened slightly. He realized he was going into shock and knew that if he let that happen, he was going to die right there in the trunk room. Then this madman would go after Melissa. He couldn't let that happen. He pushed hard on his stomach with both hands as Jack came slowly toward him. This had the effect of slowing the blood loss at the same time as increasing the pain, waking him up and keeping the faintness at bay. The knife had entered his body in his lower intestines, doing little damage initially. As Jack had dragged the blade across, it had cut through skin and muscle, but Seb's intestines had been pushed to one side. The knife had nicked his bowel before Jack had pulled it out, which increased the risk of septic shock as bacteria from Seb's gut leaked into what would normally be a sterile environment. However, that worrying possibility would take days to develop. Seb's more immediate, potentially fatal, problem was the stab wound Jack was getting ready to inflict on his throat.

Jack dropped onto his knees directly in front of Seb. He was done talking. He thrust the knife upwards at Seb's neck. Seb knew he only had one chance. His blood loss was weakening him quickly. He took his hands away from his stomach, moved his head to the right and grabbed Jack's right hand with both of his as the knife passed his left ear. Using all his remaining strength, and harnessing every ounce of adrenaline while thinking of Melissa's possible fate, he twisted Jack's hand and pushed it back toward him. Jack was physically stronger than Seb, but he was pushing upwards with the strength of one arm, while Seb was using both hands, the force of two arms, and the physical weight of his upper body to twist Jack's hand around, then push it down and forwards. Jack knew he had misjudged the situation, too confident, too quick to think Seb was weak and useless. His eyes widened as his own knife, held tight by his own fingers, penetrated the skin under his ribs and buried itself in his gut. Even then, he might have survived if he hadn't immediately pulled the knife out. A spray of blood followed it, his suddenly numb fingers dropped the knife and he fell heavily on one side.

"Call for help!" said Jack. Seb pushed his hands back onto the wound in his stomach, staunching the blood flow as best he could. He watched Carnavon twitch a few feet away. Jack's good right hand was trapped under his body. He had no means of stopping the blood leaving the wound. It wasn't so much leaking as spurting out, staining the old floorboards a rusty dark red. The knife had punctured his liver, which might have proved fatal on its own, but in pulling it out, he'd severed his abdominal aorta. He would die in minutes without treatment.

"Seb," gasped Jack, his voice weaker. He coughed and bloody pink bubbles formed at the corner of his mouth. "I'm serious. I think I'm dying. Get help."

Seb looked into Jack Carnavon's eyes.

"Please, Seb," whispered Jack, "please."

Seb wasn't sure what he believed about the soul, but as he watched Jack's eyes, he could see something shrinking, as if the life-force was preparing to depart. He knew that Jack's survival was in his hands. If he didn't call Stevie and get some help within the next thirty seconds, Jack was going to die.

He waited ten minutes. Just to be sure.

# Chapter 19

**Las Vegas**
**Present day**

Walt's house was set back from the road. After getting out of the car, Seb just stood and looked at it, wondering what was prompting such a strong feeling of deja vu. After a few seconds, it came to him.

"The Taj Mahal?" he said, smiling.

Walt walked up to the door of the pink stucco palace and glanced back at Seb before opening the door.

"This neighborhood, you stand out from the crowd if you *don't* stand out from the crowd," he said and walked in.

"No locks?" said Seb.

"No need," said Walt. "Anyone gets closer than 15 feet, they're gonna wish they hadn't."

Steve walked up to Seb's shoulder, carrying their luggage. He nodded at the open door. Seb shrugged and followed Walt inside.

Walt showed Seb to a guest bedroom bigger than any suite in any hotel he had ever seen. The bed might have slept six people comfortably. The ensuite bathroom had a shower stall with nozzles pointing from every direction. There were three sinks in a row. Seb had seen plenty of places with two, but three seemed a little odd.

"It's because of love. And sex," said Walt, gesturing toward the sinks. He was standing in the doorway, smiling. He had two glasses of cognac cradled in one hand and an unlit Cuban cigar in the other.

"You smoke?" he said. "It's the good stuff."

Seb shook his head but took the cognac and stuck his nose into the narrow aperture of the balloon-shaped glass. Rich, heady, smooth. Expensive.

"You should consider taking it up," said Walt.

"The consensus is it's bad for you," said Seb.

"Bad for everyone else, maybe. Not us," said Walt. "You said you were shot?"

Seb nodded and shuddered, remembering the sensation of tearing flesh, heat and searing pain.

"That's normally pretty bad health-wise," said Walt. "How are you holding up?"

Seb smiled and took a sip of cognac. Exquisite. He shrugged, trying to appear casual. On one level, he felt far from it. Everything seemed slightly surreal, his life seemingly wrenched out of his control by unseen hands. No one could deal effectively with the curveball that had been thrown his way. And yet here he was, a large glass of $1000 cognac in his hand, standing in a room with a genuine magician who seemed to think Seb was more powerful still - and he hadn't even told him about the alien yet. His breathing was deep, relaxed, his pulse unhurried. He felt a little like a passenger in his own body, as if the shock and panic he should be feeling was being handled by another layer of his brain.

"So you won't have any trouble with nicotine, then," said Walt, lighting the huge cigar by sucking on it repeatedly. He had no lighter, but that didn't seem to prevent a flame appearing. Seb thought back to the moment he had half-wrecked the car. It must take a hell of a lot of practise to be able to manipulate carbon dioxide, water vapor, oxygen and nitrogen so precisely you can produce an ignition point tiny enough to light a cigar. Seb suspected

Walt was showing off. He also suspected if he tried it himself, he would burn the house to the ground.

"No downside to smoking if your body is unaffected by nicotine," said Walt, letting a cloud of smoke drift between his lips. The smoke took on the proportions of the classic nuclear mushroom cloud before vanishing. "No danger of alcohol poisoning, either. You can get drunk if you like, but getting instantly sober without a hangover is occasionally useful. You ever fancied trying drugs?"

Seb just raised an eyebrow.

"Oh, yeah, I forgot you were a musician," said Walt. "Well, none of them have a downside for you now." He took another puff on the cigar, clearly enjoying it. Seb knew little about cigars, but imagined this one was probably hand rolled by Cuban virgins.

"Not that there's much point," said Walt. "In taking drugs, I mean. You wanna get high? Just do it. Why hallucinate when you can have the real thing?"

"You still haven't explained the sinks," said Seb.

"Yeah. Well, it's a sex thing," said Walt. "Seems to come with the territory. You use Manna, you generally have a high libido. Well, apart from the religious nut-jobs in the Order. Although they're probably all flicking the bean or spanking the monkey when they think no one is looking. They don't fool me with all their holy saintly shit. You get yourself a high libido, you're gonna need regular sex. And when you can look like anyone in the world, you won't struggle to get some action. When you can pleasure multiple partners without breaking a sweat...well, why wouldn't you? And when the girls turn up and see the size of the beds, the showers built for groups and the amount of sinks? Well, they adjust their expectations accordingly."

Seb said nothing.

"If you're thinking of judging me, consider this," said Walt. I've been sexually active for 83 years. Normally, there's a natural arc in the sex-drive of the human male. We're supposed to experience a decrease in libido from our late twenties throughout the rest of our lives. Not me and you, though. For a long time, mine got stronger year on year. So I found ways of satisfying it. Don't think there's much I haven't tried. Believe me, I know how to enjoy myself. And hey, my tastes are pretty vanilla compared to some. Most of the girls wanna come back for more."

He swirled the remains of his cognac around his glass then knocked it back, his enjoyment obvious.

"Some of them are interesting enough for me to let them. Not many, though."

"That explains the sex," said Seb. "But you said 'love' first. Love and sex."

Walt sighed and sat down on the edge of the giant bed. Just for a moment he looked older.

"Yeah, well, nothing in life is perfect," he said. "No one gets a blank check. Love - romantic love - is a human conceit. Animals seem to be able to do without it for the most part. This weird attachment to someone else that can change everything...what good does it do?"

Seb leaned back against the sinks. "Plenty of books, poems and songs tackle that question," he said. "You got the answer?"

Walt laughed briefly. "No, sir, I don't. And that's a pain even Manna can't handle. Barring any unforeseen circumstances, I should comfortably live for another thirty or forty years at least."

Seb wondered what a lifespan like that would feel like. Then he remembered Seb2 saying he *couldn't* die. Couldn't? Ever? Or just by violent means?

"But it's not all peachy," said Walt. "Look, I don't know you, you don't know me. For now, let me just say this. I was in love once. It lasted a long time. She got cancer and died. I got to watch."

Seb suddenly thought of Mee. He didn't know if it had ever been love, but the thought of losing her for ever? His imagination skirted around the thought, then scurried away. He turned his attention back to Walt.

"I'm sorry," said Seb.

"Yeah," said Walt. "Me too, son. Me too. It wasn't pretty." He stood up and smiled again. "On the plus side, there's all that amazing sex to help compensate. And love won't seem so important once you get the kind of perspective you're gonna get."

*And that's the first out-and-out lie you've told me.*

"Dinner's at seven," said Walt. "Then we'll go have some fun on the Strip."

The first casino wasn't on the Strip itself, but a block away. No windows or clocks same as the bigger joints. Still full of flashing lights, gawping tourists, and octogenarians feeding quarters into slots with all the enthusiasm of a prison canteen cook serving up portions of mashed potato. It was just that some of the gloss seemed to be missing - the carpets were frayed, the wallpaper faded. The croupiers were slightly older than in the big name casinos. They looked tired and bored.

Walt excused himself and went to the bathroom. Seb watched the human tide drift by, some washing up against a blackjack or roulette table and staying long enough to lose a few bucks before moving on to the next shiny, exciting prospect. Vegas was a 24-hour industry and inside a casino it was always just after midnight: late enough to convince the customers they were real players, early enough they could still hope their luck might change and this could be a night to remember. Of course, 99% woke up with a slight feeling of self-disgust, hit the breakfast buffet at around noon, then headed straight back to the tables where - as luck would have it - it was just after midnight and, hey, this could be *their night.*

Seb sipped at a coffee. The roulette wheel was almost directly below the balcony where he was sitting. He watched the faces of those setting their chips on a theoretical long shot. *At some level, they must all know the house has to win so that it can keep paying the rent, the salaries and the cost of the free drinks they keep plying us with, so why are they here?* Gambling had never appealed much to Seb. He could take it or leave it. But he knew folk who'd lost more than money pursuing the turn of a card or the spin of a wheel. Seeing a couple of relationships gone sour and hearing about a bass player he knew losing his house was all the convincing Seb needed to keep clear.

He was just wondering why Walt was taking so long when a large middle-aged woman in a shapeless blouse and old gray sweatpants sat down unasked at his table. She was carrying two canvas bags - one bulging and heavy, the other empty.

"I got a foolproof roulette system," she said, leaning forward and tugging the material of her pants out of the crack of her generous ass. Seb got ready to leave but she put a pudgy hand on his arm and fixed her watery blue eyes on him over her bifocal glasses.

"I'm here with with every penny I saved for the last five years. Gonna win myself a shot at a new life," she said. "I just need to be careful. Need to stick to my system."

She paused to order a pina colada from the waitress.

"That's why they have a table maximum," she said. "To stop people like me winning every time."

"People like you?" said Seb.

"The intelligent ones," she said, patting his arm. "The ones who've worked it out."

Seb sighed and looked over her shoulder. No sign of Walt.

"I'm Mary," she said.

"Seb." The waitress came over with a large pina colada, in a wide brimmed glass containing two straws, a tiny multi-colored umbrella and some bad-smelling thick, off-white liquid.

"So what's your system?"

"Well," said Mary, leaning forward and lowering her voice, "I come here during the week 'cause they lower the minimum bet to $1. So I put $1 on red. No real reason, I just prefer red, red's more of a feminine color than black. Don't want you thinking I'm one of them racialists."

Seb said nothing, just took a sip of coffee.

"If I win, the $1 chip goes in this bag," she said, holding up the empty bag to show Seb.

"And if you lose?" he said.

"Well, hold your horses, that's the clever bit," she said, chuckling. She was sweating and her glasses had slipped down her nose. She pushed them back up.

"If I lose, I'm $1 down, right?" Seb saw no reason to disagree.

"So I put $2 on red. If it wins, I'm $1 in profit. I've staked $1, then $2 and I've won $4. So the $1 profit goes in the bag," she said, once again holding up the empty bag. She waited, expectantly. Still no sign of Walt, so Seb sighed and gave in.

"And if you lose with your $2 bet?" he said. Mary laughed - an explosive noise pitched somewhere between an excited horse and a rutting pig. The force of her hilarity seemed to physically rock her backward on her chair and she clung onto the table for support, her glasses almost slipping off her face entirely before she caught them nimbly and dabbed at her watering eyes with a napkin.

"Oh," she gasped, wheezing, "oh, you're gonna just love this part. If I lose with my $2, it's not a problem. It's not a problem at all. I'm ready to bet again, see? And this time, guess how much I'm gonna bet? Go ahead, guess!"

"$4?" he asked, figuring she would already be $3 out of pocket, so would need to bet more than $3 to make a profit. She stopped laughing as abruptly as if he had flicked a switch. Her lips quivered and the pudgy hand grabbed his arm.

"How did you know that?" she said. "Are you working a system, too? Or are you undercover casino security?" She was sweating and looked left and right quickly before checking over her shoulder.

"Relax," said Seb. "It was just a lucky guess." She slowly released her grip on his arm and patted it a few times while staring intently at him as if gauging his honesty. After a few seconds, she reached a decision and smiled tentatively.

"Well, ok, then," she said. "But you can't blame me for being careful. Casinos hate people like me, you know. Folk who have a system. We have to remain, you know, anomalous."

Seb didn't correct her.

"And if you keep losing?" he said. Mary leaned back in her chair and smiled at him like he was a particularly slow five-year old.

"Well," she said, "this is the clever bit. I just keep betting enough to make my $1 profit. If the $4 misses, I'm $7 in the hole. So I need to bet $8 next time. If that misses, I bet $16 next time. Then $32. And so on. Of course, red will hit eventually and I'll win. As long as I don't hit the table maximum."

"What's the maximum?" said Seb.

"Here? $1000," she said. "But my maximum has to be...hold on a second." She reached into the top of the bulging bag and brought out a red plastic wallet.

"Favorite color!" she said, waving it in front of Seb. She opened it and picked out a faded piece of paper, soft with age. Unfolding it, she smoothed in out on the table and Seb saw it contained a sequence of numbers. She consulted the list carefully, breathing loudly through her mouth as her finger traced the numbers.

" $512," she said finally. "That would be my tenth bet. And you know what the odds would be for that ball landing on black again after landing on it nine times in a row?"

"50/50," said Seb. Not entirely accurately, as he knew the '0' and '00' made the odds even worse.

"Don't talk crazy," she huffed. "The odds must be enormous. I can't lose. Really I can't."

Seb wondered whether he should try to point out the huge mathematical error she was making, but she had the bearing of a true believer and he knew his skepticism would be dismissed. He decided to give it one shot.

"It won't work," he stated simply. Mary glared at him.

"Hush," she said and muttered to herself, shaking her head as she folded up her precious paper and put it back in her bag. Seb looked inside and saw it was full of $1 chips.

"Well, you just watch and you'll see," she said, standing up and grabbing both bags. She walked away, puffing, still shaking her head as she reached the stairs leading to the casino floor. Seb called after her.

"How much is your profit if the ball lands on red when you've bet $512?" he said. She turned and glared at him before answering.

"$1," she said, finally, then held the empty bag up. "And it goes straight in here." She walked downstairs toward the roulette table, then stopped and looked up at Seb, sitting at his table on the balcony. He raised his coffee cup and smiled.

"Good luck," he said.

She paused for a second, then turned away from the table and headed for the cashier's cage. Hefting her chip-filled bag onto the counter, she had a brief exchange with the bored middle-aged guy who counted her chips. He handed her something, she took it and marched quickly away, past the table she had been approaching and over to a smarter looking table, where the wheel looked like it had been fashioned from real wood rather than plastic and the seats were padded and more comfortable than the first table. The croupier was in her twenties and looked like she hadn't slept properly in the last 48 hours. This was obviously the high rollers' table. Mary waved up at him, then pointed at a sign on the table he couldn't quite read.

"$10,000 maximum," she called and laughed again, her whole frame shaking as she wheezed. She eased herself into the nearest chair and said something to the croupier, who smiled automatically and spun the wheel before expertly flicking the ball briskly in the opposite direct along its track.

"Place your bets, please," she said, automatically. Mary was her only customer. She triumphantly slapped down one chip on red, then smiled up at Seb. He hadn't been in the casino long, but this was the first chip he'd seen in that color. As the ball still shot around the outer track, he stopped the waitress by holding up his hand.

"Excuse me," he said, "how much are the purple chips worth?"

"They're $5,000, sir," she said, smiling at him. She held his gaze just a fraction of a second long enough to make it clear that her interest in him might not be strictly professional. "Can I get you a refill?"

"No..no, thanks," mumbled Seb as he stood up. Both of Mary's bags were empty. She'd just put her entire savings on red. The ball started to head for the inner wheel as Seb watched.

"No more bets," said the croupier. The ball bounced back up a couple of times, then settled. 21. Red.

"Woo-hoo," screamed Mary as the croupier passed two purple $5000 chips back to her. Seb grinned and waved. Mary beamed and waved back. She had obviously forgiven Seb his lack of faith in her system. Then again, she seemed to have forgotten her system, too. Seb looked for the waitress. Perhaps something stronger than coffee this time. Before he had got the waitress's attention, he was distracted by a shout from downstairs.

"Sebbie?" It was Mary's voice. Seb had always hated Sebbie. Never been too keen on Sebastian, either. Only Seb seemed to fit and even that never felt entirely comfortable. Maybe because he had been named by nuns at an orphanage, rather than loving parents with nine months to think about it. He looked back at the table. The ball was spinning again and Mary was sliding both $5,000 chips onto red.

"That's the table maximum, Ma'am," said the croupier. Mary nodded.

"No more bets," said the croupier. Seb headed for the stairs as the ball jogged and bounced along the polished wood. As he reached the lower floor, he heard the ball settle in one of the numbered slots, but the angle was too shallow for him to see which one. There was no scream from Mary this time. His view of the croupier's hands was blocked by Mary's bulk as he approached and there were no clues in the professionally blank expression. He reached Mary and put a hand on her shoulder.

"You ok?" he said. She turned slowly and looked up at him, the watery blue eyes blinking rapidly behind her glasses. Then she took a deep breath and started to half-laugh, half-cough, the resulting noise attracting the attention of the half dozen customers on neighboring tables as the volume increased.

"Screw the system!" she said, fighting for breath as she held up two black and gold rectangular chips, each bearing the legend $10,000.

"I'm cashing out," she said, sliding off the seat and making for the cashier cage. Seb shook his head and smiled.

"Good for you, Mary," he said. "And good luck with changing your life." She stopped and looked back at him, still puffing slightly.

"You don't get off that easy, Sebbie," she said. "You were my lucky charm tonight. I'm gonna buy you the best dinner in Vegas."

Seb smiled and held up his hands ruefully. His plans for the night certainly didn't involve dinner with a half-drunk 200 lb mid-west woman with a gambling problem.

"Sorry, Mary," he said, "I have other plans." Mary huffed and stomped back over to him. Put her hand on his arm, squeezed hard, looked up at him and said,

"I insist you join me." In Walt's voice.

Seb stood in the middle of the casino with his mouth open for a few seconds, then followed 'Mary' over to the cashier's cage, where she swapped the chips for $20,000 cash. They left together, Seb's waitress rapidly reassessing her opinion of him as she watched him follow the older woman to the exit.

"Gamblers," she sniffed as she cleared away his coffee cup.

# Chapter 20

## Albuquerque

The utility pole had taken a heavy impact, One man nudged it with his foot before kneeling and carefully prising away a splinter revealing streaks of metallic black paint. He took the splinter to a tall man waiting by the helicopter. The man frowned, squinting through the heat haze at the tire tracks leading away, then spun on his heel and boosted himself into the chopper. He dropped into a well worn leather seat and nudged the spacebar to wake up a laptop on the drop-down table. The screen stayed blank as it always did on these calls, although he knew the caller could see him.

"Well?" came the familiar, dry whisper.

"Evidence found just outside Albuquerque, sir," said Westlake. Tracks are heading west. Likely destinations are Phoenix or Las Vegas. Less likely is Tucson, Tijuana, San Diego or doubling back to Los Angeles."

There was no immediate answer. Just short, raspy breaths.

"He's in Las Vegas," came the whisper.

"That's one of the strongest possibilities," said Westlake, "but tactically it makes sense to send small teams to-"

"He's in Las Vegas." No change in the tone of the voice, no anger, just a precise repetition. Westlake knew better than to press the point.

"Yes, sir," he said. "We'll have boots on the ground in just over an hour."

"No," said the whisper. "Your orders have changed. For the present, Mr. Varden will no longer be your concern."

"He won't get away from me again, sir," said Westlake. "If I could just-,"

"No," said the whisper. "You know I admire initiative, Westlake, but I will not tolerate disobedience. Is that clear?"

"Yes, sir, that's clear." Westlake's military service had taken him to some of the most dangerous places on the planet. He had been shot twice, knifed once and tortured on seven occasions. Every man and woman he had ever commanded feared him because he never showed the least hint of fear himself, making life and death decisions rationally and calmly. Some would say coldly. And his reputation was well-founded. He had never felt fear, not for a second. Not even when he started working for the man he answered to now. The man with the whisper. The man he'd never met in person and, truth be told, hoped he never would. He might not fear him, but he knew any failure would mean his death. He respected that.

"Good," said the whisper. "I want you to bring in Meera Patel and Bob Geller."

Westlake paused.

"Is there a problem?" said the whisper. Westlake knew stating anything other than the facts would be a mistake. A big mistake.

"The surveillance team lost them last night in LA, sir," he said. "Patel first, but later both targets were re-acquired at a bar near Geller's residence. Then they somehow managed to get away unseen. They are amateurs, they're scared and they can't use their phones or any bank card without us knowing about it."

"And yet they evaded a team of highly-trained professionals?" The whisper never changed, never gave any indication as to the feelings of its owner. That flat, husky monotone might denote sarcasm, disappointment or psychotic rage, but no clues would ever be given aurally. Westlake wouldn't have put much money against the final option, though.

"I'll take over personally, sir," he said. "They will be in my custody within 48 hours."

There was a dry chuckle. A very disconcerting sound.

"Oh, I don't think so," said the whisper.

Westlake tensed. "I have the experience and resources to-"

"I do not doubt your proficiency, Westlake. But, as you said, these two are amateurs. And you had a team assigned to each of them?"

"Yes, sir."

"Then they had help. The kind of help that meant your men saw only what they were supposed to see. There are only certain parties willing to offer that kind of help in a situation in which I am involved."

"But no one knew about our involvement, sir," said Westlake. "There's no way they could know."

"But they do know. And they came straight for Ms. Patel and Mr. Geller. They didn't approach Mr. Varden."

"We can't be sure of that, sir," said Westlake. "Someone may be helping Varden too. It could be the same people."

"*You* don't know, that's true," said the whisper. "But I do. I know Mr. Varden is currently in Las Vegas. I am content for him to remain there for the time being. I intend speaking with him in the near future. He's an orphan,

Westlake. No parents, no family. You know what that means?"

"No one will miss him," said Westlake.

"Wrong," said the whisper. "He has very little to lose. Very few people he cares about and wants to protect. And you just let the only leverage we had slip through your fingers."

"I'll find them, sir," said Westlake.

"I know," said the whisper. The line went dead. A message flashed up on the screen. Westlake read his orders before stepping out of the helicopter. He gestured to his two subordinates and they jogged over.

"Prime target has been dropped for now," said Westlake. "We'll be focusing on the girl and the old man. Almost certainly traveling together, but very likely to have been joined by an unknown party or parties, possibly dangerous. They know we're coming after them, continue to track their phones and bank account activity, although I doubt they'll be that stupid. They saw us watching the station, they'll assume we're covering the airport. The most likely scenario is they left Los Angeles by car. Crawshaw, check all car hire shops for cash rentals. Davies, canvass their neighbors, find out if anyone is missing a car. If they have any sense, they'll split up at some point. Get their photos to all local law enforcement within a 1000 miles, but make sure they call it in. They must not be approached. Our orders have changed. When we find them, we watch them. Surveillance only, no contact. Clear?"

Both men nodded.

Westlake headed for the chopper. Crawshaw and Davies started to follow him, but he stopped them with a look.

"There's a car coming for you," he said. "Update me face to face in LA in 24 hours. I have some work to do."

The two men stepped back, shielding their eyes from the dust a few seconds later as the chopper's quiet but powerful rotors started to turn and the machine lifted up, pivoted in the air and headed west.

***

If the Shit Station had been quiet before Billy Joe's unexpected departure, it was morgue-like now. Carl and Chad had expected a burst of activity after the dramatic events just 36 hours ago, but apart from an initial command to wait for orders (which, translated from military jargon, meant "we don't have a clue what to do") they had heard nothing. Even though they had killed a man, then watched him jump to his feet and run away like something out of a cartoon. Neither of them had slept much, or spoken about what had happened.

When George, the retired cop who manned the security gate, buzzed them with the news, they weren't surprised. Westlake was on his way back. They guessed their jobs were on the line.

When Westlake turned up - in full uniform - with George following, they stood to attention, fearing the worst. They were the only three on duty. The Shit Station had only existed to babysit the alien. With him gone, there was no reason for the government to keep throwing money at it. Better to close it down and pretend it never existed. Both Carl and Chad had spent a considerable portion of the last 36 hours looking at worst case/best case scenarios. Worst case, military prison. Best case, laid off with a few years as security guards in the local mall to look forward to if they were lucky. George knew this was his last job - he just guessed he would have to make his government annuity stretch a bit more than he'd planned.

Westlake looked at the three men, then nodded.

"At ease," he said. They relaxed. He motioned toward the table. "Sit down."

The three did as they were told. Chad looked quickly at Carl. Carl had always been more of a talker. Carl coughed.

"Sir," he said, "if I could just explain what happened. We were completely taken by surprise, we-,"

"I've read your report, soldier," said Westlake. "I am not here to attribute blame. You were playing poker?"

The two soldiers moved uneasily.

"Yes, sir, we were," said Carl.

"Can't say I blame you," said Westlake. "You hardly had the most interesting posting in the US army, right?"

Chad swallowed and Carl tried to smile, but failed. This guy scared the living crap out of him.

"I need to complete a report," said Westlake. "Deal a hand of poker. Show me how it looked." The two soldiers looked at each other again. Chad shrugged and took a pack of cards out of his pocket, dealing two hands onto the table.

"Three players," said Westlake, gesturing at George.

"But he wasn't here, sir." Westlake just stared at them. He didn't blink. Chad dealt a third hand in front of George.

"Give me your weapon," said Westlake to Carl, holding out his hand. Carl gulped and hesitated for a second before unbuttoning his holster. He removed his gun, checked the safety was on, then handed it over. Westlake examined it for a moment, checking the rounds were correctly chambered.

"Looks like you follow the drill, soldier," he said, nodding his approval. "You look after your weapon. Make sure it's oiled, checked and loaded. Always ready to fire. Won't let you down."

"Yes, sir," said Carl.

"Good," said Westlake. He flicked the safety off and shot George in the face. The noise was huge in the small mess room. Blood and flesh splattered the wall. A wisp of smoke came up from the small entry wound in his left eye. Before either soldier could react, Westlake turned and shot Chad in the head, then dropped to one knee and pressed the barrel of the gun hard under Carl's chin. Westlake pulled the trigger and rolled away. Fragments of Carl's skull and brain rained down on the table and the floor. Westlake didn't want to get his uniform dirty. He so rarely got to wear it these days.

He wiped the gun down carefully, then placed it in Carl's hand. He stood by the door and checked the scene. Three men playing poker. Two shot dead, then a suicide by a soldier whose medical records had been recently amended to contain a schizophrenic episode in his late teens.

"No one likes a bad loser," he said, closing the door behind him.

# Chapter 21

**Las Vegas**

The restaurant was small and dark. Nothing on the menu cost less than $50. Walt ordered about $1000 of food.

"No wine?" said Seb.

"They keep a private supply for me here," said Walt.

*Of course they do.*

"So this is how you support the lifestyle?" said Seb. "Cheating casinos?"

Walt laughed. "Hardly," he said. "I'm their security consultant."

"What?" said Seb. "Seriously?"

"I cheated them for a while when I first arrived," said Walt.

The waiter appeared and filled their glasses with white wine. "Best chablis in the world," said Walt. "Wouldn't be right to drink anything else, since we're having King Crab."

The wine was sensational - crisp, dry. The slight metallic note brought back a memory from when Seb must have been five or six years old. Drinking water from a tin cup at night. The water was really cold; in a tin cup it tasted like the best drink in the world.

"How's your crab?" said Walt. Seb brought himself back to the present moment. He could only nod appreciatively around his first mouthful of the snow-white flesh. It tasted the way he had always imagined lobster might, though he'd never tried it.

"I prefer it to lobster," said Walt, doing that mind-reading trick again. Seb guessed when you lived that long, you could make some pretty accurate guesses about what others were thinking. "I have them fly it in from Kirkenes, right at the tip of Norway. The plane came in this afternoon, these are as fresh as you're gonna get on this continent."

"So how did you get the security consultant job?" said Seb.

Walt chuckled and wiped his mouth with his napkin. "Like I said, I started by cheating them. I went to see the Heads of Security for every major casino. Told them I was going to take them for $500k over the next seven days. Made a follow-up appointment for a week later."

"How did they react?" said Seb.

"They pretty much laughed in my face," said Walt. "Not one of them took me seriously for a second. I knew they wouldn't. But when I walked back in with $500k of chips from their casino, they all experienced a sudden change in attitude. Most of them were angry. A couple of them wanted to hurt me. An unintelligent response."

Walt waved his wine glass vaguely in the air. The waiter materialized and topped it up.

"The ones who responded unintelligently don't work in Las Vegas any more," he said.

"Did they have any idea how you did it?" said Seb.

"Not a chance," said Walt. "Manna is probably the most closely guarded secret humanity possesses. A lot of our power is only useful because people don't know it exists. Luckily, the only people who have suspicions and talk openly about them also believe in Big Foot and spend their weekends staring at cutlery, trying to make it bend. Nah, I just showed them what I'd cheated them out of and gave them a month to review their security footage and work out how I'd done it. When the month was up and they were still clueless, I offered to stop anyone else doing the same for a reasonable monthly retainer."

Walt named a figure and Seb whistled. No wonder he could afford to live in the Taj Mahal.

"Per casino," said Walt. "I do it for nine of them."

Seb shook his head slowly, working out the colossal sums coming Walt's way every month. "They never leaned on you to find out how you ripped them off in the first place?" he said.

Walt nodded. "I expected trouble, so I had a friend stay for a while. Someone whose talent with the source is more attuned to, er...," he seemed to struggle to find the right word.

"Violence?" said Seb.

"Self defense," said Walt.

"You had them beaten up?" said Seb. Walt hesitated, shaking his head. "Killed?" said Seb.

"God, no," said Walt. "I would never initiate anything like that. I genuinely hoped they'd just accept my services and not push me when I refused to reveal my methods. A little professional courtesy. But one casino sent a couple of big guys to follow me and when they figured I was alone, they jumped me. Pushed me into an alley. One had his arm against my throat and pinned me against a wall. The other one slipped a set of brass knuckles onto his hand. They both laughed when my friend stepped into the alley after them. He had been tailing them while they followed me around town."

"Why did they laugh?" said Seb.

"Oh, my friend doesn't exactly inspire fear on a first meeting. He can't really intimidate anyone with his bulk. He's a little person. A dwarf, I would have called him, but he prefers 'little person' and I am certainly not going to argue. He says his appearance helps. It certainly gives him the advantage of surprise. That day, he just launched himself at the one with the brass knuckles, and two seconds later the guy was on the floor, whimpering. He told the one pinning me that his friend seemed to have tripped and accidentally dislocated both elbows and broken his jaw. He suggested that terrible accidents such as this, while rare, could easily be suffered by anyone if they weren't careful. He asked the heavy if he was careful. Unfortunately, he didn't take the hint. He thought his friend must have been caught unawares and he decided he wouldn't make the same mistake. He let me go, backed up a couple paces and pulled a gun."

Walt shook his head and sipped his wine appreciatively.

"I believe the hospital report mentioned that although they had occasionally come across weapons inserted in orifices, this is the first one they'd ever seen that was still loaded. They had to exercise extreme caution when removing it. The damage to his leg was more severe and left him permanently disabled. The other casinos fell in line when they heard the news."

"Not sure I want to meet your friend," said Seb.

"Don't get me wrong," said Walt. "Barrington is a good guy. Just don't get on his bad side."

"Barrington?" said Seb, "seriously? He sounds like a library."

Walt smiled again. "You wanna bring that up with him?"

Seb reached for the wine bottle. "I think I'll leave it," he said.

Walt stood up. "Well, I hate to bring a superb supper to a premature conclusion," he said, "but work calls."

Seb stood up too, regarding what was left of his crab with no little regret. "Casino work?" he said.

Walt nodded. "When we got back earlier, I knew a new User was in town. Now someone's Using close by."

"User?" said Seb.

"User of Manna," said Walt. "I'm particularly sensitive to the presence of others with our abilities. And plenty of those end up here in the first few months after discovering a little about what they can do. Shut-eyes are the hardest to deal with. They genuinely believe they can predict the turn of a card, or where a roulette ball might fall. They don't realize they're physically changing reality to make it happen. No violence necessary these days, in case you were wondering."

Seb had been wondering. He grabbed his jacket and followed Walt out of the restaurant, noticing that no payment was offered or, apparently, expected.

Steve drove them to their destination, a well-known casino on The Strip.

"Remember my trick with the napkin?" said Walt. Seb shuddered, recalling the feeling of dread that had gripped him as the square of linen had scuttled toward him across the table.

"Don't think I'll ever forget it," he said.

"Good," said Walt. "What you've got to remember is I've been doing this a long time. Trained with Sid for 15 years, then developed those skills for more than 60 years. I'm good at reading people, too. I know how to push their buttons."

"You're going to scare them off with a napkin?" said Seb.

"The napkin is strictly for friends," said Walt. "Shows you a little of what I'm capable of. The Users who come to my town ready to break the bank without a thought about the attention they'll draw - not just to themselves, but to all of us, they get the full show."

"But you don't hurt them?" said Seb.

"No need," said Walt. "My art is far more subtle. What Sid used to do with plants, I can do with any physical object. I can make nightmares out of anything. When they're ready to listen, I let them know there's a loose hierarchy among Users. We each have our patch, we look after ourselves, but we don't tread on anyone's toes. Newer Users often get a bit of a god complex at first. Sometimes a quiet word is all that's needed to bring them back down to earth. Some need a brief demonstration of exactly how far down the pecking order they are. They generally get the message after that, realize there's room for all of us."

"Am I going to be getting this treatment?" said Seb.

"Nope," said Walt. "You don't fit the mold. Something different about you. I watch new Users arrive. It's like they're twisting the dimmer switch on a light. First just a glow, then it gradually gets brighter as they learn to use Manna. Most Users flicker and disappear, either unaware of their abilities or unable to find out how to develop them, how to replenish the supply when they need to. The tiny minority that become regular Users stick mostly close to home, are cautious about being discovered. Only a few of them develop their power more fully. Some of those join the Order and disappear off the map. The others are almost all mentored as I was. Two or three a year - in America at least - learn about Manna on their own. Their raw natural talent is always strong, but they don't develop much control, as a rule."

"Yeah, well I fixed your car after I wrecked it," said Seb.

"You did," said Walt. "And you shouldn't have anything like that kind of control yet. But, like I said, you don't fit the mold. You didn't gradually light up like a dimmer switch. One second you didn't exist, the next someone flicked a switch and there you were."

Seb thought of the glowing alien figure, the gift he had given, the way he'd just vanished. He decided he would be better off letting Walt talk and not give anything away. *I know nothing about this guy.*

Even without Walt's gifts, the new User in town wasn't hard to find. There was a crowd around one of the blackjack tables. Bottles of Krystal were heading for the table and everyone sitting or standing within 10 feet had a glass. Only one person was actually gambling. And she was winning. Winning big. The pile of chips next to her was tall and growing with every hand, much to the approval of the crowd. The floor manager was glowering from behind the dealer, looking for evidence of card counting but finding none. The casinos had protected themselves against counters ever since the MIT crowd had taken them for a ride in the 90s. When the floor manager saw Walt approaching, he nodded, smiled grimly and walked off without a backward glance.

The woman with all the chips was stunning. Wearing a low-cut black cocktail dress that made her look like she had just stepped off the set of the latest 007 movie, she held herself with an assurance common only among those who'd grown up able to get anything they wanted. She might have been a princess from a European family with her classic features, intelligent brown eyes under sculptured eyebrows and auburn hair looking like her stylist had only just stepped away from the blackjack table after a couple hours' intensive work. Seb had his doubts that any member of a royal family, however obscure, would display quite that amount of cleavage. She was paying for the drinks of about thirty hangers-on by flicking the occasional $1000 chip at a waitress and ordering more champagne. Seb thought that was pretty smart if you were cheating in some traditionally undetectable way. Lots of witnesses who were on her side, willing her "lucky streak" to last as long as possible, so she would keep topping up their glasses.

There was a king and a five showing in front of her and she tapped the table for another card. She had what looked like about $50,000 of chips riding on the outcome. *No wonder the floor manager had come down personally.* Anything above a six would bust her. The crowd held its breath, but the woman didn't even glance at the card as it was turned, signaling instead for another bottle. When the crowd saw the card and responded with gasps, murmurs and one short scream, her attention snapped back to the table. The card was the seven of clubs. Busto. As the dealer pulled the chips away, she grabbed the remains of her stack and looked sharply around the crowd. When her eyes found Walt, she froze, her gaze suddenly cold and angry. Walt nodded slightly and she stood. The crowd started to disperse disappointedly as she swept through them, heading straight for Walt and Seb.

"I'll meet you back here in an hour," said Walt before the woman reached them. Up close, she was even more stunning and the cliche about anger enhancing beauty was revealing its roots in an ancient truth. Her pulse was throbbing in her neck.

"Who the hell are you and what are you doing?" she said. Walt bowed slightly, a polite smile on his lips.

"I'd be delighted to explain, my dear," he said. "Let's go somewhere a little more private, shall we? Please follow me." He walked away and she followed with the absolute self-confidence of one who knows they have nothing to fear. Seb couldn't help feeling a bit sorry for her. He was also just a tiny bit disappointed she hadn't even glanced in his direction. Not only because of her looks, but because she was someone else who could use Manna, someone he might want to talk to. He had no reason to distrust Walt - he had saved him on the train, after all - but that didn't necessarily mean his motives were pure. *He grew up a gangster, then joined a blackmailer, it's hardly a glowing resumé.* Seb decided he would try to speak to the woman before she left town. Meanwhile, he had an hour to kill. He headed for the bar, but before he'd got halfway across the casino, a huge guy with a shaved head and an earpiece stopped him.

"Excuse, me, sir," he said. His voice was so deep, Seb actually felt it in his stomach. Seb looked up at him. At six feet tall, Seb had never felt short, but his eyes were currently level with this giant's badge, which read Casino Security.

"Is there a problem?" said Seb.

"Mr. Ford wants you to join him," said the man.

"Mr. Ford?" said Seb.

"Walter Ford, sir, he said you were working with him."

Seb nodded. "Oh, sure, ok. Where is he?"

"Please follow me, sir." Seb had to take three steps to the giant's two, making him feel like a kid trying to keep up with an adult. They rounded the corner into the corridor Walt had taken with the woman. The giant knocked at a door, paused, then opened it, gesturing to Seb.

"After you, sir." Seb walked into the room. The giant followed and shut the door behind him. Walt's office was another 30 feet down the corridor, but as Seb hadn't actually seen where he went, he couldn't possibly know that. He knew for sure he was in the wrong room now. And as far as wrong rooms go, this one couldn't have been more wrong. There was no furniture at all, apart from a hospital gurney to one side with a drip attached and small man in a paramedic uniform stood next to it, holding a needle. Two other heavily muscled men in suits - one blonde, the other with a nose that looked like it had been broken more than once - stood in the middle of the room.

"Wha-," said Seb, just as the blonde man took a quick step forward, raised his arm and sprayed something at his face.

# Chapter 22

Walt had a private office in every casino he worked for. Each of his rooms looked broadly the same. Old, dark furniture, a huge desk and one wall stacked with books floor to ceiling. No window. The woman walked to the desk, put her hands behind her and boosted herself onto it, crossing one leg so that a high heeled shoe dangled from her foot. Her dress rode an inch up her thighs and she smiled up at Walt.

"I'm a bit old for flirting," he said.

"You're never too old," she said, " and anyway, what makes you think I'm your junior?"

Walt walked around the desk and sat in the large leather chair. She was too confident, too assured. He started reappraising her as she smiled coquettishly at him over her shoulder. He nudged a trackpad on the desk and a computer screen blinked into life. He glanced at it.

"Ms Svetlana," he read. "You're Russian? Welcome to America."

She smiled. "Georgian, actually. I know it all seems the same to you, but, believe me, it's a very different country."

"My apologies, Ms. Svetlana," said Walt.

"Oh, do call me Sonia," she said, playing with her necklace, which brought Walt's gaze back to her cleavage. As she no doubt intended.

"Sonia," he said. "My name is Walter Ford. As you saw, I share similar abilities to the ones you were using to cheat at the tables. The casinos employ me to stop people like you ruining a profitable business. I have no objection to you staying in town for a while. There are some wonderful shows you might want to take in before moving on. However, I will have to insist that you stay away from gambling from now on. Unless you are willing to do so in the traditional way."

"Let the house win, you mean?" She stroked her red bottom lip with her index finger. Slowly. Walt swallowed. "Oh, I think I'd rather quit while I'm ahead," she said.

"Then our business is concluded," said Walt. "Just a word of advice. Be careful how and where you use your power while you're in this country. There aren't many of us and we respect each others' privacy, but we do look out for each other."

"Thank you, Mr. Ford, I will be sure to take your advice." He wondered if she was just playing with him. She had seemed angry enough on the casino floor, now she was compliant and flirtatious. Why? He stood up and walked to the door. As he did so, he heard her move behind him. There was a rustling sound.

"Mr. Ford?" she said. He turned. The dress she'd chosen for the night was of the kind of clingy material that led men to speculate as to the existence - or otherwise - of underwear. The dress was now on the floor, so Walt had no further need to speculate. She hadn't worn any underwear.

"No need to rush back, is there?" she said, smiling.

*** 

Seb began to tense, but as the spray came toward his face, it seemed to freeze in mid-air. Seb could see individual droplets in the fine mist. He realized they were still moving, just incredibly slowly, the kind of super slo-mo he had recently seen in a TV documentary about bees, which made every beat of their tiny wings last two or three seconds. At the same time he felt a prickling sensation in his head and the room seemed to brighten, every detail standing out. The spray, the frowning face of the man behind it, the paramedic and the other man, standing still but alert and ready; the giant behind him, close enough that Seb could feel the guy's jacket lapel touching his right shoulder. It was as if he could pay attention to everything simultaneously rather than have to focus on one thing at a time. It was dream-like in its surreality, but unlike a dream in that everything seemed more solid more real, more *there*. So when he heard the voice in his head, Seb wasn't the least surprised.

"If you're feeling wired, it's mostly because whole areas of your brain have just gone dark," said Seb2.

"You pick your moments," said Seb, marveling briefly about how preternaturally calm he felt.

"Yeah, well it seems the fact I - you - we - have been a regular human being for 32 years means we're still thinking and behaving like one. I haven't been able to communicate with you unless there's a moment of great enough stress to make you lose consciousness."

"I'm conscious now," said Seb.

"Yep," said Seb2. "We're improving. This is much more useful. Now shut up, this isn't the time. You need to win this fight."

"There are four of them!" said Seb. "One's got a needle, Blondie and Broken Nose in front look like they live in a gym and the guy behind me could kill me just by sitting on me. Hang on - don't tell me - I know kung fu?"

"Don't be a pillock," said Seb2. Mee had taught Seb many of Britain's more unusual insults and he relished any opportunity to use them. "You can only use knowledge you actually possess. So I kinda wish you had signed up for self-defense classes, but we'll work with what we've got."

"Slowing down time is a neat trick," said Seb, "but I'm still gonna be just as unconscious when that hits my face." The droplets were closer now. Seb realized he could see the giant's reflection in them.

"I didn't slow down time," said Seb2, "but the only areas of your brain now firing synapses are those essential for strategy. I've also increased your adrenaline to an almost dangerous level. Your perception of time is massively skewed because your brain is making calculations fast. Real fast. Now shut up and do as I say."

"Yes, sir," said Seb.

"Ok, two immediate problems - the spray and the huge guy behind you. Duck to your left and drive your right elbow backward."

Seb ducked to the side, wrapped his left hand over his right fist and yanked his elbow backward as hard as he could. The bony end of his elbow made contact precisely with the giant's testicles and, as Seb continued moving left, the huge figure folded in agony, taking a short, ragged involuntary breath as he hunched over. By that point, his face was squarely in the cloud of vapor. His eyes unfocused, his limbs slackened and he pitched forward as he lost consciousness. His fall took him directly into the path of the one with the spray, who spun to his right to avoid him.

"Off-balance," said Seb2. "Sweep your-"

But Seb was already doing it as pure self-preserving reflexes took over. Continuing the momentum started on his duck to the left, he put his left hand on the carpet and used it to steady himself as he swept his right leg into the feet of the unbalanced Blondie. With his weight already shifted by trying to avoid the fallen giant, the man crashed heavily to the floor.

"The neck," said Seb2. "I don't know the medical term for it, but you need to punch him on-"

"Got it," said Seb, moving forwards. He had rarely been a violent man, so he could only assume the moral center of his brain was one of the areas no longer in action as he punched Blondie in the side of his neck below his ear. His body immediately went slack.

*Two down.*

The paramedic wasn't a threat and was backing away. Broken nose was a different prospect. As soon as Seb had kicked Blondie's legs from under him, Broken nose had gone for his pocket. When Seb looked up, he saw something shooting toward him from Broken Nose's outstretched hand.

"Move to - " said Seb2, then "no! Wait, don't move. It's a taser."

It was closer now and Seb saw that Seb2 was right. Two wires snaked toward his chest, sparks already slowly moving between the barbed contact points.

"It's going to hit me!"

"I know," said Seb2, "hold still, and try very hard not to bite your tongue."

Seb braced himself as the hooked metal pierced his skin. There was a brief flare of pain. Then the sparks raced away from him, back down the lines. Straight into Broken Nose's hand. He danced like some bizarre slowed-down footage from a children's show; a wooden puppet controlled by a hyperactive three-year old, his limbs twitching and jerking, lips pulled back from his teeth and blood spurting from his mouth where he had bitten down on his tongue. After less than two seconds of frenzied twitching at 50,000 volts, he collapsed, jerked once more and was still.

"Ouch," said Seb2. Time seemed to speed up slightly as the danger receded and Seb turned to the paramedic, who'd backed up against the wall and looked very pale.

"And what am I supposed to do with you?" said Seb. The paramedic hesitated for a moment, glanced at the hypodermic in his hand, then stabbed it into his own thigh and emptied the contents into his bloodstream. He sat down.

"One," said the paramedic, "two...th..." As his head rolled forward, his shoulders slumped and his body fell sideways. After a short pause, he started snoring.

"Smart," said Seb2. "Now let's go find-,"

"Walt!" said Seb and turned and sprinted back into the corridor, vaulting the unconscious giant.

\*\*\*

Walt admitted to himself that he was tempted. Sonia was beautiful, sensuous and achingly available. He hadn't had sex for four days, and 80 years' experience of his over-developed libido meant he was ready to rectify the omission. But the contents of his pants no longer ruled the roost - once you knew you could get all the sex you wanted, you realized not every opportunity had to be quite so eagerly grasped. And his brain was telegraphing clearly the message that Ms. Svetlana had an agenda beyond seducing him.

"Who are you, really?" he said. "Why are you here?"

She took a step toward him, one hand gently cupping a perfectly formed breast.

"Wrong question," she said. "You should be asking 'what', not 'who.'"

Although his resolve wasn't wavering, Walt couldn't help but enjoy the fantasy unfolding in front of him.

"As you wish," he said. "So, Ms. Svetlana, what are you?"

She smiled and took a step closer.

"A diversion," she said.

Walt hesitated, then cursed and turned for the door. He had expected others to be interested in Seb - a surge of power like that would be felt by outliers such as himself worldwide. But he hadn't expected anyone so soon. And he had no idea who this woman was, which faction she belonged to, if any. He reached out for the handle, then gasped in pain as the metal stretched, then wrapped itself around his wrist, pulling him against the door.

Sonia smiled at him and shook her head.

"There's really no rush, Walter," she said. "We're only just getting to know each other."

Walt considered much of his manipulation of Manna close to an art form. He was proud of the creatures he could bring into being and often took minutes to slowly craft an intricate creation, either for his own amusement or to terrify a User who wouldn't comply with his request to leave town. So on one level it hurt his pride to do what he did next. On another level, it was pure expedience. He couldn't afford to lose Seb. The personal consequences didn't bear thinking about.

Ignoring the pain in his wrist and turning away from the smiling centerfold leaning against his desk, he looked toward the huge bookcase. It wasn't there because Walt was an avid reader. It also wasn't the kind of bookcase designed to impress guests with his intellectual credentials. It was there because books are made of paper. And paper, as Walt had discovered over many decades of experimentation, was his favorite medium.

Nearly three hundred books flew off the shelves toward the middle of the room, each one opening as it did so. Spines twisted and ripped as pages tore themselves out. In a whirlwind of motion, the air crackling with power, the shreds of paper and cardboard packed themselves tightly together into a mass which thickened and grew. Within a few seconds, the whirling mass had taken on a recognizable shape - a huge hand, crudely made but unmistakable, twice the size of the woman it swooped toward, its huge fingers opening as it approached. Sonia offered no resistance as the giant fist enclosed her and she disappeared from view.

Walt didn't waste any time once he had imprisoned her, immediately turning his attention to the metal holding him in place. He looked down at it - antique iron, not only practical and strong, but also one of those interior designer touches intended to lend the casino an air of opulence. Under his gaze the iron softened and became malleable, sliding away from his skin before reforming itself as a door handle. As he put his hand out to turn it, he darted a final look over his shoulder. The enormous fist held its captive firmly - no need to hurry back, she would be his guest for as long as he deemed necessary.

His hand closed over thin air. The handle had gone. He looked at the door disbelievingly. It seemed to have merged organically with the wall on either side. No hinges held it in place, the oak just melted into the plaster of the wall.

A low chuckle sounded from behind him. He turned. As he did so, the hand exploded into a million pieces. The word 'exploded' didn't do it justice - it was more like thousands of tiny fingers had simultaneously grabbed individual pieces of paper and neatly ripped them two or three times within a fraction of a second. The naked body enclosed within was hard to make out for a few seconds as a cloud of confetti drifted down around her like snow. When the flakes had settled, she shook her head ruefully and waggled a finger at Walt.

"And we could have had such fun," she said. As she took a step forward, her dress snaked up her legs and neatly peeled itself back onto her skin. "Your party tricks might scare the neophytes, but I left kindergarten a very, very long time ago."

She raised her hands. Any hint of flirtatiousness had gone. Her gaze was blank, pitiless. Tendrils of black smoke curled around her hands before focusing into something harder and stronger. Some of the paper around her sparked into flame and her hair crackled with energy. Walt had a sudden conviction that the next few seconds would be his last. He still couldn't help but be impressed by her, whoever she was. He hadn't seen such power in a long time. Lesser men might have closed their eyes. Not Walt.

***

Seb stopped in the corridor. He had no idea which way to go. He felt/heard/touched a crackle of raw energy coming from his right. The door at the end of the corridor glowed like a heat source looked at with a thermal imaging camera. He ran toward it. As he got closer, he realized the door wasn't right - no handle, no way in.

"Don't stop," said Seb2 as he put his shoulder to the door and plowed into it. The sudden lack of resistance when he had been expecting solid oak was a shock; he stumbled as he came through the door. It felt like running from a car to a house in a violent rain storm. His body was pummeled by tiny specks of force, smacking against his skin. Then he was through.

The stunning woman from the Blackjack table was in the middle of the room, surrounded by small fires. Seb felt Walt's presence beside him as he half-fell through the doorway. He stepped in front of him, just as black lightning arced from her fingertips. Time began to slow again, but there was nowhere to move unless he was willing to let Walt take the blast.

"Oh, shit," said Seb2 as the darkness reached Seb and engulfed his body.

In the room's center, Sonia's eyes widened as the situation changed. She and Walt both saw what happened during the next 5.6 seconds. For the first 2.7 seconds, Seb's body took the full force of the attack and reacted as any organic matter would if suddenly exposed to a burst of tightly-directed heat. The skin peeled away from his face and hands, his flesh bubbled, boiled, melted and shriveled to cling to his skeleton.

Walt decided he would never eat ribs again.

The next 2.9 seconds reversed the process. Seb's body sizzled like bacon on a griddle as the blackened flesh sloughed off and fell to the floor. Red, bloody, raw muscle grew back, followed by skin, hair and clothes. Sonia had the ringside view as Seb's face rebuilt itself around his teeth, which had been pretty much the only recognizably human feature left on top of his spinal cord. The final touch was his eyes, pushing back into his empty sockets with a slightly wet plopping sound.

There was a moment's silence.

Sonia moved first, spinning around and sprinting for the wall behind her. She jumped as she approached it and sailed through as if it had been an open window rather than 2cm plaster, 3cm boarding and 15cm solid brick. Outside the building, 23 floors above the street, she spread her arms and legs as gravity did its job and pulled her toward the sidewalk. Her skin darkened and stretched as she fell. Anyone looking up would have seen a dark shadow in a dark sky, nothing more. A skein of flesh flowed from her spreadeagled hands to her feet and - as her limbs continued to stretch, bones hollowing as they grew - her descent slowed significantly. She moved her left foot upwards and her body turned right gliding away from the casino. She spotted a low building four blocks away and headed for it. At the last moment, she turned into the wind and wrenched her body into an upright position, dropping onto the roof with no more impact than a medium-sized bird.

# Chapter 23

## Las Vegas

The sign outside advertised it as a Gentleman's Club, which Seb could only assume was meant ironically. He had always associated the word 'gentleman' with Alistair Cooke, the presenter of Masterpiece Theatre in the late 80s and early 90s. It was one of the few programs the occupants of the children's home were allowed to watch and Seb had always been fascinated by the well-dressed, well-spoken, well-mannered presenter. Seb looked around the table in the private booth the hostess had led them to. Three women were sat with him, two of them topless. The topless ones were kissing each other while the third one had one hand sliding suggestively up and down a champagne glass, the other hand between her legs as she looked first at the girls, then at Seb. *Nope, just can't see Alistair Cooke fitting into this picture.*

Walt came back with a bottle of fine bourbon, a woman on each arm. They squeezed into the booth. Seb was drinking beer. A cold beer really seemed to hit the spot when you'd just had your entire body burned to a crisp by a beautiful naked Georgian witch.

"Ladies," said Walt, "give us a few minutes. I need to talk to my friend." The women started to leave.

"Go have a drink on us," he called after them, then sat down and poured a shot of bourbon to go with Seb's beer.

"Gotta tell you, son, I've never seen anything quite like that. Hell of a thing," said Walt, knocking back his first shot then refilling his glass. "What did you do back there?"

"You do that, too, right?" said Seb, still slightly in shock from what had happened. He should be dead - again - but his body seemed to be able to take any amount of damage and recover. Seb2 was right, he couldn't be killed. "Heal, I mean. You can heal yourself."

"Yes I can," said Walt, draining his third shot. He started to pour another, then grabbed a champagne glass, tossed what was left in it over his shoulder and filled it with bourbon before taking a long swallow. He smiled. "But what you did was incredible."

He edged closer to Seb and put his hand on his shoulder. His hand was shaking slightly. Seb couldn't decide if he was scared or excited. Both, probably.

"I heal, sure," said Walt. "I've been beaten up, shot, knifed. Even had a hand taken off with a machete one time." He laughed and waved a perfectly whole and healthy hand at Seb. "It didn't take."

"So we can both do it," said Seb. "It's part of using Manna."

"Well, yes and no," said Walt, encouraging Seb to drink faster. Seb felt impossibly, fantastically alive. He drank.

"Thing is," said Walt, "anyone who Uses has some kind of accelerated healing. Some more than others. At one end of the scale, a broken arm might heal in days rather than weeks. When I was shot, they picked seven bullets out of my stomach and chest. I should have died within hours. Now I don't have a single scar to show for it."

"So your power is like mine," said Seb.

"Hardly," said Walt. "I thought I was a bit of a prodigy, but you just knocked me off my perch, big time. It took me six days to recover. Six *days*. You didn't even take six *seconds*. You were burned alive, Seb, I saw your bones, your skull. I don't even know how what I just saw is possible, but here you are, sitting next to me, good as new. Thing is-." He hesitated as if unsure.

"What?" said Seb.

"Well, you already know Users live longer. Manna protects us from all sickness, as far as I can tell. With serious illnesses, we know it can slow down the spread of a disease to such an extent that it would take decades, rather months, to kill us. Unnatural deaths are very, *very* unusual in Users. But it does happen, and when it does, it's always down to one of two possible causes." Walt thought for a second. "Both, occasionally."

"Which are?" said Seb.

"Brain death, or severe brain damage, is one. Your brain takes a bullet, you might be ok, but if it passes through whichever bit of you controls Manna - and the jury's still out on which bit that is - then you're dead."

"I'll try to remember to duck," said Seb. "What's the other?"

"Fire," said Walt. "It may come down to the same thing in the end - the brain destroyed by fire, but Manna can't stop the flames, so if you don't throw yourself into the nearest river, your number's up. At least, that was the lowdown before this evening. Then you got fried and came back. I was behind you, I felt the intensity of that heat. No way you should be sitting there right now. No way."

"Guess the theory was wrong, then," said Seb.

"Guess so. Or you're doing something new."

"Well, if I am, I don't have a clue how."

Walt sighed. "Yeah, I believe that. Anyway," he said, smiling, "I bet you're buzzing."

"What?" said Seb.

"Don't forget how long I've been using Manna," said Walt. "Whenever any of us Use, it just makes us want to grab life by the balls and never let go. You feeling it, Seb, my boy?" he put his other hand on Seb's other shoulder and grinned at the younger man.

Seb laughed.

"Yeah, I'm feeling it all right, Walt. In fact," he said, recalling another of Mee's favorite phrases, "it's fair to say I'm buzzing like a bastard."

"Good," said Walt. "Life is out there, waiting for us. And this isn't the movies. You get great power, you don't have to turn into a boring schmuck. You can live a little. You can live a lot."

The club's hostess returned with the girls and a fresh round of drinks. Walt gave her a $20,000 casino chip.

"Call a limo for us, Trix. Take the rest of the night off. Bring the girls and bring your magic bag."

The hostess - Trix - said something to the nearest girl who giggled and took the other away to get their coats. Then she leaned over the table, her flimsy blouse revealing breasts for which her plastic surgeon had - deservedly - won an award.

"Walt," she said, "you are a very, *very* naughty man. Now bring your handsome friend and let's go have some fun."

Fun was something Seb had never been particularly good at. He knew what it looked like, even tried joining in, but it had never felt entirely natural to him. He didn't need years of psychotherapy to tell him what he already knew. He was - effectively - an orphan, his mother dead hours after giving birth to him, his father unknown. St Benet's had been the only childhood he had known and he couldn't fault the love and care shown to him and his fellow outcasts by the

Sisters and by Father O, but all the kids had seen TV shows and read books, so they knew what a normal loving family looked like. Was it possible to miss something you've never had? In Seb's experience, yes it was, if what you were missing was a mother to stroke your hair and make you peanut butter and jelly sandwiches. Or a father to make you laugh, tell you stories and throw a baseball to you in the back yard.

There were plenty of opportunities for fun after leaving the Home. All of which were down to music. His musical talent had been recognized early and he had been allowed to skip basketball practise three afternoons a week to sit at the beat-up piano in the dining room. Some of the notes at the top of the keyboard stuck, the ivory was yellow and sticky, and the lowest notes carried on ringing tunelessly for half a minute after they sounded. One of the sisters - Barbara - had been a decent classical pianist and she'd guided Seb through early folk songs, gradually introducing some theory and scales. Then some simplified Mozart, Beethoven, Haydn. And, one unforgettable afternoon two years after Seb had first sat at a piano, Bach. The first Bach piece Seb learned, the piece Sister Barbara played to him that Fall afternoon, marked a clear turning point in Seb's life. He had enjoyed playing piano before that, realized he had some talent. What Bach did was open up his mind to the seemingly infinite possibilities of existence. It was as if he'd walked around with his head wrapped in bandages and someone had just ripped them away, saying, "This is what life looks like. This is what life sounds like, what it smells like, what it feels like."

Sister Barbara had sensed a little of what he was feeling when she finished playing the C Major prelude. She sat in silence for about a minute, then turned to look at Seb.

"That was good," he said, "play it again." So she did, then he said, "Can you teach me how to play it?" Nearly 20 years later, it was the music he had chosen to accompany his suicide.

He loved classical music throughout his teens, but could hardly avoid the rock and pop music scene in New York. St Benet's was in Brooklyn and there had been live music venues nearby. When the wind was in the right direction, you could hear the bass and drums at night and imagine the packed basement rooms, the sweat, the dancing, the excitement. No wonder the bands always seemed to speed up mid-song. Something in Seb responded to even that tiny hint of the excitement of live rock'n'roll. He took to hanging around the local music store, playing the keyboards he couldn't afford. Ted, the owner, recognized an opportunity when he saw one and gave Seb a Saturday job, demonstrating home keyboards to middle-class parents shopping for their progeny. Seb could make the cheapest piece of gear sound good, but Ted had him unleash his best stuff on the keyboards with the biggest margin. Ted sold a lot of keyboards, Seb got to play the latest gear and meet some local musicians. So when the manager of a touring band came in looking for a keys player, Ted pointed at Seb. He knew he was losing his best salesman, but he even let Seb have the rig he would need at cost and told him he could pay him back monthly from his tour earnings. Ted was a good guy.

Seb was seventeen when he joined The Backstabbers for nine months schlepping round a couple hundred second-rate bars and venues across America. He loved it. He sent postcards to Father O, Sister Barbara and the other kids at St Benet's for the first month, then he stopped. He had never been back. He'd often meant to go, had often intended to pick up a phone. But when weeks stretched into months and years, it became more difficult, then seemingly impossible. Years later, when his song Sunburst Sunday had been used as the theme tune for a daytime soap, he'd arranged with his agent for 50% of the royalties to go to St Benet's. Anonymously. He had harbored no ill-feeling toward his childhood home. It's just once you've decided to go forward and you've started putting one foot down after another, it gets harder and harder to look back over your shoulder at where you started out.

The Backstabbers had long since decided that a derisory pay check and a life of tour buses and cheap hotels could be partially compensated for by the allure of small town girls. Groupies were considered an honorable tradition by band, crew and the girls themselves, though no one could really say why. Girls offering their bodies to strange men simply because they could play a guitar didn't make much sense under any kind of scrutiny. Seb thought it was the fantasy of freedom. The band breezed into town, played up a storm and were gone in the morning to continue their glamorous lives elsewhere. The groupies never seemed to consider that their little town - the cheap hotel where they'd snorted cocaine with the drummer then shared him with the girl from the diner - was anything but unique. It was just another part of the routine for the band, alongside crappy road food and bad quality VHS porn on the tour bus. But the groupies wanted to feel special, chosen. And that's exactly how they did feel. For one night. Then it was the early morning walk home in last night's clothes, carrying their heels and hoping not to see anyone they knew.

Seb indulged, of course. He was seventeen and women were making themselves available. He threw himself into it whole-heartedly at first. But eventually he started to feel bad every morning, feel used. It was Jerry the drummer's comedic refrain on the bus: "Man, I feel used, I feel dirty. The world is a wicked and terrible place. Let's do it again." But Seb started to take walks after the gig, get back to the hotel later, alone. Keep himself to himself a little more. He tried blaming the feelings of guilt on his Catholic upbringing, but he couldn't make it stick. He loved sex, that much was obvious, but he'd like to experience it with someone who'd remember his name. Not just in the morning, but preferably during the act itself.

The drugs had been fun, too, for a while, but the torpor of a day smoking weed followed by the manic coke-fueled gigs, bourbon at the hotel and the inevitable 5am heart-hammering insomnia made for a soul-sapping routine. When the band fell apart in LA, Seb was happy to take a piano residency in a hotel, clean up his lifestyle and spend his days writing songs.

Now, at 32 years old, after reaching another turning point in his life two days previously, Seb sat in a huge jacuzzi with seven naked women and Walt. And - much to his amazement - it felt good. Real good.

Walt was pretty happy, too. "About now," he said, "any normal degenerate with unlimited funds, surrounded by beautiful women in a hot tub would probably start taking some high quality drugs. Trix here is known for her ability to procure fine Columbian product and I'm sure she didn't come empty handed, did you, Trix?"

Trix smiled and shook her head. Seb had often wondered if artificially enlarged breasts floated or sank in liquid and Trix had provided him with an answer. If she ever found herself the victim of a shipwreck far from land, she wouldn't have to waste any energy treading water. In fact, she could probably save at least three other people. Surely they were uncomfortable? He had never found "enhanced" breasts remotely arousing. They were like a traffic wreck - you might slow down to look at them but you felt slightly sick and ashamed the longer you hung around. Trix got out of the tub and swayed over to an attaché case she had brought with her, lifting it onto a marble table. Inside was a bag of cocaine crystals, a battery powered coffee grinder, a square mirror and a pile of crisp $100 bills. Trix filled the grinder and, while it was buzzing away and jittering across the table top, she started rolling a bill into a tight tube. She saw Seb watching and laughed.

"Just doesn't feel right using smaller denominations," she said.

Walt hoisted himself out of the bubbling water and shrugged on a robe.

"Come on, Seb" he said, "let's give the ladies some privacy. Something I want to show you."

Seb gently and somewhat regretfully moved one of the girls' hands from his groin and tried to think of something capable of making an erection subside quickly, a difficult feat at any time, now rendered virtually impossible by the sheer quantity and quality of naked flesh surrounding him. Even Seb's go-to image to delay an imminent orgasm - that of Woody Allen playing the clarinet - wasn't getting the job done on this occasion.

Walt, guessing Seb's predicament, laughed.

"I think you'll find you *can* control that, now," he said.

Seb thought for a second then understood. Very gently he turned his attention to his genitals and imagined his penis in its resting state. The erection disappeared. He was surprised how much more control he had over his use of Manna. It had almost been instinctive this time. He was about to get up when he decided his flaccid manhood might not be that impressive emerging from water. Especially in front of this particular audience. Sending up an automatic silent apology to any higher power, he added some length and girth to his penis before climbing out of the jacuzzi, putting on a robe and following Walt into his study.

"Form an orderly line, girls," Trix said behind him as he left the room. "There's plenty for everyone."

# Chapter 24

Walt was already sat behind his desk, studying a screen.

"I've set wheels in motion to get some information on our attacker," he said. "She wasn't trying to kill you, she was aiming for me. And I don't think I would have come back from being a human kebab the way you did."

"She wanted me alive," said Seb, "but drugged."

"Casino Security has been interviewing her friends," said Walt. "They have an array of impressive injuries - well done - and they're being treated for them. There's a very luxurious suite in the top northwest corner of the building. It's completely secure. We'll keep them there until we get some answers. The medical guy with them is in a coma and seems likely to stay that way for weeks, if not months. Whatever they were planning to inject you with was intended to keep you down for a while. She knew you were powerful, but she thought a huge hit of anesthetic would stop you for a few hours. Would it?"

Seb thought back to whatever it was Westlake had sprayed in his face. It had been incredibly fast-acting, although his Manna-enhanced metabolism had brought him out of it within minutes. But if he had been injected with something more powerful while unconscious, would he have been able to pull the same trick?

"I don't know," he said. "Maybe."

Walt finished reading, clicked the mouse and swiveled the display around so Seb could see. The woman from the casino's classically beautiful features filled the screen.

"Sonia Svetlana," said Walt. "It's her real name. She doesn't consider there's any reason to hide it. She's recently risen to the top of an organization no one's ever taken seriously - Acolytes of Satan, they call themselves. Laughable, in some ways, but brutal and, it would seem, more of a threat than we thought."

"We?" said Seb.

"Like I said, there's a bunch of Manna users that look out for each other," said Walt. "Nothing sinister, nothing you'd even call a organization. We just want to keep our abilities out of the public eye and be left alone. Other groups using Manna have agendas. The Order is religious, they usually keep themselves to themselves. There are plenty of small groups who use rituals and think they're channelling real magic - they often call themselves shamans, witches or druids. The Acolytes believe in the existence of demons and their rituals often end with the physical summoning of creatures that convince everyone attending. You and I know it's an illusion, but the thousands of believers see what they want to see. And they are prepared to fund their leaders' extravagant lifestyles. It's a pretty neat con, you've got to hand it to them."

"So what have they got against me?" said Seb.

"Well, you're not going to like it," said Walt. "These idiots have worked on their mythology for hundreds of years. They believe Satan, not God, created the world, which explains why it's such a mess. And their regular rituals, as well as being fund-raisers, are also designed to help bring about their ultimate aim."

Seb had a bad feeling about where this was going.

"Which is?" he said.

"To bring Satan back to finish what he started. Destroy the world, create some kind of hell, set up an international chain of coffee shops...I don't know what these maniacs think is going to happen. Most of them are just desperate people who want to kid themselves they know something no one else does. Something that will give them the power they crave, so they can turn their pathetic lives around. No danger to anyone, really. But the last few months has seen a change. Our friend Sonia has whipped them into a frenzy. She's something special, you have to admit." Seb could still clearly remember the sensation of his skin burning, the smell, the feel of his tongue crackling and shriveling as his lips peeled away from his teeth.

"Yes," he said. "Although I don't think 'special' is the word I'd use."

"Well, she's certainly stirred things up with the Acolytes Of Satan," said Walt. "She challenged the leader at one of the big rituals. And when I say challenged, she didn't just ask for a vote of no confidence. We don't really have any cast-iron information, but our sources suggest she may have pulled the same trick on him she tried on us. Only he did what you'd expect: went up like a roman candle and died screaming. It's the only reason we know anything about her, frankly. Even a rumor of someone with that strong an ability automatically gets flagged up. We assumed it was exaggerated. Now we know different."

"Will she be back?" said Seb.

"Unquestionably," said Walt. "She's left town now, I can't even feel a trace of her. We'll get whatever information we can out of her crew. I'm expecting an update."

"You said you thought she knew what she wanted with me," said Seb. "Well? What do you think it was?"

Walt sighed and rubbed his eyes, before standing and smiling again.

"First of all, know that you're safe here," he said. "Like I said, we look out for each other. We've set up a perimeter of Users around Las Vegas. No one with any trace of Manna gets in without being cleared first. Like I've been telling you, the way you showed up was unprecedented. No gradual process, no learning, just...wham! And there you were. So I'm buying you some time to get accustomed to Manna."

"You're not answering the question," said Seb.

"Ok, ok," said Walt. "According to Sonia, all the rituals for hundreds of years are about to pay off under her watch. Did you see the look on her face when you got in the way of her killing me?"

Seb thought back. "Yeah," he said, "now you mention it. She looked panicky, scared. Then when I survived, she looked pleased. Excited."

"Exactly," said Walt. "She really believes this garbage. She thinks she is Satan's High Priestess. And all the literature they've been churning out suggests they have to pass some great test before they can bring about Satan's new empire. They have to destroy all threats, prove themselves worthy. They've spent years trying to kill the most powerful users of Manna. They believe the energy released by their deaths brings Satan closer. And now all the planets are aligned - or some such bullshit - and they just need one powerful sacrifice to finish the job."

There was a long silence.

"Me?" said Seb.

"You," said Walt.

"Ah," said Seb. There was another, longer, silence. "I'm not sure exactly how I'm supposed to react to that information."

"Well," said Walt, putting an arm around the younger man's shoulders, "I suggest you forget about all that crap for a while and focus on what's truly important."

"And what's that?" said Seb.

Walt pointed at his study door. "Behind that door, along the hall and through the last door on the right is the room we left about 20 minutes ago," he said. "That room contains a jacuzzi and, if memory serves, seven naked women, by now coked off their tits, who are expecting a night of debauchery. I think it's important we don't let them down."

Seb, after a moment's reflection, decided he had to agree.

"Just one thing," said Walt. "Don't bother with the drugs."

"Didn't have you down as anti-drugs," said Seb.

"Hardly," said Walt. "Do whatever you want, whenever you like with whoever will let you, that's my motto. But you'll be wasting your time. Remember all those beers and that bourbon from earlier?" Seb nodded. "Feel drunk?" said Walt.

Seb thought about it for a second, checking his consciousness for that blurry feeling of well-being that usually accompanied his fourth or fifth drink. It wasn't there.

"You've had a hell of a day," said Walt. "Exhausted? Tired, even?"

"No," said Seb, thinking about it for the first time. He felt utterly awake, that feeling he used to get when he ran - there was a brief period after the first tough fifteen minutes when he felt like he could run forever. He felt that same endorphine-fueled heightened awareness now. He felt it all the time.

Walt watched Seb's face as he processed another change to his life. "Yeah, I know," he said. "We can feel the initial effects of alcohol or drugs, but Manna counteracts it pretty quickly. I think it's like the accelerated healing. These things are poisons, as much as I like them, and Manna flushes them away somehow. But hey, when you feel like we do when we're full of the real thing, why bother with anything else?"

"Fair point," said Seb. "So why bother with fine wine?"

"I've been using Manna a very long time," said Walt. "After a few years, I spent some time learning how to disarm its anti-drug and alcohol capabilities. I just like getting drunk too much, I guess. And I can sober up any time I like. But you have better things to do than spend time learning how to get drunk, right? Anyway," he said, putting his hand on Seb's shoulder and steering him toward the door, "there are always the pleasures of the flesh."

Walt's phone buzzed as they left the room.

"Go ahead," he said to Seb, "I'll catch up with you." He waited until Seb went through the door leading to the hot tub. The sound of giggling was briefly audible while Seb walked in.

"Yes?" said Walt. The voice at the other end delivered his update clearly and concisely. The guy in the coma had lapsed into a vegetative state. And the three professionals had all decided they weren't going to talk. Ever. Hollow teeth full of cyanide. Very old school. Very cold war.

He was about to put the phone back in the pocket of his robe when it buzzed again.

"Yes?" he snapped, before looking at the caller ID.

"Ford." The voice was familiar, although he rarely heard it. Given a choice, he would prefer never to hear it. He swallowed hard and stood up straighter.

"Sir," he said. His hand was shaking slightly. He clamped the phone more tightly against his ear.

"It would appear Mr. Varden is, as you suggested, somewhat of a prodigy. He will attract a great deal of attention. If he is to be useful to us, we must bring our plans forward. He must be convinced where his best interests lie."

"How long do I have?" said Walt.

"48 hours," said the voice. Not so much said, as *whispered.*

# Chapter 25

California's Interstate 15 is famous for nothing. And nothing pretty much sums up what you see while driving it. Scrub, desert, some bushes, the occasional cactus. The blacktop was more of a gray/brown top. Every color seemed to be leeched away, leaving only washed-out tones familiar to anyone who'd seen the desert camouflage uniform of US soldiers. Temperatures varied from 80-105 °F, so, while trying to fight the urge to sleep brought on by the monotonous view, drivers without excellent AC slowly baked in their own skins. Ford Galaxies over 40 years old with a million miles on the clock had no AC at all. Fortunately, Mee, Bob and Lo avoided most of the usual pitfalls by driving through the night. They stopped twice for fuel, coffee and pastries, then waited while Mee smoked a much-needed joint. No one spoke much during the long drive; Lo insisted on taking the wheel, Bob had the retired soldier's habit of snatching a few hours' sleep when he could and Meera surprised herself by dropping her initial plan of whisking Lo through a hundred important questions and, instead, succumbing to a sudden and unstoppable onslaught of absolute exhaustion.

Dawn was a pinky yellow of promise as they reached the outskirts of Las Vegas. The flashing lights were off, the tourists finally in bed apart from the hardy few, slack-jawed and dead-eyed, feeding quarters into the slots as the shadows lengthened outside. The early morning light made the whole place look grimy, tired and sick. Lo turned east away from the road as they neared the city limits, heading onto a dirt track that the Galaxie handled by throwing them around like rag dolls on its ancient shocks.

"Sorry," called Lo as Bob put a hand on the dash to steady himself and Mee suddenly bounced into view in the rearview mirror, makeup running, looking like an extremely surprised panda.

"Wassat? What?" said Mee. She was well known for her inability to string together words into coherent sentences until at least one joint and three cups of coffee had fired up her synapses.

"Nearly there," said Lo. Eight minutes' drive took them into rockier terrain, the landscape undulating slightly. As they rounded a corner, a trailer park of sorts hove into view. It looked like it had been there for decades, the newest of the seven trailers had probably rolled off the line circa 1977. The trailers were in a horseshoe formation, the open end of the U-shape closed by the hill it backed up against. The area behind and between the trailers was covered by faded gazebos, garden parasols and tarpaulin, all of it the color of the surrounding desert. Two motorcycles, a pickup truck and a minibus were parked to one side.

Lo brought the Galaxie to a shuddering stop about 30 feet from the nearest trailer. The three of them were silent for a moment, looking out through the dirt, dust and insect corpses caking the windshield. Eleven people stood between them and the trailers. Ten women and one man. All of them wearing cheap canvas pants and olive or tan t-shirts that looked like they'd been bought in an army surplus store. Each of them held a small purple flower. Bob thought he had seen similar flowers in the scrub of the Verdugo Mountains.

"Did you phone ahead?" he said.

"No need," said Lo, smiling. "Please give me a minute."

Without waiting for an answer she got out of the car and walked toward the line of people. When she was about ten feet away, she knelt in the dirt and leaned forward. Bob and Meera couldn't see what she was doing, but when she stood up again, she too was holding a purple flower. As she stepped forward, the group moved to meet her and then they were all hugging and laughing in turn, the delight at seeing her evident on their faces. After exchanging greetings, Lo turned and jogged back to the car. "Come on," she said, "they all want to meet you."

Bob and Meera got out of the car. Bob stopped and gently moved his left leg forwards and backward, bending it a little more each time. Walking eased the pain, but he avoided sitting down for long periods as it could become hard to bear. Sometimes, while walking upstairs, the sounds coming from his knee made him wonder how much cartilage was left and how much had been replaced by shrapnel. This had been the longest car journey he had made for a while and he knew he'd suffer for it. He put his weight on the leg carefully, then limped toward the waiting group, putting out his hand. "Bob Geller," he said. "Good to meet you folks."

Meera hung back and lit another joint. She had checked her stash in the car and calculated if she went to the extreme of limiting herself to four spliffs every 24 hours, she might make it for another five days before she would feel like tearing anyone's head off. She looked at the scene in front of her. They were hugging Bob now. She had an innate distrust of physical contact with anyone other than very close friends, partly because of her upbringing in Britain, but mostly because of some unwise relationship decisions in her teens. When the hugging had died down and a few looks were being directed toward her, Lo waved her over with a smile.

"Hi," said Meera, ambling over, arms crossed and a cloud of heady sweet smoke drifting up from the joint, "I'm Mee. I don't hug."

Introductions were made, then a matronly woman said she was going to make pancakes and coffee if they were interested. They were.

Ten minutes later, they were sitting in one of the trailers which had been converted into a communal dining area with two long tables and benches. The matronly woman - Jackie - brought the coffee first, in tin mugs with a jug of cream and bowl of sugar, coming back a few minutes later with a steaming pile of pancakes. Another jug contained warm maple syrup. There was a bowl of blueberry jelly, a platter of chopped fruit: bananas, strawberries, blueberries and grapes with a side of whipped yoghurt. There were no cooking facilities in the dining trailer - Bob assumed another trailer had been converted to serve as a kitchen. The food and coffee was fresh and amazingly good. Bob couldn't remember ever having had better pancakes and the coffee was strong and rich. Mee was equally impressed, but put it down to the fact that she hadn't had any hot food for nearly a week.

The food was consumed in near silence. Understandable from the point of view of the visitors, who were exhausted, but unusual in most social situations. Bob glanced up as he finished a fourth pancake and washed it down with the last of his coffee. Jackie came over with a refill, smiling. Then Bob really noticed it for the first time. Everyone was so damn quiet. And kind of happy looking. The weird thing was, he would expect a room full of silent smiling people to freak him out. He had once been invited to church by a lady he'd met buying groceries. He had gone along that Sunday, partly out of curiosity, more because he thought there was a chance he might get laid. They'd all smiled there. From the moment he walked in and was welcomed with smiles, all the way through the service which featured a sermon in which the young smiling preacher had expressed his support of carrying concealed weapons 'for Christ' and his great sadness that sodomites had turned their backs on Jesus and would go to hell. Smiles all the way through plates of cookies and weak coffee afterwards where he was asked at least nine times if he was saved. Smiles, smiles, smiles. Right up to the point where he'd asked his "date" if she believed in sex outside of marriage.

"Of course not," she said, primly, looking around her fellow churchgoers who gave her some smiling nods of confirmation.

"Well, that's a shame," said Bob, "since I was planning on taking you to bed this afternoon and having a great deal of sweaty, fun and downright dirty sex with you." There was a gratifyingly sharp intake of breath from the half-dozen people close enough to hear. "Two or three times at least," he said. His intended bedfellow's smile had finally slipped, but - to his surprise - Bob was sure he could see lust in her eyes behind her feigned shock.

He stepped in closer. "And I'd keep an eye on that preacher of yours," he said. "Think he was just a little too fired up about the evils of gay sex. Check his phone for a grindr account if you get the chance. Bit of rough trade last night, I wouldn't be at all surprised. And get someone to sort out the coffee, it's god-damn awful." He had left in silence, but, to his satisfaction, at least they weren't smiling any more.

The difference now seemed to be the naturalness of the smiles, of the silence. Firstly, the smiles weren't there all the time. If you met someone's eye, they smiled at you. And it was the kind of smile that reached the eyes. The silence was unstrained, natural. No one seemed to feel the need to fill it with small talk. It wasn't uncomfortable, it was accepting, warm. Bob rubbed his eyes. It had been an intense couple days. Maybe he was reading too much into a trailer-full of happy introverts. He finished his second mug of coffee and sighed.

Across the table from Bob, Mee belched contentedly. Even habitual dope-smokers still got the munchies and five loaded pancakes had certainly hit the spot. She, too, had noticed the silence. It was hard not to. But she found herself thinking about her Auntie back in Britain. Aunt Anita had first upset her Hindu grandparents by converting to Christianity, then scandalized them by becoming a Sister in a Carmelite monastery in East London. A nun in the family - or penguin, as she and her cousins used to call her, despite the fact that only the very oldest of the Sisters wore a habit. Aged 15, Meera had given in to curiosity and gone to visit Auntie Anita. She told her parents she was going shopping with friends. Second-generation Indian Londoners at that time were less suspicious of their children's acceptance of Western materialism than they would be by a sudden interest in Christianity.

Auntie Anita was Meera's favorite Aunt. She had achieved that honor by being able to listen without judging. Which meant Meera had kept telling her about her problems, all the way from injuries sustained by a toy unicorn, through school reports so awful that she doctored them before they reached her parents, all the way to that first boyfriend, a dreadlocked drug-dealer from a middle-class background called Edmund. She had always known him as Dog, until she found his passport. She had laughed, but Edmund hadn't. When Auntie Anita saw the bruises at the top of her arms (easy to hide), she advised calling the police, but she respected Meera's choice not to. A year later, Auntie had entered the convent as a novice. "I'm not dying," she told Meera, hugging her. Mee even hugged her back, crying. "Come visit," said Auntie.

Five months later, Mee had caught a bus and found the anonymous redbrick building tucked half a street away from a well-known soccer stadium. She had signed a visitor book in a room containing a formica-topped table covered in magazines like Woman's Own and Reader's Digest. Ten minutes later, Auntie Anita had swept into the room, kissed her and, taking her hand, given her 'the tour'. On Friday afternoons there was one room in the monastery - the refectory - where the sisters were permitted to talk between 2-5pm. The only time, barring emergencies, when the Sisters were permitted to speak. Auntie Anita put the kettle on.

"Three hours?" said Mee, disbelievingly. "Don't you go crazy the rest of the time?"

"That's the funny thing," said Auntie. "I thought I'd miss talking and for the first few months I really did. But I always preferred listening, really. 'Cause I'm so nosy." She pushed a mug of tea over to Meera and sat opposite her. She looked radiant, her eyes shining. Like a bride on her wedding day, Mee told her so.

"Well, that's what we are," said Auntie. "Brides of Christ."

Mee pulled a face and addressed the issue with the kind of implacable sarcasm only a teenager can pull off. "But no sex, and hardly any talking. Great marriage, that is. Sounds brilliant."

Auntie Anita refused to rise to the bait. "Well, I miss sex, certainly," she said, "I aways did enjoy it. Even after your uncle died there were a few memorable occasions."

"Auntie!" said Mee, protesting and reddening, putting her hands over her ears. I'm not listening to this filth. La la la la, I can't hear you."

Auntie Anita leaned forward and gently took Meera's hands away from her ears. "Don't be embarrassed," she said. "Sex can be wonderful at any age. But it's not the be all and end all. It was just one of the things I was prepared to give up, along with my privacy, owning any property, personal ambition -,"

"- and talking," said Mee.

"And talking," said Auntie Anita. "Which was the most difficult for me. At first. Because when I stopped talking, I had to listen to the rubbish swirling around my head every minute of every day. And it is *such* rubbish. Jealousy, envy, trivia, anger, hurt, guilt, shame, fantasies, memories, good and bad, all repeating themselves. To begin with, it was awful."

Mee sipped her tea and watched her auntie. Her body language was different somehow. Mee realized what had changed. Auntie Anita was almost completely still. She wasn't fidgeting, wasn't finding something to do. She was just sitting there. Comfortable.

"So I listened to my personal radio station," said Auntie Anita. "Day in and day out. And gradually I became aware of the silence behind it. Like the static behind a bad radio signal, I found silence behind mine. And it was the same silence that drew me here in the first place."

"And that's God, is it?" said Mee.

"To me, yes," said Auntie. "Others might call it something else, that's fine, but this is where God is for me and this is where I need to be."

Then she had shown Mee around the convent, a scrupulously clean, cold brick building with Victorian flagstones underfoot and dark green walls. The bedrooms - unnervingly called 'cells' - were tiny; a bed with a thin mattress, a washbasin, a desk and hard chair. A cross above the bed and what looked like a Russian Icon on the wall seemed to be the only decoration, until Mee looked closer and found a tiny framed photo of herself on the corner of the desk. Anita saw her looking and stroked her cheek with the back of her hand.

When Mee had said goodbye and walked back to the bus stop, she was almost overwhelmed by the frenetic activity and noise of the outside world. And as she watched the workers hurrying home, the cars honking in five solid lanes of gridlock, the blasts of music from open shop doorways, the billboards everywhere encouraging her to fit in by spending money on the right accessories, she had a sudden urge to run back to the convent. She had gone to see Auntie Anita because she missed her, but Mee had thought she was running away from the world, from real problems. Now she wasn't so sure. She sat at the back of the bus, rolled a fat spliff and stopped thinking about it.

"Another pancake?" said Jackie, bringing Mee's attention back to the present. Mee was full, but meals hadn't been regular lately and these pancakes were really good.

"Go on, then," she said, holding her plate up. Her lips twitched. It was almost a smile. Around the table, everyone else had finished eating. Some were drinking coffee or water, some were just sitting. Comfortable. As if here was where they were, there was nowhere else to be and that was that. Like Auntie Anita.

The sixth pancake turned out to be the limit. Mee looked at the women around them. The man was there, too, but he seemed to blend in. They all seemed to blend in, actually, with their khaki clothes. And their ready smiles. And their stillness.

A tall woman at the far end of the table stood up. She walked to the door. Lo followed her.

"I'm Diane," said the tall woman. "Welcome to the Order. Would you like to see the garden?"

# Chapter 26

**17 Years Previously**
**St. Benet's Children's Home, New York**

Seb spent eighteen days in the hospital after picking up an infection from the knife wound in his stomach. Father O'Hanoran told him later it had been touch and go for a few days, with Seb drifting in and out of consciousness, his face nearly as white as the starched pillowcase underneath. Seb guessed it must have been during that time that he thought he saw Melissa standing at the end of the bed. She didn't say anything, just smiled sadly at him. It couldn't have been her, there was no black eye, but Seb accepted the fever-born hallucination gratefully as his body healed. He knew his body *would* heal, of course, once they moved him from the ICU to a small ward. His mind was a different matter. As he moved into a more normal pattern of waking and sleeping, he found it impossible to rest properly. The first thing he thought of on waking, and the image that entered his mind as soon as he began to settle down to sleep was Jack Carnavon's pink-frothed lips as he exhaled for the last time. The awful, unavoidable, finality of death.

The police came during the second week, as soon as the doctors decided he was stable. Two NYPD officers, one a short Irishman in his fifties with no neck, the other a young, pretty black woman who said very little but looked at him throughout the interview with a keen, intelligent gaze. She looked like someone you wouldn't get away with lying to. Seb hoped his edited version of the truth would get past her scrutiny. He had read that liars usually over-elaborate, give too many details, remember the order in which events unfolded too accurately. There was no real danger of that in Seb's case, as his mind had evidently made the decision to recall parts of the fight with Jack in pin-point, laser-sharp slow-mo, while allowing other chunks of time to evaporate completely. Seb had decided to leave Melissa out of the story entirely. She needed to move on, and making a statement to the police about what Jack had done to her wouldn't help. At least, that was what Seb figured.

Sister Theresa sat in the corner, knitting. Every time Seb had opened his eyes during his recovery, one of the Sisters had been there, bringing him drinks, talking to him, reading or praying the rosary. Sister Theresa looked up at him as the two officers came in. He caught her glance. He wondered what she thought of him now.

The Irish cop was called Mahoney. "Yeah, just like the guy in that Police Academy movie," he said, "only not funny. Not funny at all." He shook his head slowly as if to emphasize his lack of comedic ability. He pulled a notebook out of his pocket and sat down, dragging a chair to the head of Seb's bed. He nodded at his partner, who took out a small voice recorder and placed it on the bedside table.

"Sergeant Dalney," she said, after pressing record and noting the date and time. "Witness is Sebastian Varden, aged fifteen." She looked at him and smiled. A professional, polite smile, no warmth. "Now, Sebastian, we are here for a statement about what happened on the evening of Wednesday 23$^{rd}$ September at St. Benet's. You are not under any suspicion at this point, we just need to present your evidence to the coroner. You've been through a traumatic event, we appreciate that, but we need you to co-operate fully. This will mean answering some questions that may be difficult for you."

"It's ok," said Seb. He took a drink of water. Dalney sat a bit further back form the bed and made very few further comments.

"Why were you in the attic?" said Mahoney, flicking through his notebook to find a blank page.

"I was tired, wanted to read rather than watch a movie," said Seb. "Jack had taken my book, so I needed to find him. I went up to the dorm -"

"And-," Mahoney flicked back two or three pages, "Steven Corser told you where Jack was. So, tell us, what was the fight about?"

Most of the interview was straightforward. Stevie had obviously already been interviewed, as Seb's description of Jack as volatile, violent and scary was barely challenged. If anything, Mahoney seemed bored, going through the motions. Seb thought they might have taken fingerprints from the knife and found only Jack's. He told them the fight was about him not accepting Jack as the boss, said he'd challenged him, called him a bully, said he was just a coward. He admitted making the first move. He told them the truth about pushing Jack and dislocating his shoulder, he mentioned the cut on the back of Jack's leg. Mahoney kept flicking back in his notes and checking. Seb told him that after being stabbed in the stomach, he had fallen. That was when Jack had come after him, said he was going to kill him. He stuck to the truth about what happened next. He described Jack trying to stab his throat, how he pushed Jack's hands away. Then how Jack had rolled away from him and he had seen the knife in Jack's stomach. How he pulled it out. The way the blood spurted.

"And what did you do? Said Mahoney.

"I called to Stevie to get some help," said Seb.

"Right after Jack pulled the knife out of his stomach?" said Mahoney. Seb hesitated. He was aware of

Dalney shifting forward slightly in her chair. Mahoney still held the notebook but wasn't looking at it. The sunlight was edging across the room and had caught his badge, making spots of reflected light dance on the ceiling.

"I passed out for a while," said Seb, frowning. "But I called out as soon as I could."

Dalney spoke then. "Was Jack Carnavon still alive when you called for help, Sebastian?" In the pause that followed her question, the only sound was the gentle *clack* of Sister Theresa's knitting needles.

"I think so," said Seb, finally. "But I can't be completely sure. I'm sorry."

Mahoney was already closing his notebook. He stood up and glanced over at his partner. Dalney hadn't moved, her clear brown eyes still focused on Seb.

"Carnavon was a mean piece of work, one of the worst," she said. "And he was trying to kill you. No one would blame you for waiting a while before calling." She leaned forward a fraction. "Is that what happened, Sebastian?"

Seb looked up at the ceiling. The light had edged in a little further and tiny motes of dust danced under the smoke alarm.

"No," he said. "I passed out. When I woke up, I shouted for Stevie." Office Dalney hesitated, then blinked slowly and stood up. She joined Mahoney at the door.

"Bad things happen, kid," said Mahoney. "Don't beat yourself up about it." As the door closed behind them, Seb noticed that Sister Theresa had finally stopped knitting.

The New York Office of Chief Medical Officer ruled there was insufficient evidence to implicate any other party in the matter of Jack Carnavon's death. Since Jack had no traceable family and any reporters following up the story were unable to get past the perpetually cheerful but incredibly vague Sister Margaret who handled all their enquiries, the incident was quickly forgotten. Or rather, it was forgotten outside the walls of St. Benet's. Inside, the boys got over the initial shock and took an unspoken decision to act as if it had never happened. Seb received a few handshakes or brief hugs from boys who managed to find him alone, but *en masse* everyone behaved as if Jack Carnavon had never set foot in the building.

Seb had no way of knowing what anyone else was thinking or feeling, but for him, the weeks following his return from hospital were the worst of his young life. He knew he wasn't a murderer, but it didn't stop him feeling like one. It was unlikely that Jack would have survived had he called for help immediately, but it wasn't impossible. And, more importantly, the responsibility would have been taken away from him if he had shouted for Stevie. It was the only thing he could have done that might have prevented Jack's death. He had chosen not to do it. And in the philosophy school book he kept going back to, turning to the same page every time, like a tongue worrying the exposed nerve of a rotten tooth, he kept reading the same quote over and over.

"A person may cause evil to others not only by his actions but by his inaction, and in either case he is justly accountable to them for the injury." John Stuart Mill.

Seb decided to talk to Father O.

Father O'Hanoran was an energetic man in his early sixties. He taught English at the school attached to St. Benet's, and was passionate about literature and poetry. His enthusiasm for his subject was such that it had an effect even on those boys who were barely literate when first arriving. Almost everyone taught by him would come to the realization, in later life, that they had been one of a lucky few to experience an exceptional teacher. Apart from his passion for his subject, he also had an undefinable quality - a kind of inner stillness - which bled out into the atmosphere around him. If he set a piece of written work to be completed in the classroom, he would first describe what it was he wanted, then he would sit down and wait for his pupils to complete the task. He didn't read while he waited, he didn't grade papers, he didn't daydream. He was just there. Present. And just his *being there-ness* had a palpable effect on the class. Difficult concepts seemed to become transparent, sentences flowed almost of their own volition, inspiration seemed available even to those who admitted freely to lacking much imagination. He was a pebble thrown into a pond - the ripples would reach you whether you were expecting them or not.

Seb knocked on his office door late one Saturday.

"Enter," said the familiar voice from within. Seb pushed open the door and negotiated the piles of books to find the desk at the far end of the room. The desk was made of heavy, polished mahogany, although it was impossible to see the wood as every square inch was covered in books or papers. The man behind the desk was reading poems by Gerard Manly Hopkins. Father O was the only person Seb had met who read poetry for pleasure. About a year previously, shyly at first, Seb had started doing the same thing.

Father O put the book down and gestured toward the chair opposite. Seb sat, unsure how to begin. The priest removed his reading glasses and rubbed his face, sighing. He pointed at the book.

"Burnt every poem he had written when he entered the priesthood," he said. "He wrote some beautiful stuff later, don't get me wrong, but why would he want to deny his past? He wouldn't have been the man he was without the experiences he wrote about when he was young. None of us would be." He looked up at Seb. "It's ok," he said. "Tell me."

So Seb told him. Everything. He didn't give Melissa's name and Father O didn't ask, but he told him what Jack had done. He told him what Jack had promised he would do next. He told him what had really happened to Stevie. He told him how Jack had stabbed him in the trunk room. Not just stabbed him, but dragged the knife across his stomach, trying to inflict as much damage as possible. He told him how he had defended himself against Jack's final attack. And, finally, he told him how he had let Jack Carnavon die there, in front of him, waiting until he was sure the boy was dead before calling for help.

Father O'Hanoran's expression didn't change throughout. He listened intently, compassionately, but didn't offer any platitudes or words of condemnation. He just let Seb talk. Seb felt his burden of guilt increase rather than lift as he finally told the truth. Father O was a good man. What did Seb expect from him? Forgiveness? He couldn't even forgive himself. How could he expect it from anyone else? Finally, he ran out of things to say. He had laid out his guilt. Now he waited.

Father O sat still for minutes, his eyes closed. Initially, Seb was shaking, but as time went by he became calmer, his breathing returning to normal. The facts were the facts, nothing could change that. But he couldn't carry on like this.

"Have you ever experienced the presence of God?" were Father O's first words after ten minutes silence. Seb felt his mood drop even further. Was that where this was heading? A religious lecture? He felt a spark of defiance rise up as he reached the limits of desperation.

"I'm not sure I even believe in God, Father," he said. Father O didn't react, just looked at him, his expression, kind, concerned but still completely calm.

"Well, for now, let me just posit two possible hypotheses," said the priest. Many boys rolled their eyes when he started speaking like this in the classroom, but Seb usually felt a secret thrill hearing someone use language imaginatively. Now didn't quite seem the appropriate time, but Father O was Father O, and he wasn't about to change his style of communication to pander to the miserable boy sat opposite. "Firstly, can you accept that the God you don't believe in doesn't exist?"

Seb let that one whirl around his forebrain for a few seconds, then nodded cautiously.

"Good. Secondly, would you find my initial question easier to ponder if I substituted the word 'reality' for the one you currently find troublesome? Like so: have you ever experienced the presence of reality, Seb?"

Seb caught himself before he went with the impulse to respond immediately in the affirmative. Again, Father O's conversational teaching style was at play here. Socratic dialogue; by asking questions, he hoped to help his interlocutor reach the logical conclusion by answering them fairly. As soon as Seb gave the question more than a brief examination, he found it wasn't quite that simple.

"Um, it depends what you mean by reality," he said.

"How so?" said Father O.

"Well, er, what you experience might be different to me. I could never know really."

Father O nodded. "And?"

"And if we can't agree on what reality *is*, I can't really say I've experienced it."

Father O leaned back, the old leather chair creaking under his weight. "Yes," he said, "quite. And much food for thought there. A couple thousand years of academic discourse hasn't solved that one yet. Let's make this a little more pertinent. To experience reality - whatever that might be - purely, would we not have to do so without preconceptions, opinions? Without filters - both cultural and personal?"

Seb thought again. "But how can we do that?"

"We can't," said Father O, and laughed. Loudly.

""Big help," muttered Seb, but Father O just smiled and leaned forward.

"Seb," he said, "I want to teach you a technique which will help you experience reality. This technique will not help you to achieve anything. You will never improve at it, because you are already perfect. But it's the work of a lifetime."

Seb looked blankly at him. "You're not making sense," he said.

"Good!" said Father O. "This has very little to do with what our societal consensus would accept as sense. However, I believe it's the calling of every human being."

Seb narrowed his eyes. "Is this some Catholic religious thing?" he said.

Father O sighed. "Religion is often a beautiful thing, but it can also be a monster," he said. "Don't think of it as a corrupt institution, however accurate that might be. Try thinking of it as a scaffold around the Truth. Sometimes it can be helpful, sometimes it obscures what it professes to reveal. Perhaps Truth, Reality, God, is ungraspable by human minds. Perhaps we can only be grasped by it. Don't get caught up in the chatter and the display, Seb. It's what's underneath that matters. I, personally, have found my vocation helpful in approaching this Mystery, but that doesn't mean it's right for you. You could equally be a Buddhist, Hindu, Moslem, Atheist. It's all just words. And what I want to pass on to you cannot be taught, only learned. Without words."

"How the hell did you get into priest school?" said Seb. Father O stared it him for a few seconds. Then he laughed uproariously and stood up.

"Seb, you're a good person. What you did was wrong. That particular combination will shape your future. But the past is dead. I don't mean to diminish the seriousness of what happened. You rightly feel remorse and I don't think what has happened will ever leave you. I certainly hope not. It will become part of you. And, whatever you believe, God's forgiveness is greater than any human mind can conceive. They taught me that at priest school." He winked at Seb. "Now go and get some sleep. Be here at 6:15 tomorrow morning."

# Chapter 27

**New York**
**Present day**

The penthouse suite of Manhattan's Keystone Hotel was furnished in such a way that suggested good taste while simultaneously making it obvious only the insanely rich could afford to stay there. There was only one suite on the top floor, a private elevator coded to respond to the thumb print of the current occupant the only way in. Sonia Svetlana was the current occupant, but even the Keystone's paranoid precautions to ensure privacy weren't enough for her. She rented the entire hotel for a year paid in advance. The owner, a career woman who had quietly built one of the biggest property empires in the country, had barely raised an eyebrow when the offer was made. A week later, all but six of the hotel staff left on 12-month sabbaticals, their bonuses generous enough to ensure none of them would have to work until their return.

The Acolytes of Satan moved in the day after the staff cleared the building. Sonia was always amused by the way Americans reacted to the name of her organization. Most assumed it was some kind of European fashion brand, as Sonia's outfits were always handmade. Some thought it must be a death metal band. On one memorable occasion, a conference room had been booked under the name *The acrobats of Santa.* Sonia, often suspected of having no sense of humor, liked to think her response on that occasion proved otherwise. She had only blinded the booking manager in one eye. Actually, the name was the idea of her predecessor, Magnus, possibly his only good idea. He called it 'hiding in plain sight' and his hunch proved to be absolutely correct.

"Call ourselves the Deltox Corporation or some such nonsense and we're heading for a fall," he said. "If there's ever a whiff of scandal, a whisper about what really goes on in our board meetings, the media will be all over us. But tell them we believe in the devil and we'll be laughed at, shunned, but never taken seriously. Put up a website, release a quarterly newsletter with small ads selling wizards' cloaks and cauldrons and we'll be dismissed as harmless eccentrics from the old country."

So that's what they'd done. And it had worked just the way Magnus had said it would. They had only ever received one letter from the US Government, and that was to remind them that, as a religious organization, they were entitled to register themselves as a charity and claim tax breaks.

After deposing Magnus in a fashion gory enough to discourage any challengers for the foreseeable future, Sonia had implemented the Light-bringer Initiative. The Initiative was simple, brutal and effective: a systematic wiping out of Manna users powerful enough to present a threat to the Acolytes. There were very few names on the list she compiled. Most Users were barely aware of the potential of their abilities. The Acolytes' successful operations in Australia, Germany and Japan were the culmination of five years of hard work, identifying, infiltrating and finding the weaknesses of these powerful individuals. A month ago, there was only one name left on the list, and a name was still all they had. Mason. Their adversary here had proved to be so obsessively secretive that he was virtually invisible. But if the prophecies were to be fulfilled and Satan returned to his rightful place of power, he would have to be found and sacrificed. So the Acolytes had decamped to America and taken over the Keystone, as the only slight lead they'd found suggested New York was where they'd find Mason. Then, just under a week ago, everything had changed.

Sonia had been awake when it happened, checking on the health of her collection. The collection currently consisted of five young men between the ages 19-24. Half of the penthouse suite had been cleared of furniture, the only decoration now a huge five-pointed star on the floor. At each point of the star stood a wooden X, made up of two thick oak beams eight feet long. The men were tied spreadeagled to these crosses. They were upside-down, gagged, their ankles and wrists tied firmly in place. Their bodies had, over the three days they had been suspended, lost their original color and taken on a gray-white, sickly hue. Under each of their wrists was a drainpipe. When she bled them, their blood was carefully channelled, joining where the system of drainpipes met, gradually filling a clay jug thought to be thousands of years old.

Blood from living sacrifices was considered essential by the Acolytes. Sonia painted the ancient symbols onto her naked body with the freshest blood available, conducting arcane rituals passed down over many centuries. Standing in the center of the pentangle, feeling the terror of the dying men around her, always produced a thrill. The sacrifices were kept alive as long as possible by attending to their essential needs, but only the strongest survived more than 72 hours. As the rituals took place every full moon, a constant supply was needed. New York had turned out to be one of the easier places to find victims, one of many points in its favor, which included good connections by air and excellent sushi. All in all, Sonia was feeling content and confident. They would find Mason, it was just a matter of time.

That night, as she neared the end of the ritual, she suddenly felt the skin of her scalp prickle and a hum begin in her brain. It was like a powerful machine starting up. Among the Acolytes, she had always been the most sensitive. She had felt it before, whenever she was in a hundred miles of someone using Manna on a large scale. This felt different. The engine in her brain screamed with energy and she dropped to her knees. The intensity was greater than anything she'd yet experienced. She knew immediately that this was new, a new User, someone more powerful than anyone the Acolytes had yet encountered. Alongside her shock - and the pain caused by the sudden awareness - she felt the thrill of knowing this individual was undoubtedly the most powerful User in the country, maybe even the planet. Mason could wait. She would need to follow the trace to its source.

An hour later, she knelt in absolute stillness as the last inverted man twitched and became still. She had followed the threads of awareness from the machine in her head toward the burst of Manna that had started it. As her eyes opened, she gasped. Because of the strength of the sensation, she had assumed the User was a block or two away, no more. But she was wrong. He - and it was definitely a *he* - was more than 2,000 miles away.

That evening, she and three senior Acolytes boarded a plane to Los Angeles. From there, she picked up their quarry's trail and left for Las Vegas. Sonia's encounter with the man in the casino was both the most humbling and the most exciting of her life. He had survived. Not just defeating the team of experts they had used to capture him, but her Manna-fueled onslaught. She had returned to New York thoughtful and focused. It was going to take more than just her power to destroy him. But she would destroy him. She would harness the combined power of all the Acolytes with her if necessary. Mason could wait. She had encountered the most powerful User in recorded history. Surely this would be enough to summon her master. And, thanks to a candid photograph taken in the Casino, she now had a name for the final sacrifice: Sebastian Varden.

# Chapter 28

**Las Vegas**

The garden turned out to be the patch of ground hemmed in by the horseshoe of trailers. Mee just stood and stared. Bob was startled by the incongruity for a second, then his military training kicked in and his gaze swept the area, first left to right, then up. In his army days, he would have been looking for entrances, exits. Checking for vulnerabilities, weak points - useful knowledge for both defenders and attackers. His military brain analyzed the information - because of the rocky hill it backed onto, the only way in or out of the garden was through the back door of any one of the seven trailers. From the north, south or west, it was hidden by the way the trailers were arranged. From the east, the rocky scree-sided hill blocked the view. Which left above. And dozens of umbrellas, parasols, gazebos and various faded pieces of material covered the entire area. From above, from a plane or helicopter, the whole place would be effectively camouflaged. But why would you want to hide a garden? Bob cleared his throat.

"Why would you want to hide a g-," he said. Then he stopped using his training and looked properly for the first time. Because of the total shade provided by the makeshift cover, the garden never saw any sunlight. Bob was no horticulturalist, but he knew enough to work out that total lack of sunlight would prevent photosynthesis. In other words, nothing could grow. And yet what he was looking at wouldn't have looked out of place in the finals of some community gardening competition. Every shade of green was on display, plus orange, purple, white, yellow, reds peeping through at intervals between the lush canopy. Bob recognized some thin leafy tendrils pointing out of the rich, dark soil near him. They were carrots, he knew that. Where the hell did rich, dark soil come from in a desert?

The woman who'd introduced herself as Diane laughed openly and goodnaturedly at the bewildered expressions on the faces of Mee and Bob.

"We forget how it feels, seeing it for the first time," she said. She walked down a grassed pathway, which neatly bisected the space before branching off in both directions to allow access to other areas of the garden. Mee hung back a little, her brain whirring with questions. Bob walked at Diane's side. He was a practical man and he was struggling with the events of the previous 48 hours. A friend had died, come back to life and moved at inhuman speed. His beautiful dog had been cruelly killed. And now he, Mee and Seb were being pursued by some kind of ruthless secret military unit, probably with the knowledge and funding of the government. And one word was on his mind, begging to be spoken. He gave in to the pressure.

"Irrigation!" he said. Diane lifted an eyebrow.

"How do you do it?" he said. "You don't have a single channel cut into the dirt here, no hosepipes coming from the trailers. And it would take gallons every day to keep this going. I saw carrots. What else do you have growing here?"

Diane thought for a moment.

"As far as I remember," she said, "we have onions, garlic, shallots, leeks, peas, zucchini, eggplant, cabbage, broccoli, bok choi, cilantro, celery, lettuce, chicory, artichokes, tomatoes, peppers, soybeans and lentils."

"Not bad," said Bob, "considering they're not getting water. Or sunlight." He stopped. There was something that had been bugging him, now he knew what it was. Underneath the canopy, the entire garden should have been dark, but it wasn't. Somehow it was being lit, but not by any kind of lighting Bob was familiar with. No one area was brighter than another and the overall effect was that of mid-afternoon sunlight. He checked for the source of it but came up empty. No light bulbs, no lamps, no nothing. Whatever technology was at play here, every gardener in the world would want it.

At the center of the garden was a section that had been allowed to retain its native quality - that of dry, thin, dusty soil. There were pebbles strewn across it. As Bob and Meera got closer, what seemed random at first revealed itself to be words, spelled out by careful placement of hundreds of small stones.

μαθαίνουν διδάσκω περιμένετε

"Greek?" said Mee. Bob turned and looked at her.

"You're full of surprises," he said. "What does it say?"

Mee wrinkled up her nose.

"I know what Greek looks like," she said, "but I wouldn't have the first clue what it says."

Diane turned to face them.

"Learn, teach, wait," she said. "It's what we try to live by."

"Is that it?" said Mee. "No big holy book?"

"No," said Diane. "No book."

"Not even a leaflet?" said Mee. Diane shook her head.

"Website? Social media?"

"No," said Diane. Mee considered for a moment.

"Now I'm confused," she said. "You're some kind of religious community, right?"

"That's as good a description as any," said Diane.

"So people join you, right? Become part of the community?"

"Yes they do," said Diane.

"But you have no books in the stores, no leaflets and no online presence at all. So how come you haven't died out? How long have you people been going? How many of you are there? And why have I never heard of you?"

"Let's sit down," said Diane. The grass was dry, the earth beneath yielding and comfortable.

"The Order is a very private community," she said. "Private, not secretive. It started between 1700-1800 years ago in the Middle East. Our founder was a hermit who devoted his or her life to discovering the nature of reality as experienced by humans. We don't know for sure whether it was a man or a woman. It's certainly unimportant. But most anecdotal accounts speak of a man, so that's the pronoun I'll use. He didn't follow any particular wisdom tradition, although it is very likely that he would have been influenced by Buddhism, Hinduism and, possibly, early Christianity, which was going through quite an upheaval at that time."

"In what sense?" said Bob.

"Well, it had been adopted as the official state religion by the Roman Emperor Constantine," said Diane. "A mixed blessing, at best. It probably ensured the survival of Christianity as a religion, but the compromises involved split the early church. There was a very strong movement by zealous followers away from the watered-down version - as they saw it. Thousands of them moved into the deserts. Small communities sprang up. Some went further and sought absolute solitude."

"And your founder was one of them?"

"In a way, yes, we believe so. But not as a Christian. Just as a hermit, a holy man, an ascetic. He spent many years alone before having some kind of experience, a vision of sorts, after which he left his cave and began to travel. During this time, he would camp just outside settlements and wait. He might remain there for a few months, during which time, local people would seek him out for spiritual guidance. Some would stay. He would move on and leave them to continue practicing what he taught."

Mee took off her sneakers and scrunched fresh grass between her toes.

"He did this for five or six years before his death," said Diane. "His followers simply kept up his work. As each community grew, one or two would feel called to move on. They did as our founder did, camped outside town limits and waited."

She waved an arm in front of her, indicating the garden and trailers.

"That's how this community began," she said, "back in 1953."

"So people come to you?" said Mee.

"Yes," said Diane. "Searchers of a certain kind always find us in the end. Some stay, some move on."

"How many of you are there?" said Bob. Diane seemed to consider for a moment. Whether it was a question she didn't want to answer or just one she didn't have a ready figure for wasn't clear.

"There are small communities near about 50 towns or cities in the US," she said. "I'd imagine there are a few thousand of us in this country." She hesitated for a moment, as if unsure how much information she could divulge. Then she took a short breath and continued. "As far as I'm aware, every country in the world has at least one community," she said. "Europe has many more members of the Order than we do in the States. But we've always been a very small organization."

Mee stood up, stretching like a cat. A low bell rang outside one of the trailers.

"Meditation," said Diane. "Thirty minutes. Please join us if you wish."

The others had started to emerge from the trailers, all carrying either a small cushion or what looked like a wooden step. They walked up the path and sat down. The wooden steps turned out to be seats designed to help you kneel comfortably for a long period, your legs tucked underneath. A couple of people had brought spare cushions or seats, offering them to Bob and Meera. Mee hesitated, then - to Bob's surprise - nodded and accepted a wooden stool. Bob stood and winced, rubbing his knee ruefully.

"I'll take a rain check," he said. Lo, settling on a cushion, looked up at him.

"Try a walking meditation," she said. "Walk as slowly as you can, aware of each step. Breath normally."

Bob shook his head. "Think I'm a bit old for this kind of thing," he said, "and you're not gonna catch me chanting. Sorry."

Lo held his gaze. "No chanting," she said, "no ritual. Think of it as a scientific experiment. Your only job is to observe."

"Observe what?" said Bob. "The garden?"

"Of course," said Lo, chuckling, "but not just that. Your thoughts, too. Just be aware of them. Don't judge them, don't push them away. Just acknowledge each thought when you become aware of it, then gently go back to walking. And breathing."

"No mumbo-jumbo?" said Bob.

"No mumbo-jumbo," said Lo.

"Ok," said Bob. "30 minutes walking meditation.
More like limping meditation, though."

He walked away from the seated group until he got
to the perimeter of the garden. A narrower grass path ran
around the entire space. He looked back at the seated
group. Some had eyes shut, some open. The silence had
deepened quickly and perceptibly. He heard the distant cry
of some kind of mountain cat, the call of a bird and an
answer from its mate, the chirp of insects and the whisper
of wind through scrub and across dust. He put his right
foot forward. Slowly. Then his left. Then the right again. He
felt a bit of a fool for the first five minutes, then decided to
try it properly. In amongst this Eden-like lushness, in the
presence of members of an ancient religious organization
who'd probably been doing this for thousands of years, he
walked slowly around their garden. At first, it was physically
and mentally difficult. His knee was still sending jabs of pain
back to his brain and his brain was slotting those regular
jabs into a cycling nightmare cluster of uncontrollable
thoughts, memories, images. Marcie in a pool of blood...the
moment in Iraq when he had realized he was lying down
when a second before he'd been standing...his daughter Kim
slamming the door...Marcie as a puppy...Seb lying dead in a
clearing...calling Kim's number and listening to the phone
ring and ring...looking down at his ruined knee and not
knowing which shreds of skin and bone were his and which
were Tom's...Seb running like a deer on steroids...Marcie.

Bob stopped on the path and shook his head, trying
to clear it. He looked at his watch. Four minutes had passed.
It had seemed like forty. Bob took a couple of deep breaths.
He wasn't a quitter. He put his right foot onto the grass,
then slowly brought the left in front of it. Before his foot
had touched the grass, he saw Marcie again, dead. This time,

he didn't flinch away, he just silently acknowledged the thought currently lodged in his brain. Emotions flickered through him - rage, guilt, despair, hope, love, rage again. He started to fantasize about tracking Marcie's killer, trapping him up in the mountains. Putting a bullet through his leg, then following the trail of blood so he could finish him. With a hunting knife. He recoiled with horror from the images welling up inside him, then he remembered not to judge his thoughts. And he tried. It was pretty much impossible. But - finally - he managed to return his attention to the walk. Left foot. Right foot. The images kept coming, the thoughts kept swirling. Left foot. Right foot. Eventually he found a rhythm. The thoughts started to seem less important. Still there, just without the fullscreen, surround sound treatment. He walked on.

The bell sounded again. Bob stood still and looked toward the center of the garden where people were stirring, picking up cushions and stools, returning them to the trailers. He realized he had lost track of time completely - it could have been sixty seconds or sixty minutes since he'd looked at his watch. Perhaps there was something in this stuff after all. He wasn't sure what, exactly, but something.

Mee sat still for a few more minutes before getting up. For her, the only shock about the last thirty minutes was how natural it seemed. Like coming home. She thought she might begin to understand what Auntie Anita was talking about. Then again, Auntie Anita wasn't as screwed up as her. And she didn't have a dope habit. And she didn't sing rock music. So, Auntie could be the nun of the family - Mee would do what she was best at.

They spent the afternoon catching up on some sleep. Mee closed her eyes as soon as her head hit the pillow. In the next trailer, Bob lay awake for nearly an hour, going over the last few days in his mind. None of it made much sense. The guys who threatened them - and killed Marcie - were obviously extremely dangerous. Still, Bob had to admit he felt more alive than he had at any point during the last 20 years. The last thought in his mind before he finally succumbed to sleep was, "No stove in this trailer either."

That evening, after a simple but delicious vegetable stew, Diane and Lo took them back into the garden. This time they went into a corner, where the lush grass was replaced by the native earth of the desert. Before anyone spoke, Diane and Lo exchanged a long look, as if they were still weighing the consequences of what they were thinking of doing. Finally, Lo nodded slightly, the two of them smiled and Diane sighed before turning to Bob and Meera.

"What I'm about to tell you rarely gets spoken about outside the Order," she said. "When someone joins us, they have usually reached a developmental stage which means they are open to understanding what we do. And why we do it. We would usually only share this information with members of our community." She stopped, seemed unsure how best to continue, then sat in the dirt and invited Lo, Bob and Meera to do the same. The women sat beside her but Bob shook his head.

"Bad knee," he said, "and today's been tough on it. Sorry."

"I understand," said Diane. "Before I go on, it might be easier if I show you something." She looked at them soberly. Bob nodded, Mee said nothing.

Diane put the palm of her hand on the ground. Her breath was slow and deep. Bringing her other hand forward, she dug her fingers into the earth, scooping a handful of soil between her palms. Bob was impressed by what he assumed was the sheer physical strength of the woman - the dirt was hard-packed, solid. Then she molded the earth slightly as if it was clay. Mee moved closer, her eyes widening. Where there had been browns, grays, yellow, suddenly there was a luscious polished red and a little deep green. Something was taking shape in Diane's hands. Mee couldn't find a way to process what was happening in front of her. Bob, having grown up in the 50s and 60s, was reminded immediately of the TV his father had kept in the den. It never had a clear picture when first turned on. Saturday mornings Bob had to tune the dial to find The Lone Ranger. At first it seemed nothing was there in the snowstorm of swirling pixels, then within a second or two, a picture would emerge; just a hint at first, then blacks and whites, some definition, then - suddenly - there was the mask, the hat, the horse as if they had been hiding in there the whole time. It was the same now. First, dirt - unformed, then a hint of something different, swirling pixels then suddenly this. An apple. As if it had always been there. Juicy, red and green, shining, like it had just been plucked from a branch. Diane held it toward Bob.

"Try it," she said.

He took the apple, half expecting it to have no more solidity than smoke. He hadn't taken his eyes off Diane's hands. He knew this was no magic trick. It felt like a apple. He sniffed it. It smelled like an apple. He took a bite and chewed the crisp juicy flesh, a burst of freshness on his tongue.

"Best damn apple I ever tasted," he said and handed it to Meera. She didn't hesitate, just took a huge bite and chewed contentedly.

"Not half bad," she said. "You know that town you're camped outside? The big shiny place with a sign saying Las Vegas? Well, they have shows. Big shows. With a bit of work, you could have a residency and a TV special.

Might have to work on the act a little, though. Apples won't cut it. I'm thinking tigers. Maybe elephants."

Diane laughed. "I wouldn't be the first to turn it into a parlor trick," she said.

"OK, spill. How did you do that?" said Bob. He crouched beside them then regretted it as a jab of pain speared his knee. "Shit," he said, which suddenly felt weirdly inappropriate. Like swearing in church. "Sorry," he said. "Like I said, tough day."

Lo took his hand and looked at him. He started to say something then stopped. She reached forward with her other hand and held her palm over his knee. Almost immediately he felt a wave of heat, as if he had spilled hot soup on his pants. Lo didn't look away from him. He looked back at her, a slight, pretty, Asian woman who appeared to be about thirty but seemed much older. The heat in his knee flared briefly then was gone. As was the pain. Completely. As if it had never been. He stood up again. Flexed his knee. Walked a few steps, then broke into a jog for the sheer hell of it. Pain-free for the first time in more than a decade. When he got back to the seated group of women, he was laughing. He sat down beside them.

"If you didn't have my attention before, you know you do now," he said. "What just happened? Why did you rescue us? And what's your interest in Seb?"

# Chapter 29

Diane looked at Meera and Bob, hesitating. Her reluctance to speak was unfeigned. She closed her eyes and took a deep breath.

"The Order is based on orthopraxy rather than orthodoxy," she said.

"Woah," said Meera. "Small words. I'm from Brixton."

"Orthodoxy means 'right teaching', orthopraxy means 'right practice'. Our founder had already seen the way religious traditions inevitably became corrupted. Even if their followers had the best intentions, arguments would break out over interpretations...look at Christianity. Started to fracture around the time of Constantine, officially divided in the eleventh century, then the Roman church split again in the Reformation. Now there are around 40,000 denominations. And they all believe they are right, or - at the very least - closer to the truth than the rest. Our founder foresaw this inevitability and decided there would be no belief system, nothing written down. Well, almost nothing. You've already read our equivalent of the Bible."

"We have?" said Bob.

"Three greek words," said Lo, pointing to the center of the garden. "Not written in stone. Written in stones, though." Mee thought this might be an attempt at a joke, but, as she wasn't sure, she kept her mouth shut.

"Learn, teach, wait," said Diane, "in that order. When we join the Order, we learn. Not by reading a book or listening to sermons, but by meditating. And meditation is just a grand word for 'paying attention' or 'being awake'. That's all it is. But practice is a lifetime's work and it's never finished. There's no goal, just what's in front of you here, now."

Lo leaned forward. Bob noticed that no one seemed to interrupt or speak over anyone else. Considering they were silent the majority of the time, when they did speak, it was with a surprising accomplished rhythm.

"Teaching is the easy part," said Lo. "We just pass on the practice of meditation and as newer members start to develop a more unitive consciousness, we teach them how to use Manna."

"Which is what, exactly?" said Bob.

"The world is full of places of power" said Lo. "Have you heard of ley lines? Thin places?"

"Nope," said Mee. "Well ley lines, yes. New-agey bullshit. I should warn you, I'm a cynic. The apple thing was cool, and Bob seems as happy as a dog with two dicks - "

Bob started to say something, but Mee held up her hand to stop him.

"I'm sure your knee feels better," she said, "but it's probably psychosomatic, sorry." She turned toward Diane and Lo. "Look," she said, "I'm just saying if you start on that tarot cards, reiki and cosmic ordering horseshit, I'm outta here. JESUS!"

Bob jumped as Mee sprang to her feet and backed away a few steps, staring open-mouthed at Lo. Bob looked too and felt his mouth go dry. Lo had gone. In her place was - seemingly - Meera's twin sister. But whereas a twin is always subtly different, this verso of Mee was a perfect replica, down to the hint of mockery always perceptible in those deep brown eyes.

"Sit down," said Lo and as Bob and Mee both stared, her features melted back to become her own again. Mee swallowed hard and sat down heavily.

"I'm sorry to have to scare you like that," said Lo, "but we need you to listen and believe us. It's not horseshit, Meera."

Meera nodded, dumbly. "Yeah yeah," she said. "Ok. I kinda got that."

Once Meera was breathing normally, Diane spoke again.

" 'Thin places' is how the ancient Celts described places where God seemed closest," she said. "And when I say the word God, feel free to substitute 'reality', 'the ground of all being', 'great spirit' or 'emptiness', whatever feels right. We don't use the word 'God' because the amount of cultural baggage it caries makes it next to useless. Our experience of reality means we just don't recognize the concept a theist believes in or an atheist dismisses. We prefer to acknowledge Mystery with silence."

"Clever way to avoid arguments," said Mee.

"Perhaps," said Diane. "But most people have felt Mystery somewhere. Often in nature - forests or mountains, sometimes in very old buildings given over to prayer or meditation. In some European countries, druids built stone circles around the thinnest places and tried to soak up or use the power they felt buried there. Our founder told us to seek out these places, he taught us that Manna can be found there. There is a thin place only a few miles from here. We visit it regularly. All users of Manna have to. It's as important as food, water, or sleep to us."

She turned to Mee. "What Lo did to Bob's leg wasn't psychosomatic," she said. "Could you show us, Bob?"

Bob rolled up his pant leg and stared down at his knee. No scarring, just smooth skin. No hint of the land mine damage that had given him pain and a limp since Iraq in the early nineties. He grinned. "If I hadn't seen it myself..." he said.

Mee grunted. "It's really healed?" she said. Bob just nodded, tears suddenly and unexpectedly in his eyes.

"It's part of what we do," said Diane. "We use Manna to heal. We also use it to feed the hungry. Every night we supply soup kitchens with hot, healthy food. The garden supplies most of the vegetables - a little help from Manna keeps it producing healthy crops all year round. Everything else we supply in the same way I produced the apple."

Meera thought back. "So, the food you've served us here? The pancakes?"

"That's right," said Diane. "No eggs, no milk. Nothing but dirt and Manna."

"Guess that explains the thing with the stoves," said Bob. "I kept wondering why you didn't have any."

"Decent tasting dirt," said Meera. "So, you can grow magic food and heal the sick. Why don't you do something with that? Plenty of hungry, sick people in the world. Why are you sitting here on your arse when you could be doing some good?" She sat back on her heels and glared - a facial expression that had rattled people twice her size in the past. It didn't seem to have any discernible effect on the two annoyingly calm women seated in front of her. She snorted in an attempt to disguise her surprise at their composure, then stood up and paced restlessly.

Lo stood up and spoke gently.

"That's exactly what we *do* do, Meera," she said. Every night, one of us makes the run around the soup kitchens and shelters in Las Vegas, delivering food to those who need it most."

"We help the sick, too," said Diane. "We visit hospitals, or sometimes just sit in Emergency Rooms for a shift. We do what we can, but we do it without drawing attention. We wouldn't ordinarily do anything as obvious as removing microscopic particles of shrapnel from a knee, then growing new, healthy tissue to mend the damage. Questions would be asked. The media would love a story like that. Occasionally, we've been careless and a healing story gets out."

"All those miraculous cancer remissions? Disappearing tumors?" said Bob.

"Yes," said Lo, taking Meera's hand and gently pulling her down to sit with them. "Luckily, the human brain is hard-wired to provide explanations when presented with insufficient data, so no one has ever come looking for us."

"Carrot juice every morning?" said Mee.

"The power of prayer?" said Bob.

"Amongst others," said Diane. "There are so few of us that we can only make a tiny contribution toward the alleviation of hunger and sickness, but we do what we can."

"Many of the so-called witches burned alive in the seventieth century were members of the Order who'd got a little careless," said Lo.

"People fear what they don't understand," said Diane. "It's a cliche for a reason."

Mee fidgeted a little. "So Manna is what? Magic?" she said, her mistrust still obvious in the tone of her voice.

"Many Users think so," said Diane. "The Order has been far more hesitant about labeling it, although there is speculation even among us. We are taught to think of it as a natural resource. Just one that is little known or understood. We had no way of comprehending what it is we were encountering until the 1940s, when one possible explanation became a clear frontrunner."

"What explanation?" said Bob at the same time as Meera said, "What happened in the 1940s?"

"Advanced technology," said Lo to Bob then turned to Meera. "You've heard of the Roswell crash?"

"Aliens?" said Mee, snorting. "You get your power from aliens?"

"Well. Not exactly," said Diane. "Manna was around before humans crawled out of the slime, so far as we can tell. As I said, we've always treated it as a natural resource. But in 1947, the conspiracy theorists had it right for a change. There was an event of some kind. We know because of what was left behind after the crash at Roswell."

"Which was?" said Bob.

"A new thin place," said Diane. "The first time it's ever happened, we believe. And it caused a stir among users of Manna worldwide. Whatever the beliefs of Users, we all felt this event take place. It was like an earthquake felt globally, we were all shaken up by it. Some Users found a way of fitting this new development into their existing world view. Many found themselves scared and confused by what had happened."

"Why?" said Mee. "If you've been using this stuff for centuries, what real difference does it make if some new place shows up full of it?"

"Three reasons, really," said Diane. "First, as I said, this was apparently an unique event in human history as far as anyone knows. Second, everything pointed to extraterrestrial involvement."

"But I thought all that was discredited pretty quickly," said Bob. "I remember the military report saying it was a barrage balloon. If anything bigger than that had landed in Roswell, someone would have found some hard evidence by now."

"The government covered it up quickly and thoroughly," said Diane. "No trace of any extraterrestrial was ever found. Most users of Manna are only vaguely aware of other Users, but the Order has always been extremely sensitive in this way. We can even sense those who have been touched by Users recently. It's how Lo found you."

Bob and Meera exchanged a look. This wasn't getting any less weird.

"If an alien carrying a new supply of Manna had arrived on Earth, we'd expect to know about it. It would be like every car alarm in your street going off simultaneously. Not something you could miss. We sensed a brief flare, a fraction of a second, so we knew where to head for. And we went."

"To Roswell," said Meera.

"Yes," said Diane. Thousands of Users made their way to Roswell the first few months after the event. Blended in with the sight-seers and alien spotters. They wanted to absorb Manna from this fresh thin place, they were inexorably drawn to it."

"You said there were three reasons people were scared," said Mee. "What was the third?"

Diane's hands were absently smoothing the dirt. Tiny blades of bright green grass pushed up between her fingers as she spoke. "The third reason was the most disconcerting of all," she said. "No one could use the new thin place. Not a single User. The most powerful people tried, the oldest and holiest member of the Order tried. Nothing. We could all feel the potential, the energy waiting. It was as if the ground itself were humming with power. But not a single soul could access it."

"It's like an itch we can't scratch," said Lo, "but it feels far worse than that. Imagine going without water in the desert for a couple days then finding an ice box full of bottles of cold water. But there's a huge padlock on the door and no way to get to the water. That's how it feels."

"An unfortunate result of Roswell was that the factions of Users hardened their positions, stopped talking to each other," said Diane. "Threats were made, there were skirmishes. For a while it looked like open fighting would break out, but the main players saw sense in the end. There's still a lingering suspicion among many Users that Roswell is being secretly controlled by one of the groups."

"Which groups? What factions?" said Bob. "Who the hell are these people and what do they want with Seb?"

"Users of Manna suffer from the same frailties as everyone else," said Diane. "Although many are loners by nature, they like the security of belonging to a group, something that provides a belief system making sense of what they can do. There are many such groups around the world. Most are harmless."

"Most?" said Mee.

"There are some factions that believe Manna is an evil power, so they must commit evil acts to keep using it," said Diane. "The Order believes that whatever we bring to our encounters with Manna taints it somehow. That's why we try to bring so little. We want to be part of Manna, not bend it to our will. Other belief systems employ complex rituals in their quest to control Manna. We have anecdotal evidence of animal sacrifices, perhaps even human sacrifices. Outside America, many such groups have grown over the centuries."

"But not here? Why not?" said Bob.

"Oh, there are groups, but they are kept small by the faction that pretty much runs the country."

"What?" said Bob and Meera together.

"This country has a proud history of striving for freedom, with some serious missteps along the way," said Diane. "But we have a concurrent history of corruption and organized crime. Our political system and these criminal groupss grew in a symbiotic way over the last few centuries."

"In other words, the mafia and the rest of them always had politicians in their pockets," said Bob.

"Exactly. Then, in the 1970s, someone carefully and systematically took overall control of all notable crime syndicates. It was an unprecedented and audacious move by a group with enough information and resources to bury every politician or gang boss of note in America."

"Oh, come on," said Meera, "no one could get away with that. What is this? The Illuminati? The Knights Templar, some shadowy group pulling the strings of puppet governments?"

"Not quite," said Diane.

"Then what?" said Bob.

"One man controls this faction," said Diane. "He has no real interest in power in the traditional sense. He is only interested in finding out more about Manna. Eventually, controlling it. He is so powerful that no one has been able to stand against him, and every User in America, sooner or later, has to pledge loyalty to him or be eliminated."

"Eliminated?" said Bob.

"Killed," said Diane. "He doesn't make idle threats. He doesn't tolerate disobedience. And his use of Manna is unmatched, anywhere. Or was."

"So you pledged loyalty?" said Mee.

"No,"said Diane. "We think he doesn't see us as a threat. Or, more significantly, as an opportunity. He can't use us in any way so he lets us be. Or, at least, he has done so far. But everything has changed now."

"What's changed? And what do you mean this loser's use of Manna *was* unmatched," said Mee.

Diane and Lo stood up, as co-ordinated in their movements as two dancers. They walked to the middle of the garden. Mee looked at Bob. He shrugged and followed them, Mee trailing behind.

The women had stopped by the stone words. Diane pointed at the last word: περιμένετε.

" 'Wait'," she said. "That's what the Order has done for nearly 2,000 years. Waited. Learned, yes, taught, yes, but mostly waited. In 1947, some of us thought the wait was over, but it was a false alarm. Then, early morning, three days ago in Los Angeles..." Her voice faded. For the first time, she seemed unsure which words to choose.

Bob stepped closer to her. "What happened to Seb?"

"We don't know," said Diane, "but we know he feels different to us. Unlike any other User we've ever come across."

"Different how?" said Mee.

"The way Manna forms within him," said Diane, "we recognize it. And if we recognize it, everyone, every User worldwide recognizes it."

"Recognizes what?" said Mee.

"The Manna he carries," said Diane, "it's similar to the earthquake we felt in 1947. Somehow, your friend is using something like the Roswell Manna."

Bob was silent, thinking. Eventually he looked up. "What exactly have you been waiting for for 1800 years?" he said. Diane didn't answer, but Lo turned toward him, eyes shining with tears.

"The Messiah," she said.

# Chapter 30

Waking in a king-sized bed with three sleeping naked women draped across him while a fourth snorted cocaine from the surface of an antique roll-top desk, Seb couldn't help smiling. He slid out of bed and padded over to the bathroom, turning the power on full in the massive shower. As he grabbed the body wash, he heard the door open. And two other bodies joined him in the steam.

"Looks like we're going to need more soap," he said, "'cause you girls are very, very dirty."

Later, the house empty apart from Walt who was preparing salad in the kitchen, Seb looked at himself in the mirror, marveling again at the way nothing seemed to have an impact on his appearance or mental state. He should look like hell, really, not like a poster boy for male grooming products. It seemed he wouldn't have to worry too much about living a healthy lifestyle any more. Up to now, he had always tried to take care of himself. The rest of the band had teased him about the relatively early nights - "it's not even 3am, man, where ya going?" - and the post-soundcheck run he'd always take before a gig. And he played it safe in other ways, never quite going as far as the others with alcohol, pot and pills he didn't even know the name of. He had partied, sure, but he'd didn't like to lose control. He remembered Mee - after their brief fling - telling him he should live a little more dangerously. "If you let yourself go a little," she said, "I think you might find you have a real gift for hedonism, Seb Varden. Go out there and get yourself laid more, say yes more, don't be so uptight." He had looked at her gentle brown eyes offset by that permanently slightly-mocking smile and decided this might not be the time to tell her he thought he was in love with her.

"Come and get it," called Walt from the kitchen. "You need your strength. Advanced training this afternoon."

Advanced training turned out to be more than an afternoon's work. Seb and Walt spent the rest of the day and all of the next working on the same thing. Walt explained what they would be doing after they walked out to the yard at the back of his property. The yard was a surprise. Seb was expecting fountains, Greek columns, a maze. Something. Not this, just a square, fenced off patch of dirt and nothing more, apart from an old punchbag hanging by the back step.

"No near neighbors," said Walt, "so no awkward questions."

There was a bench set against the fence on one side. They sat.

"This is not my area of expertise," said Walt, "but I'm not bad at it. There are at least four Users I know who specialize in this, but even they are very careful about when and where. It takes a great deal of power and a hell of a lot of concentration to do it well. We'll have to refill at Red Rock after a few tries." He shot a look at Seb. "Well, I will, anyhow."

Seb just nodded. He was a way off getting used to the idea of Manna at all, let alone the knowledge that he was carrying it - whatever it was - in his own body. Now he had a little time to relax and think, he'd half wondered why he wasn't more scared about what had happened. He wasn't an anxious person by nature, but the most laid-back guy in the world would surely expect to feel some stress about the events of the past few days. His usual calmness appeared to have been augmented by Manna, meaning he felt effortlessly present in each moment, aware of what was around him. It wasn't that he was ignoring the past or the future, he just seemed to have it in perspective. And each moment opened up many possibilities, all of which seemed to be present in his consciousness without any real effort. He felt his personality had changed. He just wasn't sure whether the change was good or bad, because there was no way to stand outside himself and make that call. He was different. But he was alive and that was enough for now.

On the bench next to him, Walt slowed his breath and Seb felt the hairs on his arms stand up as the Manna began to build. Walt's eyes unfocussed and he gazed unseeingly into the middle of the yard. Then he brought his concentration to bear on a patch of dirt about six feet in front of them. The earth moved slightly, like a stew coming to the boil.

"Ok," said Walt, speaking with difficulty, "ok. This is where it gets difficult." His breathing got faster and Seb looked away from the dirt for a moment. Walt's forehead was beaded with sweat, his nostrils flared as he concentrated. Seb remembered how easy it had been for this man to change his entire appearance - and voice - to become that of a middle-aged woman. How easy it had been for him to make that napkin move or make that beautiful paper shark in the car. But this was really costing Walt. His breath was coming in short gasps now and he seemed oblivious to anything other than what was in front of him.

Seb turned back to the scene in the yard. The bubbling dirt had risen in a column about five and a half feet high, millions of tiny specks of dirt roiling, spinning. Dust surrounded the swirling mass as its shape began to change, separating in places, stretching in others, elongating, compacting, becoming. Before long, a vaguely human shape became visible, like a child's clay sculpture: a rude, elementary sketch of a figure, misshapen, lumpen, but unmistakably that of a person. The legs were thick and ended with feet too big for its body. The torso was barrel-like, no discernible change in shape between the broad shoulders and the thick waist. The arms were heavily muscled, ending in club like hands. It had no genitals. As the dirt slowed its swirling, Seb raised his eyes to the thing's head. There was something resembling a face, but it was crude, hurried, frightening to look at. It had no hair, its ears were obviously not designed for anything other than rudimentary hearing, as they were holes in the side of its head with a lumpy curve of dirt behind them. The mouth, nostrils and, worst of all, eyes, were just also holes. As the shape settled, the dirt changed texture, smoothing itself out, lightening in color, becoming flesh. That was when Seb found it hard to look at those eyes - when the face had grown skin and become close to human. The eyes, or rather, the absence of them, the dark sockets where eyes should have been, stared back at him like an accusation. He shivered in the Las Vegas heat. Next to him, Walt held his breath for 20, 30, 40 seconds. The thing in the yard was utterly still. Walt let all his breath out in one long exhalation and slumped back against the fence. He mopped his forehead with a napkin and smiled shakily at Seb.

"Don't think I'll ever get good at this," he said. "I mean, look at the thing. It's hardly gonna win any beauty contests now, is it?"

Seb hesitated before answering and Walt laughed.

"Look," said Walt, "I'm not going to be offended by your opinion. I know what I'm good at, and this really isn't it. But it's a useful skill to develop and some Users can produce results that might be taken as human on a dark night, if you've had a drink or two."

"What the hell is it?" said Seb.

"That," said Walt, "is a homunculus. Say hello."

"A homunc-" said Seb. "A what?"

"Homunculus," said Walt again. "Technically, it means 'little human'. In the Middle Ages it was believed tiny people lived inside sperm and grew into adult humans. The same idea also appears in folklore and myths. Maybe the concept of pixies, gnomes and the like evolved from homunculi. I don't know. We call them" - he gestured at the creature - "that because they are tiny in terms of their capacities. No brain, just some kind of residue of its creator. See for yourself. Ask it a question."

"What," said Seb. He looked at the unmoving creature in the yard. Short, misshapen and utterly still, that blank stare still made him nervous. He glanced back at Walt, wondering if it was a joke of some sort.

"Go ahead," said Walt. "Ask him what his name is. Or her. Hard to tell. I was going for a he."

Seb stood up and, reluctantly, moved a little closer to the creature. It looked like something out of a low-budget horror movie. Very low budget. He moved slightly to the left and flinched as the head moved. As he stopped, the head stopped. He walked slowly from left to right. The thing's sightless eye sockets tracked him as he moved, the rest of its body still as a statue. Seb shivered involuntarily. It reminded him of an optical illusion he'd seen, where a cardboard dragon's head appeared to follow you as you moved around the room. Until you got behind it and realized your brain had been tricking you into thinking it was moving. Seb moved carefully in a circle around the homunculus. No optical illusion here, it was solid. Flesh - of a sort. It looked pallid, clammy. Worst of all, as Seb walked past the point where a human would have been unable to keep watching, the thing's neck carried on twisting, sinews and muscles stretching like old rubber bands. When Seb came back to the front, the creature's neck had gone through 360 degrees and there was a corkscrew of twisted flesh where the skin had stretched and contorted. Seb stood still and felt his skin crawl as the homunculus slowly turned its head back through the same process in reverse, untwisting its neck to face forward and look normal again. Well, as normal as a crudely-formed semi-human with holes for features can look. Seb cleared his throat.

"Hello," he said, hesitantly. "What's your name?"

Five or six long seconds passed while the thing seemed to consider the question. Then the mouth stretched open a little. This movement was horrible in itself, as it looked as if invisible fingers had reached into the creature's face and pulled open the hole where its mouth should have been. Then it made a noise, a kind of wet, grating gargling that was all wrong. The sound seemed to just form in the mouth and resonate oddly and artificially, as if the head was hollow. The voice had a slightly metallic, damp quality to it and - although it was probably inaccurate to ascribe feelings or emotion to the creature - it sounded like it was painful to produce.

"Aaarrr....iiiiiiiii," it said. "Aaarrrr.....iiiiiiiieeeee."

Walt coughed. "Er, he's trying to say Arnie," he said.

"Arnie?" said Seb. The creature nodded slowly.

"Aaarrrrr....iiiieeeee," it said.

"Bad joke," said Walt. "Actually, this is one of my better efforts. Until a few years ago, I couldn't get any kind of voice. Beyond my capabilities."

Seb realized there was something different going on. When Walt had made the napkin animal and the shark, Seb was aware of the control Walt had, the sense of a puppeteer and his puppets. This time, Seb could feel nothing like that. "You're not controlling it?" said Seb.

Walt looked surprised. "Correct," he said. "How did you know?"

"Just...feels different, I suppose."

"It is different. That's what makes it so hard. Homunculi are, to some extent, autonomous. They have a separate existence, of sorts. They can make simple decisions, but only along the lines implanted when they are created. This one is a kind of bodyguard template. If I was attacked, he would protect me. As my skills are limited, I keep things fairly simple. Arnie here can walk, but not very well and not quickly. But he's broad and his body could easily block a doorway or a hallway. His arms can move fast enough, that's where I spent the most time. Let me demonstrate. Arnie?" The lumpen head swiveled toward Walt's voice. "Hit the punchbag."

The homunculus turned and stumped across toward the door. Its steps were slow, heavy and cautious. When it reached the punchbag, it stopped, its massive feet planted a shoulder width apart.

"The big feet aren't pretty," said Walt, "but they give it stability in a fight."

The creature's right arm suddenly jabbed at the punchbag. It was, by far, the fastest movement it had made yet and Seb was taken by surprise. When the punch landed, the bag jumped backward a few feet and the 'thwack' was shockingly loud in the quiet heat of the yard. Arnie followed up with another couple jabs with its right, followed by a massive left hook which, if it had landed on human skin and bone rather than leather and sand, would had caused unconsciousness or - more likely - death. Untiring, the creature launched into a series of combinations, a flurry of punches throwing the bag from one direction to the other, dust flying.

"I've watched a lot of boxing," said Walt. "Guess if you watch it enough, you start to pick up some of the moves." Seb marveled at the way the creature was still throwing punches. He looked like he could carry on all day.

"He'll run down eventually," said Walt. "Homunculi have a short shelf life." He called over to the thing still punishing the punchbag. "Hey, Arnie! Quit it, will ya?" the creature stopped immediately, its huge arms hanging by its sides. Walt turned back to Seb. "A few hours, no more."

"And what then?" said Seb.

"From dust you came and to dust you shall return," said Walt. Noticing the expression on Seb's face, he shrugged and held out his hands, palm upward in a 'hey, don't blame me' gesture. "It has no consciousness as such. Think of it as a wind-up toy. Set it in motion and it'll do its thing until the clockwork mechanism runs down. Only in this case you can't just wind it up again, because when it winds down it falls apart. You have to start from scratch."

"Which uses a lot of Manna," said Seb.

"Yep," said Walt.

"So why bother?" said Seb.

"The autonomy," said Walt. "Homunculi have one big advantage. You can walk away and let them do their thing. Give Arnie a gun and by the time he shoots someone, I can be hundreds of mile away. And a pile of dirt with a gun next to it hardly counts as evidence." He caught Seb's look. "Hey, I'm not saying I've done it. Not saying I *would* do it. Just saying it's theoretically possible, is all." Walt gave Seb a speculative look. "Ok," he said, "your turn."

# Chapter 31

Seb wasn't sure how to start, or even if he wanted to. There was something about the semi-human look of the homunculus which gave him chills, even though he accepted Walt's definition of it as no more conscious than a clockwork toy. He had felt this way before, years back. It was the time Jack Carnavon had snapped the arm off a GI Joe at St. Benet's. He knew it couldn't feel anything, but somehow that didn't make him feel much better. He remembered wincing. He made an effort to shrug off the memory.

Arnie stood stock still in front of the punch bag. Seb was intrigued by what Walt had created, and wondered what he might be able to produce himself. He had barely begun to explore the power he now had inside him. He was briefly surprised at how unconcerned he seemed to be. Everything had changed, the world was a very different place to the one he'd decided to leave permanently less than a week ago. Perhaps that explained the laid-back way he was dealing with his continued existence. He had said his goodbyes, made what peace he could with his past and his lack of future. He had taken his own life, rather than wait for it to be taken from him by a disease with no cure. Every day since then was an unexpected bonus. Even the fact that his personality seemed to have fractured in some way didn't disturb his equilibrium. Seb2 could do the heavy lifting for now, he would just deal with life as it came.

Seb sat up, back straight, feet flat on the ground. He breathed as Father O had taught when he first learned contemplation. No effort to breathe differently, just stillness of posture and awareness of breathing. Soon, his breathing became quieter and began to deepen naturally. His heart slowed and his thoughts, drifting like clouds through his consciousness, began to lose their ability to hijack his attention, instead becoming background noise. The Bach prelude began to sound in his head as he looked at the dry dirt of the yard. Immediately, the earth began to move and he brought up the image of Arnie in his mind's eye, trying to recreate the being Walt had brought to life. The dust swirled and clods of dirt rose from the earth in a miniature whirlwind, sticking to each other as they spun. Soon, a human-like form began to appear and, as the whirlwind subsided, Arnie's twin stood before them. It grunted and flexed its muscles, in a macabre parody of competitive bodybuilders.

Walt laughed, as Seb made his creation perform an Irish jig. It was far more mobile than Arnie.

"Yeah, great," said Walt, "but you haven't let go. Cut it loose, let's see what you've got."

As Seb listened to Walt, he realized he could control the creature without giving much attention to it. He had never been good at multi-tasking before, looked like this might be one of Seb2's upgrades. He turned back toward his capering monster and broke the connection, which felt like the mental equivalent of letting go of a kite on a gusty day. He felt it go. The creature immediately dropped to the floor, leaving just a small mound of earth to show for its brief existence.

"Hmm," said Walt. "Thought so. You were controlling it the same way you controlled my shark back in the car. This is different. You can't be a puppeteer - you've got to give a bit of yourself. Don't make a puppet, make Pinocchio."

"Great, thanks for the detailed instructions," said Seb.

"Hey, don't blame me," said Walt. It's the same for all of us. We all do things differently, and a lot of what we do happens underneath the conscious level. I couldn't explain it to you any better than I could explain how my brain sends a message to my arm and my hand, enabling me to pick up this bottle, raise it to my mouth and have a drink." He took a swig from his beer in demonstration. "I mean, I could talk about nerves and muscles and synapses, but that wouldn't help you any with the practicalities, would it? Remember, Manna works *with* you. Make sure you have a clear idea of what you want. Sid used to talk about focus, about ignoring the clutter. Best description I ever heard was from some Zen teacher who'd never heard of Manna. He talked about the 'one-pointed' mind. That made sense to me, making my mind one-pointed."

"One-pointed," said Seb. "Right. No clutter, pointy brain, here we go." He turned back to the yard and let his mind return to the contemplative state. He was aware how fast this process had become. Despite having sat his ass on a cushion almost every day for the best part of two decades, he'd never found it easy. Now it seemed he could skip the 25 minutes it used to take just to get to where his thoughts weren't in total control of his scattered consciousness. From mental cocktail party to stillness took seconds.

As his mind stilled, Seb had an idea. The Bach seemed to work perfectly so far, introducing structure to an otherwise chaotic and uncontrollable power. But Walt had said he needed to put something of himself into his homunculus if it was to have any independence. He let the first few bars of the C prelude sound in his mind as he brought the image of Arnie to the surface of his consciousness. This time, as the dust began to swirl and the earth moved into its whirlwind, he started to morph the music, improvising on Bach's theme, adding a very simple countermelody of his own. It was an eight-bar sequence which resolved neatly, like tying a parcel with a bow and snipping the frayed ends from the end of the string. He broke the connection and sat back.

Arnie had a new friend. This one was just as ugly, but it differed slightly in that it had a clump of sandy hair on top of its misshapen skull.

"Wow," said Walt, "did you think it might get invited on more dates with some hair?"

"I think I know what happened. Just as I was finishing, I thought of someone I'd seen on the news and it affected what I was doing."

"Who were you-?" Walt broke off, put his head on one side and examined Seb's homunculus a little more closely. Then he started laughing. He laughed long and loud, slapping his thigh, his eyes watering, until Seb had to start laughing too. The creature looking at them didn't move, its semi-human features unsmiling under its incongruous thatch of hair. "What are you going to call him," said Walt, gasping, as the laughter finally started to subside. "Donald?"

"That's Mr. Trump to you," said Seb, which started them both off again, wheezing and crying with laughter for at least five minutes. Eventually, they gained a semblance of control.

"Come on," said Walt, "let's see what he's got. Give him some instructions."

"Take a walk, Don," said Seb, and immediately the short stocky figure began plodding in a slow circle around the yard. The sensation was very different, as Seb wasn't using Manna now. The creature was genuinely able to exist on its own. It was a disconcerting feeling, watching it walk, its long arms hanging limply by its sides.

"Hey, Arnie, come and join us," called Walt. Arnie turned away from the punchbag and came back to the spot where he had originally been created. There was a slight depression in the ground, and that's where Arnie planted his huge feet. "Arnie, meet Mr. Trump. Shake hands, fellas." The homunculi raised their arms, put out their slab-like hands and solemnly shook. It was a bizarre sight.

"He doesn't talk much, unlike his namesake," said Seb.

"Yeah, I kinda like that about him," said Walt. "Ok, you've impressed me again. I guess I'm going to have to get used to that. It took me months to produce anything that looked even remotely human. Took the best part of a year to get it to move in any useful way." He gave Seb a long, speculative look. "You're a real talent, kid. How are you feeling? Drained, tired?"

Seb shook his head. "I feel fantastic, Walt," he said. "Not sure I've ever felt this good before. Which is weird considering the situation."

"Well, don't knock it. If you feel good it's for a reason. And no need to worry about those guys on the train. Whoever they were, there's very little chance they could trace you to Vegas. And even if they did, change your face when you go out, change your whole body if you like. It's child's play compared to what you've done so far. A bit of practice, no one will ever find you if you don't want to be found."

"What about people who use Manna?" said Seb. "I thought they could tell where other Users were?"

"Yeah," said Walt, "there's no hiding from them, son, but the majority of us don't wish each other any harm, and you dealt with last night's threat pretty efficiently. I doubt she'll be back after that display." Walt took another sip from his beer and looked at Seb evenly. "Look," he said, "you're gonna have to trust someone eventually. You're in my home. Want to tell me your story?"

Seb paused for a beat. *No reason not to trust him. But no reason to trust him, either.* He took a decision. Told Walt about his illness, his trip into the mountains with a bottle of fine whisky and a sharp blade. He skipped the part about the alien...something he still needed to process and didn't want to share. He left in the part about the shooting and his superhuman speed.

"So you were unconscious - near death - and when you woke up, you were healed?" said Walt. Seb nodded.

"Only one explanation possible, as I see it," said Walt. "You must have sat your ass down on some Manna. A filling station, like Red Rock, though I've never heard of one up there. And you're a natural. A late starter, but a natural. Guess you just soaked up everything that was there." He shook his head slowly, thinking. "How the hell did you end up on that train, though?"

Seb paused again, felt cautious about saying much more. He felt bad lying to Walt, but he just didn't feel right telling anyone about Seb2, about the way he had somehow moved from one place to another. From certain death under the wheels of a van to a Superliner bedroom on the Albuquerque train. "The guy with the soldiers kidnapped me, sprayed some kind of drug into my face. I passed out. When I woke up, I was on the train. Guess someone must have helped me." Walt just looked at him

"Guess so," he said. "Well, that's some story." He looked like he wanted to ask more questions, but decided against it. He turned away from Seb and pointed at the waiting homunculi. "Now come on," he said, "let's fight."

"What?" said Seb.

"That's what these things are good for, if they're good for anything," said Walt. "So, come on, let's see what Donald has got. Put 'em up, Arnie."

Walt's homunculus raised its giant hands and curled them into huge, meaty fists. Seb's creature just stared at him.

"Ok, Mr. Trump," said Seb, "time to see what you're made of. Get ready to rumble!"

The second homunculus raised its own hands and mirrored Arnie's stance. There was none of the ducking, bobbing, or mutual sizing up that characterized the beginning of most fights. Both beings stood perfectly still, just a breath of wind lifting the edge of Seb's creature's incongruous hair, which set Walt off into another few seconds of snorting and wheezing with laughter.

"Arnie?" said Walt, "in five seconds you're going to attack Mr. Trump here. Make it good, don't want to look stupid in front of Seb."

"When he attacks," said Seb to his creature, "defend yourself. Win the fight if you can."

There was a brief pause before the fight began. Again, the atmosphere was very different to any other fight. Both of them were absolutely still. The seconds ticked down. Then, with no warning, Arnie's right arm snapped forward toward Donald's head. Donald moved backward, but still caught some of the impact on the left side of his forehead. He swayed slightly, and when he regained his balance, there was a small crater on the side of his head half the size of Arnie's massive fist. Donald clamped both hands together and swung them in a heavy roundhouse toward Arnie's neck, but Arnie was wise to the move and flexed his upper body backward, letting the blow fall short by six inches. While his opponent was still moving with the swing of his missed punch, he countered with a viscous head-butt that would have finished the fight there and then with a human opponent.

"Are you sure it was boxing you've been watching?" said Seb.

Donald took a step backward. His face looked like a lump of dough someone had pushed a fist into. His nose was gone, his mouth thrust forward, giving him a more neanderthal appearance than before, if that was possible. Sickeningly, his eye sockets no longer looked forward, but seemed to stare at each other across the chasm where his nose used to be. It didn't slow him down, though. He simply stepped forward again and kicked Arnie as hard as he could in the groin.

"Ah, that's a far more honorable way to fight, is it?" said Walt, chuckling. "Actually, that would work well against you or I, but Arnie's lack of testicles may prove to be to his advantage."

As if to prove his point, Arnie didn't even flinch, but reached down and dislodged Donald's foot, yanking it upwards. Donald dropped on the ground like a felled tree. Then Arnie stepped heavily onto Donald's pelvis - if he had one - and pulled on the foot in his hand with all his strength. There was a horrible squelch as the leg stretched, tore and finally popped out of its socket. Arnie hefted the severed limb in his hand like a club. Donald managed to get into a kind of kneeling position on one leg, supported by his arms. Arnie simply swung the leg back over his shoulder and, with the kind of swing golfers spend their lives trying to perfect, brought the limb whistling back toward his opponent. As the meaty thigh met Donald's ruined face, his head was ripped briskly from his shoulders and sent flying into the air. It sailed across the yard, hit the house wall and shattered, exploding in a shower of dirt. Simultaneously, the rest of the homunculus, including the leg in Arnie's hand, changed back into earth and fell in a shower to the ground. Arnie raised his hands in triumph. "Aaarrrrr....nnniiiiieeeee," he yelled, "Aaarrrrr....nnnii-".

Without warning, Walt's homunculus became earth, dropping to the yard floor just as Donald's body had seconds earlier. All that remained were scattered piles of dirt and a splatter of soil on the wall.

There was silence for a few seconds. "Well," said Walt, "I'm glad there's something I can do better than you."

Seb just stared into the yard, stunned by the physical violence, yet aware none of it was real. It was a strange feeling.

"Ok, you got the basics down," said Walt, "but your fighting technique sucks. Let's see if we can do something about that. You never know when you might need someone to get your back. And these guys never ask questions, don't need feeding and are absolutely loyal. Downside is, they drain Manna. Two or three more today, then I'm gonna need a trip back to Red Rock tonight. We'll see if you need to come with me." He gave Seb that quizzical look he'd flashed him a few times since they met. "Ok, let's get to work."

The rest of the afternoon was spent working on Seb's skills. First, he needed to make sure his homunculi lasted more than a few minutes. This turned out to be achievable by working a greater amount of originality into the music he used in the creation process. Second, he needed to work on his fighting skills - and this was a more telling weakness. He just couldn't match Walt's moves.

"Guess I didn't watch enough martial arts movies," said Seb. If he was going to win any of these bouts, he needed to think laterally. After a few beatings at the hands of Walt's superior fighters, he vaguely remembered watching a movie where a boxer was up against a huge wrestler. As long as the wrestler got in close, the boxer couldn't do a thing - it was down to bulk, physical heft.

Donalds MkII, III and IV showed some progress. MkIV was the one that turned things around. Although he didn't have the fighting skills to match Walt's homunculi, MkIV was unstoppable, however much punishment he was given. He just waded forward into the punches until he could wrap his arms around his opponent and start squeezing. Seb's homunculus didn't go for the death blow, just lifted his opposite number clear of the ground and waited, unmoved by the thrashing attempts at escape. Walt's creation eventually collapsed into dirt while Seb's stood for another half an hour. Walt glanced at his watch when he saw how much longer this particular Donald had lasted, then nodded, impressed.

"One more, Seb, one more," said Walt, fashioning his last beast before heading into the house to get more beer.

Seb started to create mkV, his mind already adapting quickly to the new skill, the shape spinning quickly into human form in the yard. This time, it was taller, slimmer, much more human-looking. Its body was well-proportioned, more muscle-bound man than orc. Its face was more realistic too, looking like an ugly guy who'd walked into a wall. Twice. But a man, not a monster. Seb heard Walt coming back and, with a snap decision, darted a last burst of energy toward his creation, squashing its features and forcing its body into a hunched, crouching figure. He couldn't justify why he didn't want Walt to see the improvement, he just knew he wasn't ready yet. He had never been quick to make friends, always holding back from intimacy until the time felt right. Mee had always said he'd wait so long, he'd miss every opportunity to be happy. She was annoyingly good at seeing, and stating, the obvious. It was just rarely so obvious to Seb until Mee had pointed it out.

"Wow, I actually think you've surpassed yourself on looks this time," said Walt, carrying two beers in one hand and carefully holding something metal in the other. "This guy looks like he fell out of the top of the ugly tree and hit every branch on the way down."

Seb shrugged. "Well, like you said, I can't be good at everything."

"Well, you're a prodigy whichever way you look at it. Not sure there's much more I'll be able to teach you." Walt sat down, handed Seb a beer, then tossed two kitchen knives out into the yard. "Let's make things a little more interesting," he said. "See how they get on with these."

Before he consciously knew he had moved, Seb was on his feet, white and shaking. As he stood, staring in front of him, both newly created homunculi were thrown backward as if picked up and flicked away by giant hands. In mid-air, they exploded, dirt, earth and stones pushed outwards at high speed from the center of each figure, smacking against walls and fences, breaking two windows - one in a upper story. Some of the blast headed back toward Walt and Seb, and both were left scratched and bleeding as well as covered in dirt. Walt picked himself up from the floor and began to brush himself off, looking up at Seb, who was still shaking, his lips pressed together in a tight line.

"No knives," said Seb, quietly. Walt nodded slowly. "I don't like knives," said Seb.

Walt walked to the other side of the yard and looked at the fence. Both knives were buried up to the hilt in the wooden panels.

"Yeah," said Walt, "I think I got that." He looked down at his ruined clothes and brushed some dirt from his hands. It was dusk, and the dirt looked like dried blood in the glow of the setting sun. "Something you want to talk about?"

"No," said Seb, "not really." He made an effort to recover some equilibrium and walked over to Walt. "Sorry about your clothes."

"No problem," said Walt, glancing down as his shirt began to repair itself, the material reaching out tiny threads, re-binding and repairing. In a few seconds, it looked new. "Look, no need to apologize. I don't know anything about you. You're under an incredible amount of stress, however well you think you're dealing with it. Let's get something to eat. I suggest you get an early night. I really have to get over to Red Rock, though. I'll go later - Steve will be here if you need anything." He turned to walk back into the house.

"Thanks," said Seb, "I think I'll do that. And Walt?" The older man stopped and looked back. "I was in a fight once. With a knife. I -," he stopped. "I'm sorry."

"Me too," said Walt. "I was pushing you too hard. Come on, let me show you something you'll never beat me at. You cook?"

"Not well," said Seb.

"Good. You like Asian food?" Seb nodded. Excellent. Then you have to try my Pad Thai. Worth coming to Las Vegas just for that."

# Chapter 32

Dinner was great, the conversation easy. Seb admired Walt's ability to keep the conversation flowing, to move Seb quickly away from the dark mood he was ready to sink into. Within a few minutes, he felt better, in a half hour he was laughing at a story about a gangster mistakenly putting his wife and mistress in the same hotel room. Walt had plenty of charm, no two ways about it. He was likeable, roguish, self-deprecating and funny. But Seb was slow to call someone a friend and a truckload of charm wasn't going to change that any time soon.

Walt had to make some calls after dinner and suggested Seb take in a movie. Seb wasn't surprised to discover Walt had a small movie theatre with surround sound installed in the basement. The computer system seemed able to call up any movie or TV show Seb could think of. He tested it by asking for Tom and Jerry, filtering it only to include those episodes produced by Fred Quimby with music by Scott Bradley. It still made him laugh, despite the fact he must have watched every episode hundreds of times.

Later, he sat in front of the mirror in his room, practicing changing his appearance. Walt was right, it was easy. Either he was getting better at this stuff, or this was the equivalent of first grade. Maybe a little of both. He only had to create an intermediate state of consciousness, a nudge toward the 'one pointed' mind he had needed to make homunculi. The interior music could be as simple as a single sustained bass note. Then he only had to think of someone's face, real or imagined, to see it replicated in the mirror. It was a fascinating exercise, looking into a stranger's eyes in the mirror and knowing them to be his own. Just changing the face was almost instantaneous as he pictured what he wanted. Changing the body was slower, more of a challenge, but he soon got used to it. He became famous actors and musicians, historical figures. Albert Einstein was fun, but when he managed to reproduce the current pope, he made himself feel like a ten-year old again by blowing raspberries and giving himself the finger. He experimented with a few women, but found the feeling disconcerting, particularly when he chose one of his favorite actors, undid his shirt and started admiring the magnificent breasts he'd imagined many times but never seen.

*Ok, this is getting seriously out of whack now. Time for bed.*

Seb woke suddenly, convinced he had heard his name spoken. He sat up in bed, grabbed his glass of water and checked the clock. 4:11am. He had been asleep for a little under three hours, but felt rested and alert. It was a clear night and a strip of moonlight divided his room in half with a clear, straight silver line. He sighed and swung his feet onto the polished wooden floor. He had been dreaming about Meera. He was playing a new song to her and she was listening in that intense way she had. Music was one thing she was never cynical or flippant about.

Seb stood up and paced around the room, the floorboards cool under his bare feet. He remembered Mee talking to him about music in bed one night after a gig.

"The way I see it, you can't have background music," she said. "It would be like having background sex. I suppose it's possible in theory, but why would anyone put in such a massive effort to disengage with something so amazing?" It was the reason she'd made him turn off the music before they had sex.

"It's for your own good," she said. "You really don't want to think you're taking me to love heaven, only to find I'm really digging the way the bass player went into swung eighths in the chorus. Do you?" Seb conceded that he didn't. Mee was the most amazingly focussed person he had ever met. When she decided to focus, that is. Most of the time, she seemed to exist in a hazy, detached state, her disassociation with everyday reality exacerbated by heavy pot use. Other people, when they were acknowledged at all, were slightly irritating distractions from whatever was going on behind those dreamy eyes. But music always snapped her into that incredible state of attention. And, for a while, Seb seemed to occasionally have a similar effect on her. Especially when she was listening to him playing a new song. That's what she had been doing in the dream. He sighed, heavily. They had broken up amicably, she was still his best friend, but he knew it was always going to be more than that for him. He still loved her. And he didn't know what to do with that. The knowledge that unrequited love was a very common problem didn't help much when no one had come up with a foolproof way of dealing with it. Should he tell her? And risk their friendship? Or not tell her? And - one day - lose her forever to someone else.

He padded over to the window and looked out. The sky was a vast upturned basin full of stars, the moon low on the horizon. Seb had never been able to look at stars without feeling a sense of awe. Just knowing that he was looking into the past was hard to believe, even though he knew it was true. The same few facts from school always came into his mind. He had never forgotten them, they'd never lost their brain-boggling impact. The most distant star visible by the human eye - Deneb - is more than 1500 light years away. The speed of light is 186,000 miles per second. Traveling at the speed of light, you'd be able to loop the entire Earth seven and a half times per second. *Per second.* And, if you'd got bored of circumnavigating the planet after an hour - which would be 27,000 circuits - and decided to take a trip to Deneb, it would take you 1500 years to get there at that speed. 1500 years! At the speed of light! Seb smiled. He was glad to be alive in a universe so vast, unexplored and mysterious. Thinking he saw something move below, he glanced down into the yard. There was a naked woman standing there looking at him. She waved. It was Meera.

Grabbing a robe from the back of the door, he made his way downstairs. The rest of the house was quiet. He slid open the door leading to the yard. Cold air wafted over him as he stepped out into the moonlight. The yard was lit with reflected sunlight from the orbiting moon a quarter of a million miles away, painting everything blue, gray and silver. Meera stood in the middle of the yard, her head tilted slightly to one side, that mischievous smile on her face.

"Seb," she said.

"Mee?" said Seb, coming to a stop a couple yards away. On the way downstairs, Seb had wondered what he would say if there really was a naked woman in the yard. And if it was Meera. Logically, he knew the first part of his conjecture was unlikely, the second near impossible. And yet he wasn't surprised by the reality when he saw her. He just wished he could of think of anything to say that didn't sound stupid or inadequate. But he couldn't. "What are you doing here?" he said.

"Seb," she said again, this time taking a step forward and taking his hand in hers. Her skin was smooth and warm. The pad of her thumb stroked the back of his hand. Her eyes, almost black in the moonlight, looked into his. His throat dried up. He coughed.

"You must be cold," he said, taking off his robe and wrapping it around her shoulders. Now he was just in his boxer shorts, he realized it really was cold - the desert air dropping to a cool 55 °F at night. Not uncomfortable if you're dressed, not so great naked. He realized Meera hadn't been shivering. She was holding his hand again.

"I came to tell you I love you," she said, and that's when Seb realized something was wrong. Mee didn't talk about love. She said it was nothing to do with fear of commitment, just that talk was cheap, words were easy to say. According to Mee, if she ever made it to five years in a relationship, she would consider saying the words. So this didn't make sense.

There was a sound from the other side of the building. The crunch of tires on shale. Seb looked back toward the house. Walt was back from his trip to Red Rock. What the hell was he going to say to him?

Suddenly, there was a familiar voice in his head.

"It's not what you think," said Seb2.

"What? What's not what I think? And why do I have no control over when I can speak to you? Or vice-versa?" said Seb.

"Well, there's good news on that front," said Seb2. "You should be able to speak to me any time from now on. And, hey, don't get upset about me disturbing your romantic scene here. I am you, after all."

"Fair point. Now answer my question."

"Mee. It's not her. Look at her."

Seb turned back to look at Meera. She was still smiling, the robe half-open, revealing the swell of her breasts. *Why is that so much more erotic than when she was naked?*

"Seb," said Meera again. Then he felt the pressure of her thumb disappear from his hand. As he looked at her, a sequence of events lasting less than a second, which had become familiar to him that afternoon, unfolded. Mee's 'body' collapsed inwards, skin and hair instantaneously become millions of particles of dirt. All that was left was his robe on top of a slightly raised mound of earth.

"You did it in your sleep," said Seb2.

"What? I *dreamed* her into existence?" said Seb.

"Yup."

"But she was perfect. How is that possible? I couldn't make anything better than a troll that looked a bit like Donald Trump earlier."

"That's not quite true, though. You could have, you just decided to stay at Walt's level. He doesn't have to know everything about us."

"*I* don't know everything about us," said Seb. "Am I going to be dreaming homunculi into existence every night?"

"No, I can stop it now that we know it's possible. I was as surprised as you, even though I know more about our abilities now."

"You keep reminding me you're me," said Seb, "but I don't know what you know."

"You do, it's just that our consciousness has divided. Otherwise I think we would have died on the mountain when we were given Manna. Er, something else I need to say about that, actually."

"What?"

"There's another one of us, buried deeper."

"Another me? Oh, god, tell me I'm not just suffering some kind of psychosis and this whole thing is in my head."

"You know better than that. But I can't really communicate with the other one. Let's call him Seb3, for the sake of argument. He's there, he's necessary, I think he absorbed everything we couldn't. But he's not like us."

"Not like us how?"

"He feels less human. But more human."

"Loving the meaningless aphorisms."

"Hey, a cheap shot like that might work on someone else, but you're just wasting time using it on me."

"Fair point."

"He's at such a deep level, it's hard to get anywhere near," said Seb2. "I want to get closer to him. But I can't, and I'm scared to try. There's something...ancient. And there's terrible pain. And joy."

"Great," said Seb. "That's all clear, then. Glad we had this little chat."

He heard the front door open back in the house. He picked up his robe, brushed off as much dirt as he could and put it back on.

"One more thing," said Seb2.

"Yes, Columbo?" said Seb.

"Go with your gut. I think we're right not to trust Walt."

The door slid open and Walt stepped out into the yard. He was full of energy, practically bouncing on the balls of his feet. Seb remembered how lit-up he'd been after filling up at Red Rock before.

"Beautiful night," said Walt. "Bit cold for a walk, though."

"Oh, I couldn't sleep," said Seb, stepping forward to cover the new mound of earth, although it was unlikely Walt would notice a new one among the handful they had made that afternoon. "And I love looking at the stars."

Walt stood beside him. "Yes, they sure are pretty," he said. "Makes you wonder if we can really be alone in the universe, doesn't it?"

Seb thought of Billy Joe. He remembered the touch that healed him and gave him these strange, barely explored abilities. The touch of a being from an unimaginable place. Maybe somewhere even further than Deneb. "Yes,"he said, "it sure does."

# Chapter 33

## 17 Years Previously
## St. Benet's Children's Home, New York

As Seb's body drifted inevitably back to sleep, he fell forward before jolting awake and shifting his weight on the wooden prayer stool. He half opened his eyes. The gray-blue pre-dawn light soaked Father O'Hanoran's office in surreal monochrome. Seb clenched his leg muscles and tried to find a position on the narrow stool that was even slightly comfortable. Father O seemed to be experiencing no trouble at all sitting still, he was a silent Catholic Buddha to Seb's right, his only movement the slow rise and fall of his stomach.

Seb mentally went through Father O's instructions again. *Posture upright.* He straightened his spine self-consciously, wondering if Father O was aware of the many times he had almost fallen off the stool as sleep beckoned. *Hands still, placed in your lap. Breathing normally, just being aware of your breath.* Seb wondered if anyone was capable of breathing normally when their breath was the only physical movement they were making. When his training had started, nearly four weeks previously, he had spent most of the thirty minutes seeing how slow he could make each breath. He figured he was taking two breaths a minute. He wondered if that was good. Possibly exceptional. Then he wondered what the world record was for breathing slowly, if there was one. Probably not. Then he remembered the last instruction Father O had given. *When your awareness moves away from your breath, bring it back by sounding your word.* Seb had chosen 'silence' as his word. He idly wondered what Father

O's word was for a while, then realized he had become distracted again. He sounded the word. *Silence.*

He had agreed to daily practice, thirty minutes, for one month. In five days time, the month would be up, but Seb knew he would be continuing his practice. The Christian word for what he was doing was Contemplation. Other wisdom traditions called it meditation. Father O called it Paying Attention. Paying Attention was the best description.

"That's all it is," said Father O'Hanoran had said, nudging Seb awake after the first 6:15 session. "But mysticism, the pursuit of reality filtered - for the most part - through different religious traditions, is notorious for its problems with communication. The word 'mysticism' itself is proof enough of that. It's suppose to signify an encounter with the mystery at the center of existence, but the root of the word is more commonly associated with the idea of something strange, unexplained. These days, if we say something is a mystery, we usually mean it's a puzzle. When the mystics talk about mystery, they mean something beyond our grasp, yet also the very essence of what we are. Language falls short when it tries to describe this. But here's the important bit. Language doesn't fall short because what it's describing is so complex, but because what it is attempting to speak of comes *before* language. A truly authentic encounter with reality cannot be spoken about, it can only be *experienced.*"

The first time Seb heard Father O talk like this, he was bewildered. But he had nowhere else to turn. He had expected the priest to respond to his crisis by recommending confession, penance and absolution. He had even tentatively asked if he was going to have to take more of an active role in church. Father O had left it entirely up to him. He said that Franciscans such as himself were encouraged to "preach the gospel, using words only if absolutely necessary." Sometimes the things Father O said just gave Seb a headache. But he kept coming back.

And now, sitting on a tiny wooden stool, his buttocks numb and his body cold, he unexpectedly found the constant background noise of his mind to be fading. It was as if an early morning mist was clearing as the sunlight burned it away. The gaps between his thoughts slowed. Millisecond gaps lengthened, became half a second. Then, for the first time, on a frosty morning one Fall in the half-light of dawn, half a second opened out into what might have been five, twelve, 20 seconds of pure awareness. Seb was just *sitting*. Afterwards, when he tried to recapture what had made this the single most authentic moment of his life, all he could manage was the fact that this was the only time he could remember simply being - not doing, not thinking, not planning, not judging. Just being. And it was perfect. He looked forward to many more such moments. If he had known they would only occur once or twice a year if he was really lucky, and never with the intensity of this first time, maybe he would have given up. Maybe. But probably not. Because, while it didn't help him forgive himself for what he'd done, it seemed to open out his perspective to a point where he knew that he was ready to carry on living, accepting his actions, accepting the guilt, just not obsessively judging himself or trying to rewrite history. He would take on the probably impossible challenge of accepting each moment as it came and dealing with it. Not in some New Age bullshit way, but in a grounded, pragmatic, *real* way.

Father O sighed, crossed himself and stood up, using the corner of the desk to help lever him into an upright position. He crossed to the corner of the room and flicked the switch on the kettle, fumbling in the jar for teabags. He had developed a slightly pretentious liking for Earl Grey tea at Seminary in Wisconsin and, when he left, discovered to his surprise that his palate craved the delicately floral taste. He poured two cups, knowing Seb would only drink his through politeness. He watched Seb open his eyes, noted the stillness. He waited a few minutes in silence as the tea brewed.

"Don't talk about it," he said, handing Seb his cup.

"About what?" said Seb.

"About what just happened. Words can often cheapen the experience."

"But how did you-?"

"Brother Lawrence would have called it the presence of God. Buddhists would say you had an enlightenment experience. Whatever you call it, it's as if you're wearing a badge announcing it. Just drink your tea and I'll see you in class later."

Seb drank his tea.

# Chapter 34

**Las Vegas**
**Present day**

When Seb woke up the next morning, everything had changed. He felt it as soon as he opened his eyes. Even as he emerged from the last, confused dream of the night, he knew something was different. Since adulthood he had always needed 10-15 minutes to transition from sleep to wakefulness. Coffee was usually necessary. He had always assumed he was exceptionally slow at waking until he met Mee, who seemed to pride herself on the 45 minutes it took her to manage any communication more coherent than a grunt.

But 6:30am rolled around and Seb opened his eyes, sat up, swung his legs off the bed and stood up. Wide awake, despite interrupting his sleep with a visit from a Manna-created ex-girlfriend. After padding to the bathroom, he sat upright on the end of the bed and closed his eyes, sounding his word. *Silence.*

"No real need to do this any more," said Seb2.

"I know," said Seb. "I feel that. But I want to do it. Some habits are worth keeping."

"Fair enough," said Seb2.

"It feels different. Having you here to talk to whenever I like."

"Good different or bad different?"

"You already know the answer to that."

"True. You can't judge it good or bad, it just is. Now, can you stop telling me I already know the answer to everything you're thinking? I may *be* you, but it doesn't make it any less irritating."

"Ok, ok," said Seb. "But it's not just having you here that's different. I feel like I've made a decision. It's time to go. I need to be on my own. Well, we do."

"Agreed," said Seb2. "Something I want to show you."

"What is it?"

"Open your eyes."

Seb did as he was told and found himself back in London's Richmond Park, where Mee had taken him all those years ago. Again, the sun was low in the sky and icicles hung precariously from the branches of ancient oaks.

"This really will take some getting used to," he said.

The huge park was deserted as before, the silence unnatural and unnerving. Seb suddenly had a thought. If this place existed only in his imagination, then...

A herd of red deer burst through from a copse to the west, led by about a dozen big stags, their antlers silhouetted against the swollen sun as they ran within a few feet of where Seb stood, the thunder of their hooves and the mist from their breath in the cold air bringing the whole scene to life. Seb smiled. Seeing a slight movement to his left, he turned. Seb2 was smiling as well, nodding his approval as the animals headed into the trees. He started walking toward Pen Ponds and Seb walked alongside him. As they got to the edge of the water, Seb2 ignored the bench where they'd sat on their previous meeting. Instead, he carried on walking straight onto the surface of the water and - this time - Seb accompanied him without breaking stride.

"Almost a shame no one's here to see it," said Seb as they made their way across the pond. The water felt exactly as he thought it would. It was like walking across a trampoline, each step sinking slightly before the elasticity pushed back against his weight.

"Of course it's like you imagined it," said Seb2. "You're making it happen. We just need to get you to the stage where you can reproduce this in reality. It's no different, it's just your perception that holds you back. You still think much of this is impossible. And while you think that, it will be."

"I'm much closer to believing it all than last time we were here," said Seb. They had reached the far side of the pond. The two men stepped onto the path and carried on walking.

"What do you want to show me?" said Seb. Seb2 pointed ahead, to a dense clump of trees Seb didn't remember from his day there with Mee.

"This bit is new," said Seb2. "Shouldn't be here. It isn't here in the real Richmond Park." An opening led into the wood. It was like something out of a dark fairytale, a twisted dirt path that disappeared into the gloom created by the gnarled, distorted trees, their huge branches reaching out to each other, creating a canopy through which very little of the weak sunlight could penetrate. A faint sound came from within. Seb stepped closer, surprised as he did so to feel a real reluctance to go any closer. At first it was just a vague feeling of disquiet, but as he got within a few feet of where the path entered the wood, it was close to genuine fear. He stopped.

"I know," said Seb2, "but you need to see this." He walked ahead, only slightly hesitating as he crossed the invisible border between the park and the wood. Seb hung back, reminding himself briefly that this was all happening in his subconscious, then followed.

The sound he had heard grew more distinct as he moved between the trees. It sounded like a wounded animal. More like a dying animal. A dying animal that was being tortured in its final minutes of life. The light grew weaker and he realized he could no longer see the sky through the dense canopy of knotted branches. Seb2's back was a faint shadow ahead. He hurried to catch up, tripped on a root and almost ran into Seb2, who had stopped just ahead. He was looking at something, and his face was grim.

"It's a bit of a shock the first time," said Seb2. Seb looked in the same direction. At first it was hard to see anything, but the source of the appalling noise was obviously in the middle of the small clearing ahead. As his eyes grew accustomed to the gloom, Seb could make out some sort of mass stretched out across a large stone about eight feet long, three feet wide and standing about waist high. The mass was moving, writhing, glistening. It had a shape that looked familiar somehow. The sound, a keening moan of absolute agony, was coming from one end, where a small dark hole opened and closed among the slithering mess. With a gasp of horror, Seb knew what he was looking at. It was the flayed body of a human, the limbs stretched, the muscles tearing in front of him, exposed where the skin had been removed. The hole was a mouth, and now that he had put the puzzle together, he saw two holes where nostrils should be and a pair of ghastly puckered raw craters instead of eyes.

Seb turned his back, dropped to his knees and vomited onto the hard, gray earth. His body shuddered as it ejected a stream of thin acidic material, the spasms burning his throat and chest. Seb2 just watched him, waiting. Finally, Seb stood, his legs shaking.

"It doesn't get any easier," said Seb2, "but being prepared means I don't lose the contents of my stomach now."

Seb took a few long breaths, then looked at Seb2, aware of the movement just behind him where the horror continued to unfold.

"Who is it?" he said.

"You know who it is," said Seb2. "It's us. You. Me. Seb3"

"But how? Why?"

"Because we weren't supposed to receive Manna in the way that we did *when* we did. We should have died - no normal human can act as a vessel for what we were given. Apparently, there's a good chance we would have been ready in another three decades or so."

"So why am I still alive?" said Seb, walking shakily away from the horror in the clearing, trying not to see the image now imprinted on his brain.

"Think of us as partitions in a hard drive," said Seb2. "Partitioned so we can run the software without conflicts."

"I am not a fucking hard drive!" said Seb. "What the hell is going on?" He fell to his knees, shaking. Seb2 squatted next to him and put a hand on his shoulder.

"Seb3 is what would have happened to you if the partitions hadn't been created. But the pain would have only lasted seconds before you died. This is a compromise, I don't know how Billy Joe did it." Seb looked at him blankly. "The alien?" said Seb2.

"Oh. Yeah. How could I forget? So are you saying I'm not a whole person any more?" Seb2 helped him up and they walked out of the wood, back toward the edge of the pond.

"No. Well, yes. Kinda. You're as whole as you've ever been. Gross oversimplification coming up, but here's how it works. You're the surface-level, everyday personality. 99.9% of humanity lives and dies knowing no more than the surface personality. Underneath, we have the subconscious.

We're all slightly aware of that - dreams, intuition, but mostly it does some heavy lifting behind the scenes. In your case, that's me. Having a subconscious available to the conscious mind could raise you to genius-level intellectually. Or drive you insane."

"Hmm," said Seb. "To be fair, there's no clear evidence which way I've gone."

"And deeper than the subconscious,"said Seb2, ignoring the interruption, "is the Person. The real you. No smoke and mirrors, no facade, no defenses, just a pure, unique expression of the dance of energy we call life."

"You could get your own science special on PBS," said Seb.

"Sarcasm noted," said Seb2.

"So the most real me, the most authentic...the genuine human person..."

"...Is Seb3. Yep," said Seb2. "Sorry."

They walked the perimeter of the pond rather than across the surface this time, obeying the unspoken feeling that it would be inappropriate. Seb couldn't stop thinking about the torture his innermost self was constantly experiencing. And yet he seemed to be able to carry on as normal. He realized he had absolutely no understanding of the human condition. And yet, some aspects of his life seemed to be coming into focus just as others seemed to be teetering on the edge of an abyss.

"So what do we do?" said Seb, after a few minutes silence. "Actually, let me answer my own question. I'm going to call Mee."

"You love her," said Seb2. No response was necessary.

"We've got to get away from Walt," said Seb2. "He has some kind of agenda and we need to find our own way."

"Agreed," said Seb. "I'll tell him we're leaving."

They walked back toward the huge iron gates that marked the northern entrance of the park.

"Something else we need to do," said Seb2.

"What?"said Seb.

"Stretching the software analogy a bit further, I'm trying to work out how to run a huge system, our processing power is in place, we have an operating system of sorts, but I keep looking for information that isn't there. Like the file is corrupted, or has been moved. We need to go and upgrade the hard drive."

Seb was silent.

"You really hate this computer metaphor, don't you?" said Seb2.

Seb said nothing.

"It's the best I've got, sorry."

Seb sighed and stopped walking. "Ok. I'll bite. How do we get this upgrade?" he said.

"We go and get the Manna we need," said Seb2.

"Tried that at Red Rock with Walt," said Seb. "It didn't work. And I don't seem to be running low on it like he does."

"I know. Truth is, you'll never run out. But the Manna I'm talking about can only be picked up by you."

Seb thought for a moment. "Roswell," he said.

"Roswell," said Seb2. "Then you should be able to control your abilities better. And maybe work out what you're supposed to do with it. And you'll be able to be what you're supposed to be. What Billy Joe is."

"Which is?"

"A World Walker."

# Chapter 35

Meera watched five women of the Order climb into a battered pickup, three in the front and two squeezing onto the flatbed alongside boxes and baskets full of food. The engine spluttered and coughed, then the rusty vehicle rolled away in a cloud of dust and gas fumes. Lo came up beside her.

"There will always be hungry people," she said. "We do what we can for them." Mee watched the dust cloud shrink as the truck turned the corner and headed for the Interstate into Las Vegas.

"Look," said Mee, rolling a joint carefully. She had enough marijuana to last two more days. If she paced herself. Then there would be trouble. "It's not that I don't appreciate what you did for us. Saving us, I mean."

Lo didn't answer. She had the rare gift of listening without commenting. Mee couldn't help but like her. The ability to survive being shot without any ill-effects was slightly off-putting, but, hey, Seb could do that. So no biggie. Mee shot a glance at the silent woman. Absolutely unreadable. Very annoying.

"We can't stay here. I have the band. Bob has a life, of sorts. We just need to find Seb, make sure he's ok. Really ok. The people looking for him are dangerous. I can't let him deal with that on his own. Then we can go home, 'cause we're just going to lead them to him otherwise. If those bozos are still after us, we'll tell them the truth. We saw Seb, but we don't know where he's gone."

"And if I told you Seb can look after himself?"

"That would be a first," said Mee. "He likes his own company, sure, but he's not a natural loner."

"Like you?" said Lo.

"Yeah. Like me." Just then, her pocket buzzed and she fished out her old prepaid cell phone. The call was from a number she didn't recognize. She glared at the phone suspiciously, pressed answer and held it up to her ear without saying anything.

"Mee?" said the familiar voice, and her eyes filled with tears despite herself.

"Seb!" she said. "Thank God. Where are you? Are you ok? What the hell is going on?"

"It's good to hear your voice, Mee. And, yes, I'm ok. I'm sorry I didn't call, but...well, let's just say things have been pretty weird the last few days. I'll tell you more when I see you."

"I know some of it already," said Meera. "And weird doesn't even begin to cover it. Hang on, this isn't your number. What happened to your phone?"

"Gone," he said, "but I'm staying with...a friend."

"But you've never remembered a phone number in your life. And I haven't used this number for years."

"My memory's, um, improved recently."

Seb was quiet for a moment. Mee could picture the expression on his face. She always said she could see the cogs turning when he was thinking.

"Look, I need to see you, but I'm in Las Vegas," he said. "I'll head back to LA tomorrow. Something I need to do on the way."

Mee started to laugh.

"What's so funny?"

"Well, you won't believe this, but I'm in Vegas too."

"What?!"

"Long story. Might even be as interesting as yours. I'm here with Bob." There was a pause while Seb tried to work out who she meant.

"Bob, as in Bob and Marcie? From the hills? How do you know him?"

"We have a mutual friend," she said, deciding Marcie's fate was something Bob might want to tell Seb face to face. "Come see us. I'll give you directions." She told him where the Order community was. "Or we could meet in the city," she said. "Could murder a gin and tonic right now."

"I can't come today," he said. "Somewhere I need to be. But I'll be back tomorrow afternoon. I'll come out to you."

"Deal," she said. "Don't get into any more trouble between now and then."

"I'll do my best," he said. "I'll be on this number for another couple hours. Mee?"

"Yes?" there was another pause.

"Nothing. Nothing. I'll see you tomorrow."

As Mee finished the call, she saw Bob walking toward her, a questioning look on his face.

"It was Seb," she said, smiling broadly. "He's ok. He's going to meet us tomorrow."

"You told him where we were?"

"Yes," she said. Her forehead creased as she thought about it. "Oh."

"Yeah," said Bob. "These guys have Government connections at the highest level. We don't know if they're monitoring calls. I know that's a phone they don't know about, but did you use your name? Or mine, or Seb's?"

Mee's expression changed as she considered the implications. "Oh, no," she said. "He'll be walking into a trap."

Diane walked over and joined them. Lo told her what had happened.

"We have an understanding with other Manna users," she said, "including the organization who we believe is pursuing Seb. We leave each other alone. If they know you are with us, they will keep their distance. If Seb makes it here, he will be safe."

"But if they know he's coming, they can watch the road and grab him before he gets anywhere near," said Bob.

"Exactly," said Diane. She held out her hand for Mee's phone. Mee got a notebook out of her battered backpack and made a note of the number Seb had called from. Then she handed the phone to Diane and watched as it crumbled into a fine black dust in front of her. She rolled her eyes and tutted.

"You could have just·done that to the SIM card," she said. She pouted and glared, a combination that had turned many people into stammering wrecks. Diane just ignored her.

"I'll go into town," said Bob, "pick up another cheap cell. We can call Seb, warn him, fix up another meeting place."

"No. I'll go," said Lo. "They've been watching you. It's too risky."

Bob hesitated, then nodded, agreeing reluctantly. Lo ran behind one of the trailers, then reappeared on a motorcycle, her childish figure looking incongruous on such a big machine. She roared off with a quick wave to the others.

She was back within 20 minutes with a burner - a cell phone paid for with cash with $20 credit on it. Mee took it and dialed the number. A male voice answered.

"Seb?" said Meera.

"I'm sorry," said the voice, "you must have misdialed. There's no one of that name here." He hung up.

"Shit," said Meera. She double checked the number. Definitely the one Seb had called from. "What now?" she said, looking at the others.

"Only one thing we can do," said Bob. "We've got to assume they'll try to grab Seb before he gets here. We can't warn him. So we need to watch the watchers. Set up lookouts on the outskirts of the city - the most likely place for an ambush. That way, we have a good chance of spotting them move into position. Tomorrow, when they spring their trap, we'll jump them. You lot are pretty handy in a fight, right?"

Lo smiled. "We won't kill anyone, but there are kinder ways of incapacitating an enemy."

"Just don't be too kind," said Bob, thinking of Marcie lying in a pool of spreading blood. "They don't deserve it."

"We'll make plans this afternoon, then move into place at dawn tomorrow," said Diane. "We'll have Seb back to you by tomorrow night."

\*\*\*

Six miles away, Walt stood by his desk, looking at the phone, thinking. Finally he picked it up and dialed a number he knew by heart but rarely called.

"Yes?" came the whisper.

"It's Walter Ford. Someone else knows he's here. And he's leaving."

"Yes." The whisper was weak, breathy, but the words were always precise and considered. "I know. Where is he now?"

"Packing," said Walt. "I can't talk him out of it and I don't know where he's heading."

"It's of no concern to you now," whispered the voice. "We know where he's going. Ford?"

"Yes, sir?" said Walt.

"Change is imminent. I may be calling on your services. And the services of many others. Old allegiances will be broken. We are under attack and any action we take will need to be decisive. Be ready."

"Yes, sir," said Walt. The line went dead and he swallowed hard. When he turned, Seb was stood in the doorway. *How long had he been there? Did he hear anything?* Walt forced a smile onto his face. Seb was holding the same slim bag he had arrived with. When you could make your own clothes from a handful of dirt, it made sense to travel light.

"Can't persuade you to stay a few more days?" said Walt. "You're just beginning to get used to controlling Manna. It's not an easy time, even for someone with your gifts."

Seb shook his head. "Thanks, but no," he said. "I need to be on my own." He hadn't mentioned anything about Mee to Walt. He felt bad about not trusting someone who'd helped him out, but there it was. He was going with his gut on this one - particularly now that his gut had taken on the persona of Seb2 and backed him up.

"I can't protect you from whoever's after you if you leave," said Walt. "And they seemed pretty well connected. Who can authorize a train to make an unscheduled stop? Do you really want to take that risk?"

"I have to," said Seb. "Thanks, Walt, I appreciate what you've done. Goodbye."

He stuck out his hand and Walt shook it slowly. "Well, if you're sure," he said. "You have my number if you change your mind. Still don't want to tell me where you're heading?"

"It's not that I don't trust you," said Seb, lying. "I just don't know yet. I need some time to figure things out."

"Well, when you do, get back in touch," said Walt, walking with Seb to the door, where Steve was waiting to take Seb into town. "The Users I told you about, the ones who look out for each other, they're pretty much the most powerful group in the country. And they're not all as easy-going as me."

"What are you saying?" said Seb as he opened the door of the Lincoln.

"Just think carefully," said Walt. "As a User, you can't hide, and not all of those who notice you will have your best interests in mind."

Seb thought of the look on Sonia Svetlana's face as she unleashed a burst of potentially fatal energy toward him. "Yes," he said, "I get that."

"Look, Seb, there are those I work with have a far tougher attitude than me. They might think if you're not for us, you must be against us. I wouldn't want that to happen."

Seb got into the car, opening the window as he shut the door. "Is that a threat?"

"It isn't meant to be. No."

"Funny," said Seb, "'cause that's exactly what it sounded like. Look after yourself, Walt." The electric gates slid back and the Lincoln began the short trip to central Las Vegas. Steve dropped Seb outside the Bellagio. As soon as the car was out of sight, Seb hailed a cab to the station. Within the hour he was on his way back toward Albuquerque.

Walt had received another phone call and now he was drinking. Even though he knew he would have to counter the effects of the alcohol with Manna in a few hours, he wanted to delay having to deal with reality just a little longer. He poured a very generous glass of aged bourbon, then drained it in two long swallows. He stared at the phone on his desk. He had gone for years without hearing from Mason. And now this. He looked at his watch. Eleven hours until he was needed. His glass was empty. He filled it again.

The stealth helicopter approached Las Vegas from the East. It didn't fly directly over the Order's horseshoe of trailers, but got close enough to get some excellent images. The layout was straightforward, so the strategy was easy to formulate. Just one approach by road, a track from the Interstate coming in from the south-east, following the curve at the base of the rocky hill against which they'd placed their encampment. A much rougher track was accessible leading out from the trailers to the north, but it led nowhere. Not an easy place to defend from a basic pincer movement. The sort of place you'd only choose if you expected never to be attacked.

Westlake closed the laptop and smiled grimly, remembering Mason's words an hour previously. "They won't be expecting us until tomorrow," he said. "They will be unprepared, but the element of surprise will be short-lived. You're about to break a truce that's lasted hundreds of years. So make sure it's done right. Fast and clean. No mistakes, no evidence pointing back to us. And no survivors."

Westlake closed his eyes and visualized the upcoming operation. He would brief his men an hour before starting. They were the best, he expected a perfect outcome. The only loose ends were the Manna guys. They'd need to stop the targets using their power, but he doubted he would even need them. This was what he was good at and there were few who could touch him. Mason would have what he wanted by 1am.

# Chapter 36

The atmosphere in the dining trailer was just as it had been when Bob and Meera had first arrived. A serene silence pervaded the place, despite the fact that they had spent most of the day planning an ambush for the following day.

Mee was making her way through another enormous stack of pancakes drenched in syrup. Ever since Muriel, who prepared much of the food, had told her that all the food she 'made' contained a perfect balance of nutrients, protein and carbohydrate, despite tasting like a dietician's nightmare, Mee had delightedly taken her at her word and stuffed her face with chocolate, ice cream, cookies and pie. Impossible to feel guilty when your body's telling you it just absorbed five fruits and vegetables, a handful of nuts and some brown rice. As religious communities went, this one had some perks.

Bob was sitting at the far end of the table, drinking black coffee like he never expected to need to sleep again. He was hunched over a map, triple checking everything that had already been double-checked an hour ago. Mee walked over.

"I think you've covered pretty much every eventuality," she said. He looked up and nodded.

"Can't be complacent," he said. "That's what gets you dead in these situations."

"So what do you make of this place? The Order, I mean. And what about Seb?"

Bob pushed the map away and rubbed his eyes. "I was never much of a one for magic, psychic powers, all that metal bending bullshit," he said, "but this is something else. I've been thinking about it - I spent most of yesterday talking to the folk here. They're happy to answer questions now that Diane's vouched for us."

Mee poured herself a coffee and added enough cream and sugar to give a diabetic palpitations before sitting down opposite Bob.

"What's the story?" she said.

"Well, it seems the Order is pretty pragmatic," he said. "I like them. It's not a religion as far as I can see. Not really. No worship, no need to believe in anything. They think their meditation helps them get in touch with reality, confronting the ugly stuff inside us. Not rejecting it, but not letting all that subconscious crap run their lives, either."

"You have a way with words," said Mee, smiling. Bob looked up, not sure if he was being teased. His answering smile was a little shy. He had grown to admire this fiery woman over the last few days. She never spoke about her feelings for Seb, but even someone as long out of the relationship game as Bob could see it as plain as the hand in front of his face. She was nuts about him. Bob hoped that whatever else emerged from this crazy adventure, at least Seb and Mee would stop wasting time and admit they belonged together.

"Diane told me more about their founder," he said. "Since they never wrote anything down, the stories are sketchy at best, but one thing is really clear. This guy was visited in his cave by some kind of angel, but not any kind of angel I ever heard about before. No wings, no robes, no message from God. Just handed over this power, showed him how to use Manna. And then disappeared and told him to wait. I guess he didn't think the wait would be quite this long."

"They think Seb is who they've been waiting for. Why?"

"Well, this is where it gets interesting. But not everyone thinks a Messiah is coming. Diane told me she - and many others - think they are waiting for an extraterrestrial visit. And it may have happened already."

"What?!" said Meera. "Oh, come on."

"Think about it for a minute," said Bob. "These 'thin places' where Manna is buried. People have been using this stuff for thousands of years. It never runs out. So, if it's not some mystical hocus-pocus bullshit, what is it?"

"I don't know," said Mee. "Enlighten me."

"Some kind of advanced alien nano-technology, that's the best fit," said Bob. He noted Mee's raised eyebrow, but as she wasn't walking away, he continued. "I read once that magic is just a name for stuff science hasn't explained yet. Well, Manna never runs out, very few people can use it, and the guy who learned to use it first was visited by a silent glowing creature who taught him all about it."

"An alien?" doing her best to stay cynical, but remembering what she had seen over the past few days.

"I can't think of a better theory," he said. And Roswell was the clincher."

"Why?" she said.

"Every Manna user knows about it," he said. "Apparently it's the most powerful thin place on the planet. When it first appeared in 1947, the Order thought it was what they had been waiting for. Their most senior people came here, went to Roswell to absorb it, but they couldn't do it."

"Why not?" said Mee.

"They don't know, but it didn't work for anyone. No one can use it. The Order took it pretty well, patience is something they're used to. Other Users, not so much. Diane says they've got no firm evidence, but they're pretty sure there was a cover-up immediately after the crash. Some of them think the government have been experimenting on an alien that survived the crash. Others think the alien must have died. Everyone thinks Roswell itself has some kind of protection. There are plenty of stories about people trying to dig, take samples, but the equipment they use fails when they try to break up the soil."

"Ok, back up," she said. "You think a real alien crashed at Roswell? And it was the same kind as the one who visited this bloke in a cave two thousand years ago?"

"Think about it," he said. "Manna is real, but no one knows what it is. It's magic, because science hasn't explained it yet. If we turned up in front of a caveman one day with a tablet loaded with movies, he wouldn't have a clue what was going on. But we don't think twice about it. He might learn to press the touchscreen in the right place, though. If he was shown. But he still wouldn't understand the tiniest fraction of what he was seeing, would he?"

"And we're the cave people," said Mee. "So what's Roswell?"

"If the same alien race came back after two thousand years, their technology will have moved on a bit," said Bob.

"Hmm," said Mee. "Yeah, just a bit."

"So that fits," said Bob. "All these Manna users, they feel the Roswell site is full of something similar, but they can't access it. Maybe the alien thought we would have advanced enough to use it by now. Maybe it really was an accident - a crash, and the alien didn't mean us to have it at all. I don't know. But the theory fits. And a hell of lot of the Order think that's exactly what happened."

"So why Seb? If he had been using Manna, I would have known about it."

"I don't know." Bob stood up and paced the length of the trailer a couple of times, thinking. Finally he stopped and put his hand on Meera's shoulder. She looked up at him.

"Look, I need to show you something," he said. He pulled a piece of paper out of his back pocket and handed it to her. She unfolded it, recognizing Seb's handwriting.

*Sorry it had to be you, Bob, but I knew you'd be able to cope ok. All the best, Seb. PS. Help yourself to the whisky. It's good stuff.*

"What is this?" said Mee.

"That tree we climbed back in the mountains," said Bob. "It was at the base of it. Next to an excellent bottle of whisky. Well, half a bottle. The note was held down by a knife, which was covered in blood. Seb's blood, I assume."

"What are you getting at?" said Meera.

"Why did you come to the mountain that morning?" said Bob. "Had you noticed anything strange about his behavior over the last few weeks? Any changes?"

"Well, we weren't spending as much time together as we used to," said Mee, "but that's only natural. We broke up months ago, after all."

"But you still spoke to him. You stayed friends."

"Of course. And he was still writing songs for us. But he was planning something. He said he was moving to Europe. I told him he was full of shit."

"So what was really going on?"

Mee stood up. It was her turn to pace the narrow confines of the trailer. Outside it was getting dark. "I had a bad feeling," she said, finally. "Something wasn't right. But I didn't want to push him."

"Yeah, I thought so too," said Bob. "Couple weeks back, we were walking together and he said he needed to sit down. Said he had an idea for a song, was going to make some notes. Told me he'd catch up. He almost fell over. I walked around the corner then doubled back. He was sweating and shaking. Some kind of fit, I don't know. He passed out. I was going to call 911, but he opened his eyes, started looking around, so I pretended I hadn't seen anything. He didn't mention it when he caught up."

"So," said Mee, "the note."

"Yeah," said Bob. "It was a suicide note, Meera."

"Jesus," said Mee, sitting down again. She buried her face in her hands. Despite herself, she started sobbing. Bob put his arms around her.

"I think he was really sick and had decided this was the way he wanted to go," he said. "He didn't want to hurt you. Or anyone else."

"Selfish bastard," she said, between sobs.

"But between writing that note and us seeing him, something happened," said Bob. "And whatever that something was, he went from normal guy to Manna power-user in one night. Diane said it takes years to learn to use that stuff."

"So what are you saying?" said Meera.

"I'm saying someone - or something - found Seb that night. They stopped him killing himself and they left him full of Manna."

"And you think it was another alien? These things running around LA now, are they?"

Bob shrugged, drained the last of his cold coffee. "Got a better theory?"

She opened her mouth to reply just as the door burst open and two men in black with automatic weapons burst in. They pointed their guns at Bob and Mee.

"Just sit there and put your hands on the table. Don't give me a reason to waste a bullet," said one of them. Bob and Mee looked at each other, Bob shaking his head a fraction. Outside the night was suddenly lit up, as if the sun had come out. They could feel the heat on their faces. Then the screaming started.

# Chapter 37

He knew the operation would have to be fast and precise. Mason had made made that clear enough. Westlake was not a man with any delusions: he had realized early in life that he enjoyed the act of killing, so he didn't try to dress up his pleasure with any kind of patriotic justification. His fondness for the act wasn't some kind of perverse sexual kick; far from it. It was more the professional satisfaction of completing a tidy operation with no loose ends. He wouldn't be happy until the number of corpses on the scene matched the list in his head, and the physical evidence told the story he wanted told. A job well done, a report given, a brief glow of satisfaction. Then on to the next job.

So, when his watch showed 1:11am precisely, and a buzz in his pocket let him know Teams B and C were in position, blocking any possible road exits from the Order's trailers, with team D ready on the hill behind, he felt a preternatural calmness descend, just as it always did when an operation took the final step out of his head and into reality. He motioned to the pilot to bring the chopper down. As it dropped toward the desert floor, he turned to the men waiting in the belly of the helicopter. His own men he ignored - they were proven, reliable professionals. Instead, he spoke to three men and two women sitting at the front. Two men were known to him - that lightweight Ford and, sitting next to him, the little guy - Barrington - Mason's enforcer, his gaze cold, unreadable. One of Westlake's men had made the mistake of commenting negatively on Barrington's size during an early operation. He didn't work for Westlake any more, as Barrington had broken every one of his fingers. Multiple fractures in each digit. More accurately, he didn't work for anyone any more, as Westlake had put a bullet in his head and had him buried in the foundations of a hotel parking lot. Leaving the unit prematurely didn't mean a redundancy package. His soldiers knew that when they signed up.

The other man and the two women had been brought in by Mason, so Westlake knew better than to voice any doubts about their credentials. He looked them over.

"You know what to do," he said, "but let me make this clear. No one other than the target gets to walk away, exactly as our employer has specified. You do your job, so we can do ours." None of the group, with the exception of Barrington, looked remotely comfortable. Ford, in particular, was already sweating and his hands were shaking. Westlake stared at the man until he finally met his gaze. He said nothing. Both of them knew Ford had to do what he had been told to do, if he intended to live past the next hour or so.

The pilot settled the chopper so lightly onto the ground, only the sudden decrease in vibration as the rotors slowed to a stop let the passengers know it had landed. Westlake opened the door, jumping out and watching his men fall in behind him, forming a line, the black clothes, full face masks and the dark tanks on their backs making their figures nightmarish. He flicked on his night vision goggles and watched the only two soldiers without tanks peel off to the right and head toward the trailer containing Patel and Geller. He never planned for luck in an operation, but when it came his way, he was quick to embrace it. The technology they used to observe the Order over the last few hours gave them a live feed detailed enough to pick out individual faces. The fact that Geller and Patel had decided on a cozy chat in the trailer nearest where the chopper had landed made his job easier. The Manna users stepped out behind him and he waved them forward. They stayed together as a group, stopping about 100 feet from the trailers. They quickly became very still. Westlake was not a Manna user, but experience had taught him the signs of its use. Their job was to suppress as much Manna-based resistance as possible. He turned his focus back to his crew, jogging up to join them. They were all in position. He pushed the button in his pocket, knowing each of his men would feel the buzz and immediately carry out their orders.

Twenty-three seconds later, two buzzes in his pocket signaled Patel and Geller were secure. Radio silence was no longer necessary.

"Go," said Westlake.

The first maneuver was designed to wipe out most of the Order immediately, but the use of his best men plus the addition of the Users proved how seriously Mason took the possibility of failure. Westlake knew not to underestimate the enemy, despite their appearance and hippy commune way of living. Each trailer except the one containing Patel and Geller were hit simultaneously with an particular kind of incendiary grenade banned nearly a decade ago by the United Nations. Each grenade detonated releasing superheated fireballs made up of a chemical solution designed to cling to flesh. The screaming started immediately. Westlake didn't mind screaming, in fact he often likened it to the applause of a satisfied audience at a concert. It showed things were proceeding as planned. In his many years working for Mason, the vast majority of killings had to be silent, which diminished his satisfaction slightly.

The old trailers would never have passed any kind of fire inspection. They went up like kindling. Another advantage of the grenades was the speed in which they did the damage. By the time anyone had thought to investigate a glow in the distance, it would all be over.

Three women made it out of their trailers. Westlake discovered later that another two had come out of the back, only to run into team D who ensured they got no further. The three at the front offered more resistance. Only one was alight - she rolled onto the ground and a sudden Manna-produced gust of wind extinguished the flames. Westlake looked sharply at the civilian group he had brought along. They were reacting to developments, but Westlake had forgotten how excruciatingly long the reactions of non-trained personnel could seem to someone of his background and abilities. By the time they were ready to respond, one of the women had raised her hands and a wall of earth had risen up between her and the fire heading toward her from the flame-throwers of Westlake's men. Then the wall blew apart in an explosion of dust and stones as Ford and the others finally responded. The flame-throwers found two targets and they turned into writhing figures from a nightmare, their flesh bubbling and the skin peeling away from their lips even as they screamed. They desperately tried to use Manna to heal themselves, but Westlake's group countered every attempt, and as they drew in breath to scream again, the fire burned away the linings of their lungs.

Westlake sprinted forward as the women fell, pulling the machete from his belt as he did so. With a practiced motion, he jumped just before reaching the nearest body, swinging the razor-sharp weapon over his head. As he hit the ground, the machete whistled past his ear and hit the neck of the burning woman, severing skin, muscle, bone and arteries. He kicked the head away. He had once seen a

Manna user re-attach his own head with a last scrap of consciousness, threads of flesh snaking out and snapping the separated neck onto the torso. Westlake had resolved never to make the same mistake. He noted that the nearest member of the unit had decapitated the other woman. Fire or brain-death were the only sure-fire ways of neutralizing Manna users permanently. Employing both methods ensured success.

One woman had escaped the initial onslaught, rising about 40 feet into the air on a column of earth. Her power was palpable. She glanced toward Ford and the others, recognizing the source of the most immediate threat. The ground around them suddenly buckled and split, then jerked and threw them backward like a bull at a rodeo. Only Barrington escaped the initial counter attack, rising up on his own column of earth to meet her. Westlake recognized the woman as Diane, a senior figure in the community. He had to admire her tactical thinking under duress. By lifting herself so high, she was beyond the reach of the flamethrowers, and his men were under orders not to use a single bullet, as the risk of leaving physical evidence was too great. But her indisputable talents had been directed mostly toward healing and producing food, so she could hardly be expected to be a match for Barrington, who had devoted much of his life to the study of violence, and knew a great deal about how best to inflict painful, or - if necessary - fatal damage to the human body. As his column of earth reached her, he simply punched a hole through her ribs and ripped out her heart. Knowing she had seconds to repair the damage, the woman looked down at the gaping bloody hole, only to see - too late - the blade in Barrington's other hand. Her head fell one way, her body another, the column of earth collapsing in a cloud of dust and shards of rock.

The fires from the grenades burned out quickly, just as they were engineered to do. As Westlake and his men checked the trailers and the immediate area around them, they kept a count of fatalities. Eleven dead. Every member of the community was accounted for. Their ruined bodies were lined up and Westlake called over the Manna users - all ashen-faced except Barrington - to remove the evidence by reducing the bodies to individual atoms that would never appear human, even under the most advanced forensic microscope.

"Bring them," said Westlake. The last trailer door opened, and as the final flames spluttered and died a visibly shaken Meera Patel and a grim-faced Bob Geller were brought out. Both looked around them for the bodies of their friends, confused by seeing nothing after the terrible screams of the last minute and a half.

"You bastard," said Meera, "what have you done?"

"Things have changed since we last met," said Westlake. "We need your friend, and you appear to be the only leverage we have to make sure he comes in."

"We won't co-operate," said Bob, stepping forward. "These were peaceful, innocent people. Who the hell are you and what makes you think you can get away with mass murder?" Meera didn't speak, her arms folded tight around herself, her eyes wide and her shoulders shaking uncontrollably.

"I wasn't talking to you," said Westlake. He looked straight into Meera's eyes. "Mr. Varden will come to us because of you. We don't need anyone else." He stepped sideways and the machete in his right hand swept across Bob's stomach, opening up a deep cut. Bob looked at him disbelievingly and clutched at his own flesh, trying to seal the gap and prevent his intestines spilling out onto the desert floor. In Westlake's experience, everyone cut across the stomach reacted that way, which left them unable to defend themselves against the killing stroke. Switching to a two-handed grip, he drove the point of the machete through the man's throat into his brain. Bob fell dead at his feet.

Mee let out a barely audible sigh and collapsed. Westlake gestured to his men. "Bring her," he said. He gave Ford a look and pointed at Geller's body. Walter stepped forward to remove the evidence, his face pale.

Bundled into the waiting chopper, her wrists secured to her seat with cable ties, Meera opened her eyes, then closed them again. She hadn't known Bob for long. You could know some people for years and barely notice if they left the country. Others, they seemed to have a key that opened the usual doors protecting your heart. They just got in there, kicked off their shoes and made themselves at home. And you let them do it, because you knew they were one of the good guys. As the rotors began to whine, she turned her head to one side so Bob's murderer wouldn't have the satisfaction of seeing her tears.

As the helicopter took off, Westlake sent a coded email to his employer. Less than 12 minutes had passed since they landed. Effective and efficient. He allowed himself a rare smile.

# Chapter 38

After disembarking the train in Aburquerque, Seb hired a vehicle for the four hour drive to Roswell, New Mexico. He chose a battered pickup - a vehicle the rental company said was suitable for off-road excursions. As he headed south-east, he played with the dial of the radio, only to find the one station he could detect through the hiss seemed to play back-to-back depressing country songs. He flicked it off and drove on, his thoughts whirring. Would Roswell answer any questions? Or just leave him with more?

After a couple hours on the blacktop, staring at a flat muted landscape, occasionally broken up by the appearance of a gas station, he felt himself start to doze.

"I'll drive if you like," said Seb2.

"What? You can do that?"

"Sure. I don't need as much rest as you. Couple of hours in every 24 and I'm as good as new. I usually grab them while you're asleep. But no reason I can't take over while you get some shut-eye. You're the part of us that intersects with the outside world - your consciousness is the busiest. I'll wake you up when we're close."

Seb laughed and shook his head at the sheer craziness of his life. "Yeah, sure, why not," he said. "Beats cruise control."

When he opened his eyes, the pickup was nosing into a space outside a busy diner, full of families and couples. He was hungry.

"Welcome to Roswell," said Seb2. "It'll be a few hours before it's dark, no hurry."

Inside, it was bright, clean, and the service was quick and friendly. Seb ordered the deviled eggs, apple pie and black coffee, all of which were hot and good. He looked around and felt himself relax a little. The buzz of end-of-the-week conversations sounded like a strange kind of optimistic ambient music to his ear; he could almost imagine writing a song using the soundbites grabbed from around the room.

"So he gunned the engine and"

"But the chicken wings were burned"

"We all just laughed and laughed. That damn dog wouldn't let go."

"Then we headed out to Maisie's. Have you seen what she's done to that kitchen?"

"Eight bucks for a beer, I couldn't believe it"

Seb felt a smile creep onto his face as the waitress gave him a refill. He felt normal. Sitting in a diner on a Friday evening, eating good food, folk around him talking about the stuff that actually matters. No superpowers, no miracle healing, no pursuit by shadowy military organizations. No aliens - not even in Roswell, New Mexico. Just apple pie and good coffee. It felt like the eye of the storm, he knew it couldn't last. But he was determined to enjoy it while it did.

When it was fully dark, he left, driving the pickup out of town to a dirt track, following Seb2's directions.

"How'd you know where to go?" he said.

"Internet," said Seb2. "Plus hacking into satellites. Don't ask me how. I don't understand it any more than you understand how typing something on a phone or a laptop can connect you to information 10,000 miles away. I just think it and it happens. Pull over here."

"Here" was two big red stones at the side of the track. Seb jumped out of the pickup and walked up to them.

"They're just markers," said Seb 2. "It's about a five minute walk. But we have to deal with the tripwires first."

"Tripwires?" said Seb.

"Just a turn of phrase. Manna users have been desperate to access the tech buried here for well over half a century. They may have given up on being able to do it themselves, but they want to know if anyone else manages it. You get any closer, there's enough electronic surveillance equipment planted in the bushes to open a wholesale store. Motion detectors, cameras, high sensitivity microphones, infrared beams, night vision gear. I shut down the peripheral alarm systems about a mile back."

"What?" said Seb. "So someone knows we're here already?"

"Doubt it," said Seb2. "Imagine a circle with a radius of a mile around the crash site. No one's going to worry immediately about systems failing a mile out - it probably happens fairly regularly, usually just weather conditions or local wildlife. But when I shut down the inner systems, all hell will break lose. At the center of the circle, 200-300 yards radius, the very latest technology monitors every movement, calibrated to report on everything: every rattlesnake, jackrabbit or spider that wanders across the crash site. We must be talking about hundreds of readings every minute. Years of constant information builds up a picture of normal activity. Anything bigger than a desert wolf, they're gonna take a look. Curious people get out here fairly regularly though, so no one's going to stress about human activity immediately. Particularly as Manna users see it as almost a pilgrimage. The Manna they can't have."

"But I guess most folk head out here during the day," said Seb, thinking about rattlesnakes.

"Yep," said Seb2. "And we're about to switch all their toys off. What we are about to do is a bit like poking a stick in a wasps' nest."

"Great," said Seb. "Good plan."

"Sarcasm noted," said Seb2, "but by my reckoning, we'll have 10-15 clear minutes. By the time the various Manna-heads get here to check out why all their equipment is fried, we'll be long gone."

"You sure about that?" said Seb.

"We are about to upgrade," said Seb2. "And the first thing we should be able to do is Walk."

"Walk?" said Seb.

"Capital 'W'," said Seb2. "It means consciously doing what we did instinctively when the truck was going to hit us in LA."

"Well, I can see how that would be useful. But I note you used the words 'should be able to'. Hardly fills me with confidence."

"Only one way to find out," said Seb2. Seb shrugged and headed along the track. He could feel Seb2's activity at another level of consciousness. He was aware of tendrils, threads of power reaching out across the desert floor, of electronic circuitry suddenly overloaded and burning out, the tiny hum of dozens of advanced examples of technology simultaneously disappearing.

At the end of the path was another stone, this one with letters cut into it:

WE DON'T KNOW WHO THEY WERE
WE DON'T KNOW WHY THEY CAME
WE ONLY KNOW THEY CHANGED OUR
VIEW OF THE UNIVERSE
THIS UNIVERSAL SACRED SITE
IS DEDICATED JULY 1997
TO THE BEINGS

WHO MET THEIR DESTINIES
NEAR ROSWELL NEW MEXICO
JULY 1947

"If only they knew," said Seb2. "Now step forward about ten paces. This may sting a little."

Since being healed by Billy Joe and finding himself the center of attention for various groups that would give conspiracy theorists all the validation they'd ever wanted, with power he had never dreamed of and a personality fractured into three parts to deal with it, Seb had remained an optimist. He had a strong sense of who he was and, possibly due to his Catholic upbringing (despite having been nowhere near a church all his adult life), he'd always experienced a deeply-rooted sense that everything would, eventually, work out for the best. But, as he walked into the innocent looking patch of scrub in front of him and began to feel an itchy buzz through the soles of his feet, he felt a genuine, profound moment of existential fear. He could *feel* the Manna this time, it was nothing like Red Rock. It was as if the biggest engine ever built was buried underneath the desert floor and his presence had turned the key. The ground actually began to shake and a deep *bass profundo* pedal note whispered, hummed, spoke then roared into existence, his whole body shaking with the force of it.

"Question," he said. "After this, will I still...will I still be *me*?"

Seb2 had always answered questions quickly. Since Seb2 was, in fact, Seb, he already knew the question before Seb asked it. This time, however, the long pause before he answered was an answer in itself.

"I don't know," he said. "But right now, we're broken, half-made. This completes us." The roar grew louder. Seb felt his eyes roll back in his sockets as he fell to his knees. His back arched, his head whipped backward and his arms reached out to his sides.

"Then what?" he said, hissing the words as he felt white-hot silver threads arc from the ground and touch each of his fingertips in turn, caressing and burning them.

"I don't know," said Seb2. The hum in Seb's skull crescendoed into a sudden absence of noise, a sudden absence of anything, his consciousness stretching out to embrace the edges of everything, then shrinking and un-becoming in the white noise of all knowledge collapsing into itself.

\*\*\*

The only organized group of Manna users that still kept a physical base going in Roswell itself was the Elohimians. Their founder, Jimmy Michaels, had been a mediocre Manna user who claimed his ability to heal animals and predict deaths was God-given until the alien craft came down 20 miles from his farm in 1947. He was one of the rubberneckers investigating the next day, and he recognized the power he felt there immediately. He started the Elohimians, alien-worshippers who believed their faith was being tested by the unattainable Roswell Manna. The Roswell alien was Elohim, and he would return to bestow the gift of his mighty power upon his followers when they had proved themselves worthy. At first, proving themselves worthy just meant subscribing to Jimmy's twice-yearly newsletter and buying the "rocks of power" he collected (initially from as close to the site as he could get, but later from his yard) and posted to subscribers as far away as Canada, Belgium, or Australia. When Jimmy developed a liver condition that left him unable to tolerate alcohol, all Elohimians were advised to abstain from drinking "like our glorious alien Lords". According to an early newsletter, Jesus, Mohammed, Buddha, Krishna, Ghandi and -

somewhat incongruously - Buster Keaton, were all Brothers Of Elohim, sent to our planet to spread the message of universal love. And the importance of laughter through means of silent comedy, apparently.

When Jimmy died while investigating lights in the sky and falling down a well, his son Darwin took over. Darwin had no Manna ability at all, and was completely unconvinced by his father's fledgling religion. He studied business at college, however, and came to see the Elohimians as an almost perfect model of capitalist opportunity. After his father's death, the newsletter went monthly and the subscription price went up 300%. He churned out books expanding his father's work at the rate of at least two a year, and when one of his early books, *Elohim: The Savior Of Our Sick Planet* was cited a decade later as one of the first written works to predict global warming, he found his cottage industry was bringing in a very respectable income. He embraced the internet early on and automated much of the business, bringing it into the digital domain. He knew his dad would have enjoyed the success, but was glad he didn't have to keep up the pretense of believing in "that alien horse-shit" when he was at home any more.

He kept a complex system of motion detectors set up for two reasons. One was practical: every year, he organized a pilgrimage to the site and, as part of the $10,000 price-tag on that trip-of-a-lifetime, wanted to show the faithful that, when Elohim returned, Darwin would be the first there to greet him and announce his presence to his followers. The other reason was sentimental; despite dismissing his father's beliefs, keeping watch like this allowed him to feel he was staying true to Jimmy's dream. But it was just window-dressing, really.

So when one alarm, then another, then a third, started bleeping from the den while he was fixing himself a beer in the kitchen, he dropped the bottle and ran through, his eyes wide. The first two cameras were standard tech, rugged and camouflaged, unlikely to fail, but not impossible. It stretched credulity for both to fail within seconds of each other. But the third device, buried in the desert, had cost him six figures, used military stealth technology and was in the category of surveillance equipment that the US military, who had illegally sold it to him, liked to call 'deniable'. He had been assured that anything short of a tactical nuke would simply bounce off it and the battery would need replacing a couple decades after his death, assuming he lived to 100. Without thinking of the possible consequences should Daddy's theory prove to be more than a theory, he grabbed a camera, ran to the truck and drove, knowing he wouldn't be the only interested party, but sure he would be the first on the scene. Some footage of a genuine alien and he could sell the Elohimian business and retire to Hawaii.

Even as he parked the truck as close to the site as he could get and ran past the red stone markers, he could hear an approaching helicopter. He glanced at the pickup alongside the stones. Maybe not an alien. But who could have simultaneously sabotaged three bits of tech, one military grade?

"Goddammit," he said, turning on the camera. It took a while for his eyes to adjust to the dark, but, when they did, he saw a man lying on the desert floor, curled up in a fetal position. He kept the camera focussed on the body as he moved forward. No, he wasn't dead, he was breathing. When Darwin got a few paces away, the figure rolled onto his knees, put his hands in front of him and slowly got to his feet, his back turned. He took a few long breaths in and out, then turned round. He was just some guy, nothing special. Then Darwin noticed his eyes. Even in the gloom, they seemed to pierce him. It was like looking onto the eyes of someone who'd seen civilizations rise and fall, watched planets form in the cold emptiness of space. He let the camera fall to his side. The man blinked and the moment passed.

"Who are you?" said Darwin. Then the noise of the helicopter made both of them look to the west where, only visible because of the way it was blotting out their view of the stars as it flew, it was coming in to land. Before it even touched the sand, eight figures dropped out of it, dressed in black, sprinting toward them. Two of them came straight at them, weapons drawn.

Darwin raised his hands, the camera dangling from his wrist.

"Nothing to do with me," he said, "you wanna talk to this guy." He nodded in the direction of the man he had found. When the two armed men didn't even glance away from him, he took a look himself. There was no one there. And no cover for 15 miles in any direction. He'd just disappeared.

"Shit," said Darwin.

Two incongruous figures were the last to exit the chopper. One was very tall and obviously in charge. The other barely came up to the waist of his companion. They ignored Darwin and walked to the center of the crash site.

"Well?" said the tall one. The dwarf - *must remember to call him a small person, don't want to offend him when I've got guns pointing at me* - stood very still for a moment, his eyes closed.

"It's gone," he said simply, and started back for the helicopter.

"All of it?" said the tall one, frowning.

"All of it."

"The power's gone?" said Darwin, blurting out the words before thinking. He had never been able to sense the stuff his father had claimed was buried there, had always assumed it was just another delusion.

The tall man walked up to him.

"What did you see?" he asked.

Darwin considered his options. He had always been good at negotiations, but none of them had taken place at the wrong end of a gun. He swallowed.

"Er, some guy was here," he said. The tall man took a photograph from his pocket and shone a flashlight on it.

"That's him," said Darwin.

"And where is he now?" said the tall man.

"I don't know," said Darwin. "His truck's still back there. He was just...here."

The tall man sighed and put the photo away. He spoke to the soldiers guarding Darwin.

"Make it look like he tripped and hit his head on a rock," he said. "And bring me the camera."

Darwin ran. It was human nature. He knew he wouldn't get far. He was out of condition and these guys were obviously trained killers. His last conscious thought was a silent apology to his dad, who wasn't quite as full of shit as Darwin had always believed.

# Chapter 39

## Woodbine Cafe, Earlham Street, London

By 6:57am, Marco had already been awake for two hours, dragging himself reluctantly out of a warm bed into a tepid shower, then downstairs to the cafe he had run for eighteen years with his wife, Constanza. 6:00-8:30am, the Woodbine was always busy with the same mix of transport workers, office and shop employees and a handful of bankers and hedge-fund managers who like to slum it a couple mornings every week, knowing they'd get the best bacon and eggs in town. Marco was a good cook, he stuck to the simple stuff, the food his father had told him Londoners wanted. He hadn't changed the menu in over a decade. Long before it had become fashionable, he had been brewing roasted Italian coffee and serving freshly-squeezed orange juice.

But Marco's real talent, the reason his cafe was busy even in the quiet summer months, was his memory for names. He had never been particularly gifted academically, but in his teens, he'd read a great book claiming the most successful people in business always remembered names and faces. He applied himself to the task and listened hard when someone introduced themselves, studying their face and repeating the name to himself in his head over and over. He seemed to have a natural gift for it - so much so, that people might go and work in another country for a few years, then walk back into the Woodbine only to be greeted by name, and offered their "usual". Word spread, and the cafe thrived.

So when a disheveled man in a suit materialized at the counter just as Marco was flipping a fried egg onto a piece of toast for Anna, the girl who worked at the stationer's opposite, his initial shock was followed, almost immediately, by the kicking in of his habitual memory stunt.

"Seb!" he said. "Great to see you. Such a long time. No Meera today, mm? So, the usual? Fried egg and mushroom bap, brown sauce? Black coffee, no sugar. Sit down, sit down, I'll bring it to you. What a lovely surprise."

Seb stumbled to the nearest table and sat down heavily. The conversations around him picked up again. The sudden inexplicable materialization of an American at the counter of the cafe had produced a stunned pause, but this was England, after all, and the general consensus seemed to be to pretend it hadn't happened, as it would be rude to stare. Mrs. Barclay, perched on her customary stool at the end of the counter as she sipped her weak tea, saw Seb's magical appearance occur about three feet from her nose. She glared at him for a moment as he sat down, then sniffed and returned her attention to the Times crossword.

The egg and mushroom bap was as delicious as Seb remembered. This had been one of Mee's regular haunts, although it had been weeks before she brought him in, shyly introducing him to the ebullient Marco.

"Why is it that brown sauce has never been big in the States?" said Seb2, while Seb chewed.

"Maybe it's the name," said Seb. "It hardly sounds like a delicacy."

"Says what it is," said Seb2. "It's a sauce. It's brown. What's the problem? Folks back home don't know what they're missing."

"True," said Seb. He finished up and left £10 on the table, unsurprised to find the bills in his wallet were now UK currency.

"Ciao, Seb, see you soon," called Marco as Seb opened the door. Seb raised a hand. As the door shut behind him, there was a collective feeling of relief. No one likes a show off.

"Word of advice," said Seb2. "Next time you Walk, go for a less public place. Maybe an alleyway, or behind a tree. Think Clark Kent, no need to draw attention."

"Fair point," said Seb. He found a bench outside a Polish food store, its windows plastered with posters advertising various international calling cards. "So, what's changed? Please use words I can understand."

"Ok. Primarily, you can now go where you like, when you like. The Roswell Manna was the latest nano-technology from Billy Jo's people. No one else could get it, because they were trying to run a brand new app on a 2000-year old Operating System. Imagine Windows Vista, but even clunkier."

"Wow," said Seb. "So what else can I do?"

"Hmm. You know that old expression? Show - don't tell?"

"Fine," said Seb, "show me."

He spent the morning wandering the streets, remembering those intense months with Mee before his visa had run out. He had been in London to write songs for a boy band that was supposed to be about to break through. When two of the singers had been arrested for possession, the album had been mothballed and Seb had found himself out of a job. By then, he'd met Meera and everything had changed.

Meera was a revelation. After an amazing few months of mutual discovery and unexpected happiness, she'd come back to America with him. Within a week, she had formed a band - first Crushed Asians, then

Clockwatchers. Things had started happening for her. It was only a matter of time before a major label showed some interest. But Seb hadn't really been interested in the musical direction the band pursued - Mee was more interested in the lyrics and saw the music as primarily the delivery system for whatever message she wanted to get across. She loved Seb's musicality, but it didn't fit with the sound she wanted. They parted ways professionally and, soon afterwards, personally. It had hurt, but Seb had always been confident they would end up together. He had believed that right up to the point he'd been diagnosed with a terminal condition. Then he'd decided not to tell her about it, despite knowing she would be furious.

"You think she's going to come back to you now you're half-alien?" said Seb2.

"Yeah, actually, I do," said Seb. "Now, come on, I want to buy her a falafel kebab before we go back."

# Chapter 40

Taking Seb2's advice, Seb decided to choose a less conspicuous spot to Walk to this time. He didn't close his eyes, just decided to Walk and his options opened up like someone riffling through a deck of playing cards, each card representing a different geographical location. As he looked for somewhere on the Las Vegas city limits where he was unlikely to be seen arriving, Seb became aware of other possibilities opening up. He paused the process, his options slowly revolving in front of him like tabs on an internet browser.

"What are these?" said Seb, his attention turning to a group of tabs showing potential arrival points containing inexplicable images. Some showed buildings that weren't there in others. Many had no buildings at all. A whole trench of possibilities looked like the surface of the moon, bearing no signs of life at all. Some just showed the star-filled vacuum of deep space.

"Each of these is a doorway," said Seb2. "They all lead to the same place."

"No, they don't," said Seb. "Look at them."

"The same place, but not the same universe," said Seb2.

"What?" said Seb. "You mean those Scientific America articles I read were-,"

"- onto something? Yeah. Parallel universes, different dimensions, the role of consciousness in holding together the fabric of reality. Just don't get too caught up in it. Humans currently have as much chance of understanding this as a newborn being asked to read, absorb, then write a thesis on the Theory Of Relativity, but yeah, this stuff is true."

"Humans? Last time I looked, that was me, too."

"Yeah, whatever," said Seb2. "Thing is, you could spend the rest of your life trying to understand the theory behind what's happening, but you'd get absolutely nowhere. Remember when music recording software used to drive you crazy?"

Seb thought back to the wasted hours spent installing and trying to use studio software on what was - at the time - the fastest computer he could afford. After weeks of frustration, he had eventually given up and wrenched the plug out of the wall, pushing the whole setup into a corner and throwing a sheet over it. That's how it stayed for five years, by which time the value of his entire rig was about half that of the average cell phone.

"I remember," he said.

"And remember the first time you tried a piece of software that worked?"

That had been a beautiful day. Processing power had moved on to the point when someone not particularly tech-savvy could put a laptop next to their music keyboard, plug in a mic and a guitar and make music easily, the software helping the process rather than obstructing it. In a weirdly masochistic way, Seb was glad he'd lived through the period of history when software evolved from expensive self-torture devices to affordable solutions that enabled, rather than hindered, creativity.

"Of course. Don't think I left the apartment for seven days."

"It was ten days. But you don't have a clue how that software works, right? You don't know what's going on under the hood."

"I don't want to know," said Seb.

"Same deal here," said Seb2. "I can use this software but I can't understand it. And let's be accurate, it's not software, it's wetware. Your body is alive with nanotechnology. Every human process is now automated and optimized. As your cells die, they are replaced with better, more effective, stronger cells with capabilities genetically impossible for the rest of our species. Part of your brain now allows me to do my thing alongside the usual human level of consciousness. But I, we, can never expect to understand *how* we can do what we do. At the moment, I feel like a trained monkey with a game console. I can play, I can learn. I can make some guesses about what's going on. But, ultimately..."

"You're a monkey."

"Yes. The split in your consciousness is the only way a human could use this software. Humanity has the potential - every few thousand years or so - of throwing up a genetic wildcard that can cope with it."

"At last, I truly know myself. I'm a genetic wildcard. Thank you."

"Again with the sarcasm."

"Allow me my coping mechanism."

"Of course, said Seb2. "It's either that or insanity. In fact, without Seb3, it would be insanity, followed closely by death."

Seb shuddered. He didn't like to think about the part of himself in constant agony. He didn't understand it, but he wondered what price would eventually have to be paid for fencing off part of himself. He was able to live a day-to-day existence without collapsing, solely because something prevented the pain at his core from touching any other aspect of his consciousness. Sounded like a Faustian deal - and that had hardly worked out well for Faust.

"So the doorways I can see," said Seb, "some of them lead to universes where Vegas never got built?"

"And some where Earth never developed human life" said Seb2. "Others where Neanderthals became the dominant strain of humanity. Others where the Earth never formed at all. Infinite universes."

"Infinite?" repeated Seb. "Truly infinite?"

"Truly," said Seb2. "Every time you make a decision, the universe splits into two and continues. Skip brushing your teeth this morning? New universe. Stay for one more beer? New universe. Assassinate Kennedy? New universe. Multiplied by every being in the universe capable of making a decision. Infinite."

"Ow," said Seb, finally. "My brain hurts."

"Like I said, don't get hung up on the software. We're a monkey with a game console. Let's play."

"Can I bring this kebab?" said Seb, holding the wrapped package from Mee's favorite Moroccan takeaway.

"You can bring the kebab."

Seb picked a Doorway showing a skatepark that had been half-built, then abandoned. As fast as he thought it, he Walked.

# Chapter 41

**Las Vegas**

As he rounded the corner on the dirt track a few miles from where he arrived, Seb detected a faint smell of burning. More accurately, it smelled like the charred remains of a big barbecue after a party. He increased his pace, desperate to see Mee again, but slightly nervous about what they would have to say to each other. It was going to take a while to even start to explain what had happened since that night on the rooftop in LA.

The source of the smell was a small trailer park - it must have comprised half a dozen or so dwellings arranged in a semicircle in front of a hill. The only evidence they'd ever existed - other than the slight smell - were rectangles of dark scorched earth showing the location of each trailer. Inside the semicircle was evidence of more fire amid small shoots of greenery, a flower or two, surely not indigenous. Seb stopped and looked, knowing he was in the right place, but not able to take in the implications of what he was seeing. His throat was suddenly dry.

"Seb?"

Seb's head snapped around to identify the owner of the voice. Sitting on a large rock beneath a stunted tree that provided the only shade in sight, was Walter Ford, wearing a white linen suit, panama hat and sunglasses. The huge Lincoln was parked about ten feet behind him. He had a cool-box at the foot of the rock and was drinking from a brown glass bottle. "Come and join me," he said. "A cold beer's sometimes the only thing that hits the spot."

Seb felt his hands curl into fists. The falafel kebab, having survived an instantaneous journey of thousands of miles without mishap, was now torn in half and dropped to the floor.

"Where's Mee?!" shouted Seb. "What have you done to her?!" He could feel the anger building fast. Years of daily contemplation practice had brought the benefit of being able to identify inappropriate anger and stop it poisoning his experience, but this anger felt *completely* appropriate as it swelled righteously within him.

Walt slid from his perch as the ground started to shake. Rocks, stones, tiny shards of gravel began jumping from the ground, hammering a tattoo of ever-increasing intensity. It was as if the biggest storm in history was breaking around him in the arid wilderness, the thunder provided by drumming rocks. It built into a physically painful sensation and Walt looked fearfully at the hill behind Seb as the ground seemed to roil and shift like an angry animal spotting its prey. He shouted as loud as he could over the racket.

"Seb! Seb, listen to me! I know where Meera is. She's ok! Please, stop this! We have to talk." For a frighteningly long moment, Walt thought Seb wasn't listening. He knew his Manna defenses would be be useless against power like this. Then the rumbling stopped. Walt's ears popped in the sudden silence and he looked over at Seb as his hands relaxed and his eyes stopped blazing. Walt remembered reading that metaphor in a cheap novel once and snorting. Surely 'blazing eyes' belonged in badly written romances along with 'manly torsos' and 'heaving bosoms'. But he had seen Seb's eyes, and he couldn't think of any other way of describing them. Mason's instructions had been to make Seb face facts, show him the lay of the land, intimidate him a little. Now Walt wondered who was the mark here. Was he supposed to walk away from this? Seb had changed. He could sense that flame of extraordinary talent, but it was flickering and nebulous, lost in something far more tangible, powerful and incomprehensible. His hand shook as he raised the beer bottle to his lips.

"Where is she?" said Seb. "What happened here? Where's Bob? And how the hell do you even know who she is? You said I could trust you."

"And you can, Seb, you can. Meera's fine, she's in no danger whatsoever. But listen, I don't enjoy the whole dramatic spaghetti western vibe, ok? I promise I'll tell you everything, but let's go grab a drink."

Seb had brought his breathing under control and was looking steadily at Walt. The older man couldn't read that expression, and something in the eyes made him feel like he was Seb's junior by a long, long stretch. He looked away quickly and gestured toward the car. The driver's door opened and Steve stepped out, holding open the rear door and waiting. Seb waited for Walt to get inside, then joined him. Steve drove slowly away, the big car's suspension wallowing over the uneven ground. The security glass between driver and passengers slid slowly into place.

Seb turned to Walt. "Start talking," he said.

"I never told you how Sid Bernbaum died," said Walt. Seb shifted in his seat and Walt held up a placating hand. "Look, I'm a story teller. What I need to say isn't easy - I need to tell you in my own way. And that means you need to know a little more about what brought me here. Meera is in no immediate danger. I swear she isn't, Seb. "

Seb said nothing, so Walt reached into the cool-box and opened two beers, handing one to Seb.

"I got comfortable as Sid's apprentice. He kept the bosses and the bent politicians as honest as he could and I watched and learned. Not just about using Manna, but about what makes people tick. Including myself. I found out everyone has a weakness they don't want exposed. You find it and you own them. Sex, drugs, booze, gambling, whatever. Some guys had no fear at all. That kind, you threaten their family. Or you threaten whatever it is they love. Usually money. Then they play ball. I just watched this, laid low and got better and better at controlling Manna.

"Then, suddenly, there was a new guy in Chicago. Seemed to come out of nowhere. Buying up cops and politicians, taking chunks out of Marty the Bear's extortion racket. We knew there was trouble brewing when they found Marty's head nailed to the door of the Mayor's house. The Bear had owned the Mayor for years. Sid knew he had to find this new guy. And he didn't take much finding. In fact, he came to us. Just walked into the florists one Friday morning, picked out a funeral arrangement and laid them on the counter. I was minding the store, Sid out back somewhere. This young guy, on the short side, expensive suit and overcoat, thinning blonde hair, he didn't look like anything, but he had an atmosphere about him. Like he was used to getting what he wanted. I felt something straight away, but wasn't experienced enough to realize what it was.

"'Go tell your boss I want to see him, kid,' he said. He put a business card on the counter. Tell him Michael Hamilton is here.'

"'I know who you are,' said Sid. He had this way of just appearing, always made me jump. 'What do you want?'"

"'Oh,'" said this Michael Hamilton character, acting like he knew something we didn't, 'it's just a courtesy call, Mr. Bernbaum. I'm introducing myself to potential business associates all over Chicago.'

"'You and I both know I have no interest in doing business with you, Mr. Hamilton. Please leave.' Hamilton just smiled. Now, remember, by this time I'd seen dozens of hard guys underestimate Sid and live to regret it. So I wasn't worried at all. Until I glanced over at Sid and saw straight away that he was scared. I'd never seen him scared before, but it was written large in the way he was pressing his lips together to stop them shaking. He looked like a frail old man. Then I worked out what was different, what had made me feel on edge since Hamilton had walked in. It was Manna. He was a User. And if Sid was scared, he must be powerful.

"Hamilton never raised his voice or got upset. 'It's just business, Mr. Bernbaum. Your way of running things has come to a end. The world is changing, but that doesn't mean there's nothing left for you. On the contrary, I'd love to have you on the team. You and your young friend here.' He winked at me. 'Often the younger ones see change coming first and adapt. It's a quality I admire, but it doesn't have to be solely the province of the young, does it?'

"'Leave him out of it,' said Sid. 'You've said your piece, now get out.' Hamilton put his hat back on and nodded at both of us.

"'I'll come back in 24 hours,' he said. 'I could build my organization without you, Mr. Bernbaum, but it would take a little longer. Your contacts, the nefarious way you gather information, the pressure points you've put in place...I admire your work. I admire it very much. But, make no mistake, if you do not accept my offer, I will shut you down.' He looked over Sid's floral displays, seemed to choose a wall at random and pointed a finger. Every bloom wilted simultaneously, petals floating to the ground like snow.

"After Hamilton left, Sid took me out back and made tea with shaking hands. 'Feh,' he said, 'I knew this day would come. That fool was right about one thing: the world is changing. It's always changing, and as you get older, it gets harder and harder to change with it. Sometimes you see change coming and decide you won't go along with it. His type means we go back to the old days of violence, turf wars. People will die and Chicago will become a place where decent people are scared to live. It's time to get out of the city, my boy.'

"He gave me a list of errands to run. He planned to leave town in the morning, but not before destroying everything in the shop. His whole network, all the bugged offices, hotel rooms, warehouses and homes, all the information giving him power, all gone forever. I was horrified. I thought he was crazy. But I'd sensed the power Michael Hamilton had and I could see he was someone who was going to build an empire. He just had an aura about him, he seemed unstoppable."

Walt stopped talking. The Lincoln had stopped outside a rundown bar well off the Strip. "Look, Seb," he said. "We make decisions all the time, some easy, some hard. Sometimes, one decision can determine the course of the rest of your life. Even if you regret it, it can't be undone. It sets you on a path. By the time you realize it wasn't the right path you're so far along there's no way back." He sighed heavily and shook his head.

"You betrayed Sid," said Seb. Walt didn't look at him, his eyes fixed on the back of Steve's head.

"I didn't know they were going to kill him," he said, his voice quiet and flat. "I shouted for his help outside the shop. When he came out they shot him. Five of them with machine guns. He might have coped with one. At that stage I hadn't seen how powerfully or quickly Sid's use of Manna could heal injuries, but it was obvious Hamilton was taking no chances. The bullets just kept hitting him. They fired into his body after he fell. They just kept firing until they'd run out of bullets. Hamilton stepped forward with an axe and hacked his head off, kicking it away from his body like a football. Then he walked over to me. 'Smart decision, kid,' he said. 'You just got promoted.'"

"He was your friend," said Seb. You owed him everything."

"I can't justify what I did," said Walt. "It was a long time ago. Sid was old, I was ambitious, I thought I'd be ok living with the consequences. I think about Sid every day. Every damned day. But I still look back and wonder what else I could have done. They weren't going to let him walk away, that was obvious. Why should I go down with him? What good would it have done him?"

Seb didn't answer.

"I made a decision and I learned to live with it. Never made my peace with it, but learned to live with it, ok? And I carved out a decent life for myself."

Seb was thinking about Jack Carnavon. About the look on his face when he realized Seb was going to let him die. He lived with that look every day. Bad decisions had consequences. But you could learn from them, you could try to restore some balance by doing some good, doing the right thing. You didn't have to stay on a path. Knowing he had the potential to become like Jack, someone who thought they could make decisions about life and death, had given him a constant reminder never to let it happen. And now lives were at risk again and he had the power to do something about it.

"Yeah, you got your decent life," said Seb. "But it's never too late. You can always choose to do the right thing."

Walt laughed then, but there was no humor at all in the sound. "You don't know Mason," he said, bitterly. He grabbed his laptop and got out of the car, heading into the dim interior of the bar. Seb followed him. Walt ordered more beer and sat down in a booth at the back of the room. He opened his laptop, tapped some keys, then swung the screen around so Seb could see it.

"I'm calling Mee," said Walt.

# Chapter 42

The screen showed what looked like a mid-range hotel room, spacious, clean. It could be anywhere in the world. The laptop at Mee's end was obviously on a desk in front of a window, as no lights were turned on inside, yet it was bright enough to see clearly. So she was in the same hemisphere, at least.

Mee looked washed out, tired, and angry. Seb knew his face had just appeared on her screen, as tears began to roll down her face.

"'I'm sorry, Seb," she said, wiping the tears with a tissue. "It's all my fault. If I hadn't called you, they wouldn't have found us."

"Where are you?" said Seb.

"I don't know," she said. "They used some kind of spray. I don't know how long I was unconscious for. When I woke up, I was here."

"Look out the window, Mee," he said.

"No good. They've covered it. It's some sort of tower block, I know that. I'm high up, I can see the street and other buildings, but the covering blurs everything, makes it impossible to see any details. See?" She swiveled the laptop and Seb saw she was right. He couldn't Walk to her if he had no idea where she was.

"Who's with you?" he asked.

"Paid thugs," she said, curling her lip. "Henchmen and henchwomen. Wearing black. Like they need to dress that way to let me know they're the bad guys. Idiots."

Seb smiled. That was a little more like the Mee he knew.

"Back up a little, Mee. Whatever happened wasn't your fault, ok? You've been dragged into this, and you can't blame yourself for anything anyone else does. Ok?"

She sniffed. "Ok," she said in a small voice that seemed to belong to someone else.

"Now tell me what happened."

Mee told him about Lo rescuing her and Bob back in LA, about their time with the Order. How she had quickly come to respect them and their quiet power. She told Seb the Order thought he was important, but avoided the word 'Messiah' as she thought he had enough to deal with right now. Then, her voice drained and tight, she described the events of the previous night, the wholesale slaughter of the people who'd taken them in and looked after them. She took a long breath in and told Seb about Bob.

Seb sat staring at the screen. He felt grief and rage building inside him like floodwaters battering a dam. He closed his eyes briefly.

"Breathe," said Seb2.

"Easy for you to say," thought Seb. "You don't have to." He was desperately trying to cling on to his sense of humor, before the anger overwhelmed him and caused him to reach over and squeeze the life out of this man he had briefly considered his friend.

"Mourn Bob later," said Seb2. "It's all you can do. They want you off-balance, they want you irrational. You lose it now, you're playing into their hands."

Seb took a few long breaths, sounding his word: *silence*. He unclenched his hands, then opened his eyes and looked down at the stained bar table for a few seconds.

When he raised his eyes, he looked over the top of the laptop at Walt. The older man was also looking at the table. Seb looked back at the screen, and Mee.

"What do they want?" he said, finally, his voice quiet but steady. "Have they told you that?" She shook her head mutely.

"They're not interested in me," she said. "I'm just here because they think they can use me to get to you. Don't let them trap you, Seb. Whatever's happened to you, you're still you. Don't let them use me to threaten you. I'm serious. Get as far away from these ruthless bastards as you can. Forget about me." She looked at the screen and Seb had that strange sensation of knowing she was looking right at him, but as the camera was at the top of the screen, her eyes seemed to be looking elsewhere. Her hand moved.

"Mee," said Seb quickly, "don't. I can help, I can-". The screen went blank as she broke the connection.

Walt leaned across, folded the screen down and pulled the laptop back to his side of the table.

"She's strong," he said. "I can see what attracted you to her."

Seb just looked at him. "Don't *ever* speak about Meera to me," he said. "Tell me what you want, but don't think I'm your friend, don't try to make conversation. You should have left Chicago with Sid. Or put yourself between him and those bullets. You'd be better off dead than ending up like this."

Walt was silent for a long time. Then he took a long swallow of beer and shrugged.

"I have no illusions about what I am," he said. "Now listen. Mason has Meera. He has run things in this country for about thirty years. Before I tell you what happens next, I'm going to give you some advice."

Seb opened his mouth to speak, but Walt cut him off.

"I know you don't want it. Doesn't matter. You need to know this. You can't win against Mason, so don't take him on. He is as cold as they come. You, me, Meera, Bob, the Order, we're just pieces in a game to him. He will sacrifice anyone without a second thought if it gets him something he needs. He doesn't care who has to bleed. And he's untouchable."

"No one's untouchable," said Seb.

"Think again. No one knows who Mason is. He communicates through email, text or phone calls. He runs a network of the most powerful Manna users in America. The network extends to many other countries. His attempt to remain anonymous has been completely successful. You only need one demonstration of his power to decide it would be in your best interests to join him. And he asks very little of us, really."

"Just that you murder innocent people," said Seb. As Walt raised his hands to protest, Seb cut him off. "Or stand by while innocent people are murdered. It's the same thing."

Walt lowered his hands and looked away for a moment before continuing.

"As far as I know, Mason has only been challenged once. He wiped out the challenger's whole family. The guy didn't even know it was happening, at first. An uncle in London died, I think. Then it was his wife's sister and her family. Then his parents. Then his wife. Then his children. He shot himself to deny Mason the pleasure of finishing the job. If you have anyone you care about, do as he says. If you ever want to see Meera again, Seb. Think about it."

Walt couldn't meet Seb's eyes. To know you're weak is one thing; to have someone look at you with hate, disgust and pity was another.

"What does he want?" said Seb.

"He wants you to go to New York." Walt slid one of his business cards over to Seb. Handwritten on the back was an address. "8pm tomorrow."

Seb stood up, turned and walked out without looking back. Walt tapped out an email to Mason.

**Varden will be there tomorrow. His power has increased massively, but I can't sense him any more. I don't know what he's capable of.**

Walt finished his beer and ordered bourbon. When the barmaid came over, he asked her to leave the bottle.

# Chapter 43

Seb Walked back to Los Angeles. He had 21 hours before his meeting in New York. He knew Mee was safe, for now, but he also knew she was in the hands of people who didn't have any qualms about murder.

In his apartment, he drank a glass of water and walked around the rooms he had lived in for the last three years. He felt disconnected, as if he was an intruder. He remembered feeling the same way when Mee had taken him to Liverpool and they'd visited the childhood homes of John Lennon and Paul McCartney. The houses had contained old furniture sourced to make them look as close as possible to how they looked in the late 1950s and early 1960s, when the Beatles first met. It had been a fascinating tour, but Seb remembered suddenly feeling like a voyeur, peering in at a world that had gone forever and attributing to that world some kind of magic that made it a Golden Age. They had left the tour early and gone to the pub, playing Beatles songs on the jukebox and getting gloriously drunk.

He pulled his old prayer stool out from under the piano and sat, realizing as he did so, that he was now wearing the old sweat pants and t-shirt he always wore when he practiced contemplation.

"Your clothes, your physical appearance, just thinking it changes it," said Seb2 as Seb tucked his legs under the low wooden stool and folded his hands in his lap.

"Yeah, I remember," said Seb, allowing his breathing to slow. "Tell me something useful. Fashion tips aren't going to help save Mee."

"You'd be surprised. Changing the way you look wouldn't have helped you escape notice before Roswell, but now you've dropped completely off the radar. They won't know you if you look different."

"They can't sense me any more?" said Seb. "How is that possible? Walt could tell where I was any time. That crazy Sonia woman found me quickly enough."

"The Manna you've absorbed," said Seb2, "it's completely new. It comes from a culture 2,000 years further on from the one that seeded the Earth first time around. Roswell was the third visit I'm aware of. The first visit was thousands of years before humans started walking on two legs. The Manna left then was somewhat of a marker. When humans found it, cultures started developing with a shaman, witch doctor, or priest of some kind. The second visit was supposed to coincide with a genetic wildcard being available and able to absorb upgraded Manna. For whatever reason, it didn't quite take, but that visitor left millions of Thin Places seeded all over the planet."

"And everyone who can use Manna, they're still using the Manna that was left then?"

"Right. It's self-sustaining nanotechnology, the amount of it on Earth is kept constant. Taken away from a Thin Place by a human body, the tech will shut down over time - faster as it's used by whoever absorbed it. The Thin Places automatically replace the Manna taken. And that's how it's been for many centuries. You're the next genetic wildcard, the new Manna was only left in one Thin Place, ready to seed the planet again when the time came."

"But it's gone, right? I have it all."

"Yes. Billy Joe went home after passing on Manna to you. The Manna he gave you was a bridge, not the Roswell Manna, but a upgraded version of the 2000 year-old stuff. It meant you were able to absorb Roswell without burning up. I think part of the original plan would have been that you, when the time is right, would make new Thin Places. If and when humanity is ready."

"Great," said Seb. "Looking at the way we're using Manna now, I reckon humanity might be ready in another few thousand years or so."

"Ok," said Seb2. "You can decide then."

"Oh," said Seb, thought for a few moments, then said "oh" again. "You're serious, aren't you? How long do you expect me to live?"

"To all intents and purposes, you're immortal. You *can* die, but only by deciding to do it. You'd have to release all the Manna, then you'd age, sicken and die just like regular folk."

"But until then...?"

"No sickness, no headaches, no head colds. No death."

There was a pause.

"You called me a World Walker," said Seb. "What is that?"

"Again, let me just remind you there are provisos at work here. I am still you, after all. My knowledge is very sketchy, much of it educated guesses. I think Billy Joe's arrival in 1947 didn't go as planned. It was a crash, I think the ship was a drone carrying the newest Manna. I don't think he needed a ship at all. And he arrived decades too early, although that meant little to him. He just waited. He is a World Walker too."

"Wait," said Seb. "Not just Walking from place to place, or Walking through parallel universes, but walking *from* world to world too?"

"Right," said Seb2. "Which means we should be able to do the same, in theory, but, well, remember the monkey playing a video game analogy?"

"We're still the monkey."

"Correct. If we try Walking to another planet, we'll probably be as successful as that monkey taking on a shoot 'em up designed by Einstein. No telling where we'll end up. Too much of a risk."

"I think we've got enough to deal with on this planet as it is," said Seb. "So Billy Joe is a World Walker, I'm a World Walker. Are there others?"

"No idea," said Seb2. "But logic would suggest the answer is yes."

"None of this helps me find Mee," said Seb. "What can we do?"

"Well, as you're effectively cloaked now, you can use it to your advantage. Find out where she is tomorrow and go get her."

"And if I can't find out?"

"I don't know. One step at a time."

Seb let the voices fade as he watched his breath and brought his attention to the present moment. Even as Jack Carnavon's face drifted into his mind, as it always did, it was swiftly followed by the look on Mee's tear-streaked face as she ended the call. Seb, with the discipline borne of years of daily practice, observed the thoughts, watched his own despair, anger and hope and allowed them to float away as he returned to a state of pure awareness.

# Chapter 44

## New York

Manhattan in Fall was cold. The temperature had risen sufficiently during the day to melt the early frost, but even when the sun was at its zenith, people were wrapped in overcoats, hats and scarves, plumes of mist coming out of their mouths as they hurried along the ever-busy sidewalks. As the afternoon darkened and lights started to come on around the city, the temperature plummeted again. It felt like winter had come early, but New Yorkers were used to the cold and dressed for it. So the tall guy in the smart, light summer suit got a few looks as he walked out of an alleyway in SoHo. The looks would have turned into open-mouthed gapes if anyone had seen him duck into the next alleyway, emerging two seconds later in dark chinos, thick sweater, a long, heavy overcoat, scarf, hat and gloves.

"Not that you need them to keep warm, but no point drawing attention to yourself," said Seb2.

"Where am I heading?" said Seb, stopping as he caught sight of himself in the window of a coffee shop. He seemed to have grown a beard. His skin was darker. It was a good job he was wearing a hat as he was now bald. And, apparently, he had grown a couple inches and aged about 20 years. He walked on.

"It's three blocks away," said Seb2. The address we have is an office building, but I can't find any record of the first floor tenant, although the rent has been paid promptly for the last six years."

"You're actually a vast improvement on the internet," said Seb.

"How, exactly?"

"Well, quicker, obviously, and the information is always relevant. I can only assume that's because you're not spending 80% of the time watching porn or looking at cat videos."

"You have to remember we represent an evolutionary leap forward for humanity," said Seb2. "What you have become is beyond the wildest speculations of the most maverick evolutionary biologist. So I only actually spend about 30% of the time watching porn and cat videos."

Seb laughed and stopped in his tracks, apologizing to a small Korean woman who, having used his back as a windbreak for the last 200 yards, walked straight into him. A few more steps took him to the corner of the street Walt had written down.

"Just keep walking, nice and steady," said Seb2, "but I should warn you there are six Manna users within a half-mile radius. Considering the number of Users currently in New York is 112, that's a statistical anomaly worth noting. Not a coincidence. The first one is watching from the newsstand over the street. Be subtle, remember she can't sense us."

Seb scanned the street left to right as if looking for a particular building. He spotted the woman immediately. She was trying to look like she was browsing the magazine rack in front of her. A copy of Time was in her hand and her head was bowed slightly as if she was reading, but her eyes were flicking backward and forward, checking the foot traffic on the opposite sidewalk. As Seb watched, she glanced right at him, then moved on to someone else.

"There's another one covering the other end of the street," said Seb2. "Four Users are inside the building we're heading for."

"Ok, I'm gonna walk straight past, go around the block then come back next time as me."

"Because?"

"Because they must know by now they can't sense me, and Walt must have told them I've learnt to change my appearance. But they haven't seen it for themselves. They might think he's exaggerating. If I come back looking like me, is there any way we can let a hint of Manna show? So they think my cloaking trick isn't perfect."

"Yes, I can do that. Best that they underestimate us from the beginning. Good thinking."

Seb saw the second User standing by a parking meter at the far end of the street. He went straight past him, turned the corner and walked around the block. Halfway round, he ducked behind a car and came out as himself.

"Shame," he said. "I quite liked that beard." Just before rounding the final corner, Seb2 allowed small amounts of Seb's Manna use to escape. Seb pictured the process as being like lifting the lid on a casserole to let a waft of the rich aroma into a room. Seb didn't need to look at the newsstand woman to know she had spotted him. Without him moving his head, Seb2 patched a live feed from a security camera outside a nearby store. To Seb it looked like a small window appeared to his left, showing the view across the street of the woman abandoning all pretense of reading her magazine and speaking into a mic on her coat cuff.

"Neat trick," said Seb.

"I'm full of 'em," said Seb2. "Ok, we're not expecting any physical threat from this meeting, but your apartment is lined up and ready to Walk to. You just need to think it and you're there."

"We're not going anywhere until we find Mee," said Seb. He stopped in front of a door with three brass plaques boasting a lawyer, a tax attorney and a management consultancy firm. There were four buzzers to the right, three of them labelled, one blank. "That one?" said Seb.

"That one," said Seb2. Seb buzzed, the door clicked open and he walked upstairs to the first floor. A dimly lit corridor led to a heavy oak door. It swung open as he approached. Seb walked through it and saw the retreating back of a giant of a man, close to seven feet tall. The huge figure reached a second door and held it open for Seb.

"This way, Mr. Varden," he said. Seb walked through into a sparsely furnished office. A polished wooden floor, large utilitarian desk and two lamps. No bookcases or filing cabinets. On the desk was a laptop. Behind the desk sat three unsmiling figures. The first was a woman who looked to be in her eighties, sitting bolt upright, wearing a green tweed suit. The third sat lower than the other two, despite the fact that he was perched on a cushion.

"Barrington," thought Seb.

"Got to be," said Seb2. "I suppose we should have expected to meet the muscle of the operation. What do you make of this guy?"

*This guy* was the middle figure behind the desk, a corpulent hippy with John Lennon glasses and long, greasy hair.

"The Grateful Dead fan?" thought Seb. "He looks stoned. Or bored."

"Wrong on both counts," said Seb2. "He's using every trick he knows to find out about your Manna. This whole room is swarming with nano tech he's controlling. He looks half-asleep because of his level of concentration. What he's doing is astonishing, actually. I can feel millions of approaches by his Manna, interrogating ours, feeding back information."

"And how much information is he getting?"

"Oh, I'm making sure he's got plenty to talk about once we've gone. I'm currently telling him a story he'll want to believe. They sure won't want to believe you're as far removed from them as you are."

"So what are you telling them?"

"That you absorbed the Roswell Manna - they already know that, no reason to hide it. But they'll think your body has been unable to work with what you picked up. They know you're powerful, but I'm giving them the impression you're volatile, too, that the new Manna is so far advanced, you can't predict the outcome of any significant use with confidence."

"And they're buying that?"

"Sure, pretty much. And you're about to give them the clincher."

"How?"

"By passing out for a few minutes. If you don't respond to what this hippy's doing, they'll wonder how you could be so cool about it. It'll undo all the good work I'm doing making you look weaker than you are. So I'm going to hit back, send a kind of mini-EMP at John Lennon, knock out his Manna. Probably do him some damage, too."

"EMP?" thought Seb. "Electric magnetic something?"

"Electro Magnetic Pulse. You won't be out for long."

"Fire when ready," said Seb, then slumped in his seat as he passed out. The large hippy screamed briefly and fell out of his chair. He lay on the floor, blood trickling from his nose. Barrington didn't even glance at him and the older woman merely sniffed as if unimpressed. She turned toward the door.

"Simon," she said. The huge man entered the room, grabbed the hippy under his armpit with one enormous hand and dragged him unceremoniously out of the room.

"Perhaps Walter Ford over-estimated him," said the woman.

"Perhaps," said Barrington. They both waited, watching Seb. After three minutes, his eyes started to move behind his eyelids. Then he opened them and straightened in his chair.

"Very impressive, Mr. Varden," said the woman. "You'll forgive me if we don't introduce ourselves, but discretion is one of the linchpins of our organization. Mr. Mason wishes to talk to you."

"Where is he?" said Seb. "And where's Meera?"

The woman ignored Seb's questions, pressed a button on the laptop, then swiveled it around to face Seb. The screen remained blank and the voice that spoke from the tiny speakers was no more than a whisper.

"Mr. Varden, let's get straight to business," came the whisper. "My name is Mason. Mr Ford has told you a little about me. All you really need to know is I head up a large group of Manna users in this country. We ensure our power remains unknown to the public and, as Mr. Ford told you, we keep a light but firm grip on local and national government at home and abroad."

"Where's Meera?" said Seb. "And why are you hiding? If you're scared to face me because of what you did to Bob, you should be." The response to that was a strange kind of hissing noise. It took Seb a second to work out that it was laughter.

"Hmm, got to admit he's clever," said Seb2.

"In what way?" thought Seb.

"I'm trying trace the signal. It loops between countries via various satellites, but then it comes to a dead end completely sometimes, in different places each time. It's some kind of random algorithm, no pattern at all. It's the same thing they did with Mee's call. I don't know where he is."

The whisper could have belonged to anyone. There was no discernible accent.

"I value my privacy, Mr. Varden," whispered Mason. "Miss Patel is in good health. I will open a video link to her shortly so you can see for yourself. But first, we need to talk business."

Seb said nothing, not even wanting to acknowledge this twisted maniac with a response.

"We know you went to Roswell and we know what happened there. Even before then, Walter Ford described you as the most powerful Manna User he had ever met." There was a pause. "Although, it's only fair to point out he's never met me."

Behind the desk, Barrington and the old woman were as still as statues.

"In Las Vegas, you were attacked by Sonia Svetlana, current leader of the Acolytes Of Satan, yes?" whispered Mason.

"That's who Walt said she was," said Seb. "Although most of what he told me was probably a crock of shit."

"In this instance, his information was accurate. We have been waiting for Ms. Svetlana to make her move for several months now. After dispatching the strongest Manna users in the rest of the world, she had to come here if she was to complete her collection. I have long been considered the single most powerful user of Manna on Earth, so I was always going to provide the culmination of her killing spree.

This is not pride speaking, Mr. Varden, but I would be a fool not to be aware of the nature of my own capabilities. I have led my organization for over three decades now and have no illusions. I am not here because I command respect, or affection, only fear. I offer all my associates the same choice. They join me or die. And, since I ask so little of them, almost all of them choose to join me."

"Almost all?" said Seb.

"There have been refusals along the way. Not many of them. Usually a small demonstration of my superiority convinces them of their error. If not, they die. My organization doesn't have a single weak link, Mr. Varden."

Seb remembered Walt refusing to meet his eye and wondered if that was true.

"The fact that Ms. Svetlana changed her plans so quickly when you appeared suggests one of two possibilities. Either she considers you a warm-up of sorts, a starter before she gets to my entrée, or she believes you are more powerful than me. Again, I doubt she has sufficient information to make that decision. However, I am not so vain as to assume I am the most powerful of the two of us. A truly great leader must be a realist. You may be stronger. You did, after all, absorb the Roswell Manna, even if your body may not be able to use it effectively."

"Looks like they bought it," said Seb2.

"Nice work," thought Seb.

"This presents me with an unusual situation. Ms. Svetlana needs to dispose of all challengers in order to fulfil various arcane prophecies. For such an obviously talented individual, her belief-system is embarrassingly medieval. I had preparations in place to confront her, but your arrival changes the picture considerably. She wants to take you on. That much is clear from the risks she took getting to you in

Las Vegas. She has now retreated to the headquarters she's set up here in New York. I need you to go there and kill her."

"No,"said Seb.

"I hardly expected an immediate 'yes'. First, let me briefly address your moral objections." The screen of the laptop turned on. It was full of pictures of young men. "The Acolytes have taken to performing one of their many rituals on an ongoing basis since Ms. Svetlana took the reins. These young men have all gone missing in the New York area since she and her people arrived. They are only the ones we know about, but it is likely there are many more, as the information we have suggests she requires at least 20 sacrifices every month. The victims are crucified upside-down and their blood is slowly drained until they die."

"Cross-checked those photos against police databases and most show up as missing," said Seb2. "The ones that don't have been found dead. All drained of blood."

"For Ms. Svetlana, this is just the start," whispered Mason. "Once she has completed the final rituals, which will involve your death, my death, or both, she will instruct her followers to kill all male children born within the last three months. It's some kind of perverse tribute to Herod, designed this time to bring about the rule of the Antichrist. I have no reason to lie about this, Mr. Varden. Scanned copies of all these rituals can be found on their website, where they are assumed to be of only academic interest. I assume you've checked it?"

"Hmm," said Seb2, "I guess he's not completely underestimating us. Yes, I've checked, and yes, he's telling the truth."

"So we tip off the cops," thought Seb.

"I think he's in favor of a more permanent solution," said Seb2. "The police will never be able to contain someone like her."

Seb spoke to Mason. "Ok, they're crazy, I get it," he said. "But that doesn't make me a killer. You don't seem to understand this. Not everyone treats life with the same disregard as you. Bob Geller was my friend. A good man. No threat to you or anyone else." Seb felt the anger surging inside him. He breathed more deeply and calmed himself. He couldn't help Bob now, but Mee was still out there, alive, and she needed him, despite what she'd said.

"Bob Geller was in the wrong place at the wrong time," whispered Mason. "After witnessing what happened to you in the mountains during your first, unfortunate, encounter with my people, he started doing some digging online, asking questions. He wasn't the type to let something drop. But there was another reason he had to die."

"What possible reason could you have, you twisted sadist," said Seb.

The voice from the laptop didn't react to Seb's anger.

"He had to die so you would believe I am prepared to hurt Meera Patel," whispered Mason.

Seb stood up.

"You so much as look at her wrong and I swear I'll hunt you down and kill you, you sick son of a bitch."

A thin laugh was the response.

"You see, Mr. Varden," whispered Mason, "you are prepared to commit murder after all. It's just a case of finding the right motivation. If you kill me, you believe it will stop me hurting innocents like your friend. But I've just shown you evidence of the killing of many more innocent people. You don't seem to care enough to break your precious moral code for them."

"That's different," said Seb.

"How so? The only difference is mathematical. I am not hiding anything. In the last thirty days, I have had eighteen people killed. During the same period, Ms. Svetlana and her followers have killed at least 32 people. The deaths I ordered included your friend and the members of the Order who were sheltering him and Ms. Patel. These deaths were regrettable, but necessary. I have no thirst for blood. The members of the Order had to die to stop a conflict erupting between them and my organization. They may suspect my involvement, but suspicion won't be enough for them to act against me. Which means I can concentrate on the Acolytes, without having to divert significant resources to deal with the Order."

"None of them deserved to die," said Seb.

"Yes, well, I have no ambitions to pry you away from your idealistic moral code and introduce you to reality. I merely need you to understand the lengths to which I am prepared to go. And so to Ms. Patel."

The screen, which had gone blank after showing Sonia Svetlana's roster of victims, came to life again. It was the same hotel room as before, Mee sat at the desk. This time, there were two figures behind her, both dressed in the anonymous black suits of security agents the world over. Seb recognized the taller one. Westlake. Seb's eyes narrowed. Mee was handcuffed to the chair. Her expression was tired but defiant.

"Mee, are you ok? Mee?"

"She can't hear or see you, Mr. Varden," whispered Mason. "Now I will ask you one more time. Will you kill Sonia Svetlana? If not to prevent her continuing slaughter of innocent young men, then perhaps to save your friend here?"

Seb's lips tightened, and he felt himself making fists almost unconsciously.

"You won't kill her," he said, finally. "You've done your research. You know I have no family, no close friends. Mee and I only dated for a short time. She doesn't mean that much to me. And if you kill her, not only do you lose your leverage, you guarantee I come for you."

"Cogently, and logically, argued. I agree entirely. I have absolutely no intention of killing Ms. Patel."

"Good," said Seb.

"I only intend to hurt her. Maim her. Torture her, if you like."

Seb started to get up. Across the desk, the old woman was still unmoving. Barrington met his eye and smiled.

"Don't do it," said Seb2. "Sit down. Lots of primordial instincts from your cerebellum are causing chemicals to flood the rest of your brain. Very useful when a tiger jumps out on you, but counter-productive now. You need to think clearly and calmly."

Seb sat down. "If they hurt her...," he thought.

"You'll just have to watch," said Seb2. "Don't make the situation any worse. We will find her, but I can't do anything about it immediately. You need to play along, buy us time."

On the screen, Westlake picked up something and held it up to the camera. It was a pair of garden secateurs. He grabbed Meera's left hand and place the blades around her pinky. She started to struggle, thrashing in her chair, but the other man held her firmly down. When she realized she couldn't get away, she suddenly went limp, all the fight gone out of her. Westlake waited, then Seb heard Mason's whisper come from the laptop in the hotel.

"Go ahead."

Seb closed his eyes as the blades closed over Mee's flesh, opening them again to watch her body jerking in agony, eyes rolling back in her head, her screams distorting the mic on the laptop. After five seconds, the screen went blank and the sound was, mercifully, muted. Seb felt unnaturally calm and detached. "You doing this?" he thought.

"Yes," said Seb2. "We need to get through this and make rational decisions, so I'm countering your normal responses. Don't let them see your real reaction. What good could it do?"

"I know you're right, but I still want to hurt someone," said Seb. He focussed on his breathing, trying to live with the horror he had just seen, trying not to think about what Mee must be going through, alone.

"There are many ways to cause pain," whispered Mason. "Removing fingers is effective, but it has the disadvantage of being permanent. Eventually, you run out of fingers. And toes. And other appendages. But it carries a strong visual element, which was necessary in this case. If you refuse me again, I will instruct Westlake to remove her tongue. She will never speak again. More pertinently, she will never sing again. So think carefully before giving me your final answer. Will you kill Sonia Svetlana for me?"

Seb stood. Barrington was still smiling. Seb looked at him. Barrington stopped smiling and started wincing, holding his hand up to his ear. For the first time, he spoke.

"He's Using," he said to the old woman. "Stop him."

She barely moved, but Seb was aware of a huge force building around him.

"Leave it to me," said Seb2. The old woman's eyebrows suddenly shot up in surprise as her chair flew back against the wall. The wall itself seemed to soften as she reached it and her head and body moved about six inches past the physical barrier, the bricks softening like a pillow. Then they hardened again and held her pinned in place. She looked at Seb.

"Don't," he cautioned, and she slumped.

In the next room, the massive guy grabbed the door handle and was hurled six feet backward by a huge electric shock. He twitched once then was still.

Barrington was breathing hard now, the pain in his ear becoming worse. His attempts to defend himself or attack Seb were being batted easily aside in a way he had never encountered. Finally, he could bear it no longer and shouted with pain as his left ear slowly tore away from the side of his head. When it detached completely and fell to the floor, it burst into flame and was consumed, leaving just a charred piece of blackened flesh. He clapped his hand to the side of his face and hissed at Seb.

"I'll just grow a new one."

"I don't think so," said Seb and watched Barrington's face as he realized his Manna could do nothing to repair the permanent damage inflicted by Seb's Roswell Manna.

"Very impressive," whispered the voice from the laptop. "Well?"

"Yes," said Seb. "My answer is yes. I'll kill her. Then we'll talk."

# Chapter 45

The Keystone Hotel was situated in a quiet, affluent neighborhood. The wealth and, often, notoriety of its guests was such that they appreciated the anonymity the hotel provided, blending perfectly as it did with other brownstones on the street. Security was easily arranged, as the buildings on either side were owned by the same group and used as offices. Deliveries were made through the back which had a soundproofed loading bay hidden beneath the beautifully landscaped gardens. Asked why they chose the Keystone above other, equally opulent, hotels in Manhattan, guests almost invariably used the same words: "it's discreet".

For the vast majority of New Yorkers, including every other resident of the street, the arrival of the Acolytes Of Satan had done nothing to alter the calm anonymity of the hotel. If anything, it was even quieter than normal. This was because there were only thirty occupants in a hotel which, even with its enormous rooms and reputation for exclusivity, normally saw occupancy levels average out at forty-four guests - eighty including staff. The Acolytes lived in luxury, and, as they could feed themselves using Manna, they only needed to leave the Keystone for one of two reasons: either to refill at the nearest Thin Place, which was a 20 minute walk away in Central Park, or to hunt.

Hunting in New York was not as pleasurable as it had been in Europe. Many of the longest-serving Acolytes hailed from small Eastern European countries that had gone though two or more name changes in the turbulent twentieth century. Those countries had a rich tradition of myth and folklore which appealed to the Acolytes' sense of history, ritual and theatre. The legend of the Vampire had been born in one such country. A nobleman whose family fortunes were on the wane after finding themselves on the losing side in one of the many wars common in the middle of the 1800s had developed a talent for Manna use. As he was virtually a recluse, due to a skin condition that kept him indoors during the hours of daylight, he had never met another Manna user and had received no training. The first time he had absorbed Manna in the forest near his ancestral home coincided with his first taste of human blood, taken as a suggested cure for his skin condition. He attributed his subsequent power to the blood. Thereafter, he hunted by night, slept in a darkened basement during the day, and terrorized the local population until the night they burned his home to the ground. Forced to escape, he finally met other Manna users and began to understand the real source of his abilities. His association between power and evil never truly left him, however, and he began collecting literature on the subject. Eventually, he founded the Acolytes of Satan and slowly built an organization of believers.

The nobleman's longevity was legendary - he was almost certainly over 150 years old when he died. Some believed he was nearer his 200th birthday. He assumed his leadership would continue until they had brought about the return of Satan. Or so he said. One or two very close to him suspected he had no real belief in anything of the sort, but enjoyed the prestige and privileges of unquestioned power. So it came as quite a surprise to him and his inner circle when a true believer rose quickly through the ranks, challenged him openly, and killed him briskly and efficiently, leaving only some charred bones for his former followers to dispose of.

Sonia had modernized many elements of the organization since then, but she had a deep appreciation of the importance of ritual. She didn't drink the blood of her victims, using it instead to paint runes on her skin while she performed the lengthy rites designed to focus her own Manna as well as that of the senior Acolytes, making it possible to use a combined power that would eventually break through the barriers between this world and others, opening a door for their Master.

In the penthouse at the top of the hotel, black candles burning, five sacrifices at various stages of blood loss hanging from their inverted crosses, she and 24 of the High Council of the Acolytes knelt in the semi-darkness, chanting softly, waiting for Sebastian Varden. They knew he was coming. Mason had passed on that piece of information hours ago. All they had to do was wait. Sonia smiled in the shadows.

Seb had prepared for his one-man attack on dozens of old, powerful Manna users intent on his destruction by eating noodles. Lots of noodles, then a pizza, then two steaks. Seb2 had assured him his body could store the energy without slowing him down, and the physical evidence seemed to back this up. He felt fit, rested and ready. Well, as ready as he could ever be.

Seb2 had researched the Acolytes, so Seb knew a little about the mindset of the people he was about to take on. He had read about their core beliefs and seen details of the rituals they apparently performed. Added to the information from Walt and Mason, it was a pretty unpleasant picture.

"He expects us to die, you know that, right?" said Seb2 as he finished the second steak and ordered two sundaes and a slab of Death by Chocolate cheesecake, the waitress not bothering to close her mouth as she thought disbelievingly of the amount of food he had already consumed.

"It had crossed my mind," said Seb. "But I'm out of options."

"Nothing we can do if he's right, but we need to think about what happens next if he's wrong."

"About saving Mee," said Seb.

"Yes, and yourself," said Seb2. "If you die - which I still think is impossible - it's all over, but if you live, you've proved yourself far more powerful than Mason. More powerful than anyone. We've downplayed the new Manna potential so far, but killing Svetlana and her crew will make it obvious to him. How can he release Mee, the only hold he has over us, if he knows your power is at an unheard of level?"

"We're going to have to work that out later," said Seb. He gave us until the end of the day. It's 10pm. Let's go."

Seb had carefully considered his lack of any relevant training, experience, or inclination to inflict physical damage before deciding to disregard these shortcomings. There were many Acolytes and only one of him. They had been using Manna to commit appalling acts of violence for hundreds of years. He had never heard of Manna until just over a week ago. They had carefully planned and executed the murders of many experienced and powerful Manna users. He got a bit upset when he saw videos of badly treated puppies. Since the odds were stacked so throughly against him, he settled on the only approach he could think of.

At 10:21pm, Sebastian Varden walked into the lobby of the Keystone Hotel. Veronica, a small, plump member of the Acolytes was on duty at the desk to deter unwanted attention from New Yorkers. Her matronly appearance meant she was often underestimated, usually leading to physical discomfort for those who did so.

"I'm sorry, sir," she said, "the hotel is closed until August next year."

Seb walked over and put both hands on the desk, mostly to stop them shaking.

"I don't want a room. My name's Seb Varden. I'm here to see Sonia Svetlana."

Veronica stared at him. She was slightly disappointed. Their leader had spoken of him as the most powerful User on the planet, but she could only sense a little Manna. She nodded.

"Penthouse suite, right?" said Seb, walking across the lobby. He pushed the button and the elevator doors opened. He stepped inside. "Just give her a call, tell her I'm on my way up." As the elevator doors shut, he saw the Veronica pick up the phone, still staring at him.

As the elevator doors shut, Seb looked for a button to press, then realized a small scanner on the wall was designed to recognize guests' thumbprints. It wasn't the best start.

"Wait," said Seb2. Then, "Ok, try it now." Seb held his thumb on the pad and the elevator started to move, swiftly and silently ascending.

"How?" said Seb. "Or - don't tell me - you don't have a clue, the nano-stuff did it all on its own."

"Nah," said Seb2. "Don't know if it's the quickest method, but I reviewed our last encounter with Sonia, got a hi-def image of her thumb and pasted it onto yours."

"Man, I'll never get used to this," said Seb. The elevator arrived and the doors opened. The sound of many voices softly chanting came from the room behind the big door at the end of the hall. Seb walked into the room.

The Acolytes, over thirty of them, were dressed in long, dark hooded robes, their faces in shadow. They were lining the back wall, some making arcane gestures in the air as they chanted. In front of them was a pentagram. The inverted crosses at each point now held mostly fresh sacrifices. As one victim bled out, he was simply replaced with a new unfortunate. The channels of blood gathered at the point where stone jugs were kept to collect the precious fluid. Sonia Svetlana stood naked in the middle of the pentagram. Her eyes were rolled up into her head and her voice was harsh and guttural as she led the chanting. As Seb entered, she dipped her fingers into a jar at her feet and drew a simple design across her breasts and stomach. To Seb's eyes, it looked like a Chinese pictogram, but Seb2 corrected this opinion.

"It's ancient Macedonian," said Seb2. "I just searched online, found a reference to 'curse tablets' - very similar calligraphy."

"Save the history lesson for later," said Seb, "just tell me what the hell that's for."

'That' was a huge mound of soil, spread over the penthouse floor, filling the space between Seb and the nearest tip of the pentagram. It had been roughly spread. In places, patches of the original polished wood floorboards were visible, in others the earth was about four feet high.

*Why all the soil?*

That question was answered almost immediately. Sonia was obviously from the school of villains that didn't believe in a polite chat with the hero before trying to dispatch him. She had seen Seb survive her signature killing stroke, watched the skin and muscle grow back on his bones right in front of her. She had been shocked to find anyone who could withstand her power, but she was a pragmatist first and foremost. If she couldn't kill Seb alone, she would enlist the help of all of her senior Acolytes. The rituals had been performed, the blood was pure and fresh, everything was in place. As Seb looked across the room at them, the chanting abruptly stopped and the earth started to move.

It all happened incredibly fast, but Seb was getting used to the way Seb2 helped slow down his perception of time. Internally, what happened next seemed to take about a minute. In reality it was 2.7 seconds.

The earth moved in a swirling pattern as if it was made of iron filings and a gigantic magnet was being dragged underneath the floor from the room beneath them. The dirt swirled into a cloud, becoming denser by the moment as more and more material was pulled from the outer edges into the center. A shape emerged from the chaos. Like a picture coming into sharp focus through the lens of a camera, a massive body took form. Onyx black, naked, heavily muscled and stooping slightly under the 15ft high ceiling, hairless, its eyes a dull milky gray, stood a creature out of a horror film. The difference was, no CGI monster from the most talented team of creators could ever have a fraction of the solidity and sheer *presence* of the vaguely humanoid beast in front of Seb. He could even smell its breath, rank, earthy, the stench hospitals cover with antiseptic sprays, bleach and air fresheners. The smell of death. The mouth had no teeth at all, just a long black tongue that constantly wetted its cracked, blood-caked lips. The nose was set into what passed for a face - two holes, purely functional. The hairless skull seemed to be all bone. It made no noise at all, no threats, no roars or growls. Despite its nostrils, Seb wasn't even sure it was breathing.

"Fuck me," said Seb2, his voice suddenly small, "it's a demon."

When it moved, Seb expected it to be slow and lumbering, but it sprang at him with the grace and speed of a natural predator. Even with the advantage of slowed time, he couldn't move fast enough to avoid the huge gnarled hand that shot out as the thing pounced, took hold of his head which fitted into its palm, then closed its crushing fingers on his skull. Seb screamed in pain as he felt the bones of his skull begin to splinter and fold, one tiny fragment piercing his brain, causing his legs to collapse. Almost immediately, the world began to darken around him, then -

- he Walked and was in the far corner of the room, sprawled, bleeding. The tips of his fingers tingled as the Roswell Manna began to repair the damage to his body. He didn't even have a headache. The demon was momentarily confused as its hand continued to close on empty air. Then its huge head swiveled and he sighted Seb. He ran at him, both hands now clasped together and swinging up into the air, coming toward Seb in a roundhouse blow that would have crushed his head through his neck into about the middle of his chest if it landed. His injuries now completely healed, Seb Walked again and appeared at one tip of the pentagram. He looked in horror at the young man on the cross next to him whose life was draining away from carefully made cuts on his wrists and neck.

One of the Acolytes flinched when Seb appeared and looked at him. The demon, beginning to turn, stumbled slightly, a movement totally at odds with the incredible speed and precision it had displayed up to that point.

"It's a homunculus," said Seb2 suddenly.

"What? How is that possible?"

"It's all of them," said Seb2. They're all supplying every bit of Manna they have, focussed through her. Look."

Individual threads of power were now visible, emanating from Sonia and the hooded figures, each strand as individual as DNA to Seb's enhanced vision.

"How do we stop it?" said Seb.

"We either attack the Acolytes, but that means turning your back on that thing...or-,"

Seb suddenly *knew* what to do. As the huge shape finished turning and began its sprint toward him, he ran straight at it. Even as he did it, he was aware of Sonia beginning to laugh. She knew their best chance to destroy him was to use speed and strength beyond the capabilities of any human. To her, the demon was real, summoned by their rituals, their Manna merely the fuel it drew upon. That Seb would choose fight over flight was sure, in her mind, to hand the victory to the superior being she had summoned. She watched what happened next in silence, quite unable to process the reality of what was unfolding in front of her.

Seb's decision to run straight at the threat meant the demon misjudged its next attack. It had sprung toward the point of the pentagram at which Seb had materialized, and its huge legs had already propelled it into the air when Seb sprinted straight at it. Instinctively, it lowered a knee, intending to pinion the human, then pound his head to a bloody pulp. But the knee didn't make contact. The demon dropped to the floor and was utterly still, its skin glistening in the light of the candles set into the walls.

Most of the Acolytes currently had their view slightly obscured by the presence of their leader standing between them and the unfolding action, but the ones at either edge saw Seb vanish again. Sonia could see far more clearly, but still didn't understand immediately. She watched Seb jump right at the demon and Walk again just before the impact. Her eyes scanned the room, looking for him. She realized the demon had stopped moving. It was utterly still, a statue from a nightmare. Then, more slowly than before, its great head moved as the demon pushed itself back to its feet. It looked straight at her. She stepped back involuntarily as she felt something jolt her Manna-fuelled senses. There was something wrong. As the demon moved toward her and the Acolytes, she knew. She turned and ran, jumping as she reached the wall, passing straight through it and, assuming the form her body instinctively used to simulate a kind of flight, stretched out her skin between her elongated, hollowed bones and glided across the New York skyline.

"It feels weird," thought Seb, as he looked down at the Acolytes from his new, far greater height. They were just beginning to realize they had lost control, their Manna not reaching the demon. And yet the demon was walking toward them. None of them had the requisite power to do what Sonia could do. As the demon walked on, balling its massive, head-crushing fists, they had to decide whether to fight back, or take their chances and run. They all chose the latter.

From behind the eyes of the demon, feeling quickly at home in its huge frame, Seb watched them dart for the doors in panic and disarray, tripping over their robes in their haste.

"Hardly practical, those outfits," said Seb2.

Seb knelt and put one dark gnarled hand onto the penthouse floor. Threads of white and silver lightning left his fingers and divided again and again, chasing the Acolytes and catching them all before they could escape. They all slumped to the floor unconscious.

"Is it possible to - ?"

"Yes," said Seb2. The demon shape remained still for another few seconds, during which time all Manna was drained from each Acolyte and absorbed by Seb. As the last particle of power left them, the genetic anomaly that allowed them to use Manna was subtly altered. The Acolytes' next trip to a Thin Place would result in the knowledge that their abilities had been permanently removed. They were human again, no more. Within a year, all but three would be dead. Of the three remaining, two would be in prison and the other a member of a religious order determined to try to undo some of the damage she had wrought in the previous 27 years.

The five sacrifices were all still alive, although only one had sufficient blood to remain conscious throughout. He stared in blank incomprehension as the demon fell apart, becoming a mound of earth that shook itself out like a wet dog and carpeted the floor with soil.

Standing in the middle of the dirt was Seb. He walked quickly around the sacrifices, briefly touching each one. Then he made another circuit of the pentagram, this time untying the men. By the time he got back to the first, the man's wounds were healed. When they were all untied and lying at the foot of each cross, Seb found drinking water and helped them all rehydrate as much as they could.

"Help is on the way," he told them, then left the suite before Walking to the pay phone Mason had instructed him to call from once he had accomplished his task. The phone began to ring as he approached. He picked it up.

"It's done," he said. "We need to talk."

"Come to the same office. Tomorrow. Noon," whispered Mason. "She's dead?"

Seb looked at his watch. "She's dead," he said.

"Sure of that?" he thought.

"Yes," said Seb2. "She's carrying a small package of your Manna. It will be quick. Not that she deserves it."

A little under two miles away, a smartly dressed businesswoman got into a cab and asked for the airport.

Contrary to her natural tendency toward glamor, Sonia Svetlana had elected to alter her appearance to resemble an older, slightly frumpy, executive type. She didn't feel like attracting any attention. She still felt numb about what had happened. Was her Master testing her? Could Varden be defeated? She would fly back to Europe, regroup, find new talents to recruit into the group, step up the intensity and frequency of the blood rituals. She would find answers by reading the signs in the hearts and intestines of properly prepared sacrifices. She would come back stronger. She watched the city passing by through the window of the cab. *Shame. So many cattle here.*

The taxi driver's eyes caught a movement in the mirror as the woman behind him suddenly grabbed at her chest, before sliding sideways on her seat. She gasped a few times before, horribly, going completely quiet. He drove as fast as he could to the nearest hospital.

The subsequent autopsy was written up in an eminent medical journal due to the anomalies revealed when they investigated the cause of cardiac arrest in a relatively fit woman who looked to be in her early forties with no evidence of previous coronary problems. Both arteries pumping blood around the body had clotted at exactly the same moment. The clots were large, immediately preventing any further blood flow. She had lost consciousness in seconds and was dead before a minute had passed. The clots were perfectly even, looking for all the world like they had been manufactured. The prominent heart specialist who wrote the paper almost made reference to the seeming artificiality of the clots. Almost. He had a reputation to maintain, and any hint of incompetence would do him no favors just months before he intended to retire from practice and take up one of the extremely lucrative consultancy offers he had been receiving.

No record of the patient's identity was ever found and she was cremated after post mortem photographs had been taken. A copy of the woman's fingerprints and a sample of DNA was put on record in case a relative ever came forward. No one ever did.

# Chapter 46

Barrington looked very unhappy. He had a medical dressing over the hole where his ear had been removed, because, as Seb had predicted, his Manna could do nothing to replace the missing organ. He scowled across the desk at Seb.

The old woman and the hippy were absent this time, as was the huge guy who had let Seb in the previous day. Barrington seethed silently for a good three or four minutes before the laptop beeped, at which point he leaned forward, pressed the space bar and sat back again, still glowering at his nemesis.

"Sources confirm the death of Sonia Svetlana," came the whisper from the laptop. "It seems the Keystone hotel has been abandoned by the Acolytes. They are in disarray. The crucified men you rescued from the building are all in good health. Many are in better health than they were before being abducted. Only one victim gave a statement, after which he was referred to a specialist psychiatric facility which will nurse his obviously damaged psyche back to normality. All in all, a pleasing outcome."

"Meera," said Seb. "Where is she? You got what you wanted, you're still top of the tree, the big Manna guy. You don't need me any more. I'm not interested in your power games. I just want to take Meera home."

"You're a smart guy, Sebastian," whispered Mason. "You must have thought through some of the implications of this power you've been given. I can't let you walk away. We need to find out the extent of the power given to you by our tall gray friend, then I need to decide how best to use you."

"Tall gray what?" said Seb.

"Please don't play games, Mr. Varden. The facility holding the alien was run by a government group I have controlled for many years. I know how you came by the power, I just don't know why. Considering how little we still know about Manna after thousands of years of its use, I don't expect to find out any time soon. To be honest, it doesn't interest me. But you do."

"I don't care. I didn't ask for this. I promise you, I'll walk away with Meera and you'll never hear from me again."

"That's not an option, I'm afraid. You are what this generation has started referring to as a 'game changer'. Every Manna user knows something has altered. By now, there can't be a User alive who doesn't know that the Roswell Manna has gone. When they learn that you have affiliated yourself with me, there will be no further power struggles, just obedience. There will be peace."

"God help us, every megalomaniac dictator in history sounds the same," said Seb2.

"Shh," thought Seb, "let me think."

"I want no part of it," said Seb to Mason.

"You have no choice. I intend keeping Ms. Patel as my guest for the rest of her natural life. You will never see her again in the flesh, but you will be permitted to speak to her occasionally. I have no intention of treating her badly, she will be afforded every luxury. She will never want for anything. Neither her, nor her family."

"Family?" said Seb, heat rising in his face.

"I play a long game," whispered Mason. "Looking at the longevity of other powerful Manna users, I expect to live for at least another eighty years. It is entirely possible, during that time, that Ms. Patel will die, either of natural causes, or by her own hand. When that happens, I lose the leverage over my most powerful ally. I can't allow that."

Seb felt cold and sick. He didn't want to listen.

"I imagine Ms. Patel will hold on to the hope that she can escape or be rescued. This hope may persist for some time. Months, certainly, perhaps years. Once that hope has gone, she will deteriorate rapidly, her health will decline, she will die far younger than she should. Humans are predictable that way. We all need something to live for."

"This sick bastard has done this before," said Seb2, as Seb gripped the sides of the chair.

"I will avoid this eventuality by giving her something worth living for. A child."

"What?!" said Seb, half getting up. Barrington stopped scowling and smirked at him.

"She will be artificially inseminated, there will be no unpleasantness."

"She doesn't want children, your plan won't work."

"Possibly," whispered Mason. "But I suspect she will want to keep the child when she is told who the father is."

"What the hell difference does it make who-". Seb stopped.

"Oh, shit," said Seb2. In the first days of his illness, Seb had given every kind of sample to the specialist. Blood, tissue, saliva. And sperm.

"Ah. I assume from your silence you've made the connection. Look on the positive side, Mr. Varden. You will have a legacy. A new generation, carrying your DNA. Immortality. Of course, ensuring your family line doesn't die out gives me a source of hostages that will comfortably outlive me."

Seb could barely form a coherent thought. He sat in silence for a few long minutes. Finally, he spoke.

"You'd do that just to make me work for you?" he said. "Control those lives, make prisoners of children?"

"I am prepared to do whatever is necessary. And please don't think I would baulk at causing those children pain in order to keep you in line. Everyone has a price or a weakness, Mr. Varden. Those of us who rise to the top do so because we identify and exploit the flaws in others. I need you to understand your position. Do you?"

"I think you've made it clear," said Seb.

"Then our business is concluded, for now. Barrington will give you a cell phone. This is how I will contact you when I need to. Keep it with you at all times."

Barrington slid the phone across the desk to Seb. He was still smirking.

"I'd rather die," said Seb, quietly.

"Speak up, please, Mr. Varden. Do we have an agreement?"

"I said I'd rather die," said Seb, feeling the truth of it. Now it was Mason's turn to leave a long silence before finally speaking.

"That is also an option," he said. "Less complicated for me, certainly, although not as interesting. However, as you must appreciate by now, I am a practical man. Your death would be an acceptable, if regrettable, alternative to your accepting my offer."

"Then that's what I choose," said Seb. "Give me a day to settle things. I was pretty much there, anyway."

"What the hell are you doing?" said Seb2. "At least think this through."

"I don't need to," thought Seb. "We have to save Mee." He spoke aloud.

"I will trade my life for hers," he said. "I have to know she's safe."

"That's possible," whispered Mason. "But if you are dead, how can you trust me to keep my word?"

"That's my problem," said Seb. "I'll think of a way. There's a pizza place on the Upper East Side. Send Walt there tomorrow evening. I'll tell him how we're going to do this."

"You appreciate your head will be separated from your body and both parts burned up?" whispered Mason. "There will be no opportunity for trickery. It doesn't matter how powerful you are, if the brain and body are utterly destroyed, you will die."

"Hey, I almost died a couple weeks back," said Seb. "It's not that bad."

"You have until tomorrow night, Mr. Varden. You may wish to reconsider your decision during that time. Ms. Patel will have a long, healthy life. As will your children. If you choose the second option, those children will never be born."

"Send Walt," said Seb, getting up. "He'll tell you how it's going to play out."

# Chapter 47

Seb spent the next day on a world tour any travel agent would have sold their soul to provide. From the Zhangye Danxia Landform in Gansu, China, with its breath-taking multicolored mountains, to an Orthodox monastery 1300 feet atop a natural sandstone rock pillar in Greece. He breakfasted at the base of an ancient redwood in Yosemite, had mid-morning coffee in a packed market in Istanbul, walked through a Japanese bamboo forest where tall green stalks waved over his head like living tower blocks. He spent an hour on a beach in Peru, the only human for miles around. He paddled in shallow pools inside a huge cave, lush with exotic vegetation, in Hang Song Doong, Vietnam. He swam in the Dead Sea and watched a rainbow over the Victoria Falls in Zimbabwe. He saw the sun go down over Paris from the top of the Tour Montparnasse, saw lights dancing on the Eiffel Tower. Apart from three hours in the afternoon, he spent the day as if it might be his last.

The three hours were spent in the Syrian desert, his body automatically adjusting to the heat and screening out any harmful UV rays in the harsh sunlight.

"This is where the founder of the Order is rumored to come from," said Seb2.

"I know," said Seb. "It seems fitting, somehow." He walked up an incline to the mouth of a cave. Bones around the entrance hinted it may have housed some kind of animal, but their dry, brittle condition suggested it had long since been abandoned. Seb sat in the shadows and held out his hand. A plate, jug and glass took shape, the jug full of ice-cold water, the plate seeming to grow fresh sushi directly from the white china base. Seb ate slowly, savoring each mouthful. Then he looked at the empty plate and it became sand again. He sat, his mind becoming still, silent and focused.

***

When he arrived at the pizza restaurant, Walt was already in a booth, drinking bourbon and nervously folding and twisting a paper napkin.

"You gonna make that attack me?" said Seb as he slid into the chair opposite.

Walt half-smiled. "I wouldn't dare," he said.

"Mason tell you what was going on?" said Seb.

"Yes," said Walt. He stopped playing with the napkin and tossed it onto the table. "You trying to make a point?"

"Maybe," said Seb. "There's always a choice. Always, Walt."

"What kind of a choice is death?" said Walt. "Giving up. What good can you do dead?"

"I might not be able to do any good," said Seb, "but I won't do any harm, and sometimes that's the best option."

Walt stared at him steadily, shook his head, then drained his glass and called the waiter over for more. "You're making a mistake, kid, that's all I can say. All for a girl? You're young, it might seem to make sense to you now, but give it 10, 20 years, you're gonna feel differently, trust me. No one's worth dying for, Seb."

"I'm not sure you entirely believe that yourself," said Seb. "That's why I wanted you here."

"Whatever," said Walt. "You do what you've got to do. But you've been given an amazing gift. Manna makes us better, better than them-," he waved his arm to include everyone else in the restaurant. "And you have the Roswell

Manna. You were given that for a reason. You're gonna throw all that away? You're crazy." He shook his head in disgust. Seb could see he had been drinking for a while, and wasn't using Manna to negate the effects.

"I'm no better than anyone in here," said Seb. "Neither are you. You forget that, it makes it easier for you to carry on helping that psychopath. But I can't forget it. I won't. I've made my choice."

Walt didn't answer, just drank his bourbon and looked across the table.

Seb stood up, reached into his jacket and tossed an envelope at Walt.

"There's a construction site in the Bronx," he said. "The address is in that letter, along with details on how this needs to go down. Sun up is 6:26am, I'll arrive then. Make sure you're there with Meera. I won't be alone, I need someone to drive Meera away, and I won't let you near me until I know she's safe."

"What's to stop you killing me and walking away with Meera?" said Walt.

"Two things," said Seb. "Firstly, I don't want to spend the rest of my life looking over my shoulder. Secondly, I give you my word. By now, you should know that's enough." He started to walk away, then changed his mind and returned to the table.

"Make one thing clear to Mason," he said. "If he tries tracking Mee, puts a bug on her, or has anyone nearby ready to follow her, I'll know about it. Ask him what happened in the Keystone hotel. Tell him I will know if he plans to double-cross me, and if he does, you all die. I know Mee will die too, but it will happen quickly and painlessly. I can make sure of that. But the rest of you will die slowly in the kind of agony you can't even begin to imagine. And then I will devote the rest of my life to hunting down Mason and doing the same to him."

Seb leaned across the table and looked into Walt's eyes.

"Understood?" he said.

"Yes," said Walt.

"I'll see you at dawn," said Seb, and walked out.

# Chapter 48

Seb had often been awake at dawn, not because he was an early riser, but because most shows finished in the early hours, and if the band wasn't staying overnight, they'd board the tour bus and get back on the road. Some of the best musical ideas he had ever come up with had come to him while half-dozing on the Interstate as the first thin sliver of red light began to warm the landscape. He still had hundreds of pieces of scrap paper in the apartment with fragments of lyrics hastily scribbled down, many indecipherable. He thought of it as a haunting time of day, unformed, full of mystery and possibility.

An hour before dawn, an old station wagon arrived at the building site named in Seb's instructions. The occupant got out, walked over to the site, then returned to the vehicle 12 minutes later. During this time, the sound of a large engine could be heard within the site itself, a sound which continued to rumble. As the sky slowly lightened, colors and textures bled into the scene like someone turning the color dial in an ancient television set. The occupant of the car was revealed to be a man in his sixties, dressed in the plain black habit of a Catholic priest. He was gripping the steering wheel tightly, taking long deep breaths as if to calm himself.

A second vehicle arrived at 6:35am. It was a black SUV, the privacy glass making it difficult to see the occupants. It stopped near the site entrance, opposite the station wagon, about 50 feet away. Both doors at the front opened. Two men stepped out and stood still, their breath making wisps of smoke in the cold. It was Sunday, so no interruptions were anticipated.

The older man in the station wagon watched intently as another figure appeared, this time walking out of the site entrance. The newcomer approached the two waiting by the car.

"Where is she?" he said. Westlake took a step back and opened the rear door. A few seconds later, Meera emerged. She looked older, her eyes still sparking with feisty intelligence, but her face drawn and pale. She was wearing jeans and a sweatshirt, no coat. She was shivering, partly from the cold, partly through fear. Her right hand was bandaged. She looked up at the man approaching from the site.

"Seb," she said.

"Mee," said Seb, a small smile on his face. "Are you ok?"

"I've had better weeks," she said, trying to smile back. "Didn't I tell you to stay away, you stubborn idiot?"

"You did," he said.

"Well, you're even more stupid than I thought, then," she said.

"I love you too, Mee," said Seb. She started crying then, silently, her eyes never leaving his face. Seb turned to Walt.

"Take her over to the car," he said, pointing out the station wagon. "She leaves now."

Walt walked up to Mee, who promptly punched him in the face as hard as she could. Walt staggered backward, blood pouring from his nose.

"You broke it," he said as the nose straightened itself and the blood turned transparent before sinking into his skin like moisturizer. "You really are charming. But not much point trying to hurt me."

"Good point," she said, and kicked Westlake in the balls. She winced as her sneaker collided with something far harder than the testicles she had hoped to crush. Westlake rapped his knuckles on his crotch, which sounded like someone knocking on a door.

"Had dealings with your type before," he said. Mee suddenly launched herself at him, screaming. As she shouted, she pummeled him with her fists, not caring about the pain from her missing finger, trying to reach his face with her nails. He fended her off with smooth, practiced ease.

"Don't you lay a finger on him, you vicious bastard," she yelled. "Don't you touch him, you do what you like to me, just leave him alone, don't you dare-." She slumped suddenly as Westlake sprayed a puff of something from a small bottle into her face. Walt caught her. Westlake turned to Seb and shrugged.

"You want this to go down smoothly, this is the best way. She'll only be out for a couple minutes."

Seb shrugged right back at him, the distaste he felt barely concealed.

"Take her to the car," he said. "I want to see her leave."

Westlake nodded at Walt who hoisted the unconscious woman over his shoulder and walked over to the station wagon. The driver got out and Walt's eyebrows went up at the unexpected sight of a priest.

"Who the hell are you?" said Walt.

"An old friend," said the priest. "Sebastian asked me to help him."

"*He* might trust you. Why should we?"

The priest looked at Walt, his expression unreadable, but gentle. "He made me swear to treat everything I heard or saw as if it was protected by the sacrament of confession," he said. "I don't like what I'm seeing, and I'd strongly suggest you give some thought to the state of your immortal soul. You are a precious child of God just as much as this girl is. But you needn't worry about my telling anyone anything. As far as I'm concerned, this morning never happened."

"Good," said Walt, as the two of them laid Meera onto the rear bench of the car. He walked back to Westlake, who went to the trunk and handed him a flamethrower. He hoisted the harness awkwardly over his shoulder. Westlake went back into the trunk and produced a large axe. Then the two men walked to the site entrance and joined Seb.

The priest waited for Seb's nod, then got back into the station wagon and started the engine. Meera stirred in the back and opened her eyes. She propped herself up on one elbow and looked quizzically at the man in the driver's seat.

"You're the guy in the photo," she said. "The photo Seb keeps on his piano."

"Father O," said the priest, turning and smiling at her over his shoulder. "I need you to trust me. It's going to be all right."

"How?" said Mee, pushing herself into a sitting position as the car moved away. She looked out of the window and saw Seb walking through the site entrance, the two men following. "How can it ever be all right again?"

Father O'Hanoran put the car in gear and drove away. Mee looked over her shoulder but Seb, Walt and Westlake had disappeared into the building site. The last she thing she saw before the car rounded the corner was diesel smoke rising from behind the fences. Her tears blurred the scene, but she didn't wipe them away.

# Chapter 49

Walt looked at Westlake as Seb led them a hundred yards into the site to the edge of a pit. Two large mechanical diggers stood near the side. The engine noise and smoke was revealed to be coming from a cement truck, the huge mixing shaft slowly rotating to keep the concrete in its liquid form. It had been backed up to the edge of the hole, ready to start on the foundations.

"What's he gonna do, build something?" said Walt.

"Shut up," said Westlake, his eyes never leaving Seb's back.

Walt opened his mouth, then thought better of it. Although Westlake had no Manna ability, he was the closest thing Mason had to a second in command, so antagonizing him was never going to be a wise option. He had also once seen him snap a man's neck while making a phone call. Seb stopped near the edge of the pit and turned to face them. He said nothing.

"Let's get this over with," said Westlake, taking grip of the axe and stepping forward.

Seb held up a hand. "One more step and I'll superheat that plastic box between your legs so that it melts onto your genitals." Westlake visibly paled, and hesitated. He had a very high tolerance for pain and a below average libido, but enough imagination to decide to do as he was told.

"We wait," said Seb. "I know I can't trust you, I assume you're having Meera followed. However, I allowed for this when I planned this morning's adventure." He pulled out a cheap cell phone and held it up. "If I don't get a call on this phone in -" He glance at his watch, "- four minutes, I'm going to reduce both of you to your composite atoms and spread them all over Manhattan."

Walt put the flamethrower on the ground and held up his hands.

"Look, Seb, think this through," he said. "There's no need to rush this decision. Why not take a few weeks and really consider your options? No one's going to hurt Meera, she's just insurance. But do you really think she can hide from Mason when you're gone? By doing this, you're killing her as well as yourself."

"I'll take that risk," said Seb.

"Ok, you think you can out-smart Mason, I get it. But what if you're wrong? What if-"

Seb held up a hand. "Shut up, Walt," he said.

They stood in silence, the only sound the steady rhythmic chug of the truck's engine. Finally, the cell rang. Seb held it up to his ear, listening intently. Then he smiled, turned it off and tossed it into the pit.

"Ok," he said, "I'm ready." He walked over to the truck, pushed a button at the rear, and the trailer lifted, liquid cement pouring out of the back into the hole. He came back to Walt and Westlake, turned his back on them and knelt on the edge, without saying another word. Westlake hoisted the axe and walked forward. Without knowing why, Walt looked away.

The next few seconds seemed to pass extraordinarily slowly to Walt. There was no scream, just a grunt from Westlake as he swung the weapon. Nothing else could be heard above the noise of the engine, but when he looked again, Walt saw Seb's body on its side, his head about four feet away. Blood was still pumping out of the neck.

"Don't just stand there," said Westlake. "Burn it up."

Walt walked forward as Westlake backed away. He pulled the trigger that released the gas and simultaneously ignited it. A jet of flame roared out of the nozzle.

They stayed long enough to make sure it wasn't a bluff of some kind. Then they kicked what was left into the bubbling cement, turned off the truck's engine and walked away. Westlake sent a message to Mason and they drove back into the city.

***

The priest drove for about five minutes without stopping, then took a right into a parking lot, swiftly climbing four levels before backing into a space. Meera sobbed in the back. The priest made a phone call.

"Good to go," he said. "This feels weird. Thank you for doing this. Goodbye." Then he closed his eyes for about ten seconds. When he opened them again, he turned and grinned at Meera.

"It worked," thought Seb.

"Of course," said Seb2.

"Can't quite believe they bought it," said Seb.

"Hey, a homunculus that smart could have spent a week with them without being caught. He was something else."

"He was me. You. Whatever."

"Not a person. A complex sub-program designed to emulate one. If an AI programmer could have met it, he'd have passed out."

"Yeah," said Seb. And Walt and Westlake just covered the evidence - or lack of it - with concrete."

"Enough patting on the back. Now life is going to get really interesting."

"Why?"

"Better ask her. Hope she'll be pleased to see you."

Meera watched the priest turn around and grin at her. Something about that grin. It just didn't seem to belong on that face. But it sure looked familiar. Then she forgot to breathe for ten seconds. The priest's face blurred, moved, the features softening like clay, the whole body shifting, the clothes changing color. The grin stayed put. But when it was on the new face, Seb's face, it suddenly belonged. She laughed, burst into tears, then leaned forward and punched him on the arm. He started laughing too. She climbed into the front seat, sat on his lap, threw her arms around his neck and kissed him like she had never kissed anyone before. When they finally broke apart, they looked at each other for a minute or two.

"Couple of things," said Seb. He put his hand flat on the faded walnut veneer dash. It changed to leather under his fingers, the interior of the vehicle remaking itself in seconds, the changes spreading out from his fingers and increasing in speed and scope as they encompassed every last inch of the car. She looked at the badge on the steering wheel. Apparently, they were now sitting in a BMW. Mee looked at him google-eyed

"What *are* you? What are we going to do?" she said. "Where are we going to go?"

"I'm a World Walker," said Seb. He held up his hands as she started to speak. "I don't know much more than you. As for the other questions, I really don't know. There's so much to tell you, Mee. But first, we need to get away. Far away." He smiled at her gently and put his hand on her face. "This might feel a little strange. Hold still."

Meera felt her skin tighten, then slacken strangely, the roots of her hair tingling. She looked in the rear-view mirror and gasped. Then she looked back at Seb and gasped again. Then she giggled until she thought she wouldn't be able to stop.

Mason had people stationed at every exit of the parking lot within a minute of the station wagon pulling in. Barrington was on the fourth floor, his cold, blank stare scanning everyone coming through the doors. After 20 minutes, a team swept the entire parking garage, reporting back that no station wagon had been found. Barrington's report insisted the priest and Patel must have got past one of the less vigilant members of Mason's team. No one could answer Mason's question as to how that was possible. The search continued for a week but no trace was found. Mason kept a low-key worldwide search active permanently. He hated loose ends.

Barrington, meanwhile, never once gave another thought to the octogenarian couple who had shuffled past him on their way into the mall. The old boy, with a Florida tan and bony wrists, had stopped and spoken to him.

"No school today, sonny?" he had said, and ruffled Barrington's hair. If he hadn't been so intent on finding the priest and the girl, Barrington might have considered stopping the old bastard's pacemaker, but he didn't have the time. He just briefly glared at the frail, watery-eyed nightmare in the blue shirt, with his elasticated tan pants pulled up to his ribs. He never saw the old guy turn around and look at him after he'd taken a few steps. He never saw him smile. And he never saw him kiss the old woman with him like a teenager and, his hand tightly holding hers, both of them smiling broadly, stroll out of sight.

## THE END

# Author's note

## Get The World Walker Prologue FREE!

If you're reading this, the likelihood is you just finished The World Walker. My first novel. So, before I go any further, let me thank you. Thank you. I would love to be able to write more books, and you are instrumental in making that a possibility. Don't let the responsibility weigh too heavily on you. If you *really* enjoyed it, I'd love you to leave a review on Amazon. And maybe visit http://http://eepurl.com/bQ_zJ9 to sign up for news on more books and occasional blogs (not many, I'm lazy *and* I'm going to be spending my free time writing the next World Walker book. Yes, there will be another one.) I'm even on FaceBook and twitter, apparently. I'll send the prologue to everyone who signs up above. It tells the story of Simeon, the founder of the Order. In the end, it didn't get included because I wanted to get straight into the action. But if you enjoyed the book, I think you'll like it.

I used to enjoy Stephen King's author's notes as much as his books. More, sometimes. I liked the sincerity, the directness. As readers, we were reminded that the rich work of fiction in which we had just lost ourselves was not the work of some kind of super being, just a regular human being. Well, perhaps not *completely* regular, in Mr. King's case. Every time I read one of those notes, I felt that itch. The itch I hadn't yet scratched, making itself known again. But I never did anything about it. Mostly because, as Ray Bradbury put it, "writers write". Every interview with a writer suggested they wrote because they had no choice. If they couldn't get in front of their computers, typewriters or yellow legal pads with *that brand of pencil* every day, their lives would fall apart, their marriages would break up and they would end up living in a cardboard box, drinking lighter fluid and shouting at pigeons. Hand on heart, I couldn't make the same claim. I wrote, sure, but I always enjoyed the sensation of *having written* far more than actually *writing*.

It took me an age to realize many writers feel the same way. I don't know why this information took so long to sink in. After all, one of my favourite writers, one of the few I had read in my teens, twenties, thirties *and* forties is Douglas Adams, and he seemed to hate the act of writing. When he wrote the radio series, *The Hitchhiker's Guide To The Galaxy*, he was famously locked into a hotel room by the producer until he finished it. But, somehow, he managed to author some of the funniest, most thought-provoking books of all time. He also once said, "I love deadlines. I love the whooshing noise they make as they go by."

Don't get me wrong. I have written before. Scripts, sketches, lots and lots of songs. The occasional short story. I had small successes along the way, but nothing to get excited about. I had notebooks full of ideas for novels. But the longest thing I'd ever written was around 10,000 words long. I had no idea how writers sustained an idea for so long. And who'd want to spend all that time trying when the vast majority of first novels never get published? I didn't have that much confidence, but I admired those who did, the talented few who made it.

Then ebooks came along, a novelty at first. When Amazon launched the Kindle, it obviously wasn't going to be a novelty for long. And so a new era began. Writers were publishing their own books. When that first Kindle came along, I was an early adopter. My job at that time involved an awful lot of flying, as I was playing piano and singing in

Scandinavian bars most weekends. I used to buy dog-eared paperbacks from thrift stores, read four or five every weekend and leave them in airports, bars and restaurants for the next reader to discover. The Kindle did wonders for my back as I could now lift my carry-on baggage unaided. After re-reading every Sherlock Holmes story, some Dickens and every cheap classic I could find, I started filling it with thrillers, fantasy, science fiction, magic, religion, philosophy. When I hunted the Kindle store for new books, I sometimes came across writers I'd never heard of before. Their books cost me less than a good cup of coffee. I bought some. I'll be honest, many of them weren't so hot. I got a bit more discerning, read reviews, tried a sample. And I found some great stuff out there. Wool, by Hugh Howey, was one I remember. And The Martian by Andy Weir. Now both of them have big publishing deals and The Martian is a movie starring Matt Damon. Self-published books! Everything has changed.

The final convincer (although it took me another four years to start writing, but, hey, I'm a slow learner) was meeting someone who wrote ebooks. Ebooks that sold enough to make him a living. Pot boiler political thrillers, high-octane, violent. Eminently readable, and tens of thousands of readers had discovered this and were buying his books. Murray McDonald. He's even written a scifi novel - The God Complex. You'll find him on Amazon. Just having a friend who described himself as "a writer" without blushing was a new experience. Finally, I had first-hand, undeniable, evidence-based findings: it's possible to write books and make a living at it. For real.

I started writing. I still had those old notebooks, but I'd been inspired by an interview with science writer and presenter James Burke, during which he was encouraged to make predictions about the next forty years of technological progress. He foresaw the rise of nanotechnology leading to a society of abundance, without poverty or hunger. I wondered if our age-old hierarchies of the haves and the have-nots would be permitted to be up-ended quite that easily. Then I speculated what the world would look like if the technology already existed, but, for some reason, was only available to a few. Next, for some reason, Roswell, New Mexico, 1947 popped into my head. And, suddenly, it was hard to write my notes fast enough to keep up with the alternative world that was springing into being.

Seb and Mee aren't done yet. Mason haunts the World Walker without us ever finding out much about him, but I know much more than I'm letting on. He'll be back. As will Walt, who fascinates me. I know I'm doing that author thing now, talking about the characters as if they were real. They *are* real! Sonia Svetlana turned up halfway through the first draft without ever featuring in my notes. She was such a powerful character, I wrote her into the story much more fully. Scared the crap out of me, I don't mind admitting. And the Order has always been more than the sum of its parts. It's not going anywhere.

I'm writing this note in a cafe. I've overdone the caffeine today, so it's afternoon tea for me. How civilized. I finished the novel four days ago and sent it to a few friends and family members to check for errors and let me know if it made sense. One of them - Neal - read the whole thing in two days flat and loved it. *Really* loved it. His enthusiasm gave me a glimpse into the way authors feel when their work makes a real, tangible connect with someone else. What a rush! So if this book ends up sinking into obscurity, Neal was wrong. But if enough readers feel the way Neal does, I might end up being able to say, "I'm a writer" without caveats or embarrassment. So, one more time, before I start work on the next book, thank you, whoever you are, for reading this one.

Ian W.Sainsbury

Norwich

February 9, 2016

21990561R00245

Printed in Great Britain
by Amazon